THE BEST NEXT Thing

Un PROFESSIONALLY YOURS

The Best Next Thing

NATASHA ANDERS

Natasha Anders

Also By Natasha Anders

The Unwanted Series

The Unwanted Wife

A Husband's Regret

His Unlikely Lover

Alpha Men Series

The Wingman

The Best Man

The Wrong Man

The Broken Pieces Duet:

More Than Anything

Nothing But This

A Ruthless Proposition

Promises of Forever

ISBN: 978-0620899420

Cover: Designs By Sweet 'n Spicy Designs

Editors: Melody Guy and Suzanne Jefferies

Formatting: Paperhearts Publishing

For Carmelita and Cheri-Lee.
Thanks for being such awesome friends.
Maybe I'll name a couple of characters after you guys in the next book.
Maybe.

Prologue

The shroud of darkness was accompanied—as always—by a terrifying inevitability. Each excruciating exhalation left her with even less air in her lungs. And while she fought to breathe, he was right there, applying ever more pressure.

His sinister voice promised, "Tonight's the night you die, Charity."

No!

The panic and helplessness were familiar companions as she clawed her way back to the light.

Charity awoke with a gasp and immediately kicked off the suffocating, restrictive bedcovers. Her nightgown was soaked through with sweat, her hair drenched, and she shivered uncontrollably. She swallowed down the small, distressed sounds coming from the back of her throat while she fought to regulate her breathing.

"Get yourself together." She hated the woman she became every time she had this nightmare. "It's over. You're okay. You're safe."

She counted to ten, first in English, then in French and then —just for the hell of it—in Japanese, until she was sure she had a handle on her emotions. It was an odd quirk of hers; that ability to count to a hundred in several different languages, none of which she could actually speak or truly understand.

"He can't hurt you," she told herself. "He can't hurt you. He's gone. He can't hurt you." Some nights it took longer than others to convince herself of that fact. But it was easier tonight. Perhaps because she hadn't been asleep very long.

She got out of bed, dragged her nightgown over her head and dumped it on

the hardwood floor, before padding, naked, to the en suite. The sweat dried rapidly as the cold air hit her overheated flesh. She was still shivering uncontrollably as she stepped beneath the punishingly hot spray of her shower.

The nightmare would be back, maybe not tonight or tomorrow, but eventually.

It was inescapable.

Chapter One

Absolute rest.

That was what the doctor had ordered. Which was bullshit. Miles Henry Hollingsworth wasn't a man who could sit on his arse and do nothing all day long. But his mother and sister had been concerned, and he knew that they would badger him endlessly if he didn't take that prescribed "mental and physical" break. Miles was a bloody weakling when it came to denying the two most important women in his life.

Which was why he had finished any outstanding business and left his COO,

Bryan Yoshida, in charge of Hollingsworth Holdings Inc. Miles's younger brother, a recently promoted junior exec, would assist Bryan. Hugh was eager to grow and learn, but Miles had been reluctant to give him more responsibility. Not because the young man was incompetent, but because Miles had a hard time ceding even the slightest control to anyone else. Bryan was Miles's most trusted friend and colleague. The man would be a patient and wise mentor to Hugh.

Consequently, Miles had boarded the corporate jet and fourteen hours later, here he was, at his isolated holiday home on the Garden Route in the Western Cape of South Africa. It was after three in the morning, pouring with rain and colder than a witch's tit, but the weather suited his mood. He could have followed the sun and gone to his villa on the Amalfi Coast, but the Western Cape in winter was exactly what he was looking for. He knew the nearby tourist town would be quiet at this time of year, and he would be alone but for the staff he kept on retainer.

The only individuals with whom he would have to interact would be Amos Moloi, the gardener; his driver, George Clark; and the dour live-in housekeeper, Mrs. Cole. The woman had worked and lived there for nearly three years, and nobody knew much about her other than she kept to herself for the most part, got her work done almost as if by magic, and excelled at wish fulfilment. No matter how crazy the request, Mrs. Cole could arrange it.

Recommended by his attorney, the woman was a gem, and Miles guarded her jealously. This house was more hers than his. She lived here full-time, while he visited once or twice—if he was lucky—a year. There really was no need to have her here all year round but for the fact that Miles was afraid he'd lose her to a better position if he offered her only part-time employment. He'd rather pay her handsomely and retain her services full-time than lose her. When he found someone he could trust to do a job the way he wanted it done, he'd move heaven and earth to secure their loyalty.

He had forgotten to let her know he was coming, but he had faith that Mrs. Cole wouldn't miss a step. The house would be fully stocked and operational in no time at all.

God, he was exhausted.

His arrival to the house was quiet and there was no sign of

Mrs. Cole when he disabled the alarm and stepped into the dark kitchen from the basement garage. While Miles thought nothing of waking her, he didn't feel like interacting with anyone at the moment and wanted to avoid her till morning.

He allowed George to carry his bags to his room before dismissing the man for the rest of the night. He needed a hot shower, some food in his belly, and sleep. Lots of it. *Years* of it.

ABOUT FIVE MINUTES after George left, Miles made his way down the long passageway from his suite to the huge rustic, country kitchen. He needed a sandwich or something before showering and crawling into bed. He hoped Mrs. Cole had stocked some of the basics. She had her own private wing, complete with a kitchen, a sitting room and study, so her personal grocery supply likely wouldn't be stocked in this kitchen. Still, he hoped there was something edible at least.

He stopped dead in his tracks when he got to the kitchen and blinked at the sight that met his eyes.

The previously dark room he had walked through a few moments before was now brightly lit. A tall, shapely, unmistakably feminine figure stood framed—with her back to him—in the door of the large refrigerator. The mystery woman was wearing a pair of loose exercise shorts and a long-sleeved T-shirt. She had strong, lean legs, leading to gorgeous firm thighs, and a round shapely bum, the lush fullness of which tapered into a tiny waist, slender back, and narrow shoulders. Her long, long hair cascaded almost to her waist and rippled with every move she made. She hummed softly to herself as she rummaged around in *his* fridge.

Miles had no idea who this trespasser was or what she was doing there, but she gave him an instant, aching hard-on even before he saw her face, and he didn't like it. Not one bit. This was not conducive to a peaceful holiday. He didn't need the distraction of an unwelcome attraction to some intrusive stranger who had no business being in his house. At best, she was related to one of the staff—Mrs. Cole's daughter, perhaps?—at worst, she was a trespasser. Either way, she was not welcome.

She turned, her slender arms full of ingredients, and shut the fridge door behind her with a cheeky hip thrust. She lifted her head and hissed in shock when she saw him, and he took petty satisfaction in startling her as much as she had stunned him.

She had brown eyes, he noted grimly, so dark and intense it was hard to differentiate between iris and pupil. Those disturbing eyes were set beneath lovely, perfectly arched dark brows and between thick, long lashes. Her face was a delicate oval, with lush, pink lips, a slightly dented chin, and high, perfect cheekbones. The only things marring all that perfection was the slightly crooked nose—but it gave her an appealing approachability—and an oddly shaped scar on her left temple, just beneath her hairline. Her hair tumbled over her shoulders, past her breasts, wrapping around her like a cloak, and he marveled at the silken stuff. He'd known a lot of gorgeous women in his lifetime, but he couldn't remember one ever having hair like hers. It was lovely. A sleek, black cascade that he wanted to wrap his fist in.

There was a lovely dusky brown tone to her velvety looking skin, giving her a Middle Eastern or North African—possibly both? —appearance. She was singularly beautiful.

And familiar. *Very* familiar. She had to be related to Mrs. Cole. He didn't usually pay too much attention to his housekeeper. Not enough to notice details about her appearance...but her eyes were unmistakable. This woman had the same striking eyes.

"Who the hell are you?" He finally found his voice, and was pleased to note that it didn't betray an ounce of his fascination with her. He sounded cold and in control. "Why are you here? What are you doing in my house?"

CHARITY BLINKED at the man glowering at her. Why was *she* here? Why was *he* here? She had received no word of his arrival. Why had nobody notified her? Warned her that he was coming?

Gosh, he looked awful. He was a trim figure of a man, but had enough depth to his shoulders and definition to his body to make him appear bigger and stronger.

Usually.

Currently he was a husk of his former self. Too thin and also much too pale. It was summer in the UK, why was he so pale? His impeccably tailored suits always fitted him like a glove, yet this one hung from his frame with room to spare.

She looked at her armful of groceries and grimaced, feeling at a disadvantage. She had kissed the notion of sleep goodbye after her nightmare and had been about to make herself a sandwich when her boss had scared her nearly to death. Aware that she looked completely unprofessional, she straightened her shoulders, tilted her chin, and schooled her face into its usual expressionless mask. There was nothing she could do about the way she was dressed but, even though she felt defenseless being seen without her usual armor in place, she did the best with what she had.

"Mr. Hollingsworth, sir, I wasn't expecting you tonight." *Or at all.* "Can I fix you something to eat?"

He scowled at her suspiciously before an expression close to disbelief settled on his face.

"Mrs. *Cole?*"

She didn't respond, merely kept her gaze level, and her face impassive. He raked his incredulous glance up and down her body, and she strove not to cringe beneath that scorching appraisal.

"Perhaps a sandwich, sir? I'm sorry, my refrigerator is on the fritz and the electrician hasn't been in to fix it yet, and I've been keeping my groceries here for the time being. I'll remove everything as soon as possible, of course."

Miles was having a hard time reconciling the barefoot goddess in front of him with the prim, practical Mrs. Cole, whom—for some reason—he had always assumed was closer to fifty than thirty. Yet this woman standing in front of him in those tiny shorts didn't look much older than thirty. But her slightly aloof demeanor, her voice, the absolute professionalism, despite the way she was dressed, were hallmark Mrs. Cole.

This was...*bizarre.*

Miles would move heaven and earth to secure an accomplished employee like Mrs. Cole, confident in the knowledge that once she was working for him, he wouldn't have to do anything more than check in on her occasionally. That's the beauty of hiring the best.

Mrs. Cole ran the house efficiently from behind the scenes, employing cleaning and catering services as needed, and communicating through texts and emails whenever she could. All while keeping herself determinedly invisible. She was like a phantom—the legendary Mrs. Cole who appeared only when needed and disappeared into the woodwork when her task was complete.

It was easy to understand how he had not noticed this striking woman before. And yet, the transformation was still mind-boggling. How could the difference in dress and hair be so profound that it felt like he was looking at a completely different woman? In fact, Miles doubted even Vicki or Hugh—both usually a hell of a lot more observant than Miles when it came to people—had any idea what she really looked like.

She was still talking about the refrigerator and he forced himself to focus on what she was saying.

"I don't give a damn where you keep your groceries, Mrs. Cole," he said, forcing the incredulity out of his voice. If she could maintain her professionalism under these awkward circumstances, then so could he. "Just make sure I'm fed on time, the house is clean, and I remain undisturbed. That's all I require."

"Will anybody be joining you, sir?"

"No."

"And might I inquire as to how long you'll be staying?"

"Six weeks at the very least." He sensed her surprise even though her expression remained stuck in neutral. He had never stayed here for longer than a week or ten days. His siblings and their friends usually stayed longer but the siren song of work always called him back sooner rather than later.

"And yes, I'd like a sandwich."

"Very well, sir." So much aplomb in that crisp voice. "Would you like me to bring it up to your room?"

"I think that would be best." He gave her another frowning once-over, before shaking his head, annoyed with her for being so disturbingly different. He trusted that she'd go back to her normal self by morning so that he could attempt to dismiss tonight as exhaustion playing tricks on his mind.

He left without a backward glance, and Charity heaved a relieved sigh. She dashed into her room to scrape her long hair back into a bun and drag on a skirt. She didn't allow herself to speculate over what he must have thought about her sloppy appearance, and definitely didn't allow herself to dwell over the heat she'd seen smoldering in his steel gray eyes while he had been dragging his gaze over her face and body.

He hadn't recognized her, that much was clear and having him see her like that, without her usual protective shell in place, had left her feeling raw and defensive.

Just get through tonight, she urged herself, heading back to the kitchen to quickly assemble a grilled ham and cheese sandwich. She added a side salad and a mug of hot chocolate with marshmallows—his favorite nighttime drink—and placed everything onto a breakfast tray. She took a moment to compose herself, allowing tranquility to blanket her shattered nerves. After another deep breath, she felt centered enough to calmly walk the long, dimly lit corridor to his suite of rooms.

There was no response to her initial knock on his bedroom door. After another perfunctory knock, she turned the handle and stepped into the room. It was illuminated by the bedside lamp, which shed only enough light for her to see that Mr. Hollingsworth was sprawled out and fast asleep in the center of his luxurious king-sized bed. She tried not to wince at the sight of the stripped-down bed, reminding herself that nobody had notified her of his imminent arrival. Impossible to be effective if she wasn't kept appraised of the family's intentions.

She stared at her employer for a moment, wondering if it was best to let him sleep, but he was still wearing that hopelessly wrinkled gray pinstriped suit—and he had requested this sandwich. Charity had worked for him long enough to know that he would be displeased if she didn't follow his instructions to the letter. He was an exacting, cold man who had no time for, or patience with, bad service.

She set the tray on the bedside table and cleared her throat awkwardly.

"Mr. Hollingsworth, I brought your sandwich," she said. Nothing. Not even the flutter of an eyelid. *Crap*. She raised her voice, "Mr. Hollingsworth. Your sandwich."

Still nothing. She closed her eyes and inhaled nervously. She was going to have to touch him. She wiped her suddenly clammy palms on her skirt and swallowed back the bile that had risen in her throat. This wasn't ideal. She should leave. Maybe he'd wake up on his own.

"Mr. *Hollingsworth*!" She practically shouted in a last-ditch desperate attempt to avoid touching him. That did the trick. He leaped out of the bed like it was on fire and stood staring at her with wide eyes, his chest heaving as he assessed the situation, searching for the threat. When he realized that there was none and registered her presence, he stood upright and glared at her.

Charity tried her best to appear unfazed even though his violent reaction had nearly sent her rabbiting out of the room like the coward she was. She held her hands clasped in front of her in an effort to hide their trembling from him.

"Mrs. Cole? What the *fuck*? Christ, you had me thinking the house was on fire!" She had never seen the usually unflappable Miles H. Hollingsworth look so completely pissed off before, and she couldn't help taking a step back, preparing to flee if the need arose. Her breathing shallowed, and she tried to quell her instinctive fight or flight response, not sure if his reaction would worsen.

He raked his hands through his hair, furrowing it into messy peaks, and after another deep breath, his anger visibly dissipated, leaving him looking even more exhausted. Charity allowed herself to relax and took a step forward again.

"I'm sorry, sir. I thought you'd want me to wake you for the sandwich." She gestured toward the tray, and his piercing gaze followed the vague movement of her hand.

"Yes. Of course. Thank you, Mrs. Cole. That will be all."

Resisting the usual urge to curtsy in the face of all that British reserve, Charity nodded before asking, "What time would you like breakfast served in the morning, sir?"

"I doubt I'll surface before noon. Prepare something light at one."

"Yes, sir. Goodnight, sir." She backed out of the room but kept her eyes deferentially downcast while remaining acutely aware of his penetrating, unflinching gaze as she retreated.

She escaped the room with a relieved gasp and leaned back against the door for a moment as she gathered herself. She took a few, wobbly steps toward the kitchen but paused, swore beneath her breath, and nearly kicked herself as she remembered the bed. She couldn't, in good conscience, leave him to sleep on an unmade bed.

Five minutes later, she was knocking on his door, hating the fact that she was disturbing him again, but she took too much pride in her job not to.

"Come." There was no hesitation in the familiar command. Not for the first time, Charity shocked and amused herself by picturing him using the exact same word and intonation in bed with one of his lovers as he commanded her to climax.

Somehow, she couldn't picture Miles Hollingsworth as a

passionate, hot-blooded lover who lost himself in the act of sex. Instead, she envisioned him as a cold automaton barking orders at the woman beneath him while he heaved away methodically inside of her. The thought sent a shudder of revulsion and fear down her spine, and her amusement faded almost instantly.

She let herself into the room and blushed like a schoolgirl when she saw that he had divested himself of his shirt, shoes, and socks in the last five minutes. He was seated on the edge of his bed, with half a sandwich in one hand and the mug of hot chocolate in the other.

Whoa! Mr. Hollingsworth might have lost too much weight since she'd seen him last, but he still had an impressive chest. Wide shoulders with well-defined pecs lightly dusted with downy looking dark hair that tapered down a pretty decent six-pack toward the waistband of his trousers...

She jerked her eyes to his face, which was wearing one of his trademark frowns.

"I brought fresh towels and clean bedding. I'll just..."

"Leave it."

"But..."

"Leave it, Mrs. Cole," he repeated, the words ripe with irritation. "I'm knackered, I don't want to sit around waiting for you to get those military corners just right. All I need is the duvet and a pillowcase. You can take care of the rest tomorrow. Towels in the bathroom, if you please, and then leave me alone."

Butthole. Charity fought to keep her annoyance out of her expression. She nodded and carefully placed the linen at the foot of the bed, before making her way to the attached bathroom. She neatly placed the towels on their racks, replaced the toilet paper, and put his favorite soap, shampoo, and conditioner in the shower.

When she returned to the bedroom, it was to witness him

polishing off the last of the sandwich and washing it down with the hot chocolate.

He noticed her hovering and jerked his head toward the tray. "You might as well remove this."

He had barely touched the salad, and she bit the inside of her cheek to refrain from commenting. He had clearly been ill but hadn't eaten the healthiest thing on the tray. It wasn't her place to say anything. Instead, she gathered up the tray and once again bade him goodnight.

"Mrs. Cole." His voice halted her retreat right at the door, and she lifted her eyes to meet his cool, gray gaze. "No more interruptions."

"Yes, sir."

After she left his room, she fled to the kitchen. It was her haven, and she felt safe and in control here. She picked up a pen and some paper and sat down to make a list of everything she needed to get done in order to take the house out of snooze mode and get it one-hundred-percent operational again.

She always did the cooking, and while she had cleaning staff in once every fortnight when the Hollingsworth family wasn't in residence—preferring to do most of the light cleaning herself—she would have to arrange for them to come in at least twice a week with Mr. Hollingsworth there.

She made a mental note to text Amos later to let him know the boss was back. The elderly man usually joined her for breakfast a couple of times a week when the Hollingsworth family wasn't in residence, and she wasn't sure what the straitlaced Mr. Hollingsworth would think if the gardener showed up at the kitchen door in the morning expecting breakfast.

She usually ordered massive amounts of food online when she knew the family was coming on holiday, and she liked to have their menus planned—first day to last—weeks ahead of time. But she would have to "wing it" this time. God, how she hated spontaneity when it came to her job. She liked to know exactly what she needed to do and by when it had to be done. This upheaval would probably require a physical shopping trip to Knysna—the closest big town—because delivery for online orders tended to take longer. The prospect of going to town had her stomach in knots. She hated leaving. Hated being out in public. She always felt at risk...

And visible.

She even did her clothing and cosmetic shopping online. Books, movies, music, all the things she needed were delivered right to her doorstep or straight to her tablet. She enjoyed the isolation—venturing out to the closest town once a week—and liked having only a few trusted people in her life. It kept things uncomplicated.

Safe.

Charity prided herself in anticipating what Mr. Hollingsworth and his family would need before they even realized it themselves, and she knew him well enough by now to predict what food he would want and what personal toiletries he would require—she even knew what brand of condom he favored. It was her job to make his stay pleasant and stress free and, as he had been ill, it was more imperative than ever to ensure this particular visit was smooth and problem free.

She put down the pen and rolled her neck, trying to keep her growing headache at bay. No point in even attempting to get any more sleep tonight. There was way too much to do.

THE THUNDERING RAIN WOKE HIM.

Miles opened his eyes and was momentarily confused by his gloomy surroundings. His body clock told him it was later than it appeared and a glance at the bedside clock confirmed that it was nearly eleven in the morning. It felt earlier because of the miserable weather. He sat up and disentangled himself from the bunched-up duvet, a silent testament to his restless sleep.

He made his way over to the glass doors that led into his private corner of the extensive garden. A glance out confirmed it was coming down in sheets. And an ominous roll of thunder in the distance told him that the weather would last for a while. The verdant garden was a dramatic counterpoint to the grim weather. But that was the beauty of the Garden Route; because of the rain it was usually lush and green in winter. Rain had been scarce over the last few years, but from what he had heard, this winter had seen welcome relief from the drought.

He turned away from the view and went to the spacious walk-in closet. He was gratified to note that his closet was stocked with clothes from his last stay as he didn't feel like rummaging through his suitcase for something to wear. Mrs. Cole would undoubtedly unpack everything for him later. He grabbed some stuff, tossed it onto the rumpled bed, and went to the bathroom. He needed a long, hot shower to clear the remaining cobwebs from his head.

He was so tired, a bone-grinding weariness that made it hard for him to focus on anything for too long. It was that, in addition to his mother's and sister's insistence, which had made him agree to this enforced rest. He couldn't do his job effectively without focus. He had nearly lost millions of pounds on a bad investment a couple of weeks ago. It had been an appalling error in judgment, something that would never have happened had he been his normal self.

As he stood beneath the pulsating spray of the shower, he

contemplated the sobering reality that—thanks to his bloody stupidity and stubbornness—his life had nearly been snuffed out by a microscopic bug. He inhaled deeply and coughed when he held the aromatic steam of the shower in his damaged lungs for a beat too long.

Damn it.

The doctors had warned him not to rush his recovery. They hadn't been happy to hear he intended to leave the country and even less happy to learn that he was headed to a cold, damp climate.

Not heeding their advice had landed him in this mess in the first place. He had been so obstinate, so sure he knew his limits better than his healthcare providers. He should probably have learned from his previous mistake and stayed home...or gone someplace warmer. But he liked *this* place, and because of Mrs. Cole, he knew that he'd be comfortable and allowed to recuperate in peace.

Mrs. Cole with her shapely, mile long legs and that ridiculous length of hair. With her velvety looking skin and her—

Fuck!

He glanced wryly down at his eager—and entirely inappropriate—erection and grimaced. This was crazy. And definitely not what he had in mind for his stay here.

He shook his head, impatient with himself for dwelling over a moment that he sincerely hoped would not recur. He was here to get healthy and strong in both body and mind. And that meant Mrs. Cole needed to remain the unobtrusive and efficient employee she had always been. Someone he knew he could rely on to always get the job done.

By the time he made his way to the kitchen, Mrs. Cole—who always seemed to have an eerie precognitive awareness of his movements—already had his brunch waiting in the solarium. She was nowhere to be seen but his boiled egg, toast, and coffee were all warm. Which meant she must have laid it out moments before. He allowed himself a final—he hoped—moment of speculation about her unexpected youth and attractiveness, before pushing the errant thought aside. Mrs. Cole and her peculiarities were not his business. As long as she maintained her efficiency and tact, he would set last night's revelations aside.

He picked up the ironed newspaper and went straight to the business section, before thinking the better of it and putting the entire paper aside. He considered the egg for a few moments and, for the first time in more years than he cared to recall, he wanted something else for breakfast.

A creature of habit, Miles had a soft-boiled egg with whole wheat toast, coffee, and orange juice for breakfast every day since he was twenty. It was a perfectly adequate meal, and he did not see the point of having anything different. But today it held no appeal. He frowned down at his plate and looked up, wondering if Mrs. Cole's ESP would kick in, and she'd pop out of the woodwork with something more appetizing in hand.

He waited.

Nothing.

He shook his head, amused by his nonsensical flash of whimsy, and picked up his spoon. He held it poised above the shell, before swearing and pushing himself away from the table. He rarely entered the kitchen but—for the second time in less than twelve hours—he found himself back in Mrs. Cole's domain. The large, expensively equipped, homey room was scrupulously tidy and disappointingly empty.

"Mrs. Cole?" His voice was low and could barely be heard

above the raging wind and lashing rain yet, despite that, she drifted into the kitchen by way of the pantry. Her hair was parted and pulled back into a severe bun at the nape of her neck. As usual she wore no makeup, but today Miles could appreciate the flawless, smooth skin of her face, which gave her such an ageless quality.

She wore her usual uniform of a knee-length black circle skirt, combined with a black cardigan buttoned over a white blouse, with the sharp points of the prim lace collar folded over the top of the cardigan's round neck. Thick, opaque black tights and sensible lace-up black brogues completed the horrendous ensemble.

Clothes fit for a nun.

But where before he had found it easy to ignore the disturbing, dark depths of those haunting eyes, the long, thick lashes, the lush fullness of her heart-shaped mouth, he was finding it difficult to dismiss that intriguing loveliness that morning. Despite the matronly outfit, her beauty was distinct and unmistakable. And he remained astounded that it had not truly registered with him before now. However, her obvious reserve was enough to keep anyone at bay.

And he was grateful for that.

His eyes drifted down to the wedding band on her left hand —he vaguely recalled Jim, his attorney, mentioning that she was divorced. Or was that widowed? He couldn't recall, but for the first time Miles wondered what had happened to the ex/late Mr. Cole.

"Did you need something, Mr. Hollingsworth?" Her tone was as frigid as the winter storm pummeling the house, and he fought back the unusual urge to grin. She clearly didn't like having her territory invaded.

"Yes. Pancakes."

"I beg your pardon?"

"I want pancakes. Not what you've given me." Even to his own ears he sounded petulant but, *goddamnit*, if he never saw another boiled egg in his life it'd be too soon. He didn't understand this sudden desire for change—maybe it had something to do with nearly dying. This was the kind of thing people usually experienced after a brush with death, wasn't it?

She gaped for a few seconds before she could disguise her reaction.

"Of course, I'll have that ready for you in a few minutes." She started to turn away from him, but when he sat down on one of the bar stools beside the marble-topped central island, his action was enough to stop her in her tracks. She turned her head to pin him with her unnerving gaze, for a second, before angling her body back toward his.

She folded her hands primly at waist level and pursed her lips.

"I'll bring your pancakes to the solarium," she told him with pointed emphasis. "Would you like bacon with it?"

"Bacon. Yes." He nodded and very nearly complied with her implicit command before stopping himself. "I don't mind waiting here. In fact, I think I'll eat here in the mornings. Mealtimes needn't be extravagant affairs. Not when I'm the only one here."

"But..." For a moment she looked set to argue, and he braced himself in anticipation. But she hesitated, and he could see her mind ticking over before she nodded curtly. "As you wish, sir."

Miles was disappointed that she had backed down. He had been looking forward to sparring with her. He eyed the straight line of her spine as she started on the batter for his pancakes and wondered at his sudden bizarre urge to pick an argument with her. He curbed the immediate impulse to goad her but it was still there...just a breath away.

Fortunately, George chose that moment to interrupt. The man came stomping into the kitchen by way of the back door. He had a raincoat thrown over his upper body and brought the noise and cold of the storm in with him.

"Cats and dogs out there, Mrs. Cole," he said jovially, as he swung the coat from his shoulders. "Are you sure you want to head out in this mess?"

"Head out to where?" Miles asked, and George's head jerked at the sound of his voice.

"Aah, good afternoon, sir. I didn't see you." The man looked confused to find him sitting there, and Miles was annoyed that everyone seemed so flustered by his presence in the kitchen. It was *his* house, wasn't it?

"Head out to where?" Miles disliked repeating himself, but since George was still gaping at him, he clearly needed the prompt.

"To town. For supplies," Mrs. Cole replied for George, calmly stirring pancake batter.

"Supplies?" Miles was momentarily confused by that statement. Why would she need supplies? He was the only one here. He didn't need an army's worth of food. "We don't need supplies. I'll eat what you eat."

Mrs. Cole coughed and deliberately diverted her eyes to the pancake batter. Miles felt his face go hot, and he frowned. He wasn't used to being put in his place with a look. That was usually *his* go-to move.

"After the, uh...pancakes," he said, the words sounding lame and unconvincing even to his own ears.

"*My* groceries are low, sir. I'm afraid they wouldn't last a week if I were to feed you as well." The emphasis on the possessive pronoun was clearly there to serve as a reminder that the food in the house had been bought with her own money, for her personal consumption, and his face went even hotter.

He forced the chagrin aside and nodded coolly.

"Yes, of course. It was a thoughtless suggestion." It pained him to admit as much.

"I usually have the pantry stocked in advance when I know you're coming." Another jab. Mrs. Cole disliked being surprised.

Got it.

"Fortunately for me, you're adaptable," he said, with a grim smile. "It comforts me to know that I can show up at any time of my choosing and depend on you to have this place up and running in no time at all."

Translation: *My house. I can damned well come here whenever the hell I like.*

She injected a fair amount of frost into the smile she sent his way—*message received*—good to know they understood each other.

"Of course, sir. As soon as I have the supplies, everything will be in order."

"I'm glad you're here, George, then I won't have to repeat myself." Miles diverted his attention to the older man, who had been watching his frigid exchange with Mrs. Cole with interest. "My stay this time will be somewhat different. I have been...ill, and I'm here to recuperate. I won't be leaving the house much, and as such I won't be requiring your services too often. That said, I would prefer you remain accessible for the duration of my time here. Clear?"

George nodded smartly in response to Miles's question.

"Mrs. Cole." She had been busy pouring the batter into a hot skillet, and her back stiffened even more—how was that even possible? —and she cocked her head in a manner that indicated she was listening, even though she kept her eyes on the pancake. "Meals will be informal. I will eat breakfast in the kitchen. And lunch and dinner in the living room instead of the dining room. I would prefer heartier breakfasts than boiled eggs and toast. Feel free to surprise me. I came here for solitude and rest. As such I would prefer not to have the cleaning service visit too often while I'm here. Since I won't be using the entire house, I'm sure you can manage. Understood?"

"Understood." She flipped the pancake expertly as she said the word. They were all silent for a moment while she finished the pancake and slid it onto a plate before starting the next. "Will you be needing anything from town, sir? The weather service says the rain will continue for the rest of the week. And that means we probably won't be able to do another shopping run for a while."

"Why not?"

"The river will likely burst its banks, which can lead to localized flooding. The bridge linking us to the main road could be washed out or even away. And if that happens we could well be cut off for weeks."

"Has it happened before?" he asked. His brow lowered as he contemplated that troubling possibility.

"Yes."

"And you've been trapped here? Alone?"

"Amos was here the first time it happened," she said, with a dismissive shrug.

"The first time? How many times has this happened?"

"Only twice since I've been here." She slid a plate, laden with a stack of pancakes and a few rashers of bacon, toward him. Momentarily diverted, Miles took a moment to stare at the perfectly golden and fluffy stack of pancakes and the beautifully crisped bacon. He swallowed down the saliva that flooded his mouth and nodded in thanks.

Reaching for the syrup, he drenched the pancakes and shoveled a forkful into his mouth. His taste buds sang in ecstasy, and he bit back an appreciative moan. He could not remember the last time he'd had pancakes. It had always seemed like such a frivolous meal to him. Vicki had often tried to coerce him into having some of hers, but he had always preferred his boiled egg.

But *this*...this was glorious.

He washed the mouthful down with a sip of coffee and had some of the bacon.

Christ! So fucking delicious.

He schooled his features into impassivity, but it was hard when he was enjoying the most amazing food of his entire life.

He hadn't had an appetite in weeks but suddenly—after just two bites—his body felt like it was coming alive again. He ducked his hands beneath the counter in an attempt to hide their trembling from George and Mrs. Cole. He was embarrassed by his reaction to what was essentially an extremely basic meal.

He stared at the plate fixedly for a moment, resisting the urge to scarf it all down like a barbarian and, after composing himself, lifted his fork and began eating again.

"What happened the second time the bridge washed out?" he asked, hoping neither of them found his behavior odd.

But when he looked up, it was to find that Mrs. Cole had turned away to clean the stove, while George had sat down at the banquette in the cozy breakfast nook. The elderly man was reading a newspaper and ignoring them as he sipped from a cup of coffee that Mrs. Cole must have provided while Miles was having his come-to-Jesus moment.

"Everything was pretty much the same, only it didn't take us by surprise that time. We knew what to expect, and I had stocked up in the expectation of exactly such an event."

George grunted, and Miles's gaze swung to the man, who was staring at them over the top of his newspaper.

"Not quite the same as the first time, Mrs. Cole. Amos was in the Eastern Cape for his uncle's funeral."

"Well, Amos lives out in the cottage, so it's not like we see each other all the time. I barely saw him the first time it flooded. We'd check in on each other periodically to make sure everything was fine, but other than that I might as well have been alone."

Isolated in this huge house by herself? That must have been tough. He was amazed he hadn't received her resignation immediately after that. He paid her handsomely. But to be completely cut off in the middle of winter? No amount of money could coerce Miles to endure anything similar.

"Do you need anything?" Mrs. Cole asked again, and Miles shook his head.

"No." The word came out more curtly than he had intended. "Thank you."

"You won't be needing any...uhm, medication or anything?"

His eyes narrowed at the hesitant question. He hated how weak he probably appeared to them.

"I said I don't need anything." He felt a pang of regret when she jerked at his abrupt response. Her dark eyes shuttered, and she gave him her back when she turned away to wipe the already clean counters.

"But I think I'll come with you." His tone was gentler but, judging by the way her shoulders tensed at his words, Mrs. Cole didn't like that idea.

Her next words, steeped in formality, confirmed that displeasure, "I'm sure that's not necessary."

"It probably isn't but, nevertheless, I insist."

"You've clearly been ill and should stay out of the cold, wet weather."

He felt his teeth clench as he fought the urge to tell her to mind her own damned business.

"No need to concern yourself with my health, Mrs. Cole. I know my limitations."

His physician would get a hearty chuckle out of those words.

"Very well, sir. We'll leave in half an hour." The words were forced through tightly gritted teeth, and Miles bit back a grin. The prickly Mrs. Cole was proving to be unexpectedly entertaining. He didn't respond and refocused his attention on his mouthwatering breakfast.

Fortunately, they left him to his silent enjoyment of the meal. A good thing since the delicious food soon rendered him incapable of coherent speech. He polished off his breakfast in no time and was tempted to ask for seconds but managed to restrain himself. He needed to gain weight and regain his strength, but overindulging could well see the pendulum swing in the other direction, especially since his exercise options were limited while he was still so weak.

He thanked Mrs. Cole quietly and got up.

"I'll meet you in the garage," he murmured, and left without further word. He had a bucket load of medication to take and would prefer not to have anyone witness that.

Chapter Two

"Sorry to keep you waiting."

Her employer's voice held no inflection whatsoever, but Charity knew he wasn't the slightest bit sorry that he had kept her and George cooling their heels for nearly fifteen minutes. She was riding shotgun in the massive SUV that was rarely used for anything other than shopping.

George leaped out of the car to open the sliding door with an obsequious little bow for their boss. The gesture looked vaguely sarcastic to Charity. She never could figure out the relationship between the two men. George didn't seem nearly as deferential as he should, and Mr. Hollingsworth always seemed to tolerate it with gritted teeth and a stoicism that ran contrary to his usual assertiveness.

Mr. Hollingsworth took the seat behind hers, and the hairs at the back of Charity's neck immediately stood on end. She should have anticipated this possibility and now regretted her decision to sit up front. Having someone directly behind her, close enough to sense but not see, made her feel horribly defenseless.

She shifted her body to the right, ostensibly to face George in the driver's seat, but really to keep Mr. Hollingsworth in her peripheral vision.

He had been behaving oddly all day. Mr. Hollingsworth was usually a creature of habit. And she had found his predictability comforting, but the unexpectedness of his demand for pancakes that morning had totally unnerved her, and she didn't like it.

"Where are we headed?" he asked, his voice curt.

"Knysna," George responded cheerfully while clipping his seatbelt. "Buckle up, everybody."

Charity was already belted in, and she knew the friendly reminder was for Mr. Hollingsworth, who hadn't even attempted to reach for his seatbelt. An aggrieved look flashed across his face. The fleeting expression made his usually austere features boyishly petulant before it smoothed over and he assumed his usual façade of icy indifference.

He said nothing but found the belt and did as he was told.

Charity hid her smile behind a polite cough and fixed her eyes on George's grizzled profile. The refreshingly frank man was in his mid-fifties, of medium height, and solidly built. His short, black hair was liberally sprinkled with salt, and he always sported a roguish silver stubble. His weathered, dark brown skin wrinkled attractively around his eyes and told the tale of a man who spent a great deal of time outdoors and who laughed frequently.

George lived in town and, though he didn't have to, often popped in to check on Charity throughout the year. Especially during winter. He was contracted to do any driving errands she required of him, an amenity of which she made regular use.

Charity liked the blunt, no-nonsense man and felt safer when he was around. She regretted that he did not stay on the premises when the Hollingsworths were in residence. She always felt like George was in her corner, and it was such a comfort to have someone she could trust implicitly around. Especially when the Hollingsworths brought strangers on vacation with them.

After today—unless Mr. Hollingsworth needed George to take him somewhere—she and her employer would be alone. And the prospect of being alone with him all day, every day, filled her with dread.

"Why Knysna?" Mr. Hollingsworth asked, as George carefully navigated the dirt road toward the old, wooden bridge that led into town. "Riversend is closer."

"Riversend's supermarket may not have some of the ingredients I'll need, they stock only the basics. Knysna has more variety." Charity didn't like explaining herself. He didn't usually care about these things, trusting her to handle it efficiently. That's what he paid her for.

"I told you, you don't have to make any special effort on my behalf. If the weather is as unpredictable as you say, wouldn't it be better not to chance the drive to Knysna? What if the bridge washes out before we get back? I say we go to Riversend and make do with what we can get from their local grocery store."

Charity inhaled impatiently, counting silently to ten in German before pasting a fake smile on her lips and nodding.

"As you wish, sir," she said, forcing the words out past the clenched teeth of her strained smile.

"I haven't been to Riversend before," he stated, leaning back —seemingly content now that he had gotten his way—and folding his arms across his chest. "We've always just passed through it on our way to Knysna or Plett."

"Nothing much to see, really," George weighed in on the conversation, more relaxed now that he had successfully reached the tarred road that led into town. "A few shops, one restaurant, one pub. And completely dead in winter."

Charity felt that was an unfair assessment of the town George called home. It was quaint and while it was quiet—which she appreciated—it didn't lack charm. The restaurant had changed management a year ago and was becoming quite popular with locals and tourists alike. Charity wasn't one to eat out at all anymore, but she had heard about the splash it was making on the local scene. And it had been hard to miss how crowded it always was on her weekly forays into town.

The citizens of Riversend were friendly and never seemed particularly perturbed by the "keep away" vibes Charity deliberately exuded. But they respected her desire for solitude, and Charity appreciated that about them.

Mr. Hollingsworth and George continued to chat amicably, while Charity watched the wet, green scenery slide by. She mentally reviewed her grocery list, eliminating things she knew the local store didn't stock and considering possible alternatives.

The sound of her name in Mr. Hollingsworth's mellifluous voice startled her from her thoughts, and she was jerked back to the disagreeable present.

"I'm sorry, I didn't catch that," she said, trying to keep her expression as neutral as possible.

"I asked if you come into town quite often," he repeated.

"Not often. Once a week for uh..." Her voice petered out, as she considered a reasonably honest substitute to what she had been about to say. "Gym."

"Gym? There's a fully equipped gym at the house."

"Yes. I use that regularly as well, but there are special classes I like to attend on Wednesdays."

"Like Tae Bo, you mean?"

Tae Bo? Did people even do Tae Bo anymore?

"Something like that," she murmured.

"My daughter, Nina, is a big fan of that Zumba thing," George offered conversationally. "She's tried to get me to go to a couple of classes with her. But I've seen it on the TV. Just a lot of jumping and bumping and gyrating, if you ask me."

"Is that what you do, Mrs. Cole?" Mr. Hollingsworth asked, his deep voice utterly serious. "Jumping and bumping and gyrating?"

Charity pinched her lips between her teeth and refused to reply to the borderline inappropriate question.

Seeming to recognize the impropriety himself, Mr. Hollingsworth's color heightened. He cleared his throat and diverted his attention to his driver. "How is Nina these days, George?"

Charity very much doubted that Mr. Hollingsworth had ever met Nina Clark, but George talked about his only child often enough that anyone who knew him would be at least loosely familiar with her antics.

A disgruntled frown settled on George's face, and his jaw tightened.

"Pregnant." The word was succinct and teeming with fatherly disapproval. "Thirty-two years old and she finds herself pregnant and single. Can you believe that? And she won't tell me who the father is. But at least I'll be a granddaddy. The rate she was going, I wasn't sure I'd ever be one."

Mr. Hollingsworth made a suitably sympathetic noise, and that was enough to set George off. He ranted about Nina and the mystery man who had gotten her "into trouble," rhapsodized about his impending grandfatherhood, and updated their employer on the local gossip.

Thankfully that let Charity off the hook again and she

relaxed somewhat and dragged out her tablet to adjust and recategorize her shopping list.

WHEN THEY REACHED the tiny town, Miles found himself at loose ends. Mrs. Cole clearly didn't want him to accompany her, that much was evident from the way she leaped from the SUV before George had even brought it to a complete standstill and—her shoulders hunched against the cold wind—proceeded to walk at a brisk pace toward the supermarket.

Miles was left to either jump out and run after her—a humiliating prospect since he wasn't sure he would catch up with her in his current condition—or explore the town. An equally unappealing thought considering the weather. And since the place literally consisted of one main road lined with shops and a few streets branching off that led to the suburbs, he was pretty sure it would be a very short walk. Not that he had the energy for anything more than that. There was the beach boulevard that, George had informed him earlier, had undergone something of a facelift and rejuvenation thanks to a recent injection of local and foreign investment into the community. But Miles wasn't certain many of the beachside stores would be open in weather like this.

He was still debating his next move, when George exited the vehicle and opened the sliding door for Miles. His choices were limited to staying in the van with George or wandering around aimlessly. After a brief consideration, he chose the latter and stepped down onto the wet curb.

Fortunately, it had stopped raining, but he nonetheless gratefully accepted the closed, black umbrella that George silently handed him.

"Text if you need me," George instructed him, and climbed back into the SUV. Miles watched as his driver lifted a tattered paperback and leaned back to read. Feeling thoroughly dismissed, he looked left and then right, wondering which direction would yield the most interesting results. Foot traffic was relatively light, but there were enough people on the streets giving him curious looks to let him know that this was the kind of small town where strangers were viewed with both interest and suspicion.

He coughed and decided to go in the same direction as Mrs. Cole. He wasn't following her, but if he happened to see her, he could perhaps accompany her on her shopping excursion. He laughed bitterly at himself. How goddamn pathetic that he had been reduced to following around his housekeeper because he felt so lost and weak. He, a man who commanded his own empire, didn't know what the fuck his next move was going to be, and he was hoping that finding Mrs. Cole would give him some direction at least.

As he walked, his chest drew tight in the frigid air, and he stopped frequently, both to catch his breath as well as to regain his strength. He was grateful for the umbrella, which he was unashamedly using as a walking stick. He doubted he would get very far without it.

What he had believed would be a short, unchallenging walk, was now becoming a nearly insurmountable distance, and he could hear the familiar, horrible wheeze forming in his chest as he battled to breathe. He staggered a little before righting himself, casting a humiliated look around to be sure no one had seen him. Thankfully, everybody seemed preoccupied with their own concerns and, while curious at first, most of the townspeople were now ignoring him.

He leaned on the umbrella and was about to admit defeat

and reach for his phone to call George—who was parked just three hundred yards away—when he spotted an A-frame advertising chalkboard ahead. Parked beneath an awning to protect it from the rain, the board sported blue, green, and red chalk curlicued writing to advertise the day's specials. He had been so focused on his colossal struggle to breathe and walk at the same time that he hadn't noticed the restaurant at all.

He wasn't hungry after that delicious brunch, but a cup of coffee while he caught his breath would be most welcome. It took more strength and willpower than he would ever admit to anyone, but he made it to the restaurant, which was open and teeming with customers

A smiling young man welcomed him, led him to a table right beside the window and handed him a menu and a wine list, before assuring him that his waitress would be with him shortly.

He sat down with an appreciative sigh, pretty certain his wobbly legs wouldn't hold up much longer and glumly contemplated the menu as he considered his appalling weakness. He had possibly been precipitous in inviting himself along this morning. He had always been the kind of man to run instead of walk but this fucking illness had humbled him and—while he would never admit it to anyone—it had terrified him as well.

He inhaled deeply, grimacing at the twinge in his chest and let out the breath with a slight cough. Just a huff but it still irritated him. He was ready to get back to normal, but normal seemed a long way off.

He barely had time to register the contents of the menu, when a middle-aged waitress, with neatly pulled back red hair, approached the table. She placed a glass of water on the table in front of him and offered him a perky smile.

"Good afternoon, I'm Suzie, I'll be your server today. Have you had a chance to look at our drinks menu?"

"Just a coffee."

"Cappuccino or—"

"Coffee. Black." He knew he sounded curt but didn't much care. He was trying very hard to hold back what felt like an impending coughing fit and wanted her gone before that happened.

Suzie's face fell and the smile dropped from her lips. Her eyes went cold and Miles could practically see her sticking him into the "difficult" category. That was fine. He was difficult. And demanding. And an arsehole who was used to getting his own way.

"Of course, sir. I'll have that for you shortly." She turned away, and he latched onto the water and sipped it slowly in an effort to hold back the coughing. After a few undignified splutters into the water, he managed to control the tickle in the back of his throat and put the glass down.

He perched an elbow on the table and dropped his forehead into his palm.

Seriously, *fuck this*! He was so damned over it.

He turned his head—transferring his chin into his palm—and stared out at the wet street. Dark rain clouds were hanging ominously low, promising more downpours to come.

He liked this place. He always had. He had never been here in winter, but he found himself appreciating the gloomy weather. In fact, even though the cold and damp were likely detrimental to his physical recovery, he did believe that the tranquility and the spotty Wi-Fi would bode well for his eventual recovery, along with his emotional and mental well-being.

He snorted at that notion. His emotional state wasn't something he generally considered. He didn't have time to sit around contemplating his feelings. He was a busy man, who had scraped his way up from nothing to unimaginable heights of wealth and prosperity.

So what if he didn't get to enjoy said wealth and prosperity himself? That wasn't why he had worked so hard to earn his first million pounds before the age of twenty-seven. It wasn't why—seven years and countless millions later—he still wasn't content to rest on his laurels. He *never* wanted to go back to having nothing and, more importantly, he wanted his siblings and his mother to continue enjoying the life he could now provide for them. And if that meant never enjoying it himself, the sacrifice was well worth it.

Suzie—a slightly less bright smile on her lips—interrupted his grim thoughts.

"Your coffee, sir. Are you ready to order?"

"Coffee's fine for now," he muttered, and she nodded and retreated with almost indecent haste. Miles checked out the place while he waited for the coffee to cool. It was quaint. Very country cottage with its floral mismatched crockery, spindle-legged cushioned chairs, and warm colors. It was also surprisingly busy for a week day. Most of the tables were occupied. Some people were clearly there to catch up on some work, laptops open and phones out. Others were socializing, chatting and laughing. It felt remarkably urbane for a sleepy town like Riversend, and Miles took a curious look at the menu.

Pretty standard breakfast fare. But the dinners and desserts appeared to be absurdly sophisticated. He raised a skeptical eyebrow and wondered if the food was up to par. It was one thing to promise "*yuzu* and rosé *panna cotta*" and quite another to deliver anything remotely as complex.

He flipped to the back of the leather-bound menu to read up on the chef, and his other eyebrow lifted to match the heights of the first when he read that she—Olivia Chapman—had trained in Michelin-star restaurants across Europe before settling down here.

Who knew?

He set the menu aside and took a sip of coffee. His eyes tracked back to the street outside. It was starting to drizzle. He watched as people scurried to get indoors or under cover before the inevitable downpour.

His phone buzzed in his pocket, and he eagerly reached for it, hoping it was Bryan with an update. Logic told him it wouldn't be Bryan, who had promised Miles weekly reports during his six weeks of forced "vacation." Miles had insisted on daily updates but Bryan—not one to be bullied—had point blank refused that demand.

It wouldn't even be Hugh, who was so eager to prove himself to Bryan, that he would never contradict the man's orders. Not even for Miles. The company would have to be verging on bankruptcy before either man called Miles for advice. Not a comforting thought...but Miles trusted Bryan implicitly. Even if he didn't often show it.

He finally managed to fish out his phone and frowned when he saw Vicki's face and name on the screen. She never called, preferring texts and every social media app on the face of the earth to actually picking up the phone and talking. The fact that she was calling immediately set off alarm bells.

"Vicki? What's wrong?"

"What makes you think something is wrong? Maybe I miss you. Maybe I'm worried about you." His sister's tart voice made him grin, and he relaxed. It didn't sound like anything was drastically awry.

"Are you?"

"A little...but mostly I want you to call off your goon. He's driving me insane."

"What the hell are you talking about?"

"This musclebound oaf"—Miles heard an offended masculine "Hey, now!" in the background and his grin widened—"you hired to follow me around. I swear to God, he barely lets me go to the bathroom alone."

"Then he's doing his job."

Vicki was a florist, specializing in cutesy, kitschy, animal arrangements, and her shop had been robbed just before Miles had been hospitalized. Ill, and barely thinking straight, he had asked his security team to assign someone to watch his little sister. His mother and brother both had low key security details. But he wanted someone massive and intimidating to be Vicki's shadow at all times. His sister was sweet and fragile and a little naïve, and he had blamed himself for not following his gut and pushing the security issue harder with her before the incident. She had flashed him her gentle smile and told him she didn't feel comfortable with people following her around, and he had melted like butter and been more relaxed with her security. And then some bastard with a gun had roughed her up, vandalized her store, and robbed her.

Miles wasn't allowing that to happen ever again.

"Miles, he went into the ladies' room at Harrods to check if it was empty before allowing me to go to the loo."

"Was it empty?"

"*No.* He then demanded the women there leave." Miles heard the male voice say something in the background, and Vicki blasted an impatient breath directly into the phone. Her next words were evidently aimed at her bodyguard. "I don't care how *polite* you think you were, Tyler! It was still rude."

"Vicki, let me talk to him."

"Tell him he was way out of bounds, Miles," Vicki said, her

voice edged with frustration. There were muffled noises as she handed the phone over.

"Sir?" The deep voice on the other end had a Texan twang to it.

"It's Chambers, right?" Miles asked.

"Yes, sir."

"Keep doing what you're doing. I want her safe."

"Of course, sir."

"Good man. Now let me speak with her again."

"Did you tell him, Miles?" Vicki asked.

"I told him to keep up the good work."

"Miles, come on, this is ridiculous. The store was robbed. It happens. If you want to help, stick this guy on shop security or something. I'm just a regular woman. I can't have this...this *person* following me around like I'm some pop star or...or heiress or something."

"You are an heiress," Miles corrected her, striving for patience while he took a sip from his coffee. "You're *my* heiress."

"Ugh! That's just... it's just..."

"Vic, just bear with me, okay? When I'm feeling better, I'll ask the security company to be less obvious with your detail. But while I'm here and not able to keep an eye on things myself, it would really ease my mind, and probably aid in my recovery, if you'd humor me for now."

Pulling the sick card was a low blow, but he knew she would feel obliged to acquiesce to his request. Especially when he never usually asked her for anything.

"Okay," she muttered begrudgingly. "But I'm not happy about it."

"Noted."

"So how are you feeling?"

"Fine."

"Miles." The impatience in her voice told him she was probably rolling her eyes as well.

"A little tired after the flight," he admitted. "But you know how peaceful this place is. It's even quieter at this time of year. I think this will do me the world of good."

"You should have gone someplace warmer and drier."

"It's not damp here, just cold and rainy."

"Cold and rainy is the definition of damp."

"The house has central heating," he muttered, aware of how defensive he sounded. "And it's not like I'm going to be wandering around in the rain."

"You sure about that? I know how much you enjoy your long, meandering hikes."

"I'm here to rest."

"Make sure that you do."

Miles couldn't help but smile at the words. His sister was seven years younger than he was, but she sometimes fussed over him like she was the older one.

"How are Hugh and Mum?"

"If this is your sneaky way of trying to find out if Hugh's pulling his weight at the company, I'm totally not telling."

"If I wanted to know that I'd ask Bry—"

"He wouldn't tell you either." She sounded so smug.

"Probably not, but he's more likely to have an actual answer to my question. You wouldn't know."

"I know stuff." Her voice was breezy and unconcerned, and Miles could imagine the careless wave of her hand as she said the words. "I just have more interesting things to obsess over."

"How *is* Sullivan doing?"

"We broke up. Your henchman made him nervous."

Good. Miles knew better than to say the word out loud, but his sister's last boyfriend was an arsehole who lounged around doing nothing much of anything as far as Miles could tell. Vicki had called him "creative" and "sensitive," which Miles had translated to "lazy" and "useless." The guy hadn't worked in the entire time that Vicki had dated him, always banging on about his muse not speaking to him. Miles still wasn't sure if the guy was a painter, a writer, or a musician...his "art" had been an amorphous thing that never quite solidified into anything identifiable.

But while Miles had opinions, he never interfered in his siblings' love lives. Unless they came to him for advice, he trusted them to figure it out. That didn't mean he hadn't taken the time to have a long, extremely one-sided, conversation with each of Vicki's boyfriends, warning them of what would befall them if they hurt her in any way.

He did the same with Hugh's boyfriends. Nobody was hurting his baby brother and sister. Not on his watch.

If Vicki having a bodyguard meant a break from the endless stream of arty, unemployed hipster types, then Miles was all for it.

"Tell me," Miles began, as another thought struck him. "How old would you say Mrs. Cole is?"

"I don't know..." Vicki sounded distracted, and her next words, once again meant for Chambers, confirmed that. "*Don't* touch that! Why do you have to fiddle with everything? Aren't you guys supposed to be strong and silent and stationary or something? Ugh. Miles. This is the worst thing you've ever done to me."

"I'm sure it's not that bad and if it keeps you safe, then that's just the way it's going to be for now. Now, about Mrs. Cole."

"What? I don't know...forty-five? Fifty? She sort of fades into the background, and you don't notice too many details about her. It's weird, right? Now that I think about it, she could be in a room with us and we wouldn't notice her unless she spoke. That's some serious ninja skills. But I always thought it was just part of her job. To be invisible or something. I don't think I could even tell you what color her hair is. Gray, right?"

"Black," Miles supplied without thinking, then winced. Luckily Vicki didn't seem to notice, she was still musing about Mrs. Cole.

"Or does she wear a cap? I can't really picture her. The harder I try the fuzzier the image. So weird. It's like I've been huffing 'shrooms and—"

"What do you know about huffing 'shrooms?" Miles interrupted, and she coughed delicately.

"Like how I imagine it would be if I'd been huffing 'shrooms," she amended, before prudently changing the subject. "Why are you asking about Mrs. Cole? You're not thinking about firing her or anything, I hope. She's brilliant."

"Of course not."

"Then why ask?"

"No reason."

"You always have a reason..."

"What's that? Vicki? *Vicki*? You're breaking up...I...you... hear me?" Miles got a childish kick out of faking the bad connection. He had always wanted to do that, especially since he knew his siblings did it to him all the time.

"You're so full of crap." Vicki sounded unconvinced but, Miles chuckled and disconnected the call before she could say anything more.

The phone pinged a second later, and he lifted it to read the text from his sister:

VICKI
I heard you laughing before you hung up You didn't fool me at all.

MILES
Don't know what you're talking about.

VICKI

VICKI
Love you, big bro Stay healthy

MILES
Don't gove Chambers too much shit. He's just doing his job.

VICKI
Not making any promises

He was about to put his phone away when, purely on impulse, he called up Bryan's number. His friend would surely want to know how he was feeling after his long flight. And if talk happened to drift to business? That would be par for the course for them.

The phone rang once before it was picked up.

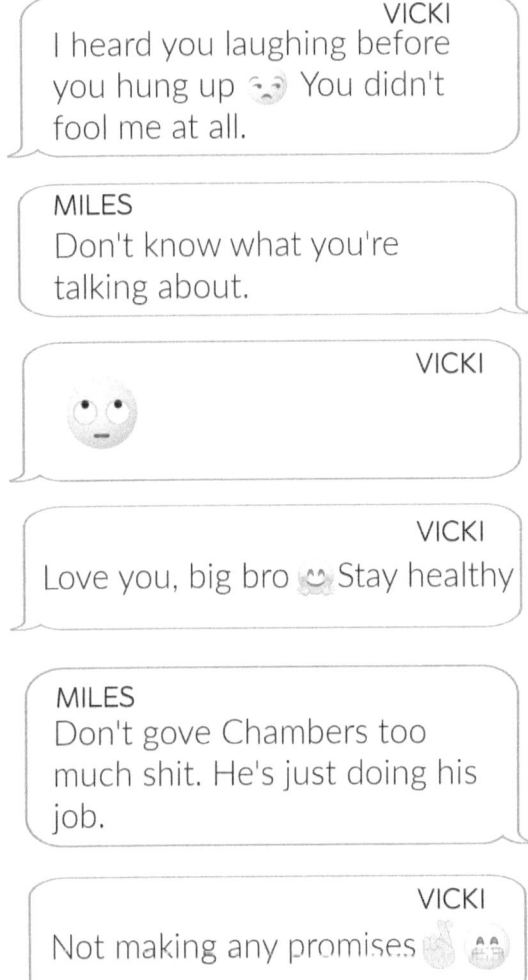

"No!"

"Bry—"

"No, Miles. We agreed, I'd give you weekly updates. It's barely been thirty-six hours since we last spoke."

"Can't I call to touch base with my buddy?"

"*Are* you calling to touch base with your buddy?" Bryan asked, and Miles grinned.

"Maybe I want to know how Hugh is doing? Has he fucked anything up yet?"

"No more than expected. Your brother is fine. He'll do well. And don't think you can call him to find out about the Lambert contract either. He's under strict instruction to say nothing to you."

"I wasn't calling about the Lambert contract," Miles lied. He had *hoped* Bryan would drop a breadcrumb or two.

"Of course not, you're touching base with your buddy. I'm fine. But my golf game is off. I lost to old man Fitzhugh on Sunday. Can you believe that? I think I need a new nine iron."

Christ, Bryan knew that Miles hated it when he talked golf. It bored him to tears. He was happy to let Bryan schmooze potential investors on the golf course. In addition to

loathing the sport, Miles wasn't too great with people. He left the socializing to his more personable COO.

Bryan was still droning on about golf, and trapped in a conversational noose of his own making, Miles sat back and listened. He knew that Bryan was doing this intentionally, but he wasn't about to satisfy his arsehole friend by begging for mercy. His eyes kept drifting toward the decadent looking chocolate cake that took pride of place in the cake display. He may have to reward himself with a slice after this phone call.

GEORGE HELPED Charity load the groceries into the back of the SUV. She had serious doubts that what she had bought would last her and Mr. Hollingsworth more than a couple of weeks. But she would place a few online orders and hope that they managed delivery before any of the more severe storms predicted for the next week set in.

Carla, the assistant manager, had strolled through the store with her. The friendly woman had kept up a constant stream of one-sided conversation, shattering Charity's concentration and forcing her to utter the occasional nicety in response. It had been trying and was one of the reasons Charity preferred not to shop in Riversend. Too many people trying too hard to be her friend. Her reticence seemed to bounce right off them, and they were all so earnest in their attempts to befriend her that it was impossible not to like them.

But a trip to Riversend always exhausted her, mentally and emotionally. It was draining to behave like a normal human being when she had all but forgotten how to be one.

She was relieved once the last grocery bag had been lifted into the SUV and she could climb into the front seat next to George. He always seemed to sense how desperate she was for solitude and silence after a trip into town and kept his comments down to a minimum.

He had the vehicle started and halfway down Main Road before Charity remembered her employer.

"Where's Mr. Hollingsworth?"

"Saw him pop into MJ's earlier. Wobbly as a newborn calf. I didn't think he'd make it that far, truth be told. Never before seen a man fight so hard to keep himself upright. It was admirable."

He slowed the vehicle down as it drew abreast of the restaurant but swore softly when he realized that there was nowhere to park.

"Circle the block, I'll go in and get him," Charity suggested, and George nodded, stopping long enough for her to hop out.

Charity spotted Mr. Hollingsworth at one of the window tables, but he didn't see her, his attention focused on whatever he had in front of him. Sighing, because that meant she would have to go in, Charity threw back her shoulders and entered the warmth of the restaurant.

The *maître d'*, a familiar looking young man, smiled when he spotted her.

"Mrs. Cole. How lovely to see you. Will you be having lunch?"

Seriously, how did everybody know her name? And why were they always so warm and welcoming? It was sweet and unnerving and really uncomfortable.

"Uh. No...thank you. I'm just here to speak with my employer."

"Your employer?" The *maître d'*, identified as Ricardo by his discreet name tag, looked blank for a second, but when his eyes drifted to Mr. Hollingsworth's table, a troubled frown settled on his face. "*That's* your boss?"

Clearly, Mr. Hollingsworth had *not* made a good impression during the short time he'd been here. Not if the look on Ricardo's face was anything to go by.

"Yes." She tossed him a fleeting smile before hurrying toward her boss's table. She could now see what had him so wholly absorbed—a huge slice of dark, moist chocolate cake.

"Mr. Hollingsworth?" Her voice seemed to startle him, and his gaze snapped to her in an instant, rooting her to the spot.

"Mrs. Cole." His voice was glacial. "Done with your shopping?"

"Yes. We're ready to leave."

"Join me for some coffee," he said, ignoring her statement.

"George couldn't find a parking spot, so he's circling the block."

"This cake is sinful. I can't finish it by myself. Would you like to share?"

Share? Did he not recognize how out of bounds that suggestion was? Friends, intimates, *lovers*, shared slices of cake. And they were none of those things.

"You could take it home, sir."

"What's your rush, Mrs. Cole?"

"The weather, sir."

His lips thinned. No arguing against nature.

He nodded and the curtness of the gesture was reflected in his voice, "Of course. I'll settle my bill and meet you outside."

Feeling thoroughly dismissed and unutterably relieved about it, Charity hastened out of the restaurant. She acknowledged Ricardo's cheery goodbye with an awkward nod.

She stood beneath the awning, stamping her feet to ward off the cold while she waited for George. To her relief, the SUV took the corner back onto Main Road before Mr. Hollingsworth exited the restaurant and after navigating a snag in the traffic, George double parked beside an ancient VW and left the engine idling while he waited.

Charity chose not to wait for Mr. Hollingsworth and dashed across the short distance to the SUV, gesturing at George to stay put when it looked like he was about to exit the vehicle to assist her.

The rain was starting to come down in earnest now and, by the time she hopped into the front seat, she was soaked. An icy stray droplet slid down the neck of her blouse. She shuddered at the sensation of ice water slipping down her back and had a horrible moment of panic as the sensation triggered the memory of a sharp, cold blade skimming down the exact same path as that frigid droplet.

The recollection was disorienting and for a second, she was back *there*. In *that* moment. With *that* man...helpless, terrified, and so alone.

The sound of the door slamming mercifully ripped her back to the present, and her eyes darted around the cab of the SUV in horror. She was grateful to note that George had exited the vehicle to open the door for Mr. Hollingsworth and that neither man had been present to notice her tiny lapse.

These moments of blind, helpless panic were becoming less frequent, but Charity knew it was past time to seek professional help. Staying here, isolated, and voluntarily cutting herself off from the people who loved her the most, had seemed like a solution before, but she knew it was nothing more than cowardice.

Lightning sparked in the sky ahead, streaking from one black cloud to the next like a mischievous sprite playing tag. It was closely followed by a massive, rumbling boom.

George slid the door open for Mr. Hollingsworth as the echoing rumble faded away.

"That was loud." Miles Hollingsworth, connoisseur of the dry understatement.

"Storm'll be on us very quickly," George said, as he got into the driver's seat and buckled up. He slanted a speaking glance to the back, and Mr. Hollingsworth fastened his seatbelt with a sigh.

George wasted no time getting them back on the road, and they were just exiting Riversend, when the sky opened up.

"Good thing we didn't go to Knysna," Mr. Hollingsworth pointed out, and Charity gritted her teeth, hating that he was right.

"Definitely," George agreed. "Weather forecast says this is only going to get worse."

"Best make haste back home then, George."

GEORGE ONLY STAYED LONG ENOUGH to help Charity unload the groceries. He parked the SUV, asked if they needed anything more, and left in his own late model Toyota.

"I think I'll retire to my room for a spell, Mrs. Cole," Mr. Hollingsworth said, moments after George left. He looked wrecked, and Charity couldn't help but feel concerned. His eyes were sunken, his cheeks hollow, and he looked a thousand times worse than he had before they had left the house. The small amount of activity had clearly been too much, too soon.

"I'll call you for dinner," she told him, tempted to ask if he was okay, even though she knew he'd shrug off her concern. Or worse tell her—rightfully so—that it was none of her business.

"When might that be?" The words seemed dragged out of him—he was definitely flagging fast.

"What's your preference?"

"Sixish?" Three hours away, that gave her time to swim a few laps before starting dinner.

"That's fine, sir. Anything in particular you'd like me to prepare?"

"No soup or broth, of any kind. Nothing bland—not that

your cooking is ever bland. But if I see anything steamed or boiled I think I may well expire from sheer boredom."

She clasped her hands in front of her and nodded, "Noted, sir."

"And dear God, if I'm to be here for six weeks, I'd much rather we relax the formalities. Call me Miles."

That disconcerted her, and her hands tightened around each other so much she feared the whites of her knuckles had to be showing.

"I don't think...I'm not sure that's proper."

"Who's to know? And I'm not sure 'Mrs. Cole' suits the informality we're striving for either. I'll call you Chastity."

She cleared her throat awkwardly. "That's Charity, sir."

"What?"

"My name. It's Charity."

"Right. Okay. Sorry about that. Charity it is then."

She shook her head, feeling panicked. "No. Wait..."

He sighed. A long-suffering expression on that arrogant, much-too-thin, face.

"I don't think I feel comfortable calling you by your first name."

He moved closer and held her eyes captive with his penetrating stare. "Why don't you try it and find out for sure?"

She took an involuntary step back. She hated to feel crowded. Invading someone's space was a classic bullying tactic, and Mr. Hollingsworth seemed to do it unconsciously. A character trait that threw up massive red flags for her.

"Excuse me?"

"Try it. Say my name and see if it makes you uncomfortable."

"I'd rather not do that...Mr. Hollingsworth."

"*Jesus.*" He shook his head in disgust and stepped back,

giving her some much-needed breathing room. "Fine, if you feel so strongly about it, call me Mr. Hollingsworth, but just give the 'sir' a rest, would you? I feel like a sixth form school teacher, every time you say it."

"Thank you, Mr. Hollingsworth."

"But I'm calling you Charity."

She didn't like that at all. She hated hearing her name on his lips. It sounded *much* too inviting, even when it was being delivered in that crisp, no-nonsense English accent of his.

She maintained a stoic silence, hoping he would glean from that how much she disapproved of this entire conversation.

His smile was purely a predatory parting of his lips. "Buck up, Mrs. Cole. It's just a word."

She preferred the formality of being called Mrs. Cole, it kept him at a distance. It kept *everybody* at a distance. He scrutinized her for a second, before appearing to see something in her determinedly neutral expression that made him shift his shoulders in displeasure.

"Alright, have it your way, Mrs. Cole. We'll keep things formal."

She nodded, the gesture stiff, but couldn't resist responding, "As you wish, *sir*."

His lips tightened for a second before he opened his mouth. She held her breath, wondering if he was going to call her out on her low-key insolence. But he seemed to reconsider what he'd been about to say and, with an impatient shake of his head, he swiveled on his foot and strode from the kitchen.

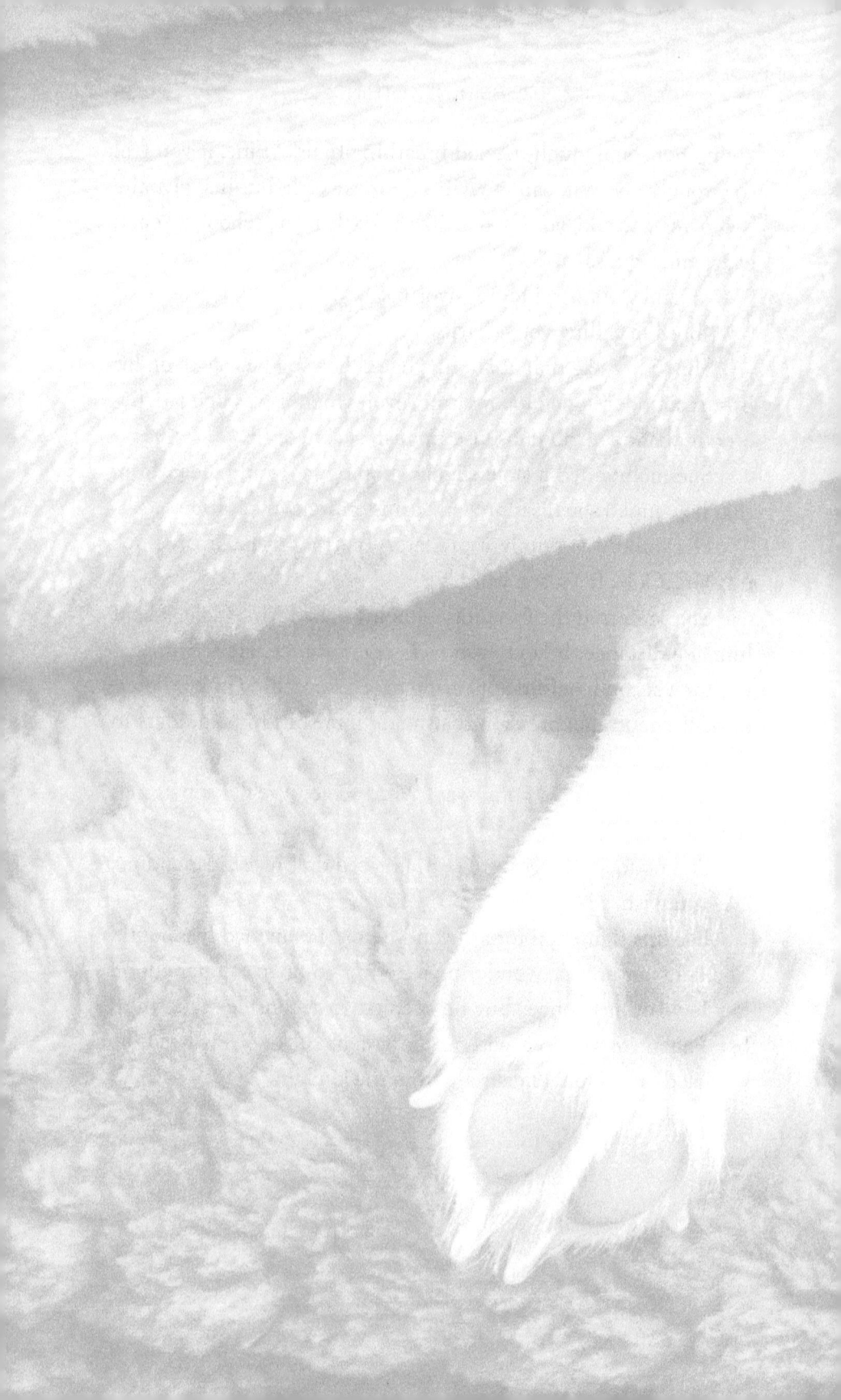

Chapter Three

A rumbling boom shook Miles from his restless sleep. He sat up disoriented in the darkness. He reached toward the nightstand and found the bedside lamp.

But nothing happened when he flipped the switch.

"*Shit!*" He felt around for his phone and was relieved when he found it almost immediately. He hastened to activate the flashlight.

The miserly beam of light quelled his rising claustrophobia and he got up, just as a bright white flash of lightning lit up the entire room for a second, making the darkness so much more oppressive when it faded.

The thunderous clap that followed actually rattled the windows. The wind was picking up, and a weird clattering sound, a noise that he couldn't quite identify, rapidly gained intensity until it was almost deafening.

Hail.

"Fuck me," he grunted, unnerved by the severity of the storm, and tentatively made his way to his door. According to his phone, it had just gone six and he wondered when the power had died.

If the lingering warmth of the central heating was anything to go by, it couldn't have been too long ago.

The house was eerie in its silence, and all he could hear was the wind and the dull roar of hail hitting the roof and cobblestones outside.

"Mrs. Cole?" he called, once he had stepped out of his room and into the hallway. His voice sounded ridiculously timid, and he shook his head, disgusted with himself, before calling again. This time his voice was louder and more assured. "Mrs. Cole?"

Better. But there was no still response. The beam of his flashlight barely penetrated the blackness of the hall yawning ahead of him. Everything not illuminated by the dim light was shrouded in absolute darkness.

Where the hell was she? And why was he so bloody hesitant to walk down this fucking hall?

Another shock of lightning lit the way ahead, and he was relieved to note that there was nothing lurking in the shadows. He immediately berated himself for even allowing the notion to cross his mind. Despite his love of epic fantasy books, Miles wasn't one for ridiculous flights of fancy, so he wasn't sure where the hell this was coming from.

He should have been prepared for it, but the resonating *crack* that shook the paintings on the wall, made him jump. He swore again, before throwing back his shoulders and confidently striding down the hall toward the kitchen.

The sprawling house was built on one level. It had an underground garage— Miles preferred building down rather than up. His architect had argued that building a second floor would capitalize on the panoramic views, but Miles had been adamant. One level, and a basement, or he'd find a new architect. The kitchen and pantry divided the family's sleeping and living areas from Mrs. Cole's private rooms.

"Mrs. Cole?" Jesus, he sounded like a broken record but he hadn't expected to find the kitchen empty. The next flash of lightning lit up the large room long enough for him to establish that Mrs. Cole was definitely *not* here. There were sliced vegetables abandoned on the counter next to the stove. The large knife she must have been using for the task was tossed to the side. She had clearly been in this room when the lights went out.

He turned to exit the kitchen back the way he had come but banged his knee against one of the stools at the island. His clumsiness sent the stool toppling with a loud crash that rattled him almost as much as the thunder that followed.

His phone chose that moment to die, and Miles froze on the spot.

The darkness was absolute and oppressive. He could feel it closing in around him. The air was thick and stifling. His breathing sped up and he was embarrassed by the short harsh gasps rasping from his throat.

Disoriented, Miles stood—helplessly adrift—in the kitchen. Because he had been in the process of turning when he'd knocked over the stool, he wasn't quite sure where the island was, or where the stool had fallen, or even where the doorway to the hall was right now—although he was certain that it was directly behind him. And he *hated* the idea of having his back to that cavernous black hall.

He shoved his phone into his rear trouser pocket for safekeeping and tried to figure out what his next move should be. Thankfully, it didn't take long for his eyes to adjust. And he was able to identify shapes in the darkness within moments. He remained unnerved by the blackness though. Especially with the accompanying discordant symphony of the violent storm raging right above them.

The wind was increasing, the rain intensifying—although it had stopped hailing—he could hear the faintly ominous ticking and scraping of branches on the kitchen window. The branches belonged to the giant old yellowwood tree that offered such welcome shade in the summer. He'd had no idea the damned thing was so close to the kitchen window. He was surprised Amos hadn't trimmed back the branches yet. Miles would speak to him about it in—

What the fuck was that?

A low, howling sound...coming from the back door that led out to the garden. It was faint, but it was noticeable because it was anomalous. It didn't fit in with any of the normal storm sounds. It sounded like an animal.

Miles swallowed and leaned toward the sound, trying to hear it more clearly over the whistling wind. The howl had lapsed into whining. It was insistent and urgent. And... *Jesus*, accompanied by faint, scratching sounds. Someone or *something* was trying their damnedest to get into the house.

Coming down to the basement garage during a blackout always made the hairs on the back of Charity's neck stand up. And tonight, was no exception. Well, it was decidedly worse thanks to the frightening violence of the storm. They rarely had weather-related blackouts, but this storm had been touted as the worst in ten years and, sure enough, the lights had flickered out with the first lightning strike. If the dramatic display of sparks outside the kitchen window was anything to go by, the lightning must have struck the transformer. Mercifully this particular storm was accompanied by torrential rain.

Several years ago, in severe drought conditions, a similar storm—without the rain—had resulted in raging wildfires that had ravaged the surrounding area. Fanned by gale force winds, the fire had decimated over a thousand homes in Knysna, destroyed sixteen thousand hectares of fynbos and forestry, ravaged the wildlife and—tragically—killed seven people. It had been terrifying. Charity and the citizens of Riversend had been on high alert, waiting to hear if they would have to evacuate. But the fire—one of the worst in South Africa's history—had been contained before it came to that. They had been fortunate. Eight thousand others had been forced to abandon their homes in terror.

It had brought home how alone she and Amos were out there. George had offered to stay with her in case they needed to evacuate. But because she knew he would prefer to stay close to Nina, Charity had assured him they were fine, and she would drive them out if need be. Even though the prospect had terrified her. She had seen harrowing clips on the news of people driving through burning forests. The fire had spread so quickly. She couldn't imagine being forced to drive through something like that.

She shook her head, disgusted with herself for allowing these grim thoughts to creep in and unsettle her. She focused on the immediate problem—she needed to switch on the generator. She would hate for her boss to wake up to a dark and cold house. The light from her handheld searchlight bounced off the wall, creating unsettling shadows as she walked toward the state-of-the-art generator that Mi—Mr. Hollingsworth—had installed a few years ago.

The rain sounded louder down here, lashing against the

high, narrow windows and drumming against the garage doors. She didn't like it, it sounded like something ferocious and powerful was battling to get inside.

The wind tossed something substantial against the garage doors, and the loud bang cemented her feet to the polished concrete floor. It sounded like someone's angry fist thumping furiously against the metal.

"Charity, open this fucking door!"

The harsh, familiar male voice seemed to echo around the cavernous garage, and Charity's chest heaved as she found herself fighting for breath. For a horrifying second the voice seemed so real, so *close*; she instinctively went into a crouch and covered her head with her arms.

Stop it! Stop it! STOP IT!

He's not here. He's not.

She counted: *Ten, nine, otto, sett, roku, go, quatre, trois, zwei, eins...*

Again. Her breathing regulated, her heartbeat slowed, and she gradually—sheepishly—lowered her arms and unfurled her body. She picked up the searchlight from where she had placed it on the floor and swallowed heavily. God, nights like these always brought out the worst of it.

She shook herself and resumed her walk to the generator. As she reached for the switch, she heard a clatter from upstairs and froze again. Her breath snagged in her chest.

Oh God...what was *that*? That hadn't been one of her imagined threats, that had been real and—

Crap! He must be awake. And walking into the furniture, if the noise was any indication. Feeling silly and a little guilty for dallying down there when the man was floundering his way around in the dark, she flipped the switch and the generator sputtered to life with a whir. It took a second before the light flickered on, accompanied by the beeps and buzzes of various appliances coming back to life.

She hastened her way back to the stairs leading to the kitchen door, hoping her boss hadn't damaged himself or the house too badly in the dark.

WHEN THE ROOM lit up again—so brightly it hurt his eyes—Miles thought it was lightning and braced himself for the thunder that would shortly follow...but the light stayed on, and Miles blinked a couple of times as he tried to figure out what was going on. A door opened to his left, and he swiveled toward it. His senses still heightened, and his reactions on a hair trigger. He belatedly recognized it as the door leading to the basement garage and the tall, familiar figure of Mrs. Cole stepped through it a moment later.

Her head was bowed, her focus on the magnificent, heavy duty searchlight in her hands—no pussy phone flashlight for her—and she didn't immediately notice him.

"Where *were* you?" Okay, so maybe his question sounded more than a little accusatory, and her head snapped up in surprise.

"Mr. Hollingsworth, are you alright?"

"Of course, I'm alright," he snapped, then felt like an arsehole. "Sorry, just on edge. I wasn't sure where you were."

"I had to switch on the generator. It doesn't automatically kick in when the power goes out."

Of course! The generator. Miles had forgotten about the expensive generator. He'd had it installed a couple of years ago because the series of regulated, rolling blackouts, implemented by the national power company, had become all too commonplace.

"I'm sorry, I should have anticipated a power failure and left a flashlight in your room."

"I had my phone," Miles said, then grimaced before admitting, "it died. What the bloody hell *is* that?"

THE QUESTION CONFUSED CHARITY, and she stared at him in puzzlement. He appeared uncharacteristically frazzled. His hair was standing up in tufts, he must have slept in his clothes because they were wrinkled and in disarray. His eyes looked wild and, if it didn't seem so implausible, Charity would think he had been slightly freaked out by the dark.

Now—after that sharp question—he was glaring at the back door almost resentfully and stalked toward it. She bent to right the upended bar stool that had probably been the source of the noise she had heard earlier, before following him cautiously, uncertain of his unpredictable mood.

He stopped at the door and put his ear to the wood.

"Do you hear that?"

Charity tilted her head, trying to hear what he was hearing.

"I'm sorry, I'm not sure what—"

"*There*!"

She shut her mouth at his interruption and then frowned, listening more closely. She moved nearer to the door, now able to hear the strange moaning noises he was referring to.

"That's odd, right?" he asked, his penetrating gaze bore into her eyes.

"It's unusual," she acknowledged, and crept even closer until she was standing almost right beside him. She was acutely aware of—and very uncomfortable with—his proximity and was about to take a side step to allow for more space between them, when the moaning started up again. Louder and more insistent this time.

Miles—*Mr. Hollingsworth*—reached for the lock, and Charity's breath snagged.

"No, wait," she whispered. "You don't know what's out there."

"Only one way to find out," he stated, looking grim.

"What if it's a wild animal? Amos spotted a troop of baboons in the area not too long ago. Trust me, you don't want to mess with baboons, we had a nasty encounter with one that broke into the kitchen last winter. It was aggressive and terrifying. Even animal control had trouble subduing him."

Her words made him pause and consider. "Would a baboon be dumb enough to be out in this weather?"

"They could be seeking shelter."

A frown settled between his straight, dark brows, and he grunted and shook his head. He extended his hand toward the lock again.

"Surely a baboon would be noisier and more insistent than this?" His words were followed by a gigantic, reverberating rumble that made them both jump.

"*Fuck* me!" Mi—*Mr. Hollingsworth;* she wished he had never invited her to call him by his first name—swore vehemently. "Where the hell did that come from? There wasn't any lightning was there?"

"We were must have been too distracted to notice it."

"Stay behind me, Mrs. Cole," he advised, once again diverting his grim focus to the door.

Stay behind him? That was priceless since—given his current state—she could kick whatever was outside's butt a lot more efficiently than he probably could. She was reassured by the knowledge that she was—temporarily at least—physically stronger than him.

"I'm done being a cowering ninny." Matching action to words, he grabbed the handle and turned the key in one motion. He threw back his shoulders, yanked the door open, and invited the full might of the storm into the kitchen with them.

The frigid, gale force wind immediately swirled around them, dumping icy sleet at least five feet into the kitchen. Charity hissed and cringed away from the cold, but he muttered something foul beneath his breath and stepped forward, his head bowed as he focused on something out of her line of sight.

"Mrs. Cole, grab a towel. *Quickly*," he called, and Charity—alarmed by the urgency in his voice—leaped into action and seized the closest thing at hand, a tea towel, and braved the cold wind and sleet again to hand it to him. He had something clutched protectively to his chest. He tugged the towel from her without a word of thanks and covered the tiny, wet thing he held cradled in the crook of one arm.

Charity carefully navigated the slippery, wet floor to shut the door behind him. He was saying quiet, soothing things to the wrapped bundle in his arms, and she turned to see what he was holding.

"I think it needs a warm bath, Mrs. Cole."

"What is it?" she asked, hoping it wasn't a baby baboon. The last thing they needed was Mommy and Daddy Baboon looking for their offspring. One thing Charity had learned after the incident last winter was that if a baboon wanted in, it would damned well find a way in.

"A puppy," Mi—Mr. Hollings—*he* said. "Poor thing looks like it's on its last legs, we need to get it warmed up fast. A bath and a blow-dryer, if you have one."

"I try not to use too many appliances during a blackout. We

only have so much fuel for the generator. And we don't know how long this blackout will last. It could be days and if we're cut off we can't—"

"A few minutes won't do any harm, Mrs. Cole," he interrupted her, the uncompromising grimness in his voice brooked no argument.

Charity clamped her lips together and folded her hands in front of her. "Very well, sir." She turned away to get the dryer from her room

"Not sir." The reminder sounded like an afterthought, and she didn't bother to acknowledge it as she left the kitchen.

He went back to talking to the puppy, his voice gentle. She didn't think she'd ever heard him speak so quietly before. It did strange things to her chest. If anyone had asked her to describe her employer before now, she would have used words like *brusque, frigid, unemotional...terrifying*. Never *kind* or *sweet* or *tender*. And yet he was being all of those things right now; to a wet, probably tick and flea riddled, helpless little pup.

Granted, two to three weeks a year over a period of three years, was hardly conducive to truly getting to know someone. Especially when Charity herself had done her utmost to remain unobtrusive and had rarely spoken to him at all. She had drawn her own—probably erroneous—conclusions about the man. But his coldness had been such a contrast to the friendly warmth of his younger brother and sister, it had been hard not to judge him accordingly. Her inherent mistrust of powerful alpha males didn't exactly help.

And while him showing kindness to one puppy didn't make her change her opinion of the man entirely—it shook her previously rock-solid preconceptions somewhat.

She was returning to the kitchen with the blow-dryer when

his voice, coming from the guest powder room, stopped her in mid-stride.

"In here, Mrs. Cole."

She pushed the ajar door open all the way and found him hunched over the sink. The puppy—much smaller than she'd anticipated—stood shivering in the deep basin, immersed in filthy, soapy water up to its neck. It resembled a skinny, brown drowned rat and stared at Charity with big, pleading eyes.

"She's absolutely filthy," Miles said, his focus on the pathetic little pup.

Mr. Hollingsworth! She corrected herself sternly. But she had been finding it difficult to think of him as such since he had invited—commanded?—her to call him by his first name that afternoon. It was like a niggling ear worm that she couldn't rid herself of.

Miles. Miles Henry. Miles H.

Miles smiles for miles.

Ugh. So frustrating.

"She has fleas and I've already removed a couple ticks the size of apple seeds from her ears. I fear there may be more."

"No doubt, there *will* be more. But once you hand her over to the SPCA, I'm sure they'll take care of the problem."

"There'll be no talk of handing her over to the you-know-what right now, Mrs. Cole," he said, with a pointed look at the top of the dog's head. His unspoken implication that the scruffy, shivering, miserable looking bag of bones could understand them, was both ridiculous and oddly sweet.

His flash of whimsy confused her, and she wasn't sure how to respond.

"Besides," he continued, sounding self-conscious in the face of her silence. "We probably won't be able to get her out to a vet for a couple of days yet."

"More like a week."

"*A week?*"

"That's usually how long it takes to get the road into town operational again. We won't be very high on the priority list after a massive storm like this. I've been following the news, there are already reports of widespread flooding in the informal settlements and wind damage in town. Emergency and municipal services will be stretched thin. Nothing we can do but wait. Especially if we're not in any immediate danger."

"This is untenable. How the hell can you stand to winter here alone?"

"I don't mind it."

"You should. At the very least you should have asked for a raise. Or danger pay or something. I had no idea it was this bad out here in winter. Floods and fucking wild animals. *Jesus*."

"It's not always like this. We've had a couple of dry winters recently."

"And fires. You were here for that fire a few years ago." He sounded shaken, as if the thought hadn't occurred to him before now.

"Yes." Her reply was matter-of-fact, and he looked as if he was about to say something. Likely ask her for details. He hadn't asked when it had happened, he had probably—*rightly*—assumed that because she hadn't mentioned it at the time, it hadn't directly affected them. But her anxiety and stress had been very real, and she could see the dawning realization in his eyes as he stared at her in absolute horror.

"That must have been terrifying."

"We were unaffected."

"The bushveld around this place is a tinderbox during a drought...it could have gone up in seconds."

"It didn't."

"Did you and Amos stay in town during the worst of it? In case of evacuation?"

"We were ready for that possibility."

"But you remained here?"

"You should probably finish bathing that dog. Her shivering is getting worse."

Her words diverted his attention to the pup. He made an apologetic sound to the mutt and swooped her up in a hand towel. Not any old towel, mind...but one of the premium 600 thread count white Egyptian cotton towels Charity put out only when the Hollingsworth family and their guests were in residence. Charity tried hard not to wince.

She attempted to school her features into impassivity, but knew some of what she was feeling must have crept into her expression. Fortunately, he was wholly focused on the dog, and it allowed her some time to beat back the cringing horror she felt as she watched the beautiful, soft and fluffy towel go black with grime.

"I'm sorry."

His apology took her by surprise, and she lifted her gaze from the towel to meet his eyes, which were now unflinchingly trained on her. Okay, so maybe she hadn't hidden her dismay quite as effectively as she had hoped.

"That's fine, I'm sure it'll wash out after a good soaking in some bleach and detergent."

The mystified expression that crossed his face, told her that she must have misunderstood the reason for the apology. The man usually kept his every thought and feeling on lockdown, so Charity was unsettled to suddenly find herself able to read his expressions so clearly.

"What?"

"The towel?"

"*What*?" he repeated, the impatience layered into the question was a lot more in keeping with the man she thought she knew.

"What was your apology for?"

"For not contacting you after the fires to find out if you and Amos were okay. I assumed, because I didn't hear from you, that things were fine."

"They *were* fine."

"I should still have enquired. And I'm sorry for not knowing how dire things can get here during winter. Nobody should work in these conditions. Perhaps I should consider shutting the house down during winter. You could come in once a week or something to keep things ticking over, but staying here during the worst of it is ridiculous."

She didn't know what to say to that...no *wait*, she *did* know what to say to that, but chose to keep her own counsel for now. Instead, she met the puppy's gaze. The little dog was snuggled against his chest, wrapped in the ruined towel, and only the three black dots of her eyes and wet nose were visible. She was no longer shivering and looked quite smug in her contentment.

"We can discuss this after you've taken care of the dog. I have to finish dinner."

She turned away before he could say anything more and returned to the kitchen. His words kept bouncing around in her head. They felt ominous, threatening...more oppressive than the storm raging away outside. Where would she stay if he decided to close the house for winter? If he meant for her to check on it once a week, he must intend for her to remain close by. The closest populated area was Riversend. Charity didn't want to live in Riversend. She didn't want to live close to anyone. She liked it here. This was her home. She felt safe here.

And what about Amos? He had plans to retire back to the

Eastern Cape eventually, but for now he was happy and content to live and work here. Closing up the house for winter would force Amos to retire earlier than he wanted to.

She was chopping onions for a ragout, and her vision was so blurred—from the onions, of course—that she could barely see what she was doing. She stopped, afraid of cutting her fingers, and took a moment to compose herself.

This wasn't her home. George and Amos weren't her family. This was *his* house. And they all worked for him. She had fooled herself, for three years...fooled herself into thinking of this place as a safe haven. But she should never have stayed this long. She had never meant to stay for years. She had come here at the lowest point in her life...and she had developed this persona. This *Mrs. Cole*: ageless, sexless, efficient, invisible. Mrs. Cole had made her feel safe. And Charity had stayed. And had refused to listen to the gnawing voice in the back of her head. The one that told her that she should move on, move out...heal.

But she had stagnated here and had become invisible, and unrecognizable, even to herself.

And now—faced with the very real, very alarming prospect of having to leave—she found herself feeling *terrified*. Alone.

Hunted.

She placed her palms flat on the marble surface of the kitchen counter and lowered her head as she fought to regulate her breathing.

Snap out of it, Charity!

One deep cleansing inhalation of breath, a slow count to ten, and a gradual release of the air in her lungs, and she felt better.

Centered.

Nothing was decided. It had been mentioned in passing. Almost impulsively. Everything was going to be fine.

"Something smells good."

The dark, masculine voice, coming so unexpectedly from behind her, nearly an hour later, disconcerted Charity. But she managed to curb her immediate fight or flight instinct in response to being startled. She braced her shoulders, forced all expression from her features, and turned to face him.

He had stepped into the kitchen, puppy tucked into the crook of his arms. The sight of the dog brought a quick, involuntary smile to her lips.

"Oh, that's clever," Charity said. He had used some of his legendary ingenuity to fashion a sweater for the dog out of one of his tube socks. He had cut a hole into the toe of the sock and two others below that for her head and front legs. The sock was very roomy on the tiny pup.

"Perhaps one of my socks would be a better fit," Charity suggested, and his gaze dipped to her sensibly shod feet.

"If you wouldn't mind donating a pair to the cause, that would be much appreciated." He lifted the snoozing puppy slightly. "She cleans up rather nicely, wouldn't you say?"

No. Charity wouldn't say. Not at all.

The puppy wouldn't be bringing home any beauty prizes. The bath hadn't improved the nondescript brown of her partly wiry, partly fluffy coat...But she was adorable in the way all dogs were, with the earnest pleading eyes and the sweet expression and the hopeful wag of her fluffy tail. She appeared to have some Yorkie, Chihuahua, and Maltese poodle in her, and Charity doubted she'd get much bigger. Considering her tiny size right now, it was a miracle she had survived out in this weather for so long.

"I wonder if her mother and siblings are out there," Charity mused. She hoped that if they *were* out there, they had found some decent shelter to weather this storm.

Miles—*damn it*! She was just going to consider him as such in the privacy of her thoughts—looked horrified at the notion and took a step toward the back door. Recognizing his intention, she stepped in front of him and shook her head.

"If they were out there, we would have heard them by now. More than likely, this little one—"

"Stormy," he interrupted her, and she blinked, not sure why he was stating the obvious.

"Yes. Because of the stormy weather, they've probably found shelter and she got separated from—"

"No...her name is Stormy."

"You *named* her?" She couldn't disguise the dismay in her voice. He was going to find it incredibly hard parting with the dog if he'd named her already.

"She needs a name and I wasn't going to call her 'Dog' or 'Hey You'...I thought Stormy was apt."

"But—"

"Do we have anything to feed her?"

"I don't keep a supply of dog food in the pantry, no."

"No need for facetiousness, Mrs. Cole. I meant chicken or fish...something we can steam with some veggies. I remember reading somewhere that unsalted steamed chicken and rice would be the easiest on a sick pup's little tummy."

Tummy? Seriously?

"I'll prepare enough chicken and rice for the next few days."

"She'll need to eat three to four times a day."

"You seem to know a great deal about this, do you have a dog in London?"

"Stormy's my first dog."

"You're keeping her?"

"I don't see why I shouldn't. I'll get her shots up-to-date... make sure she's healthy, and I'm certain she'll be well enough to travel long before *I'm* cleared to work again."

The dog—*Stormy*—gave Charity a haughty look. Oh, she *knew* she'd just landed in the lap of luxury. Skin and bones, a little mangy and probably still sporting more than her fair share of ticks, she was already carrying herself like a princess.

And Miles... *damned* if he didn't look completely besotted with the mutt.

"I'll take care of her food. I doubt she's house-trained so we're going to have to keep her confined to a bathroom or something."

"I'll sort something out. No need to concern yourself, Mrs. Cole."

Hard not to worry. If he changed his mind about Stormy, Charity knew she'd be the one left as the dog's primary caregiver. Miles seemed in love with the pup now, but who knew if that would last?

She ran her damp palms down the front of her skirt and nodded.

"Very well, sir." He winced at the word. "Let me know what you'll need for her and I'll do my best to procure it."

"I know that, Mrs. Cole. Now, what's to eat? I'm *starving*."

Chapter Four

Stormy was a quiet, undemanding dog, and Miles worried that she may be sicker than she looked. But until he could get the hell out of this house, there was no way to know. Her appetite seemed fine, but she slept a lot and stuck close by his side. He was beginning to think he should have named her Velcro instead.

His impulsive decision to keep her had been out of character for him. Usually he would have handed the pup over to Mrs. Cole with the instruction that she took care of it and kept it out of sight until they could pass the responsibility on to the SPCA. But one look at the pathetic scrap of a dog, so clearly ill and malnourished, and he had felt an immediate affinity toward it.

And now here she was; lying on the couch next to him despite his housekeeper's critical glares whenever she spotted the dog on the furniture. The pup was wearing one of Mrs. Cole's socks—a much better fit for her—and her head was resting on her tiny front paws while she stared up at him in devotion. Her ears were lopsided, one up and one down, giving her a rakish appearance, and her limpid black eyes were ridiculously expressive, especially with their dark "eyebrows".

According to the Internet research he had managed to do during his extremely limited allotted "Wi-Fi time", puppies her age were balls of mischievous energy. But Stormy spent her days sleeping and shadowing his every move.

He decided to crate train her and found a small, wicker shopping basket that she couldn't climb out of to use for that purpose. It worked well as a temporary crate, and she was content to be left in the basket for a couple of hours here and there. She seemed to consider it *her* space. He fashioned a ball out of a pair of his socks and hoped that it could work as both a pacifier—since it carried his scent—and as a toy.

He knew Mrs. Cole didn't quite approve of the entire set up and couldn't figure out why. But her reticence and his extreme awareness of their employer/employee status, prevented him from asking.

Mrs. Cole had been right about the blackout lasting for more than a few hours. They were still using the generator now—three days after the massive storm had blown the transformer box. Nobody could come out to fix the box because the bridge had washed out. And according to George, who was in daily contact with Miles, it was scheduled to be repaired "sometime before the weekend", which was of no help at all, since it was currently Monday.

Miles could now see why Mrs. Cole was so damned precious over his use of electricity. She entered rooms, moments after he exited them, to turn off the lights, or the television, or whatever the hell else he had thoughtlessly left running. It was unnerving how rapidly she seemed to materialize to do those things, before fading right back into the woodwork as if she'd never been there.

It was like living with a disapproving ghost, and his curiosity about her grew every day. He had never again caught her with her hair down, or dressed in anything other than her regular, boring apparel of skirt and blouse, combined with those sensible, ugly black brogues. The shoes seemed too heavy and chunky for her slender legs.

Not that he'd noticed her legs...*much*. Well, his eyes were always drawn to the ugly shoes and just naturally followed the length of her shapely calves to the hemline of her skirt. He only *sometimes* allowed himself to recall how they looked even farther up, past the knees, to those firm, beautifully toned thighs and...

He shook his head and muttered a curse, drawing Stormy's concerned gaze to his.

He was developing a serious case of cabin fever. His mind was restless and venturing into dangerous, no-go zones.

"Let's go for a walk, girl. See if we can find your mum."

It was the best thing to do. He wasn't a huge reader and had pretty much blasted through his audiobooks already. Television was out of the question as Mrs. Cole had allocated precisely three hours for television watching in a bid to conserve electricity. He was saving those hours for later. When he had asked her how many hours she had, she had told him that she rarely watched TV. Which he found hard to believe. What the hell else was there to do out here?

Stormy was a sharp little girl, and they'd been on enough limited outings in the short time that he'd had her for her to recognize the word "walk". He took her out every four hours for toilet breaks, relishing the opportunity to stretch his legs. It was cold and rained intermittently, and it probably wasn't good for either of them, but both he and the pup enjoyed their forays out into the vast garden.

Today, wasn't as blustery as the last few days had been, and

Miles wanted to walk along the lakeshore and take the opportunity to search for Stormy's mother.

The house had a private beach about a mile long. During summer, his siblings and their friends made good use of both the beach as well as Miles's forty-five-foot sloop that remained moored year-round at their private jetty. He figured he could easily walk up and down the flat, sandy stretch of beach without getting too winded.

"Mrs. Cole?" he called, before entering the kitchen. She didn't like being startled— he had picked up on that pretty quickly. As a result, he had taken to announcing his presence before intruding upon any areas he deemed her domain. And the kitchen was very much Mrs. Cole's territory.

She looked flushed and flustered when he walked into the room a moment later, and his eyes narrowed. She was standing by the sink, patting her pristine hair, a dull red flush darkening her cheeks, and she couldn't quite meet his eyes.

Something was up with her.

Miles assessed her appearance, wondering what could have caused such an uncharacteristic reaction in his usually unruffled housekeeper. A quick scan around the spacious, bright room solved the mystery almost immediately.

A pot of tea, next to a half full cup, sat on the round table at the cozy banquette in the corner of the kitchen. She must be on a break. A gossip magazine, the likes of which he would never have imagined Mrs. Cole reading, lay open beside the dainty porcelain cup.

The bright red headline screeched:

"Mermaid Pregnant with Chris Hemsworth's Love Child."

He fought back a grin but was immediately distracted when his gaze dropped and he caught sight of her ugly, unwieldy shoes. They were tucked beneath the table, with her thick, white socks stuffed into them. His eyes tracked back to Mrs. Cole and trailed down her slim body, lingering over those beautifully shaped calves again, before finding themselves helplessly drawn to her small, delicate feet.

Ten perfect toes, topped with frosted blue tips. The shade was a surprisingly whimsical choice for the monochromatic, buttoned-down, stern woman standing in front of him.

Miles swallowed in a bid to moisten his abruptly dry throat. He had never found feet particularly erotic before...but right now, these elegantly arched soft looking beauties were seriously revving his engine.

He was staring, he knew he was staring...he should stop fucking staring before his dick went from half-mast to a full, proud salute.

He cleared his throat and jerked his gaze back to her deer-trapped-in-the-headlights stare and said the first nonsensical thing that popped into his head, "How does one copulate with a mermaid, do you suppose?"

Her jaw dropped and he felt his own face heat at the inanity of that question. But before he knew it, even more stupid words spilled from his lips, "I mean, which parts go where? It's not like there are corresponding bits. No inserting Tab A into Slot B as it were."

He sounded like a bloody fool.

"Well, you're overlooking the most common mermaid trope," she said, after a long, measured pause. "They can take on human form for limited amounts of time. I would assume that's when the...uh...copulation takes place."

The word "copulation" wasn't sexy, but hearing it spill from her lush lips was like a spark to tinder. He was embarrassingly erect in seconds.

Fortunately, he was wearing a baggy sweatpants, and his

errant hard-on wasn't noticeable. Still, it was damned awkward standing in front of his stalwart housekeeper sporting wood with her name on it.

So inappropriate.

"I uh...we..." He dropped his gaze to Stormy who was curled up in the crook of his elbow. "We're going for a walk. On the beach. I was looking for something to fashion into a lead and collar for Stormy. Any suggestions?"

A small frown settled on that smooth brow.

"I don't think you should do that. It's slippery and perilous out there. You could fall."

Did he look so fucking frail to her?

"I assure you, I'll be fine, Mrs. Cole."

"It's also freezing and raining. I don't think you or the dog..."

"Stormy," he reminded her.

"I don't think either of you are ready for a walk like that yet."

"It's not your concern."

"On the contrary, it totally *is* my concern. If anything happens to you, Amos and I would have to find you and get you back to safety. In these conditions, emergency services are an hour away at best. Likely longer with the bridge out. Anything could go wrong. What if it rains harder? The water levels would rise before you could get back here in time and you could be washed away. And who knows how the cold will affect your chest? You may be—"

"*Enough*! Mrs. Cole, you are out of line," he snapped, pissed off because she was also right. He couldn't chance taking a solitary hike in his current condition. But he fucking *hated* having his housekeeper treat him like an errant, sickly schoolboy.

Who the hell was in charge here anyway?

He glared at her while she stared back, her face serene and inscrutable, not a hair out of place...

He sighed.

Without a bloody doubt, she was in charge. This tall, ageless, mysterious—*barefoot*, a tiny voice reminded him breathlessly—stern woman was one-hundred-percent running the show. That's why he liked having her around. With Mrs. Cole in charge, their vacations had been stress free. But he wasn't currently on vacation, and that appeared to be unsettling the equilibrium of their usually uneventful non-relationship

"Your concerns have been noted, Mrs. Cole, and if you find me collapsed in a heap five hundred yards from the house, feel free to tell me you told me so. Now, do you have anything I can use as a leash or not?"

STUBBORN MAN!

Charity kneaded her bread dough more vigorously than usual, imagining that it was Miles Hollingsworth's face. He had been gone for half an hour already. She had watched in concern as he and the puppy—who had pranced alongside him wearing another sock sweater and slapdash rope slip lead—painstakingly made their way to the jetty. He had turned right before the wooden dock in order to access the beach, and Charity had lost sight of him after that.

He wasn't her responsibility, she was here to cook and clean and make his stay as comfortable as possible. She was *not* here to police his every move and make sure he took his fricking medicine. She lifted the dough and slapped it down on the granite counter with enough force to send flour exploding in all directions.

"Damn it," she cursed, annoyed by the mess and blaming

him for that too. The last three days had been so uncomfortable for her. She had done her best to remain out of sight, but he seemed to actively seek her out, which unnerved her. Especially since he never appeared to have any reason to do so, sometimes he just sat in the kitchen and watched her work. She *hated* that. She felt awkward and out of sorts having him in her space.

But she couldn't prohibit him from coming into his own kitchen.

She could tell that he was bored and restless but—again—it wasn't her job to keep him entertained. Happily, training the dog took up a lot of his attention. But the pup was a fast learner and slept often, which meant that he found himself at loose ends for large chunks of the day.

His walks around the garden had gotten longer each day, and she supposed it was inevitable for cabin fever and boredom to force him to venture farther afield.

But he still seemed so weak.

She shook herself and wiped her forehead with the back of her wrist.

None of your business, Charity, she reminded herself. *Absolutely none of your concern if the damned fool man wants to kill himself!*

Still, she kept lifting her eyes and taking peeks out of the back window. Hoping to see him plod his way up the back garden path toward the kitchen door.

Instead, all she saw was Amos who caught her eye and waved at her with a happy grin. He had popped in earlier with a few cut proteas for decorating the house. She waved back, her thoughts still on her boss. She barely noticed when Amos drifted out of sight again.

She still had no real clue what was wrong with him, and she

wondered what manner of illness could have laid her previously infallible-seeming boss so very low.

She once again reminded herself that it was none of her business, but it was hard not to speculate. Part of her wanted to ask, reasoning that it would be better if she knew, in case of relapse. The other part didn't want to know. She didn't want to care or be concerned over what could possibly happen to him out here in the wild with no medical assistance close by.

Her phone chimed, and she wiped her hands on a tea towel and reached into her apron pocket. She didn't often receive messages. Over the last six years, all but the most stubborn of her friends and family had given up on her. With good reason...she had retreated, kept them at bay. Been uncommunicative and emotionally, mentally and physically distant.

Only her sister, parents, and best friend had remained in contact. They were her tether to the "real world", as she had started to think of it. This wasn't her life. It was temporary. Yet temporary had somehow gone from "just a few months" to *three* years, and she still wasn't sure how that had happened.

Life here was so...uncomplicated.

She checked her message. It was from her sister, Faith.

> FAITH
> Cherry, we need to talk. I know you hate unannounced calls, so fair warning. I'm calling in 5, 4, 3...

Her phone rang.

Charity swallowed past the lump in her throat as she stared at the device. She hadn't spoken with her sister in months.

"Hello?"

"Cherry, you okay? You sound sick?" Charity fought back both a smile at the sound of her sister's voice and a swell of revulsion at the nickname.

He had used it often. Sweetly at first, then more and more mockingly until—by the end—she had cringed every time he said it in that sickeningly tender, taunting way of his.

Cherry baby, you're mine. All mine. My cherry *little Cherry.*

"Uh...I'm fine," Charity said, beating back the memory of that voice. Of how he would call her...playfully stretching the nickname out over several syllables while he hunted for her. He had taken a sweet—somewhat silly—nickname, bestowed upon her by her loving family and he had weaponized it. Turned it into something ugly and repulsive.

"Look, Gracie's birthday is coming up, and I want you here."

Charity was well aware that her niece was turning six next month but had hoped she could get away with sending a gift and making a phone call.

"Faith, things are crazy here. My boss showed up unannounced and..."

"We're having a party," Faith interjected. "And she's asked if you'll be here."

"The timing is—"

"I told her you would be here," her sister interrupted again.

"My boss has been ill. I can't simply up and leave without warning."

"Charity, it's been three years." Her sister's voice—gentle and laden with empathy—undid her. So much sympathy, love, and understanding.

But Faith didn't understand, not really. None of them did.

"I won't pretend to know why you've felt the need to uproot and move to the middle of nowhere. I thought after Blaine... you'd want to pick up where you left off with your career. Instead you put your life on hold to become a frikken *housekeeper*. I recognize that you needed the space, and we thought we were doing the right thing in giving it to you. But we shouldn't have done that. You need us. You need your family. We should never have allowed you to grieve alone. Because you haven't healed at all, have you? You can't move past this. We *all* miss Blaine, Cherry. We all loved him as much as you did, and we're all grieving his loss. But when you left, it felt like we lost you too."

They thought that she grieved for him. Missed him, *loved* him...that man. Her husband, Blaine Thomas Davenport. The man who had beaten her, kicked her, raped her, abused her almost every day of their three-year marriage. The man who had tried to kill on her that last horrific night.

Her family thought he had been a good man, and they mourned his loss.

Watching them cry over him had proven impossible to do, and Charity had begged her attorney, the only person on this earth who knew her truth, to help her find a place to hide. To lick her wounds in private. Mr. Lanscombe had found this position for her...he'd practically had it created for her. He had known Miles's family attorney and had called in a favor.

And Charity had fled.

Something that she should have done during those three long years of abuse. She hated herself for not leaving him. For making every excuse under the sun until she had run out of excuses and instead found herself acknowledging that she was weak, stupid, and powerless. It had been her lowest point. He had owned her after that.

Body and soul.

"Cherry?" She snapped back to the present at the sound of her sister's voice and realized that her face was wet with tears. She stared blindly out of the kitchen window and was alarmed to see Miles coming up the path. He caught her gaze and his brow lowered, but she turned away and scrubbed the edge of her sleeve over her damp cheeks.

"Faith, I can't come. I have responsibilities here," she said, hoping her sister wouldn't hear the betraying husk in her voice.

"Cherry, you have a family who loves you, please come home."

A familiar refrain.

"I'll consider it. If I...if I can find a way to..." Her voice tapered off when the backdoor opened, and she kept her face averted, not wanting Miles's perceptive gaze to spot any trace of tears on her cheeks.

"Everybody would love to see you. Sandra and Paul will be there too. They've been so lost since...since *it* happened. It would be wonderful if they could spend time with you again."

Charity knew that, and it was the main reason she did not want to go to her niece's party. Sandra and Paul Davenport, her husband's parents. She had stopped thinking of them as her parents-in-law around the same time she had comprehended that they knew about Blaine's abuse of her.

They were her parents' best friends. Of *course*, they would be at the party. Beloved Aunt Sandra and Uncle Paul.

Maybe if you'd stop making him so *angry, Charity.* Her mother-in-law's gentle suggestion, offered in an oh-so-helpful tone of voice, drifted through her mind. This after a particularly bad beating. He had broken her ribs that time, and Sandra had taken her to the hospital, offering some explanation or excuse for the injury that the doctors hadn't questioned.

"Faith, I have to go," Charity said, knowing she sounded abrupt but unable to do anything about that. She hated having Miles here to witness any part of this call. It felt like an intrusion. "I love you. Hugs to Gracie."

She disconnected the call before her sister had the opportunity to say anything more. She cleared her throat and took a moment to compose herself before turning to face her boss.

He wasn't paying her any attention. Instead, he was guzzling down a bottle of mineral water while Stormy enthusiastically did the same at her water bowl. After finishing half of the bottle in one go, he lowered it to wipe his forearm across his lip. The move was so unlike the fastidious Miles Hollingsworth that Charity couldn't help but stare.

He caught the stare and lifted his shoulders.

"I'll have to remember to take some water along next time."

"You look..." She paused and considered her words. Hot, sweaty, wrung out, and not at all like his usual self. In fact, she would go so far as to say he looked really, *really* good. Despite his thinness and his sick bed pallor. His black hair—so much longer than she was used to seeing it—was wild and damp. The thick, unkempt mane framed his face attractively.

He was tallish, five nine or ten, and sparely built. Some would probably be generous in their use of the word "average" when describing Miles Hollingsworth. Charity would be the first to admit that perhaps he was beautifully, boringly average at first glance. In fact, the only thing about him that wasn't average was a hawkish nose that dominated his narrow face and would have most people struggling to call him even passably handsome.

But there was something about him...about those plain features. A sharpness to his cheekbones and an edge to his jawline. Something in the piercing and aloof chill of his striking steel gray eyes. That penetrating stare, combined with that overbearing nose, was what made him seem so unapproachable.

That reticence was the very reason Charity should stay as far away from the man as possible. Yet *something* about him appealed to her in ways that she found unsettling and tried to keep suppressed. And while it had always been there, this tiny tug of attraction, she had never truly admitted it to herself before this moment.

But that terrifying acknowledgment had her keen to slam the lid on this simmering attraction that could boil over if she didn't maintain her vigilance and her distance.

"The Ice Man", that's what the media called him. Cold, calculated, and cutthroat. He was pretty much the antithesis of her late husband.

Blaine had been almost godlike in his beauty. Tall, with a perfect body, perfect face, pale green eyes, and perfectly coiffed sandy hair. He had been so warm and approachable. Everybody's favorite guy.

Just *perfect*.

And rotten to the core.

"I look?" Miles prompted her softly, and she blinked. She hated that she had noticed how good he looked. She didn't want to notice that about him, or about any man for that matter. She didn't think she was ready for that. For sexual awareness. Especially not awareness of someone who had so much power over her life and immediate future.

"Uhm...cold. You look cold. And wet."

"It started drizzling about five minutes ago. Light and annoying but pretty effective at soaking us through."

"That can't be good for you."

"Probably not, but I feel fantastic. It was an invigorating walk. We both enjoyed it."

He took another thirsty gulp from his bottle, this time keeping his perceptive, unsettling gaze on her face. "You have something on your cheek."

He brushed his long, slender index finger over his own cheekbone.

Charity self-consciously lifted her hands and scrubbed them over her face. The corners of his lips lifted when he met her inquiring gaze, and he shook his head.

"Despite just about rubbing your skin raw, you still missed it."

"What is it?"

"White powder. You been snorting coke while I was gone?" The words were so deadpan, Charity's jaw dropped in shock at the question. His lips kicked up even more at the edges, revealing the shallow dimple in his right cheek.

"*No*, of course not," she gasped, and this time he snorted. The sound somewhere between a laugh and a sigh.

"Relax, Mrs. Cole, I was joking. I can see that it's flour." He indicated toward the island behind her, where the overworked dough lay forgotten on the counter.

"Oh," she said, feeling like a complete idiot. He stepped toward her and lifted his hand. She froze and then flinched when his thumb touched her skin for a millisecond.

"There," he said, not seeming to notice her reaction. "It's gone."

He took a deliberate step back, his movement telling her that he had most certainly noticed her reaction.

"I'm sorry." The apology stunned her. "I shouldn't have done that. It was uncalled for."

. . .

Fuck!

He shouldn't have touched her. He wasn't sure why he had. It had been improper behavior. But the gesture had been unconscious and not intended to do anything more than remove the smudge of flour from her cheek.

But it had shocked and...*frightened* her. And the very last thing he wanted was for her to feel unsafe around him.

She had looked so fucking sad when he had first walked into the kitchen, and Miles had teased her to get that tragic look out of her eyes. It was the first time he had ever seen the usually stalwart Mrs. Cole so vulnerable, and he didn't like it. Not one bit. The depth of sadness and despair he had glimpsed on her face had made her seem young and completely defenseless.

He hated it, and he wanted to know what had caused it.

"Was that your family? On the phone?" he asked, and then could have kicked himself for opening his damned mouth. It was none of his business.

She didn't say anything, merely patted her hair—checking for errant strands that were never there—and turned back to her work station at the island.

"Do they live close by?"

Fucking hell, shut up, Hollingsworth!

He was about to change the subject by asking about dinner, when she replied, "No. They don't."

"Where do they live?" Now that she'd responded, the topic was fair game as far as he was concerned.

"Nowhere near here."

"Do you see them often?"

"No." Her response was cold and delivered with an air of finality that encouraged no further questions.

Miles watched her closely for a second, her smooth, clinical mask of indifference was back in place, but there were fine cracks forming. He could tell from the slight tremble of her long, elegant fingers as she cleaned sticky dough off the marble counter. And from the white line forming around the tight press of her full lips. If he pushed her, she would break...

But he found that—despite his curiosity—he didn't want her to break. He wanted to know more. But only if she was willing to tell him.

And why should she ever want to confide in him? He was nothing but a paycheck to her. And his current curiosity and boredom, and frustration did not entitle him to know her secrets.

He cleared his throat, not sure what to say next. He should leave her to her privacy. But what if she cried again? He didn't like the thought of leaving her alone to cry.

In the end, she was the one who broke the silence. "How was your walk?"

He latched on to the question gratefully.

"We didn't get very far. It took us fifteen minutes to get to the bushwillow tree"—a feat that usually took him under ten minutes—"and because we were both already flagging at that point, I thought it best to turn around. Didn't want to give you the opportunity to say 'I told you so'."

"Oh, I wouldn't have..."

"I was joking, Mrs. Cole." Again—as with his off-color comment about the flour earlier—she looked so confounded at the notion of him having a sense of humor, that Miles found his amusement fizzling.

Jesus, he knew he could be a crabby bastard at times, but he wasn't *that* bad, was he?

She had removed the raw dough from the counter and was meticulously wiping the surface with a damp cloth.

"You're not going to finish the bread?" he asked. A topic

change seemed prudent, and it might as well be about something mundane.

"I ruined the dough, I'll have to start over."

"Do you—" He slammed the brakes on the question he couldn't believe he had almost asked and swallowed audibly. Her eyes swung up to his; uncharacteristic curiosity lighting the dark, dark depths of that beautiful limpid gaze.

"Do I what?"

He considered his options for the rest of the day. It was still too early for television, Stormy would soon pass out and sleep for a few hours after her walk, he had no more audiobooks, the Internet was down, work was off limits...he could grab a book from the extensive library, but he usually needed to be in the right frame of mind to do any reading.

That left sleeping, exercise—not the ideal option after his walk—or staying here. With a woman who clearly preferred her own company to his.

Nothing else to it, he might as well complete the question, "Do you need a hand?"

She looked confused, as if she couldn't quite comprehend what he had asked.

"I know I'd probably be as useful as tits on a bull, but I've always wanted to try my hand at baking bread."

Her gaze shifted from confused to assessing, as if she were trying to gauge his level of sincerity.

"Have you really?"

The complete lack of anything resembling credulity in the question made him wince, and he shook his head, "Okay, not really. But it would be interesting to try."

Another long stare, and Miles was proud of himself for not squirming beneath her intense scrutiny.

"You're bored, aren't you?"

Her astute question nearly made him smile, but he kept a poker face and maintained unflinching eye contact. "Out. Of. My. Fucking. Mind."

It wasn't a good idea. It would be best if he stayed out of her way, and the lines between them as employer and employee remained clearly defined. But the power had been out for three days. The weather had kept him confined mostly indoors. And she could tell that the restrictions were starting to chafe at him. Miles Hollingsworth was a workaholic, she knew that, she had seen it whenever he had come on "vacation" with his family. His siblings always had a blast, but Miles tended to remain glued to his phone, or his laptop, earphones practically a permanent fixture on his head, studying headlines and staying abreast of stock market trends.

His idea of relaxing appeared to involve sipping the occasional brandy while listening to what she assumed were financial podcasts. He was a workhorse whose only apparent passion was finding and fixing broken things. And then selling them at immense profit.

Sure, that was a gross oversimplification but how else did one explain what he did?

And now *he* was the broken thing in need of fixing. And he didn't seem to have the first notion of how to go about that. Then again, neither did Charity. She had been broken for so long, it was hard to remember being whole and undamaged.

Her teeth raked over her lower lip as she considered his request. This was his house, his kitchen, and she was his employee. He would have been well within his rights to demand instead of ask.

But he hadn't. He had offered her a choice.

She exhaled softly and nodded. "Fine, get cleaned up, and we'll get started on the bread."

His eyes smiled at her. And it was remarkable. His expression didn't change at all, but his steel gray eyes lit up and crinkled at the corners. She had never seen him do that before and she found it disturbingly appealing. Flustered, she shifted her attention to the puppy standing at their feet. Stormy was patiently waiting to take her cues from Miles.

His gaze followed hers and this time, the smile traveled to his lips. They quirked, showing off that dimple, and the dog's tail thumped slowly at the change in his expression.

"But first I have to feed and crate this one, she's bound to be exhausted after our walk."

"You can bring her basket here and leave it there"—she pointed to the doorway separating the kitchen from the hallway — "that way she won't get anxious."

"I will, thank you."

He turned away and left the kitchen, Stormy close behind him, and Charity released the breath that she had been holding.

She didn't like the idea of him being underfoot, but she could imagine how frustrating the entire experience had to be for him and part of her job was to ensure that he was content and enjoying his stay here.

That was the only reason she had agreed to his absurd request. Part of the job, really.

Nothing at all to do with the gentle look in his eyes when he had caught her crying. Even less to do with the appealing cant of his head and the almost puppy dog pleading in his eyes when he had asked her if he could help.

This was Miles Henry Hollingsworth. Modern age marauder. Present day pirate. He didn't do puppy dog eyes. She must have imagined it.

Chapter Five

Miles loved the squidgy feeling of the raw dough between his fingers. Kneading bread wasn't something he had ever imagined himself doing, or even liking, but this was ridiculously enjoyable. He had followed Mrs. Cole's careful instructions to the letter. She hadn't touched anything but had told him which ingredients to get, how to mix them, and then how to knead the lump of gooey dough until it was "springy"—her word—to the touch.

"Stop poking at it," Mrs. Cole rebuked, when he stuck his finger into the soft, elasticky stuff...

Again.

He liked watching the dent he had made disappear as the dough swelled back into shape.

"Just testing the springiness," he said.

"For the fifth time?"

"I like to be sure."

She didn't roll her eyes, but she wanted to. He could tell.

And he couldn't imagine it at all, Mrs. Cole sinking to such juvenile depths. It made him desperate to see her actually do it.

"I never had playdough as a child," he confided, and she threw him a look of sheer and utter disbelief. "No, it's true. Our parents didn't have the money to waste on such frivolities. And later, after my dad died, mum started taking extra shifts at the department store where she worked and needed my help around the house more. Whatever money she had for toys—which wasn't much—went to Hughie and Vicki."

She opened her mouth seemingly to say something but then shut it immediately. He didn't like that. He wanted to hear whatever it was she had to say.

"Out with it, Mrs. Cole," he commanded her, while surreptitiously sticking his finger into the dough one more time. Her reproving stare told him she hadn't missed the move and made him feel like a kid caught with his hand in the biscuit tin.

"How old were you?" she asked him. The question, coming in an uncharacteristically timid voice, surprised him somewhat. He wasn't sure what he had been expecting, but that most certainly was not it.

"About eleven. Hugh and Vicki were six and four respectively."

"That's a lot of responsibility for an eleven-year-old to handle."

"I managed."

"I can't imagine how."

"I did, and that's all that matters." He regretted his brusqueness when she retreated completely. Her face went blank as she took a measured half-step back.

Mrs. Cole clearly required more tact than Miles possessed

"Of course. Well…the dough needs to prove for a couple of hours before it can go in the oven. I'll call you when it's ready."

And just like that...he was dismissed. That didn't sit well with him. He wasn't the type of man who allowed himself to be dismissed by his employees.

"What if I peel the potatoes?"

"No potatoes tonight."

Well, *that* wouldn't do at all. "I like potatoes."

"Variety is the spice of life."

"Trite, Mrs. Cole."

"But true, Mr. Hollingsworth." Her pithy comeback made in that deadpan voice amused him, but he didn't think she'd appreciate his amusement at her expense and curbed the instinct to smile.

"What's for dinner then?" he asked.

She removed a roll of cling film from one of the kitchen cupboards and unwound a strip. Miles watched, fascinated, as she tore off a piece and covered his recently kneaded dough with the plastic. She dropped a clean tea towel on top of that and dusted her hands in a satisfied manner before answering his question. "Lasagna. Honey roasted carrots. And salad."

"With bread?"

"Way too many carbs. The bread is for tomorrow's breakfast."

He currently didn't give a damn about the added carbs. He had been ravenous since arriving here—was it really only five days ago?—and had fully indulged in all the delicious foods she had been cooking. He knew he should care more. But considering the amount of weight he had lost, he imagined a few extra carbs would do him the world of good.

"I need the carbs," he pointed out, and she eyed him in that long, considering manner of hers.

"You do."

He thought she would leave it at that, but instead of

diverting her eyes, she continued to stare at him. He waited. Wanting her to ask, even though he wasn't sure he would answer.

"What happened to you?"

"Ignored my doctor when he told me to take it easy. Thought I could work through a cold, only it wasn't a cold and I was a stubborn fool who found himself lounging in the ICU for few interminable weeks."

"ICU?"

"Yes."

If she wanted more, she would have to ask. Her mouth opened, the lips rounded as she formed the start of a word. Her forehead furrowed as she considered what she was about to say… a soft breath escaped those full lips, before she pursed them shut and bobbed her head slightly.

"You can prepare the salad."

"Right." He was disappointed by her lack of follow through. But Miles, more than most people, understood the desire to keep one's nose out of others' business.

He didn't like talking about himself, and he wasn't sure why he wanted her to ask…perhaps because he recognized the soul deep loneliness in her. He often considered himself equally isolated. But he was a loner by nature. A loner who had never been as completely cut off from the world as Mrs. Cole appeared to be.

And while he wasn't an overly affectionate or demonstrative man, he didn't lack love in his life. Not with a sister who forced her hugs on him, a brother who unashamedly hero-worshipped him, and a mother who always meddled in his private life.

But this woman, despite the phone call he had inadvertently walked in on a few hours ago, seemed wholly alone. And that bothered him. He was honest enough with himself to admit that he would not have given her mental and emotional well-being a moment's consideration under normal circumstances. In fact, he had given her very little thought during the three years she had been employed by him. But right now—with little else to occupy his mind and his time—Mrs. Cole was an enigma. And Miles fucking *loved* solving mysteries.

One more lap!

Her lungs were burning, her legs and arms felt like they were about to fall off, but experience told Charity that half a mile was the magic number to help her fall asleep again after one of her nightmares.

And, thanks to her sister's phone call earlier, her brain had dredged up the worst of them tonight.

She woke up covered in blood. So much blood! Was she bleeding? He didn't usually make her bleed...well not this *much.*

No! Charity focused on the burn. Physical pain of *her* making. That horrific moment was three years in the past. It had no bearing on her current reality. Blaine was nothing to her but a bad memory now.

Such a bad memory.

Half a lap to go.

Focus...focus...*focus*!

Her hands slammed into the wall, bringing her body to an abrupt halt. Water fountained violently up around her and crashed onto the coping tiles. For a split-second, she was tempted to flip and do another lap, but she knew her physical limitations. That was it for her tonight. A hot shower and, hopefully, she'd manage another two hours of sleep before getting up to fix breakfast.

She levered herself out of the pool. Thankfully her arms, wobbly after the relentless workout, supported her weight. Her hair, too long to be contained by a swim cap, had been plaited and wound into a large bun. But the long, thick rope of her braid had lost its anchor and tumbled to her waist.

She should cut it but...

I want your hair jaw length, Cherry. It's classy.

She shuddered and grabbed up the thick fluffy towel she had left on the bench beside the half Olympic size indoor pool. There was an outdoor pool as well. Purely recreational. But this one was for swimming laps. And Charity made full use of it whenever her employee and his family were not in residence.

Her breathing was heavy and echoed around the large room. The water, only now starting to settle after her exit, was slapping against the pool wall. Those sounds, combined with the rhythmic drip of moisture from the end of her braid to the floor, and the sighing rustle of the towel against her skin and the fabric of her swimming costume, were comforting and familiar.

But the quiet squeak of rubber against the tiled floor was unexpected, unwelcome, and intimidatingly intrusive.

She froze.

Her instinct was to crouch, to make herself small and invisible...but she refused to do that. Not this time. And after that split-second of indecision and absolute terror, she lifted her chin to look and then exhaled the breath that had snagged in her throat.

The man silhouetted in the doorway did not frighten her.

She could not see his face, the light coming from behind him was brighter than the dim illumination in the natatorium, but she recognized the breadth of those shoulders and the arrogant assurance in his stance.

Besides, no man could be frightening with a scrawny puppy sitting splay-legged at his feet.

He did not frighten her, but his intrusion did make her feel uncomfortable and exposed. Vulnerable in a different way.

She lifted her towel and held it up in front of her body, shielding herself from his view.

Her message was clear, but he didn't turn away as she had hoped he would.

"I'm sorry, Mrs. Cole. I wasn't expecting to find you here. Not at this hour."

"I could say the same of you." She winced as soon as she said it. He could go where he pleased at any hour of the day or night.

"I couldn't sleep. It was swimming or hot milk. And this was the more appealing option. What brings you here at three in the morning?"

"I had a nightmare." The words were out before she could think the better of it.

"About?"

"The boogeyman. The pool's all yours." She wrapped the large, sheet towel securely around her body, and tucked the ends in at her chest. When he didn't move, she edged toward the door. Her wet feet slapped against the floor, echoing around the massive room.

As she drew closer to him, and her eyes adjusted to the light, she saw that he was wearing swim trunks. The squeak that she had heard earlier had come from his rubber-soled sandals.

She swallowed dryly at the sight of his bare chest, trying hard not to notice too many details. She told herself that if she wanted him to respect her desire for privacy during this awkward moment, she should allow him the same privilege. She tore her eyes away from the subtle shading of dark hair on his well-defined—but not grossly exaggerated pectorals—and lifted her gaze to his face...to find *him* blatantly staring at her legs. The towel ended just below her crotch, leaving everything else bare to his, very interested, eyes.

Heat crept up her body, inching from the tips of her toes, turning her legs to mush, and pooling heavily in the neglected cleft between her thighs. The warmth moved upward, swirling pleasantly in her stomach, beading her nipples, and finally blooming on her face. She lifted her hands to her chest, holding the towel close, not wanting him to recognize her bewildering reaction for what it was. *She* barely recognized the sexual attraction—it had been so long since she'd felt anything similar to this.

She was confused and not sure how to feel about it. Part of her reveled in the awareness; it felt like the resurrection of something she had believed forever lost to her. A part of her that had been slowly and torturously murdered by Blaine. In the three years since his death she had stopped thinking of herself as a sexual being. And during their marriage...She flinched away from the recollection, not wanting to remember how he had hurt and punished her for having normal sexual urges.

But another part of her hated that it was Miles who stirred these feelings. She told herself that it was because she hadn't been around any virile, single men in years. She shouldn't have cut herself off from the world so completely. Perhaps if she'd been around men, these feelings would have reawakened sooner. Proximity and lack of other distractions could be the driving factors behind this sizzling awareness she suddenly had of him as a healthy, virile, and, extremely sexy man.

She even found his slimmer physique hot. It emphasized the hardness of his body and the cut of his muscles and spoke of how well he had taken care of himself before his illness.

Her breathing had shallowed, and she knew that it was evident to him. He didn't move out the doorway when she took another step forward. She muttered an apology beneath her breath, and angled her body sideways to shuffle past him.

Don't do it! Her inner voice screeched at her. But she unwisely ignored it and crept past him. The doorway wasn't narrow, and neither of them were particularly broad but somehow, she got close enough to feel his body heat, smell his divine cologne, and—ever-so-lightly—brush against his chest as she sidled by.

The contact made her freeze. Made them *both* freeze and she stood there...in front of him, head bowed and eyes shut. Stood quivering like a nervous gazelle, not wanting to move away from his heat or the electrifying touch of his bare chest against the backs of her hands. She was hyperaware that if she dropped her hands, dropped the towel...a thin layer of spandex would be the only thing separating his bare skin from hers. And, *God*, she so badly wanted to drop her hands. Her nipples were hard, painful points and craving that contact.

He leaned toward her, and she felt his hot, uneven breath washing over her cheek and ear, stirring the damp strands of hair that had escaped her braid.

His hands lifted to grasp her upper arms, and she lamented the fact that she wore a long-sleeve swimsuit. She wanted to feel those hands on her naked skin.

Wanted it.

Needed it.

Burned. For. It.

He inhaled deeply, his chest expanding against her knuckles, and she fantasized about exploring the contours of that magnificent torso. But before she could do anything, he exhaled and spoke...

His voice, a broken, hoarse whisper, delivered the words directly into her ear, "Goodnight, Mrs. Cole. Sleep well."

He shifted her gently to the side, and for a split-second, the movement brought her fully against him, and she could feel his heavy, thick erection even through the towel.

It should frighten her. Should send her rabbiting back to her rooms. But once he had her set aside, her eyes darted downward and she could see the clearly delineated ridge of his hard penis pressing up against the fly of his swim trunks. Even as she watched, the tip crept past the waistband of those low-riding trunks. Her greedy eyes widened, but before she could get a proper look he had turned away and was striding toward the pool, Stormy following him.

He muttered a curt "stay" to the dog and dove cleanly into the water. He surfaced halfway across the pool, impressive for a man who was recovering from what seemed to be a respiratory illness, and his body cleaved through the water, his strong shoulders and arms making quick work of the eighty-two-feet distance. His legs churned up a substantial wake, and Charity imagined those strong, muscled thighs threshing beneath the blue water.

She wanted to straddle them, capture them between her thighs, and hold him still while she claimed his hard length into her clenching, thirsty pussy.

Oh my God! What the hell was going on with her? He was her boss. The wrong man to fixate on. What a ridiculous time for her body to decide to wake up and want again.

It was nearly four in the morning—she'd had a terrible nightmare; her defenses were down. That had to be why her emotions were going haywire. He was a (near) healthy man, she was a healthy woman, and their physical closeness and lack of clothing had merely resulted in a predictable physiological response between them.

That was it.

Tomorrow they would pretend that this never happened and continue on as normal.

She hoped.

EIGHT LAPS—ALL he could manage at the moment—and one frigid shower later, and Miles's hard-on was only now beginning to subside. Why hadn't he moved out of the doorway? What the bloody fuck had he been thinking?

He had been riveted by the look of absolute longing in those damned seductive eyes of hers. Her lashes were so dark and thick she always looked like she was wearing black liner around her eyes...it added to her mystique and her unique beauty.

He should have turned around and left when he had spotted her, but he had been captivated by her grace and power as she sliced through the water like a sleek, human torpedo. And when she had levered herself out of the pool—*God*, he had been lost. Tall, lithe, and toned; her body was magnificent. Her long, long legs were sleek, muscled and beautifully shaped. She had turned away for an instant to grab her towel and unintentionally presented her perfect behind to his ravenous gaze. Round and firm, his hands had clenched with the need to touch, squeeze, and caress it.

He had frozen, stunned by the strength of his lascivious reaction, while his eyes had drunk it all in during that too brief moment before she had wrapped the towel around her. Her bathing costume zipped up the front like a wet suit, and it hadn't been closed all the way, forming a tantalizing open V over her firm, high breasts. Revealing the shadow of her perfect cleavage. Her nipples had been tight and hard from the cold air, and his mouth had watered embarrassingly at the sight of them.

And that hair…

Jesus! He glanced wryly at his cock, hard again thanks to this compulsive stroll down memory lane. He hadn't bothered going back to sleep. It was nearly six, and he had given up on sleep. Instead, he was on his bed lying on his back and staring at the ceiling. Wearing nothing but boxer briefs and fantasizing about his housekeeper.

She hadn't been immune to the sizzling sexual tension electrifying the air between them. He knew she hadn't. She could have waited for him to move, and he *would* have moved, once he picked his jaw up from the floor. But she hadn't waited. Choosing instead to slide past him and shocking the hell out of him.

And then she had stopped. Right there. In front of him. Her body brushing against his with every shallow breath. And he had wanted to taste her. Any part of her. The soft skin beneath her ear had called to him…

And he had been so close to answering that call when Stormy's cold nose on his leg had jerked him back to his senses.

He cupped himself now and gave his hardness a slow stroke through the soft cotton of his boxer briefs as he fantasized about that arse. Those nipples. Imagining those long, strong legs wrapped around him as he took her.

He exhaled on a slow, shuddering breath and slid his hand under his waistband. His palm found his hot, aching length and he fisted himself…

An enquiring whine made him jerk his hand back guiltily.

His head whipped to where Stormy sat up in her crate beside the bed, watching him with a quizzical tilt of the head.

"*Seriously*? Do you have to stare?" No way he could continue with the pup's curious, innocent gaze on him, and he shut his eyes for a moment, before resignedly sliding off the bed and striding to the bathroom for another long, icy shower.

His doctor would not be happy with him.

Two hours later, when Miles ventured to the kitchen for breakfast, he found the banquette table set as it had been every day since he'd informed Mrs. Cole of his intention to eat in the kitchen. Stormy trotted to her plastic bowl filled with chicken and rice, also diligently set out each morning, and began to snuffle her way through her breakfast.

Miles, meanwhile, sat and glared at what was on offer: one boiled egg, two slices of whole wheat toast, a cup of coffee, and a glass of orange juice.

What the fuck? Was this punishment for the pool? For being turned on by her?

Or...was she irked because he hadn't taken her up on her unspoken offer? Because he had done the only sane thing and shifted her aside before either of them could act on what was simmering between them?

"Mrs. Cole?" He didn't raise his voice, he knew she was close. He could still smell the fresh floral fragrance of her soap. It lingered in the kitchen and wrapped around him like a seductive cloak.

She didn't magically materialize like an efficient wish-fulfilment fairy, and his frown deepened as irritation began to replace his initial confusion.

"Mrs. Cole!" he inserted some volume into his voice. But the added effort garnered no reward. The only sounds in the kitchen were Stormy's disgusting wet chewing noises and the irritating tick of the yellowwood's branches against the kitchen window. The weather was miserable as usual, overcast, cold and blustery. But at least it wasn't raining. Yet.

"Mrs. Co—"

"*What,* for God's sake?" Her exasperated, agitated voice, more than her bad-tempered question, startled him. And he found himself gaping as the door to the garage was shoved open to reveal a less-than-pristine Charity Cole. She was glaring at him; her hair coming out of its bun, her usually white apron smudged with...Was that *grease*?

"What's going on?" he asked. He pushed to his feet and took a couple of steps toward her, but she hastily positioned herself behind the island. Clearly using it as a physical barrier between them.

Miles chose not to be offended by that and instead focused on her agitation. He was rather alarmed at the state of her. If it had been anyone else, he wouldn't have thought twice about the slight disarray, but for his housekeeper this seemed entirely uncharacteristic. He braced his palms on the counter and watched her intently.

"I was refueling the generator when a-a..." She clenched her fists, and he wondered if she was biting back a few choice curse words. He smothered a grin when she threw back her head dramatically and inhaled deeply before continuing in a fierce, controlled voice, "A *spider* crawled up my l-leg."

She shuddered, and Miles valiantly fought back a chuckle as he watched her swat at her skirt again.

"Lucky spider." He shouldn't have said it. But the thought had popped into his head and out of his mouth without passing through his usual tact filter.

Her head flew up, and she nailed him with a glare so venomous he was shocked he didn't simply wither on the spot.

"Why did you keep calling me? What was so damned urgent it couldn't wait a few minutes?"

Well then. It seemed that Mrs. Cole had gone on a short break—probably still cowering from the spider somewhere—and had left this ill-tempered, sarcastic, *fascinating* creature in her place.

Charity, he presumed.

She seemed to recognize the impropriety of her question, and her face shuttered almost immediately as she withdrew back into herself.

Noooo. He wanted Charity to stick around a little longer.

"I'm sorry, Mr. Hollingsworth," she murmured, patting at her hair again. He was starting to loathe that bloody gesture and all that it symbolized. "I'm a bit flustered. I'm not particularly fond of spiders."

"That's fine, I'm sure it must have been a deeply unpleasant experience."

"Deeply," she agreed with a nod, unable to prevent another full body shudder. "What can I do for you?"

God, talk about a loaded question. He could think of so fucking many things he wanted her to do for him. With him. *To* him.

"I was wondering about the egg."

She stared at him blankly. She was standing across from him, and the island between them felt like no real barrier at all.

"The egg?"

"The *boiled* egg?"

"What about it?"

"I thought I'd made my feelings clear."

"I thought you may have been exaggerating to get your point across. So, you really never want boiled eggs again? *Ever*?"

"No. I mean, of course I do, but..." Well, this was a bloody absurd conversation. He could think of so many other things he wanted to say to her right now. But here they were, discussing fucking boiled eggs.

But Miles hadn't built an empire from scratch by pussy-footing around, and he decided to take the matter in hand, "Are you angry with me?"

"What?" Her eyes grew as round as saucers.

"Because of what happened at the pool this morning?"

"Nothing happened."

"Are you angry because nothing happened then?"

She looked appalled by that question. "Of *course* not. Look, Mr. Hollingsworth, I—"

"Miles."

"No."

Damn it.

"I'm sorry for not moving aside." His apology was quietly sincere. "I fully intended to, and I'm not entirely sure why I didn't. It wasn't well done of me at all."

Her shoulders lifted and fell on a soft sigh.

"I wasn't myself last night," she admitted, her voice dropping to a whisper. "The nightmare unsettled me and...well...I'm sorry too. You caught me in a moment of vulnerability."

"Well, that makes me feel like a bloody predator," he said, doing nothing to disguise his grimace from her.

"No, that wasn't my intention at all. The thing...what happened, it was mutual. I knew you would move if I'd only stood my ground. But I wanted...I needed—"

Her voice trailed off and looked down and fixed her stare at the counter between them.

"Charity..." The sound of her name seemed to startle her, and her eyes shot up to meet his. He held her gaze, not wanting her to mistake the meaning of his next words, "*I* wanted and *I* needed too. And while I apologize profusely for the circumstances, I cannot apologize for that."

She shook her head, her eyes still entangled with his. He watched her slender throat move as she swallowed.

"Your breakfast is probably cold by now, I'll fix something else." Her voice was brisk, her words impersonal, but her eyes were still dark, liquid pools of vulnerability.

"That's not necessary. Why don't you get changed? I'll have my egg and take Stormy out for a quick walk."

And give both of them some much needed breathing room.

She hesitated—clearly not too happy to leave him eating a cold breakfast. Even though he deserved it for being such a picky bastard.

"If you're sure?"

"Positive," he reassured her, trying very hard not to look at her mouth when she sucked on the full lower lip uncertainly.

She nodded and walked away before he could say another word.

Miles sighed and looked at Stormy, who was waiting at the back door. Her tail wagged when he made eye contact. She was such a bloody good dog, so eager to please. She'd had some unfortunate bathroom accidents these last few days, but they were few and far between. He guessed that growing up on the "street", so to speak, had toilet trained her to a certain extent.

Still, he didn't want to test the puppy's bladder. He grabbed his egg, peeled it at the sink, and bit it in half as he opened the back door for the pup. He tried not to wince at the rubbery texture of the now cold egg and did his utmost not to gag when the cold, gelatinous yolk filled his mouth. The greasy slide of it down his throat was nearly his undoing, but he persevered with a queasy gulp. Yeah, he was pretty much done with boiled eggs for the foreseeable future.

He chased the disgusting thing down with a half slice of dry toast before Stormy had even clumsily squatted on the wet grass.

"Morning!"

The unexpected sound of the cheerful male voice coming from behind him, startled Miles. Stormy emitted an adorable purr of a sound that he reckoned was supposed to be a growl, but was cute as hell instead of remotely threatening.

Miles swung around and grinned at the sight of the familiar face peering at him from the other side of the low hedge bordering the back garden.

"Amos! Good morning, how are you?"

Because of the inclement weather, he hadn't seen the gardener since his arrival. The elderly man was clad in green workman's overalls and was holding a rake in one hand and a pair of garden shears in the other.

"Can't complain," Amos responded with a grin, his white teeth a dramatic contrast to his dark, wizened skin. But, seconds after his initial sanguine response, he proceeded to do exactly that, "This weather—*ai ai ai*—it's so bad for my bones. Nothing but rain all day, every day. And the cold, I tell you, my knees don't like this cold. But at least today my phone says there won't be rain, just this wind. But I told myself —'Amos, go trim the hedges while you can'. So here I am."

"Do you need any help with the hedges, Amos?" Miles asked, hoping the old man would say "yes". He needed the exercise and an excuse not to go back into that house and seek out Mrs. Cole.

Amos, however, looked quite offended by the question.

"I complain about my old bones, Mr. H, but I never said I can't do my work."

Shit.

"I know that you can do the work, Amos...I just need something to keep myself busy."

"I only have this one pair of shears."

Miles wasn't too certain of the veracity of that statement, but he let it slide. Amos, like the intractable woman inside, clearly did not want him underfoot. It was humbling how much of a nuisance his employees appeared to think he was.

"Right. I'll leave you to that then."

Amos nodded and threw him a friendly grin before ambling away toward the front of the house. Miles sighed and stared at the closed back door. He supposed he could always re-listen to one of his audiobooks. Or play fucking *Candy Crush* again. The app that Vicki had jokingly installed on his phone had remained untouched for nearly two years. But in only four days, he had already reached Level 275. He would probably be a lot farther along if not for the infernal in-app purchases, which required a Wi-Fi connection. At least he hadn't yet succumbed to using his precious, if spotty data, to purchase gold bars for boosters.

He hoped that by the time the Wi-Fi was restored, he wouldn't have a bona fide addiction to the game. He didn't want to wind up spending real money on a frivolous, time wasting app. The thought made him pause and he glowered before digging his phone out from his back pocket and swiping until he reached his sister's number.

She answered immediately. "Seriously, Miles, you're the only person in the world who still makes phone calls. Well, you and Tyler. You're like old men stuck in young bodies."

He chose to ignore that, "How much money have you spent on this *Candy Crush* game?"

"What?" The question floated to him on a tiny, incredulous laugh.

"You heard me."

"I did, but it was such a ridiculous question it bore repeating. And because of that, I'm thinking you either, A—really, *really* miss your beloved baby sister. Or B—you're bored out of your ever loving mind over there. And judging by your very offensive snort at option A, I'm going to guess that it's the latter."

His sister often portrayed herself as an annoying flake, but she was intelligent and perceptive. He sometimes wished Hugh had more of her smarts and she had more of Hugh's ambition. Her flower shop was doing well, but with her business acumen she could do so much more. She had point blank refused to work for the family company. Preferring to do her own thing. And Miles respected her for that, even if he wished she were less content with just a tiny corner flower shop in Earl's Court. But his siblings were the way they were, and Miles loved them regardless.

"The electricity has been out for four days. And the bridge into town was damaged, and the transformer can't be fixed until that's repaired. We're running on generator power, and Mrs. Cole has banned all non-essential electrical equipment, like the Wi-Fi router and television."

"She thinks *Wi-Fi* is non-essential?" Vicki sounded gratifyingly aghast at that. "That's positively medieval! You're the boss, tell her you need Wi-Fi."

He felt like a fucking teenager snitching on Mrs. Cole and also a little guilty because he knew that her rules were in their best interests, but cabin fever—combined with tedium—had led to this new low.

"*She's* the boss around here," he said, shocked by how sulky he sounded. There was a stunned silence on the other end, followed by a hastily stifled giggle.

"Is big, bad Miles scared of mean, old Mrs. Cole?" she mocked him in an annoying sing-song voice.

Hell. He was never going to live this down.

He made a very bad situation about a thousand times worse when he unthinkingly corrected, "She's not old."

This time the pause that followed was loaded and lengthy.

"She's not?" Vicki's eventual question was much too damned nonchalant for his liking, and he made a noncommittal sound.

He was starting to agree with her on the merits of text messaging. At least then, he'd have time to think before he responded. Ordinarily, he rarely voiced an impulsive word.

But he hardly recognized himself anymore. Lusting after his employee, speaking out of turn, adopting puppies, changing his breakfast routine...playing bloody match three games on his phone. He didn't know what was happening to him and he didn't like it one bit.

"Vicki, I have to go."

"Wait, so how old *is* Mrs. Cole?"

"I'll speak with you again soon."

"Miles, tell me...is she like forty? Thirty-five?"

"Take care."

"No. Miles—"

He disconnected the call with a huge sigh, feeling harassed. His phone beeped, and he gritted his teeth. He should have known she wouldn't let it go. He lifted the device.

VICKI

Thirty? Younger? Seriously? Younger than thirty? She doesn't look it. Or does she look it? 🤔 Have you seen Mrs. Cole out of her Mrs. Cole suit? Send pics!!!!! 📷👩

Her "Mrs. Cole" suit. It was an uncannily apt description. Because he was starting to understand that Charity wore that uniform, that persona, as some kind of disguise. And it made him desperate to know why.

He tapped out a hasty message to Vicki:

MILES

Tell Mum I'll call her on the weekend XOXO

VICKI

Miles!!!!!!!!!!!! 💩

He switched off his phone, ignoring the poop emoji that followed her many exclamation points.

He shoved his hands into his trouser pockets and watched

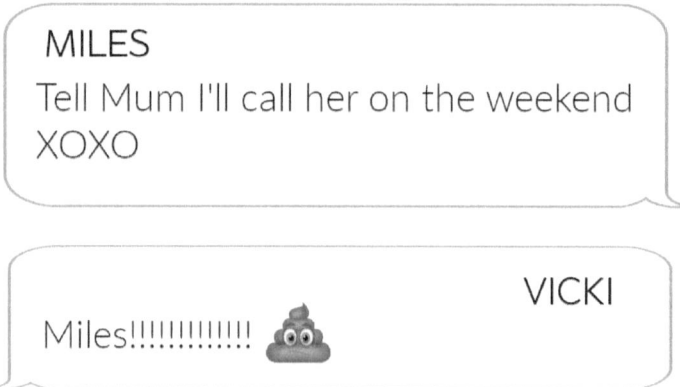

Stormy chase leaves around the yard, while his mind was furiously occupied elsewhere. He glanced at the house and saw the kitchen curtain twitch, as if someone had quickly ducked out of sight when he lifted his head.

He sighed deeply and was pleased when the inhalation didn't result in an automatic cough. Despite the cold weather, he was getting stronger and healthier. The fresh air, exercise, and Mrs. Cole's cooking were working their magic.

Despite the inconvenience of having his housekeeper inexplicably transform into a goddess, his decision to come here hadn't been too misguided. He looked at Stormy who mistimed a lunge for a leaf and went tumbling head over paws.

"And who knows what would have happened to you if I hadn't been here?" he told the dog, bending a knee to rub her lopsided ears.

The backdoor opened as he was pushing to his feet.

"Good news," Charity called from the doorway. "George says they're repairing the bridge tomorrow and Thursday. Once that's done, they'll send an emergency team out to fix the transformer on Friday. Hopefully we'll have power by the weekend."

Fantastic. Maybe if he were able to leave the house more often, he would stop fixating on her so much.

He stared at her gentle, smiling face, his eyes on her full lips and even white teeth. He recalled the long legs hidden beneath that drab skirt and the perky breasts so effectively disguised by that boxy blouse.

And then he considered the young woman who had hidden herself in the middle of nowhere for three long years. Three years of harsh winters filled with pillaging baboons, wildfires, power outages, floods and isolation. And summers catering to entitled, rich arseholes—yes, he included himself, and *definitely* Hugh and Vicki in that—not much older or younger than her. With nobody but two elderly men for company.

He shook his head. *Maybe* he would stop fixating on this stunning, mysterious woman, once the power and the road were restored.

But he very much doubted that.

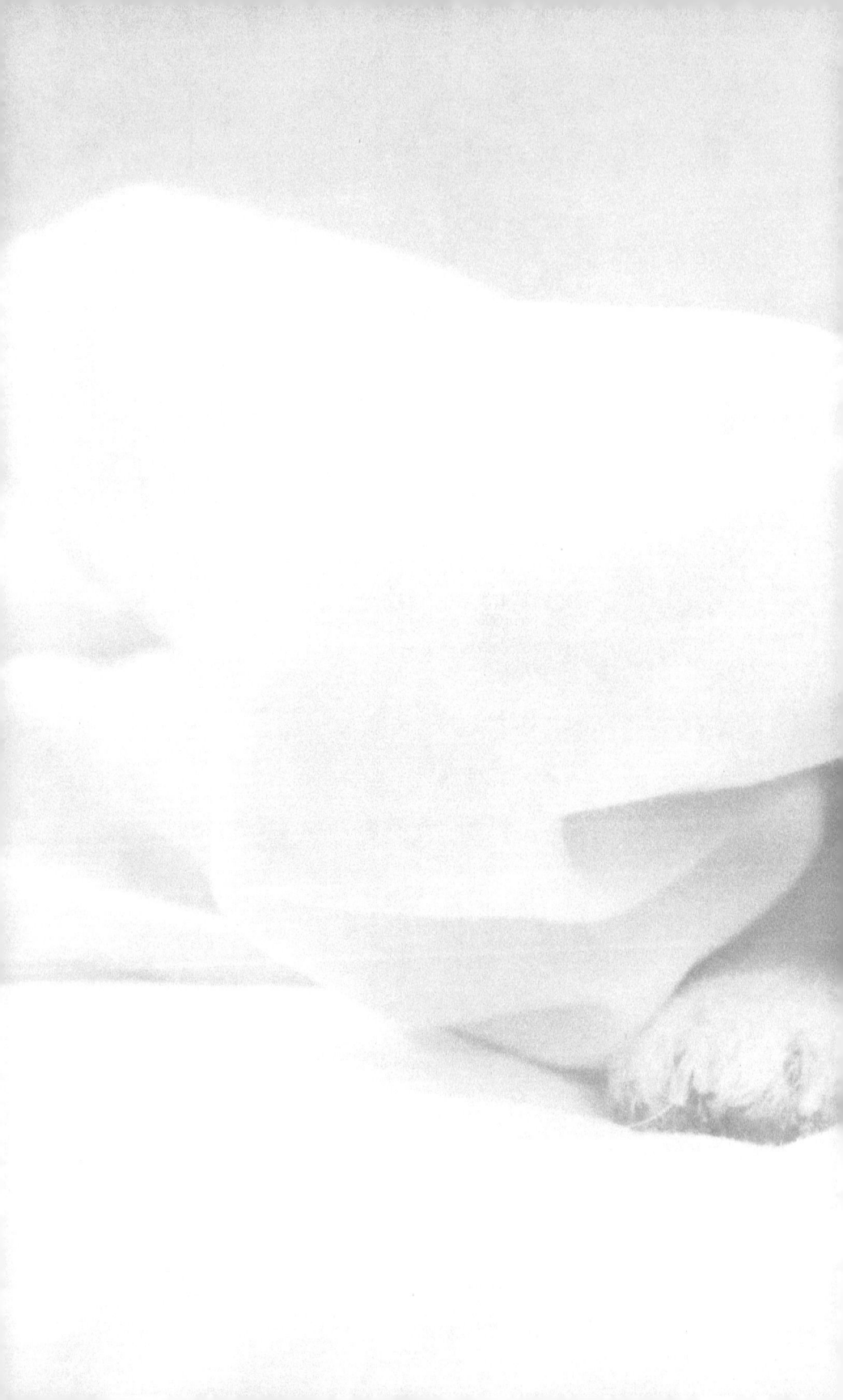

Chapter Six

"Stormy, get *back* here!" Miles called in an urgent undertone as Stormy darted down the hall with a pair of his briefs in tow. With the road restored, he had managed to get her to the local vet. And since then—thanks to her vaccination shots, a deworming tablet, a healthier diet and regular walks—she had found a new lease on life. And a mischievous streak a mile wide. In fact, it was safe to say, she was hell on four legs.

The huffing sound she made as she fled through the kitchen and made a beeline for the housekeeper's quarters definitely sounded like mocking laughter to his ears.

In the six days since their poolside encounter, Miles and Charity Cole had fallen into a rigid, formal routine. It was not conducive to a relaxing, healing atmosphere, and Miles tried his damnedest to steer clear of her.

He couldn't say that avoiding her helped. Not when his every waking moment, and most of his sleeping ones, were filled with recollections of her rising from that pool like a fucking fertility goddess.

He hadn't been so perpetually horny and frustrated since his early teens, and it was driving him insane. He had tried to distract himself with other things. Focused on getting fit, training Stormy and—despite Amos's protestations—hard physical labor like trimming the yellowwood in the back yard and chopping wood for fire.

Stormy darted through the ajar door leading to Charity's rooms, and Miles's pursuit came to an abrupt halt. It was after nine, she usually retired to her side of the house by eight-thirty. Miles had never, *ever* infringed on her privacy before. In fact, he had no idea what her rooms looked like.

He stared at the warm light spilling from the doorway into the dark hallway and cocked his head, listening for her inevitable reprimand of Stormy for the intrusion.

She hadn't warmed to the friendly pup, rarely acknowledging the dog's presence or referring to her by name. Miles figured she wasn't a dog person. He couldn't imagine her being very impressed with Stormy's uninvited presence in her rooms. He could hear the faint sounds of music and talking. The television perhaps?

Shit. What if Stormy peed in Charity's slippers or something similarly horrid?

Miles swore beneath his breath. He wondered if he could sneak in, grab the pup, and sneak back out without being spotted?

He glanced down at himself. He had been in the en suite, stripping for his shower, when he had returned to his room for a fresh razor blade. He had just caught a glimpse of Stormy—the sneak—dashing off with his clean briefs in her mouth, and immediately gave chase. Consequently, he was barefoot and wearing nothing but his unbuttoned jeans. Not quite dressed for company, and he couldn't imagine what his housekeeper would say if he entered her private quarters naked but for a pair of low riding jeans.

Still, who knew what Stormy was getting up to in there? He shook his head and, before he even realized his mind had been made up, his feet were carrying him toward the door. He flattened his palm against the wood and slowly pushed it open. The well-oiled hinges didn't make a sound and he popped his head around to do a quick recon of the area. The door opened into a cozy open-plan kitchen and living room. Charity was seated at the round dining table, her back to the door, laptop open and books spread out in front of her. His eyes darted around the dimly lit room, but Stormy was nowhere in sight.

That was when he realized that Charity was talking. Her voice was a gentle hum against the backdrop of the jazzy music coming from her laptop, and he strained to hear what she was saying.

"...so much trouble. I appreciate it, honestly, but you *have* to stop bringing me these gifts. What would Miles say if he knew of your infidelity?"

"She's done this *before*?" He couldn't prevent himself from uttering the incredulous question and, sure enough, at the sound of his voice, Stormy's furry little head popped up over the back of Charity's sofa.

As for the woman herself? She gasped in horror, shoved to her feet, and swiveled around to face him.

She was wearing fuzzy slippers and a thick, comfy looking robe. A *pink* robe. The soft, feminine color was flattering against her exquisite brown skin. Her hair was bound in a loose, soft braid that framed the oval of her face attractively.

She was absolutely stunning.

She had one hand clutched at the neck of her robe, holding the two sides protectively closed, while she stared at him through wide, shocked eyes.

"M-Mr. Hollingsworth!"

"Uh uh, none of that now, Mrs. Cole. You're so busted! Don't think I didn't overhear you referring to me as Miles ten seconds ago."

Her face bloomed with color, and he suppressed a grin.

"I'm sorry for intruding, but my dog has absconded with one of my delicate unmentionables. Not for the first time, it would seem."

Her full lips twitched, and the almost-smile encouraged him to continue in a similar dry vein. "So, am I to assume that you have an impressive collection of my odd socks and undies?"

"I do *not*," she denied. "I return them every morning while you're out on your walk."

"How long has this been going on?"

"These past four nights or so."

He sucked a resigned breath in through his clenched teeth while he considered that information. "This is my fault. I've been leaving her uncrated while I shower. And she's always in the room, right where I left her, when I return from the bathroom."

"Oh, these visits are usually very fast. She drops her "gift", begs for a treat, and then dashes back out. I probably shouldn't have rewarded the behavior. Would I be correct in assuming you thought you'd misplaced the missing items?"

His eyes dropped to Stormy who had bounded off the couch and was now at his feet, rolling around on her back. She stopped in mid roll and watched him with a comical tilt to her head, mouth open and tongue lolling.

"Quite," he said, with a chuckle.

. . .

CHARITY FOUND it hard to catch her breath with Miles right there, in her private domain. He was shirtless and shoeless, her gaze dropped to those long, masculine bare feet, and she wondered how the hell she could find the sight of his unshod feet so sensuous. Perhaps it was the way his toes kept digging into the plush pile of the rug—as if he were enjoying the texture of it—or maybe she just liked how earthy and approachable it made him seem.

Her gaze skittered up to his chest and then darted away. In the week since she had seen him in his swim trunks, he had put on even more weight and muscle mass. Those broad shoulders now had more power to them, as did his long, corded arms. And his chest...*God*, after a week of being around him, having him within touching distance but never allowed to indulge in what was becoming an obsessive need; the urge to pet and stroke every inch of that naked expanse was much stronger in her tonight.

She watched him all the time. When he was working in the garden, chopping wood, walking with Stormy. She *loved* seeing him with that dog. He was endlessly patient with the pup. A far cry from the curt, commanding man she had considered him to be in the past.

And it was bizarre, but the more she looked at him, the less ordinary he appeared. Nothing about him had changed and yet, from one breath to the next, he had transformed into something utterly beautiful. She didn't understand how it had happened... but now when she looked at him, all she could see was a dangerously attractive man, with striking eyes, strong features, and an irresistible smile.

Right now, he was using that smile on Stormy who was still

on her back, her tongue lolling from her grinning mouth. His eyes, usually so unfathomable were soft with affection.

"You *know* you've been bad, don't you, you naughty little bitch? That's why you're flirting with me like this."

For a shocking moment Charity *absolutely* believed the words were aimed at her, and she didn't quite know how to react to them. But good sense reasserted itself seconds later, and she coughed to cover up her irrational misconception.

The sound drew his notice, and he eyed her curiously.

"Sorry," she coughed again, for emphasis, and circled her forefinger in front of her neck. "Ahem, frog in my throat."

"Do you need some water?" His eyes were grave with the beginnings of concern.

"I'm good. Thanks. You never raise your voice at her," she said, thinking it prudent to change the subject. "Even when she frustrates you or disobeys you."

"Of course not," he responded, sounding shocked. The thought of raising his voice to the dog had clearly never occurred to him. "That would scare her."

Such a simple answer. And yet it said so much about his character.

His eyes roamed around her small home again, and landed on her textbooks and notepad on the kitchen table. She had been studying when Stormy had bounded into the room.

"What are you doing?"

"Paperwork," she lied. This was too personal, something she hadn't shared even with her family. But she had kept up with her studies, and continued to pay for her practice number, in the hopes that she could one day step into the career that she had abandoned in favor of Blaine.

"Paperwork?"

"Yes." She hoped he would respect the finality in her voice and not probe any further.

"Okay." A long pause before he dislodged some of the gravel in his throat and refocused his attention to the snoozing dog on the floor. "Come on, Monster Mutt, it's bedtime. I'm sorry for the intrusion, Charity."

Her throat went dry at the sound of her name in that quiet, gruff voice but this time she didn't protest his use of it. There was no point in clinging to that extra layer of decorum. It had been hard enough thinking of him as Mr. Hollingsworth *before* his dog began bringing her his underwear as gifts.

"I didn't mind," she said, feeling her lips tilt upward in a small smile. It had been so long since she had smiled spontaneously that the movement felt unfamiliar. "She was just being friendly."

"I didn't think you liked her. Well, dogs in general actually."

"I like dogs. But I didn't think it was prudent to become too attached to her. In case you changed your mind."

There was a short, awkward silence and Charity wondered if she had offended him.

"Why would I change my mind?"

"You're a busy man. I thought maybe, after you had time to think about it, you'd decide you didn't have the time for a puppy

"I wouldn't do that."

"I've come to appreciate that. And I apologize for the unfair assumption."

He looked uncomfortable and acknowledged her apology with a curt nod. He bent to scoop Stormy up, and Charity felt a pang of envy as the dog snuggled against that strong, beautiful, *naked* chest.

"Have a good night, Charity."

"You too."

He turned to leave, but Charity spotted the abandoned cotton boxer briefs on her sofa and grabbed them without thinking.

"Miles."

He whirled around at the sound of his name. His intense gaze honed in on her face.

"Yes?"

"Don't forget these." His eyes dropped to her hand and his cheeks actually flushed.

"Christ," he muttered, and yanked the underwear from her hand. "I'm so sorry. Truly. They're clean, I put them out to wear after my shower."

"You *do* know that I do your laundry, right?" He seemed so charmingly flustered that she couldn't resist teasing him. He shot her an appalled look, his face a study in consternation and mortification.

"Fuck...I...goodnight."

"Goodnight...*sir*." Oh, she was feeling so damned brave. She already knew that this blushing, near naked man, with the puppy clutched to his chest didn't scare her. And now she was testing the limits of her courage by teasing him. She couldn't remember the last time she had teased a man. Or just enjoyed being around one.

"Watch it, Mrs. Cole. Or I may ask you to teach me how to make pancakes tomorrow."

"I can do that." The impulsive words were out before she could stop them. But when she considered them, she recognized that she was happy enough with the offer. She was even looking forward to it.

"You can?"

"Sure. But not tomorrow."

"Oh yes, because of the cleaning service, right?"

The cleaning service would be in for their fortnightly visit tomorrow. And they would probably stay all day. Charity had already informed Miles that his breakfast would have to be a hit and run affair in the morning.

"I thought, if it's a nice day, I'd take Stormy to the beach," he said. "Would you like to join us?"

"I have to oversee the cleaning staff." She didn't really have to, because they were employed by an independent company, and would have their usual on-site supervisor accompanying them. Charity always felt superfluous when they were here. They were so fast, efficient, and reliable.

In fact, she usually took the day off when they were scheduled to come.

"Let me know if you change your mind. Stormy and I would both enjoy your company."

He left before she could reply.

BACON, one egg—sunny side up—mushrooms, and toast. Aside from the hot breakfast awaiting him at his usual spot in the kitchen the following morning, there was no sign of Charity.

Miles tried not to be disappointed by her absence and sat to have his solitary breakfast. He didn't know why he had expected to see her this morning. Perhaps because last night had felt like a breakthrough in their odd relationship. A tacit acknowledgment that perhaps they were ready to explore the limits of what they could say and do to each other.

But—if not for his plan to go to the beach—this day would probably have followed the usual pattern. Breakfast alone, spend time with Stormy, chat with Amos, try to engage Charity in conversation. And fail. Walk and lunch alone. Watch Charity clean the kitchen, offer to help. Get rejected.

End of part one.

Listen to one of his recently purchased audiobooks, try to convince Charity to watch some television with him. Fail again. Play with Stormy, swim, contact his siblings and mother, have dinner. Alone. Bedtime.

End of part two.

Rinse and repeat.

He had come here for the isolation and had resigned himself to the tedium that was bound to accompany that isolation. At least Stormy offered a welcome respite to that tedium. He shouldn't want more. But he did. And he had since the moment he had set eyes on Charity stripped of her armor that first night.

But that wasn't her problem, it was his. And he should respect *her* desire for solitude and let her do her job without interference. God knew, he was trying, but every so often—like last night—he felt like she enjoyed his company, that she was as intrigued by him as he was by her.

And the confusing signals were driving him fucking crazy.

At least today, thanks to the rare crisp and clear day with which the weather gods had gifted them, he was looking forward to something a little different. Stormy's first visit to the beach.

He would drive himself, not something he often did, but he had been keen on trying out his Land Rover on some of the challenging off-road terrain. He sighed, put Charity firmly out of his mind, and finished his breakfast.

It's just a day at the beach. You deserve a day off. Be brave...

Be brave.

She had been so proud of herself last night. Proud because she had borderline flirted with her employer.

How had she become this person? This timid woman, who considered a mild bit of flirting daring. She, who had once lived for her next thrill. Her parents had been so happy when their wild child had settled into her perfect life, with her perfect husband.

Now here she stood listening while Miles's voice drifted farther away as he headed to the garage with Stormy. He was conversationally telling the dog all about the day he had in store for them, and Charity's body leaned toward the closing door as she listened to him speak.

She had stepped into the kitchen just as he and Stormy were exiting through the basement door, and she had wavered. Part of her eager to go after them, but the other—*terrified*—part urging her to stay put and not risk opening herself up even further to him.

He was her boss, he was too disturbingly attractive...He could hurt her. Emotionally. Mentally. Physically.

Let him go.

...

No. Be brave, Charity.

"Do you two have room for one more?"

Miles sucked in a quiet, relieved breath at the sound of the hesitant voice behind him, and he schooled his features into rigid neutrality before turning to face her.

"A-always." The word stumbled over his suddenly numb tongue as he took in the familiar, yet wholly *unfamiliar*, sight of the woman who had begun to occupy his every waking thought.

She was wearing a pair of snug, faded jeans and a black and red plaid shirt over a white tank top. She had a down jacket flung over one arm, and her unbound hair was streaming over her shoulders, down her back, to her waist. It was everywhere. A gorgeous curtain of silky, messy tresses. A slouchy red beanie futilely attempted to tame the mass, but all it did was give her a bohemian appeal. She was wearing red gloves and dark brown hiking boots on her feet.

Stormy gave a happy whine at the sight of Charity, and Miles cast a wry look at his dog.

You and me both, girl!

He was so fucking pleased to see her. He yanked open the passenger door before she could change her mind and she offered him a grateful smile before climbing into the cabin.

Miles shut the door behind her and turned away to compose himself. He felt like a teenage boy on his first date, terrified he would do or say something to offend her or scare her off. Or just plain humiliate himself.

He placed Stormy into the doggy booster seat he had purchased—along with a shit ton of other pet paraphernalia—once he had been able to get into town again.

"So where are we headed?" she asked, as he climbed into the driver's side.

"I thought we could go to the beach in Riversend, close to the river mouth. I hear it's nice there."

"*Klein Bekkie*? It's very beautiful. You've never been?"

"No. Vicki and Hugh have gone a few times, and they always talk about how untamed it is. And how great the surf is. I've seen pictures, it looks like a long stretch of beach, perfect for walking. I thought it would be a great place to focus on Stormy's recall."

He felt like he was chattering inanely, but she seemed interested.

"What do you mean, her 'recall'?"

"Getting her to return to me on command. According to the research I've done, it's a fundamental training tool. And important especially in emergencies. I mean, take last night as an example, I would have been able to stop her in her tracks with just a word."

And if he had, they would not be here this morning. So he couldn't quite regret Stormy's embarrassing invasion of her room last night.

"Think she's ready for that?" Charity cast a doubtful glance over her shoulder at the dog.

"She's the right age for it. And she's clever enough to get it pretty quickly." He didn't want to sound too smug, but he was sure his dog was a genius.

"I haven't been to Klein Bekkie in a while," she said, after a short pause. "It's quiet during winter—usually just joggers, surfers, and kite surfers around. Oh, and anglers. The fishing is pretty good there. Especially at this time of year. There will probably be some other people walking their dogs as well."

"Well, she *does* need to be socialized," Miles said, with a glance back at the dog. Stormy was staring at them with a huge grin on her endearing face. She was panting with excitement. This was only her third time in a car, but she seemed quite at home in it.

He turned on the ignition and, when the engine roared to life, the Bluetooth sound system immediately synced with his phone and his most recent audiobook blared to breathless life:

Dendroignis the Abhorrent, violator of maidens, demolisher of kingdoms, pillager of riches, scourge of the four sovereignties of

Terra Arbor, will lay waste to our dwellings if apposite safeguards are not—

"Shit!" He fumbled for the dial and muted the bombastic speech. "Sorry."

"What was that?" Charity asked as he navigated the vehicle out of the garage.

He focused on clearing the structure before answering her question. "An audiobook."

"I gathered that much. It was very...descriptive."

"The author does bang on but—" He shrugged offering her a small smile and appreciating how she had turned in her seat to give him her full focus. "I like it."

"What's it about?"

"It's a space opera."

"Like *Star Wars*?"

"A bit darker. Very medieval and graphic."

"Medieval? In space?"

"Well, their world, *Terra Arbor,* is primitive. They're fighting over land and resources, using swords, burning pitch, and trebuchets in battle. That kind of thing."

"So...no spaceships?"

"Of course they have spaceships, but..."

"How can they have spaceships but still not have evolved beyond sword fights and medieval battle tactics? What about medicine? How do they treat the gaping sword wounds?"

"Their ship, the *Arbor,* was part of a larger colonial fleet—humans fleeing a dying earth in the year 2250—and it crash-landed on a massive, habitable planet—"

"Of all the planets, in all the solar systems, amidst billions of galaxies, in an infinite universe, they crash-landed on a habitable one? Fortuitous..." she inserted dryly, and he shot her an unfathomable look, before continuing.

"The rest of the fleet continued on their journey, because once the ships land, they're no longer able to take off. They become temporary hubs for the two thousand people who populate them. The ship is meant to house them and protect them, until their new planet is terraformed and suitable for human habitation. The fleet promised to send a rescue mission back for the *Arboreans*, but that was over five hundred years ago.

"Meanwhile, the colonists on the crashed ship learned to adapt to life on Terra Arbor. But resources are scarce, and tech has degraded badly. They inevitably broke off into clans, and formed kingdoms to keep the gene pool diverse. They created a primitive free-market and trade-based society. But there were outliers, those who wanted to control resources and amass power. *Dendroignis the Abhorrent* is the descendant of one of those outliers."

His voice trailed off in embarrassment as he recognized that he was being overzealous in his eagerness to share his favorite author with her. He sneaked a glance at her—she was watching him with an enigmatic smile on her full lips.

"Is it a series?"

"Uh, yes. This is the fifth book in the saga. It started with *Alpha Gen*, the original stranded colonials."

"So you don't have one hero to root for?"

"The first book was mostly world building. A prologue of sorts, it gave us an insight into the struggles the original generation faced. The next book skipped two hundred and fifty years ahead and showed us how everything pretty much went to hell. Books three to five focus on the current generation. The series follows one particular clan, the *Cedarians*—all the clans are named after trees—which is why the outlying tribe named itself *Dendroignis*, which literally translates into 'tree fire'."

Charity couldn't stop staring at him. He reminded her of an excited little boy telling her about his favorite toy. The story sounded frankly ridiculous, but the delight he took in it was charming to witness. She let him continue on about these fictitious clans, their spirit trees, and their mortal enemies the tree burners or whatever. And she couldn't prevent a silly smile from creeping onto her lips.

Miles Hollingsworth was kind of adorable when he was geeking out, and she kept him talking with the occasional leading question.

She was happy she had summoned up the guts to join him and Stormy that morning. It felt good to be out of the house again. She hadn't left the premises aside from that one shopping trip to Riversend on the day after his arrival nearly two weeks ago. He had gone into town to get Stormy checked out after the power outage but, with the exception of his daily walks, he had also been pretty much housebound.

Something he said drew her back to the conversation.

"Wait, so there's magic?"

"No, just powerful elemental forces at play."

"But you just said the fire starter guy was a mage."

"The planet contains powerful mystical and elemental forces and the Dendroignis outliers have learned to harness them. But the current leader of the Cedarians, Willow, is a first-generation weather mage. She draws her power from the cedar trees Alpha Gen planted five hundred years ago. Something in the soil has mutated them into powerful..."

And on he went... this story sounded crazy and convoluted. The author had clearly been unable to decide if he wanted to write sci-fi, or fantasy, or good old-fashioned mythology. So he had thrown everything but the kitchen sink into the story.

Aaaand now there were...

"Dragons?" *Seriously*?

"Well, not dragons as we know them," he explained earnestly. "A native species of flying reptile. Willow has leaf-bonded with a hatchling. I think the connection between her and *Delonix*—the hatchling—is going to be a serious game changer."

"How many books are in this series?"

"Ten. The author, Michael Quinn, has written several epic series before this one. I've read them all, but this is my favorite."

"I see," she said faintly. "And you like this space opera stuff?"

"They haven't all been space operas. The last one was straight up fantasy."

She honestly wouldn't have taken Mr. Straitlaced Hollingsworth as someone who enjoyed anything as fantastical as this. She'd only ever seen him read newspapers. Then again; he often sat in isolation—a pair of headphones clamped over his ears—while his siblings and friends laughed and played. She had always believed that he chose to cut himself off from them because he was dour and unfriendly and a workaholic. But she now understood that this was his way of relaxing. All those times he had been lost in one of these insane stories.

This man: rescuer of stray pups, avid fan of over-the-top fantasy fiction, sudden boiled egg naysayer, recent frequenter of her most erotic fantasies, was *nothing* like the cold, calculating person she had originally believed him to be.

"Do you only listen? Or do you read these books as well?" she asked when he took a breath between raving about dragon bonds and the discovery of a new and hotly contested continent.

"I don't usually have the time, or patience, to sit and read a book. I can't remember the last time I read one from start to finish. I often multitask when I'm listening to a book. It's a more efficient use of my time. We're here."

The last two words surprised her and she glanced out to see that they were, indeed, pulling up to the dirt parking area at Klein Bekkie. There were only three other cars in the lot. The half hour journey had flown by. She had been so riveted by his retelling of the bizarre space saga, that she hadn't paid much attention to the passing scenery.

"You ready for your beach debut, Monster Mutt?" he asked over his shoulder as he put the vehicle in park. The pup whined in anticipation and he grinned—a wide, open, boyish grin. He turned to Charity and gave her the full force of that smile, dimple and all, and it stripped her breath away.

"She loves the lake and I'm keen to see how she takes to the ocean," he told Charity, his gorgeous smile remaining firmly in place.

"I'm sure she's going to love this too," Charity said her voice faint, as she tried to find the breath he had stolen from her with that gorgeous grin.

A deep, purring, oh-so-sexy sound of approval rumbled from his chest, and he opened the door and leaped from the Land Rover. She was still unbuckling her seatbelt by the time he had rounded the front of the vehicle and opened the door for her. A little flustered by the consideration, she didn't give herself time to think before taking the hand he offered, and stepping to the ground on wobbly legs. His hands weren't as soft as she would have imagined. The last week or so of wood chopping and garden work had formed a few callouses on those capable, broad palms, and she loved the feel of the rough texture of his skin on her own.

She shuddered as she imagined them exploring other, more

sensitive, parts of her body and helplessly clenched her thighs at the thought. Thank God, he seemed to remain oblivious her reaction. Instead, he released her hand almost immediately and turned back to the vehicle for Stormy. The pup's excited whining was turning into yelps of approval, and he chuckled.

"Cool your jets, Stormy girl," he said, as he lifted her from the booster seat and snapped a leash to her harness. He clipped a bag of treats to one of the belt loops of his well-fitted, low-riding jeans, donned his backpack, and beamed at Charity. "Ready?"

It was breezy this close to the ocean, and Charity's hair was starting to lift and play around her face. She regretted not bringing a hair tie and swept the length over her left shoulder and tried to anchor it in place with her scarf.

She grabbed up her own backpack and shrugged into it before nodding.

"Ready."

Stormy was tugging at the leash, while Miles waited for Charity to join them.

His eyes ran over her face. "You cold?"

"It's nippy but not too bad."

A long strand of her hair escaped the imprisoning hold of the scarf and danced on the wind. He leaned forward and very slowly—clearly projecting his intention and giving her ample opportunity to back away if she chose—reached out and tucked the hair behind her ear.

She stood her ground and allowed it. Happy that he had—by the excruciating slowness of his movements and the question in his eyes—*requested* permission to touch.

"Let's go."

Chapter Seven

Miles appreciated Stormy's clear enjoyment of the exciting new sights and sounds around her. They were walking downstream along the slow-moving river, toward the beach. There were a few random anglers scattered about, all of them utterly focused on their lines. Several of the men looked up and nodded as Miles and Charity passed.

Stormy, after initially pulling at her lead, finally settled into a cheerful trot alongside Miles's heel, happily obeying his unspoken commands to speed up or slow down. Charity didn't speak much, she seemed content to take in the scenery, occasionally pointing out water fowl with descriptive names like "black-winged stilt", or "white-faced whistling duck", and his favorite, the "maccoa duck". It was his favorite mainly because of Charity's reaction when she spotted it.

She grabbed his arm to halt his movements and leaned toward him with such urgency that for a split-second Miles thought she must have injured herself. An instant later, she pushed the length of her body against his side to get closer to his face. For a breathless, exciting moment he was utterly convinced she was going to kiss him.

Instead, disappointingly, she placed her mouth close to his ear to whisper, "Look! Over there. Maccoa ducks."

His eyes followed the straight line of her arm and extended index finger to spot a family of happily bobbing ducks. Weird looking, squat things with brown bodies, black heads, white markings on their faces, and magnificent blue bills.

"We're lucky to see them, especially at this time of year. There are no females in this group. They're probably nesting already. I'm really surprised they're here. They're rarely found on rivers, I assume because of the recent rains, and because this part of the river is fairly sluggish, it offers some good eating. They're on the near endangered list and are quite shy."

"You know a lot about this stuff," he murmured.

"Not really. I'm just interested in my surroundings and do a lot of reading in my downtime."

"You probably have a lot of that. Downtime, I mean."

She was still staring at the ducks—a dreamy, faraway look on her face. He wondered what was behind that reflective gaze.

"Penny for your thoughts?" he offered, his voice hushed. He did not want to spook her or the contentedly bobbing ducks.

A smile crooked the corner of her lips, but she kept her eyes on the birds.

"A penny? Hmm...what with the currency conversion, that's slightly more than they're worth."

"I'm sure that's not true."

"I was considering your statement. About me having a lot of downtime. Seems it would be bad form to agree with your employer about having little, to nothing, to do when they're not around. Wouldn't want you to reconsider my worth or anything."

"Now now, Mrs. Cole," he said, his voice light. "You know you're priceless."

The smile faded and a troubled frown fleetingly settled on her face before she smoothed her expression and turned away from the ducks. "Let's get to the beach, Stormy's getting impatient."

Disturbed by the depth of sadness he'd seen on her face moments before, Miles hesitated, but she moved onward without waiting for him to follow. He remained rooted to the spot and watched the enigmatic beauty walk away from him. It was a pleasure to witness her graceful gait. She had her gloved hands tucked into the pockets of her down jacket and strands of her hair escaping the confines of her scarf and riding on the breeze behind her. Lending her an ethereal vulnerability.

Stormy whined and strained against her leash, eager to follow Charity. Miles complied, taking a few hurried strides to catch up with the woman.

The river mouth widened and shallowed when they reached the beach, and the fresh water flowed placidly into the gentle embrace of the ocean. Well, *currently* gentle. Miles imagined the ebb and flow of the waves would be a lot less tranquil once the tide rolled in.

The scenery changed dramatically at the beach. The lush greenery of the trees and shrubs along the riverside opened up to a long stretch of pristine white sand dunes, dotted with hardy fynbos, and a flat shoreline, perfect for sunbathing during summer.

The beach was empty and, despite the relative warmth of the day, a light mist was hovering just above the ground. Miles could see a jogger coming toward them, still so far off, he was nothing but a dark speck in the distance. He could just make out a smaller speck—probably a dog—keeping pace with the jogger.

As Charity had predicted, there were a few kite surfers dotted along the shore, some in the water, and several still unloading their kites. A lone kayaker was paddling out beyond the surf. A couple walked hand in hand down the beach. They had their shoes off and pant legs rolled up, but maintained a respectful distance from the gentle, lapping waves. Miles imagined the water had to be freezing.

This place was paradise and Miles inhaled deeply—happy that he was able to do so with relative ease—enjoying the salty tang of the fresh air. He looked at Charity who was watching him with a smile.

"Why haven't I ever come out here before?" he wondered out loud, and her smile widened.

"I like coming here, especially in winter. It's so peaceful. I often run on the beach."

Of course, she did. Miles was starting to understand how important fitness was to her. She swam often and, in the last week, he had spotted her heading out to the lakeshore in running gear before dawn every day. He was usually out in his private garden at that time, waiting for Stormy to do her business.

Charity had no idea he knew, and he didn't want to mention it in case she felt uncomfortable or considered it an infringement of her privacy. He did not want her to feel like he was spying on her. The fact that he had seen her had been altogether unintentional...

The first time.

After that he had looked forward to those furtive glimpses of her every morning. She always seemed so unguarded and carefree in her running gear, with her hair tied up in a long, swinging ponytail. And he enjoyed seeing her like that.

He didn't say anything in response to her comment and unclipped the dancing Stormy's leash.

The dog yapped joyously and took off down the beach at a precipitous pace, barking all the way.

"Oh fuck! *Stormy*!" Panicked, Miles took off after her, calling her frantically. The dog didn't acknowledged him and, terrified that he was going to lose her, Miles tried to keep up. But he could feel himself flagging, the walk had already taken a lot out of him. He staggered and would have fallen if not for the firm hand that latched onto his elbow. He was unsurprised to find Charity standing beside him. She had kept pace with him for the humiliating, short distance he had managed to run.

He refused to be self-conscious about that. She was currently in much better shape than he was. He knew that. Still...it would be nice not to be seen as a lame duck by this woman anymore. He doubled over, his hands on his knees, while his breath wheezed in and out of his bellowing, hurting lungs. He could hear Charity making soft, encouraging sounds above him, one of her hands was stroking his back in soothing circular motions.

He lifted a limp hand.

"S-Stormy...please...get..."

"Stormy's fine," Charity said, her voice calm. She handed him an open bottle of water, and he grabbed it and gratefully gulped the cool liquid down. "Easy, Miles. Small sips."

He complied.

"She thought you were playing a grand old game with her," Charity said. "She's stopped running, and she's watching us now, probably wondering why you're not playing anymore."

Miles looked up and sure enough his naughty little shit of a dog was standing a few yards away, staring at them with a quizzical tilt of her head.

"Sit down," Charity commanded him. "She'll come to us."

It went against his every instinct not to go after the pup, but when Charity sat down, grabbed his hand, and tugged him onto the sand beside her, he was unable to resist. Both because her hand felt amazing in his and because he literally didn't have the strength.

Charity was on her butt with her knees bent and spread, the backpack tucked between her thighs. She opened the top and rummaged inside before producing a couple of Granny Smith apples.

Miles accepted the one she offered him. She scrounged some more and found an extra bottle of water, which she uncapped and took a thirsty gulp from.

Stormy inched closer.

"Ignore her," Charity advised. She took a hearty bite from her apple and made a "yummy" sound while she chewed. It was meant to entice the dog and in no way supposed to be sexy, and yet Miles found himself mildly turned on by the throaty sounds and the way she was smacking her lips. He was unabashedly staring at her, enjoying the unintentionally erotic way she chewed and swallowed that damned fruit. Loving how every few seconds she had to brush her hair from her face. Worshiping the curve of her cheek and the smooth, silky looking expanse of her throat. Adoring how great she smelled and wishing he could bury his nose in the hollow of her throat and just inhale.

She was focused on Stormy, but Miles—content now that he knew his dog wasn't running for the hills—was entirely absorbed by Charity.

He was so captivated that it was a shock when she swung that sultry, dark gaze toward him and caught him staring. The smiled faded from her full lips and her wide eyes bounced back and forth between his before they dropped to his mouth.

She licked her lips. And Miles suppressed a shudder and bit back a groan of longing. Not taking his eyes from hers, he leaned toward her until their lips were a mere hairsbreadth apart—and then waited. Giving her the choice...praying he wasn't reading her wrong but not wanting to assume. Not when his position as her employer gave him so much authority over her. This had to be her choice and, if her decision went contrary to what he wanted, he had to respect that.

She lifted her free hand to palm his cheek, and his breath hitched in his chest. Her thumb ran back and forth over the edge of his jaw, abrading on his two-day-old stubble.

"I've never seen you unshaven before this stay." Her voice was contemplative and didn't give him any indication of her feelings. But right now all he could focus on was the delicate brush of her lips against his as she formed the words.

"I..." The word emerged on an embarrassing, throaty rumble, and he cleared his throat before speaking again. "I'm trying something new."

"A beard?"

"Piracy."

Her lips parted on a delighted smile and without any warning she bridged the infinitesimal gap between his mouth and hers and kissed him. Her mouth was soft and tart from the apple but still the sweetest damned thing he had *ever* tasted.

He made an anguished sound that he didn't recognize as his voice, and his hand went up to cup her neck just below her ear. He waited, wanting to see what she would do next, but she kept the kiss light and innocent. He didn't want innocent, he wanted to be the fucking pirate he had jokingly referred to earlier. He wanted to plunder, pillage, and pursue. He wanted to ravage her mouth with his and leave no doubt as to his intentions.

But he reined it in, sensing that she needed a lighter hand. He didn't want to ruin the possibility of more with her.

She sighed softly, the sound laden with a sadness that confused him. Alarmed him. Why would she be sad? Yes, this was less than he wanted, but it was also *so* much more than he'd expected. Didn't it mean the same to her? Was that why she sounded so damned desolate.

She drew back and shifted away from him. The movement was small but deliberate. Where before there hadn't been space to squeeze an envelope between them; now the air circulating in the chasm she had placed between their bodies felt ice cold.

Miles couldn't take his eyes off her. With her arms caging her bent knees, and her hands clasped tightly together, she appeared to have closed herself off both physically and emotionally. And it was frustrating to witness.

She stared at the ocean. Not acknowledging him, or what had just happened between them.

Stormy whined and Miles looked at the puppy who was sitting with her back to the water and watching them. More specifically—ravenously eyeing the apple core that Miles had dropped in the sand when Charity had kissed him. He picked up the sandy core and dropped it into a poop bag, before looking at the dog again.

"Come," he called, snapping his fingers to punctuate the command, and Charity made a soft snorting sound. His eyes jerked back to her face and—even though she was still gazing at the ocean—that smile was back. Relieved that she still seemed to be in good spirits, he waited for Stormy to obey him, before refocusing his attention on Charity.

"What's funny?" he asked, lifting Stormy into his lap and fluffing her ears affectionately.

"I'll tell you some other time," she said.

"When?"

"When I think the time is right."

Well, what the fuck did that mean?

"Do you enjoy being an enigma?" He tried to sound teasing, but instead the note fell flat, and he sounded curt and a little resentful instead. That was all it took to chase the smile from her lips.

She looked at him, her eyes somber. "No. And I don't want to be considered a challenge either. A fun trophy to hunt."

"Is that what you think is happening here?"

"I'm not sure what's happening here, I'm merely telling you what I hope it's not."

"It's not that."

"We'll see." She pushed to her feet and stepped away from him to dust sand from the seat of her jeans. "I thought you were going to work on that naughty dog's recall. And if what happened earlier is any indication, she definitely needs it."

He supposed that meant the subject was closed.

For now.

Stormy was being a brat. Charity tried not to laugh at Miles's comical frustration as he tried his best to teach the puppy to "sit" and "stay". She sat like a champ, but "stay" was a problem. She seemed to know exactly what Miles wanted and stayed put about 50 percent of the time. But the instant anything more interesting came along, she took off in pursuit.

Thus far; she had been diverted by a tangle of rotting seaweed, chased a flock of seagulls, and followed a crab into the waves only to run away in shock when the water had "chased" her. The latter, of course, had resulted in a fun—for her—game of keep away with the waves.

Miles appeared both exasperated and entertained by her. More often than not, he had an amused grin on his face while he was issuing half-hearted commands or reprimands.

Charity couldn't take her eyes off him. But whenever he glanced over at her, she shifted her attention to the puppy, not wanting to be caught staring. She liked watching him. With his unruly, windswept black hair, and his dark stubble, despite the faded jeans and that dark blue hoodie, he definitely resembled the pirate he had jokingly claimed to be earlier.

Her fingers—the same ones which had so enjoyed stroking his prickly stubble—lifted to trace her still tingling lips. She knew that he had wanted more than that soft kiss, but he hadn't made any protest when she had moved away from him.

She contemplated the kiss. She had liked his lips; curved, firm and smooth, she had enjoyed how mobile they had felt beneath hers. She had daringly traced the seam of his mouth with her tongue, but he hadn't taken it as an invitation to stick his tongue down her throat. He had merely allowed her to explore as she pleased.

But she regretted not taking the time to discover more. She still wanted to touch the chest that so fascinated her, wanted to feel his weight on top of her, and his thighs between hers...her nipples hardened at the exciting thought. And she very nearly forgot herself and touched them.

Her breathing accelerated, and the long-neglected inner walls of her pussy tightened in anticipation. She wanted to feel him there. Inside her. Hard. Hot. She wanted him above her... No *better*; beneath her, and she wanted him to command her to *come*. In that deep, controlled voice.

The thought of it excited her, *thrilled* her. But also terrified her. How could she be so helplessly aroused at the thought of allowing any man such control over her again?

How dare you touch yourself while you're sucking my cock, you little whore? I didn't say you could come!

She was nearly overwhelmed by the surge of nausea that hit her at the uninvited, repulsive memory. And she shuddered in all-consuming horror.

Her burgeoning arousal was immediately dampened.

She could never again trust anyone to have such absolute dominion over her mind, body, and soul.

Never again.

Stormy's shrill barking wrenched her from her horrific recollections, and she looked up to see what had stirred the pup into such a frenzy. Charity recognized the huge scarred dog—a boxer—before she even registered the jogger who had stopped to shake hands with Miles.

Stormy, showing more wisdom than Charity would ever have given her credit for, dove behind Miles legs and barked at the man and dog from between his calves. The boxer, so much more well-behaved than the pup stared off into the distance, ignoring everyone around him, while his owner—Charity's self-defense instructor—Sam Brand, shook Miles's hand.

"Hey, I heard you were in town," Sam said by way of greeting. Not even a hint of wind in his voice to indicate that he'd just been full on running over sand dunes.

"Yes, I arrived a couple of weeks ago. Stormy, *sit*!"

Shockingly the pup obeyed and stopped barking, but she continued to voice the occasional kittenish growl at Sam's dog, Trevor. The larger dog tossed her a disdainful glance before looking away again.

"Sorry, Sam, she's a former stray. Showed up in the middle

of a storm. I've been attempting to train her. With limited success."

"That's okay, Trevor is used to little dogs with Napoleon complexes. He won't hurt her. Training takes time and patience. The veterinary practice offers puppy training and socialization classes on Wednesdays if you're interested."

"I might look into that. Dr. McGregor, right?"

"That's the one. He's my future father-in-law."

The familiarity between the two men surprised Charity. She hadn't realized that they were this well acquainted. They were both English, maybe it was an expat thing?

"Sam, I take it you know Charity?" Miles asked, and Charity, who had been hovering about a yard away, nodded and smiled awkwardly when both men looked at her.

The two men were similar in height, both a couple of inches under six feet. But while Sam was blond and sported a healthy tan, Miles was dark and—even though he wasn't nearly as pale as he had been two weeks ago—still had residual sickbed pallor. The winter sun had added some color to his face, and Charity was once again struck by how much healthier he looked.

"Of course, I know her. She's my star pupil. How're you doing, Charity? We missed you these last few sessions. You know how much everybody enjoys watching you kick Grey's butt."

Greyson Chapman—still quite new to town—was the other instructor.

"Pupil?" Miles asked, his brows beetling.

"Self-defense," Sam said. "We do a combination of MMA, Muay Thai, boxing, and Krav Maga. Any rough and ready way to get a woman out of a nasty situation really. Charity has a real knack for it."

"That's what you meant by those special Wednesday classes?" Miles watched Charity closely, and she fought hard to keep a discomfited flush at bay. She preferred to keep her private business, private.

"Yes."

"So *not* Tae Bo?"

"Tae Bo?" Sam laughed, sounding genuinely amused by Miles's incorrect assumption. "She's taken a real shine to MMA in particular and could probably kick your arse in about seventy-five different ways."

"Of *that* I have no doubt." The admiration in Miles's voice flustered her. She couldn't remember the last time anybody had sounded so *proud* of her. Not even her family. Lately all she got from her parents or sister was disappointment and confusion. Not that she could blame them. Blaine had ruined everything, even her relationships with her family.

Sam's next question—aimed at Miles—jerked her right back into the present, "How are you doing after your brush with death?"

The dramatic turn of phrase startled Charity. She knew he had spent some time in the ICU but, despite that, it had never occurred to her that he could have died from his illness. She found the possibility more than a little distressing.

"Fuck off, it was hardly a brush with death, Brand."

"Weeks in ICU, hooked up to machines? That sounds pretty dire to me."

"Who the hell told you that?"

"In my line of work, information is power, my friend."

"And in *my* line of work a rumor like that can, and will, result in plummeting stock prices and nervous shareholders."

"Fortunately for you, it wasn't common knowledge."

"I commissioned Tyler to guard Vicki, *not* to divulge my private information to you." Miles sounded only mildly annoyed. In fact, he sounded amused. Blaine would have considered something like this a humiliating breach in confidentiality. And then he would have gone home and taken his anger out on Charity.

"Tyler would never leak a client's business to anyone. Not even to me. You know that's not how we operate. I have other means."

"I was ill," Miles confirmed, with a dismissive shrug. "I'm here to recuperate. And I left the company in capable hands."

"Your brother's?"

"*Jesus*, no. Bryan's. Hugh is assisting him. They've got it covered."

"You've been calling them every day, haven't you?" Sam asked, on a laugh, and Miles grinned.

"I speak with Bryan once a week but after a very brief, uninformative update, he starts talking about his fucking golf swing or his tennis serve. He knows I find both sports tedious and will do anything to avoid hearing about them."

"Good for him."

"Yeah, even my assistant won't tell me anything other than 'it's all fine'."

Sam laughed again. "How's Tyler working out?"

"Swimmingly, if the amount of complaining Vicki has done since he's started is anything to go by."

"That's my boy." Sam nodded. "Listen, my fiancée, Lia, would have my balls if I don't invite you around for dinner sometime. She's been on me to give you a call since she heard you were in town. She's keen to meet you. Charity, I know she'd love it if you joined us as well."

The latter seemed tacked on as an afterthought, and Charity smiled politely and uttered a noncommittal sound in response to the invitation. She would *not* be joining them for dinner. How would that even work? She was on nodding acquaintance with Lia McGregor and on friendly but impersonal terms with Sam. And Miles was her boss. It would be awkward as hell. What would they talk about?

She was saved from a proper response by Stormy. The pup, emboldened by the fact that Trevor appeared wholly disinterested in her, ventured out from behind Miles's legs and confidently trotted up to the bigger dog for a sniff.

When she couldn't reach his butt, she went onto her hind legs in an attempt to make his acquaintance in the time-honored canine way. Trevor, realizing what was happening at his rear, turned smartly to face her.

Stormy yelped and fell over backward before scuttling back behind Miles's legs.

Both Sam and Miles hooted at the pup's antics but Charity was, once again, captivated by the way the laughter transformed Miles's face. The lines and angles shifted attractively; previously smooth surfaces wrinkled and creased, the dimple deepened, his teeth, so white and straight, contrasted strikingly against the dark stubble.

She fell a little bit in like with her boss in that moment, and the consequences of that recognition alarmed her.

He and Sam were shaking hands again and Charity, still shaken by her revelation, automatically smiled when Sam told he'd see her soon.

"Let's go, Trev," he called to the dog and, with a final wave, took off at a breakneck speed over the dunes.

Stormy started to give chase but skidded to a halt and tumbled butt over head when Miles uttered a sharp, "*No*! *Stay*!"

He slanted a disbelieving look at Charity before lavishly praising the dog for her obedience and giving her a treat.

"I didn't think she'd listen," he admitted.

"I think your tone of voice shocked her into obedience," Charity said, with a laugh.

"Too sharp?"

"It worked."

"Let's head back. I think she's flagging." He raised his eyebrows at her before lifting his shoulders with a sheepish smile. "And I *know* I'm flagging a lot."

She liked that he was confident enough in his masculinity to admit to that.

"You're able to walk a lot farther now than when you first arrived. It's pretty impressive how fast you're recovering."

"Glad you're impressed. *I* feel like it's taking fucking forever to get back to normal."

"You have to be patient."

"Patience has never been my strength. I'm an instant gratification kind of guy."

Somehow, she doubted that. It took patience to build a business from scratch into a multimillion-pound organization. He had to be patient to be a father figure to his much younger siblings and still keep their love and respect. It took a boatload of perseverance to maintain his good humor and affection while dealing with a mischievous puppy. And he had shown admirable restraint earlier, when he had so clearly wanted to kiss her, but had waited for her to make the first move.

It seemed to her that the only person Miles Hollingsworth did *not* have patience with was himself.

She considered that fact while they retraced their steps back to the land rover.

"Should we stop for lunch somewhere?" Miles asked, after he had maneuvered the vehicle back onto the road.

"I can't think of any pet friendly places in Riversend," Charity said.

"Then I suppose we'll have to venture farther afield," he said carelessly.

"I don't see why not," Charity agreed, not wanting their day out to end just yet. "The cleaning service will be at the house for a few more hours."

"Then let's see where the road takes us."

Chapter Eight

The road "took" them to a quaint farmhouse kitchen style restaurant off the N2 just outside of Knysna. They provided under cover seating for pet owners and their four-legged charges in their courtyard. Charity took an instant liking to the place, which was a working farm with a thriving cottage industry eatery. The menu—outlined on a chalkboard at the entrance—was small and consisted of wholesome country foods. Sunday roast served daily, chicken pie and veggies, as well as lamb chops with mashed potatoes, and "farm fresh"—as the menu boasted—peas. Their dessert options were limited to milk tart or dark chocolate cake.

As was to be expected on a random Tuesday afternoon, the restaurant wasn't very busy. There were only a handful of patrons inside and none outside. A truculent young man led them to their table and provided a couple of glasses of water.

"Your server will be here soon," he muttered, before skulking off. Charity raised her eyebrows at his surly attitude, but since he wasn't their server, chose not to comment.

Miles didn't seem to notice the guy, he was too busy making sure his dog was comfortable. He put Stormy's "travel cushion"—as he called it—down on one of the chairs and after two turns, the pup flopped down and passed out.

"I'm always amazed by how fast she switches off," Miles marveled, an undercurrent of amusement in his voice. "I found her comatose with her head in her food bowl the other night."

"I nearly tripped over her in the den two days ago. She was fast asleep in the middle of the floor, stretched out in that superhero pose, you know the one?"

Miles chuckled and nodded. Stormy often lay with her front paws outstretched, head tucked between them, her tummy flat on the floor and her hind legs splayed like a frog's. It looked comical but it was her favorite way to sleep.

Charity watched Miles's face soften as he ran a gentle hand over the puppy's head. The dog barely seemed to register the touch. Charity's insides melted into a pool of comfortably warm goo. The pleasant shudder of excitement that accompanied the giddy sensation felt familiar. A long-ago echo of something that could only be described as romantic interest.

Every instinct she had screamed at her to distance herself from him. And from this unwanted and painful awakening of feelings that she had believed were dead and buried. She had known, of course, that she was sexually attracted to him. But the possibility of forming a romantic attachment was inconceivable.

But instead of skittering back into her shell or distancing herself the way she knew she should, she folded her arms on the table and leaned forward, keen to learn even more about this intriguing man. "I didn't realize you knew Sam Brand so well."

"I've known him for about six years. His company handles security for Hollingsworth Holdings. As well as personal security for my family."

"And for you."

"To a certain extent. I don't have a security detail or anything like that."

"Why not?" Surely a man as powerful and wealthy as Miles Hollingsworth, chairman of the board to one of the most successful holding companies in Europe, would need some form of personal protection?

"I'm *reclusive*." He used air quotes to frame the word "reclusive" and his tone was light, but the tongue in cheek response didn't satisfy her. It seemed negligent of a man in his position to allow himself to be so vulnerable. Charity knew how swiftly someone who meant to do violence could strike. From one second to the next, you could go from seemingly fine to prone, in pain and powerless.

"You shouldn't be so flippant about your safety," she heard herself berating him, and instantly wished the words back when he pinned her with a searching look. She had sounded too grim and her intensity didn't match the tone of the conversation.

"Uh...I'm not," he said, after a long pause. "When I know I'm heading into an unknown situation, or into a crowd, we always take extra precautions. I don't take unnecessary risks. Not in business and not with my life."

"You did with your health." She pointed out.

He grimaced and rubbed the back of his neck sheepishly. "You got me there. It was stupid. It felt like a cold and I ignored it but it kept getting worse. I saw a doctor when my concentration became impaired. He suggested I take time off and I—foolishly, I admit—disregarded him. I took the medication he prescribed and kept pushing myself. It was a fucking *bug*, I thought I had it under control. Right up until the point I found myself waking up in the hospital with my mother and sister crying at my bedside like I'd already died."

"What did you have?"

"I had the flu..." He waved his hand when she started to say something in response to that. "Seriously. That's how it started. Influenza Type B. Sore throat, runny nose, chills, the works. It all felt manageable, and I worked from home because I didn't want to spread it and debilitate my entire company. But when I work from home, I tend to overdo it. I schedule international conference calls at all hours, work on contracts till late into the night, research new acquisitions...I wasn't joking earlier when I said I'm reclusive. That's pretty much my life. And it was easier to ignore my symptoms without anyone around to nag me about them."

"But your sister and brother must have checked up on you. Your mother?"

"They're used to me being fine. Hugh was adjusting to his new role in the company—he's just been promoted to a junior executive position and is assisting my COO. He had a lot on his plate. And Vicki was traumatized, she was mugged a day or two before I was hospitalized. My mother was taking care of her. *I* just had the flu."

The statement was telling. It seemed like his family relied on him to be the strong one, to take care of them when they were sick or in trouble. Miles was the previously infallible head of the family.

"How's Vicki?"

"She's fine." He shook his head with a wry chuckle that attractively accentuated his dimple. "She *hates* that I had Brand assign a close protection officer to her after the mugging. I imagine she must be making the poor guy's life hell."

"So why were you hospitalized?"

"Are you ready to order?"

They both looked up when their server—a woman who looked around seventy—spoke.

Charity had been so engrossed in the conversation that she hadn't even noticed the woman approach. And she definitely hadn't given any thought to what she would eat. And, judging by the startled look on his face, neither had Miles.

"I think I'll have the chicken and mushroom pie," Charity decided impulsively. "With milk tart for dessert."

"Same for me. Pie. But I'll have the cake for dessert."

"Anything for the pup?" The server—Estie, according to her name tag—asked with a twinkly smile. Miles grinned appreciatively at the question.

"I think she's fine for now. Thank you for asking."

The polite *thank you* surprised and charmed Charity. He wasn't a rude man. Just abrupt and to the point. He didn't usually seem inclined to bother with social niceties like minding his p's and q's.

Estie shuffled away, her fuzzy slippers sighing against the ground as she walked.

"She's wearing bunny slippers," Miles muttered, his voice choked, and his eyes shining with suppressed laughter.

"I know."

"That's fucking ridiculous."

"I like it," Charity confessed. A giggle burbled from her lips, and the lighthearted sound surprised her. She couldn't remember the last time she had made that sound. Or when last she had just wanted to laugh with someone.

"Me too," Miles said, a chuckle escaping, and the happy sound matched her effervescent giggle. That seemed to surprise *him* as much as her laugh had shocked her. He blinked for a moment, before shaking his head and laughing again and this time, she joined him.

They exchanged shy glances after the uncharacteristic bout of shared laughter, and Miles cleared his throat before taking a sip of water.

"Well?" Charity prompted him, and when he looked confused she reminded, "You were going to tell me why you were hospitalized."

"I started coughing...I was disoriented and dehydrated, despite drinking what I thought was a fair amount of fluids. When my brother found me, I was incoherent and confused. Turns out I had bronchitis, which—left untreated—developed into bronchial pneumonia. By the time I was hospitalized, I was facing the very real possibility of acute respiratory distress syndrome. Which could have resulted in permanent lung damage. I was fortunate that my stubbornness didn't get me killed.

"It was a little...humbling. I'm healthy, I stay in shape, I eat all the right things. I can't remember ever being seriously ill, not even as a child. A cold here and there, sure—but *nothing* like this. It was a wake-up call. I hate being so bloody incapacitated, but I know I have no one to blame but myself."

"Why did you choose to come here? It's cold and wet and miserable this time of year. And I'm sure you had other options in more tropical settings."

"It's cold and wet and miserable," he repeated. "But it's also peaceful. And it holds one very important advantage over my other holiday homes."

She considered that comment but couldn't figure out what that advantage could be.

"What?"

His lips quirked and he gave her a hooded look that she could not decipher.

"It has *you*."

"Oh."

Was that a come on? She flushed, not quite sure what to make of that comment. But ridiculously flattered by it, no matter what it meant.

"And before you read anything shady into that," he clarified quickly. "By you...I mean *Mrs. Cole.*"

The clarification confused her, and her brows knitted as she considered his words. "We're the same person."

"*Are* you?"

No...they weren't. And it was alarmingly astute of Miles to pick up on that. Charity felt more exposed than she had in years. And it terrified her.

Terrified and *exhilarated* her. It felt wonderful to be seen again. Recognized as an attractive woman who had very little in common with the ageless, sexless, frosty persona she had created out of fear and desperation.

Before Mrs. Cole, she had been Charity Davenport, grieving widow of the saintly Blaine Davenport. And further back still, she had been the pastor's wife—smiling, serene, and counselling to others, while screaming and dying on the inside.

She hadn't been just Charity in so long. She didn't even recognize that free-spirited, happy, confident woman as herself anymore. She was no longer that woman-child, ridiculously in love with the charming boy next door. How shocked people had been at the match. How disapproving his parishioners, that their beloved pastor had married someone so very *wrong* for him.

She couldn't go back to being the person she had been before marrying Blaine. She had lost that Charity somewhere along the way. But she was no longer Mrs. Davenport either...the broken woman of Blaine's creation.

And she now recognized that she would have to move on from Mrs. Cole soon. That reality terrified her. Mrs. Cole had been a cozy security blanket and had kept her safe while she healed from her emotional wounds.

But Charity needed to reclaim her freedom and find out who she was now. She had to mend fences with her family and confront the demons of her past. A part of her had always clung to the hope that she would one day—at the very least—follow the career path she had once chosen for herself.

Why else would she have hung on to her practice number all these years? She still attended the obligatory chiropractic seminars and conferences a few times a year. She had done so even during her marriage, when she had—at great risk to her well-being—lied to Blaine about where she was going and what she was doing. And she had been studying in the hopes of taking her re-entrance examinations at some point.

These were the actions of a hopeful person. Someone who wanted more. So much preparation, in the belief that someday she would find the strength and courage to pursue her dreams again.

"Should I offer a pound this time?"

Miles's wry question snapped her back to the present, and she met his amused gray eyes in confusion. "What?"

"For your thoughts?"

"It's quite a coincidence that you and Sam Brand wound up in the same random place on the Garden Route," she said, clumsily steering the topic back on course.

She wasn't ready to talk about herself yet. Not with him. She wasn't sure she would ever be ready to discuss her most intimate thoughts with this man. He was too...*everything*. Too powerful, too wealthy, too sexy, and too increasingly attractive for her peace of mind.

He dimpled at her.

"Not that coincidental," he said, graciously allowing the

subject change. "His former business partner, Mason Carlisle, grew up in Riversend. And, before he sold his half of the business to Sam, Mason was their company's de facto client liaison officer. He often spoke about this part of the world. I was in the market for a holiday home and thought I'd look into this "slice of heaven" as he so eloquently and accurately described it. I fell in love with the location and built my house before either of them even considered moving here."

"Oh."

"Pretty mundane, right?"

"Here you are, my lovelies. A nice home-cooked meal for you to enjoy," Estie's chipper voice filled the comfortable silence that had fallen between them, and they looked over to see the woman shuffling over. She epitomized everybody's idea of a grandmother—round, matronly, and silver-haired with a twinkle in her eye and apples in her cheeks.

The woman slid two plates in front of them, and they gawked at the amount of food that had been piled onto the dish. It smelled and looked wonderful.

They thanked her and watched as she shambled away.

"Bet she chain smokes and swears like a sailor in her downtime," Miles muttered, and Charity choked back a laugh.

"Probably wears leather and has a tattoo that says 'Daddy's Little Bitch' on her left boob," Charity added somberly, and this time Miles was the one who choked.

"Toy boy thirty-six years her junior." Miles flung the words down like a gauntlet.

"Pothead," Charity happily countered.

"Estie, or the toy boy?" he asked.

"They smoke together."

"Probably right before she bones that kid like that there's no tomorrow."

Charity covered her face with both hands and shook her head.

"*Stop*! Oh my God," she laughed. He joined her and when the laughter died down, they grinned at each other a little goofily.

He cleared his throat and picked up his fork. "Eat up before it gets cold."

Charity happily complied and the first mouthful of pie was divine.

"This is *so* good," she moaned, scooping up another bite. Miles watched her eat for a moment before digging in. His eyes widened, and he stared at her in shock.

"It's pretty damned tasty," he agreed with her.

While they ate, they chatted amiably about the weather, Stormy, and Miles's attempts to help Amos in the garden. Safe topics—cautiously tiptoeing around the questions they really wanted to ask each other.

Several pretty brown hens wandered into the garden and slowly meandered toward their table. They were busily bobbing their heads, scratching and picking at the ground, cheerfully clucking as they got closer and closer to where Charity and Miles were seated.

Charity watched them with a delighted smile and glanced over at Miles to share her enjoyment of the unexpected moment with him. But he looked less charmed by the chickens than she would have expected from a city boy. Instead, he appeared downright horrified.

"What's wrong?" she asked, alarmed.

He didn't immediately respond, but glanced queasily at his plate before swallowing.

"Do you..." he began faintly, before clearing his throat and starting again. "Do you think we're eating one of their siblings?

Or, God forbid, *offspring*?"

He was starting to look green around the gills, and Charity bit her lips, fighting back a laugh.

"P-probably *more* than just one," she joked, her voice shaky with suppressed laughter. The look he shot her was so appalled, that she immediately regretted teasing him.

"Shit, I should have ordered the lamb," he muttered. He had no sooner uttered the words than a cute fluffy white lamb gamboled into the courtyard.

"Fuck."

Charity covered her mouth with her hand, attempting to hide her smile from him.

"Perhaps you should consider converting to vegetarianism," Charity suggested, her tongue firmly in her cheek. She knew how much the man loved a medium rare steak.

He winced, eyes still on the frolicking lamb, and shook his head in what looked like self-disgust. "I tried. When I was younger. But I didn't have enough strength of conviction. I'm happy enough to eat meat and chicken but only prepackaged and refrigerated and store-bought."

"They were all alive once," Charity pointed out, once again finding herself charmed by another unexpected facet of this interesting man.

"I know it doesn't make sense. I never order lobster either. I fucking hate it. And I avoid those restaurants with the tanks of live lobsters. The thought of them being cooked alive—" He left the sentence unfinished, but his shudder said it all.

He glared at the table, and Charity leaned forward to shift his plate aside.

"Save some space for dessert," she suggested gently, and he heaved a sigh and slanted her an unreadable glance from beneath those dark, furrowed brows. Her breath caught at the intensity of that look, and she found herself quite unable to do anything but stare helplessly back.

He opened his mouth to reply, but Stormy chose that moment to open her eyes. She immediately spotted the lamb and chickens and was on her paws and hysterically yapping in under ten seconds.

Miles shifted his penetrating gray stare to his dog, and Charity heaved a relieved sigh, before pushing her own nearly empty plate to the side.

The hens, startled by the onslaught of barking, squawked indignantly and waddled away fussily. The lamb toddled forward on stilt-like legs, seemingly curious about the noisy creature making all the fuss. Bleating plaintively, it ignored Stormy's frantic barking and shoved its face toward the dog's chair.

Miles grinned, and when he stroked the lamb's velvety looking muzzle, Stormy calmed down almost immediately, clearly trusting her human to know best. She cautiously sniffed at the strange creature standing so close to her, but when the lamb baaed again, Stormy yelped and leaped into Miles's arms.

He laughed, that same carefree laugh he had shared with Sam Brand earlier, and Charity swallowed painfully. She wasn't at all happy with the way his laughter made her feel and didn't know how to deal with it.

The lamb bounced away and disappeared around the corner. Stormy stopped barking and curled up on Miles's lap with a contented sigh.

Miles chuckled quietly. "She seems a little smug now, doesn't she?"

"She probably thinks she scared them off."

He shook his head and fondled the dog's ears.

"Crazy mutt," he grumbled beneath his breath, his voice loaded with affection.

Charity didn't respond to that. She aimlessly fiddled with her water glass; twirling it, running her index finger along the rim, tracing patterns in the condensation on the smooth, cold surface. Miles allowed the silence to grow, and for a long while there was nothing but the sounds of birds chirping, chickens clucking in the distance, a cow mooing, and the wind gently susurrating in the grass and the leaves of the massive wild fig trees dotted around the courtyard.

"Are you divorced or widowed?"

The question seemed to come from nowhere and, after allowing the soothing sounds of the farmyard to lull her into an unguarded and relaxed stated, it unnerved Charity. But it was just a question. Personal, sure...but no more so than any of the ones she had asked him today.

"What makes you think I'm either?" she replied with a nonchalance that surprised and impressed her. Her emotions were in complete upheaval, and she did *not* want to discuss her marital status.

Not with Miles.

Not with anyone really. But especially not with him. Not when she was starting to feel so many *things* around him. Physical things. Possibly even emotional things.

Bringing her marriage into this moment—this formerly tranquil, and happy, moment would ruin everything.

Her response seemed to flabbergast him, and his brow lowered.

"I'm sorry, I always assumed...I thought...wait, so you're *married*?" He sounded so dismayed that Charity actually found herself tempted to smile, despite the uncomfortable subject matter.

"No. I'm not. I'm widowed..." She paused before honesty compelled her to add, "but I should have divorced him."

His gaze sharpened.

"Arsehole, huh?" he sympathized.

She hesitated, so tempted to say yes. But years of pretense, of going along with the world's belief that Blaine Davenport was a stand up, great guy had left her without a voice. And she stared at Miles helplessly.

"Did he cheat on you?" He immediately shook his head and made a self-conscious noise in the back of his throat. "I'm sorry. I shouldn't pry."

"It's not that, it's just..." She worried the inside of her cheek with her teeth. "One shouldn't speak ill of the dead. Right?"

"I don't see why not. Especially if the dead guy was an arsehole. And it's not like I knew him. So, speak your mind. Was he a cheating bastard?"

"He was a-a—" Another hesitation. She sucked in her breath and met his level, non-judgmental gaze. Nobody had ever had a bad word to say about Blaine. Not to her. Not to anyone. People always sang his praises, spoke about how committed he had been to his parishioners, to his community, to his faith, and to his wife.

And it had rendered her completely mute. Both during her marriage to that smiling, handsome monster, as well as after his death. When everybody had been so very *devastated* by his loss. When they had naturally assumed that she must be devastated too. She had been compelled to keep her relief and exhilaration at finally being free of him hidden behind a veil of insincere mourning.

And when she had been unable to keep up the pretense any longer, she had begged Mr. Lanscombe, her and Blaine's attorney, to help her get away from that stifling life of lies and regret. He had come to her with this position less than a week later.

It had astonished her; how easy it had been to just up and leave. For so long she had been petrified of what Blaine would do to her if she tried to leave him...and suddenly, she could just go. Without any fear of repercussions. The reality of her newfound freedom had been staggering and overwhelming.

And utterly terrifying.

"He *was* a bastard," Charity admitted beneath her breath, and she immediately smacked a hand over her mouth as if trying to cram the words back in. But they were out...hovering in the space between them. They sprouted wings and took flight and were out in the world before she could call them back.

Four words. Each one brutally weighted down by so much sadness and despair that she felt unburdened and lighter than air once they were out.

The freedom that she should have rejoiced in after his death finally unshackled by her quiet admission, and Charity's lips lifted in delight.

"A total bastard. I *hated* him, and it's an awful thing to say but I don't miss him at all."

Miles didn't respond. His face remained impassive but his eyes were kind...even understanding, and the lack of anything resembling censure in that gaze made her choke up.

For so long, she had kept those words locked in a metal box in her heart, terrified that if she spoke them, if she confided in anyone, they wouldn't believe her. She had been petrified that they would judge her for saying such an awful thing about the man they thought they knew and loved.

But here *he* was: Miles H. Hollingsworth. The most unlikely confidante in the world. And while he didn't—*couldn't*—comprehend how much this moment meant to her, he had allowed her to speak her truth in an entirely safe environment.

Her eyes flooded, and she looked away self-consciously, terrified that she would break down in front of him.

The hot tears burned the back of her eyes, and she shut them in a futile attempt to force the scalding moisture back. She slowly counted to ten—using every language in her arsenal—while keeping her breathing measured and under strict control.

She was so focused on her internal struggle that she jumped in fright when she felt his roughened palm close over her forearm. It wasn't skin on skin contact, she was still wearing her jacket, but it was contact nonetheless and it was unexpected.

But not unwelcome.

"It's okay."

The quiet words nearly undid her. And she withdrew her arm from his hold and covered her face with her shaking hands. Not wanting him to see the tears that finally overflowed.

"I'm sorry," she muttered, her words so muffled behind her hands that she wasn't sure he could hear them.

"Don't be sorry," he replied, his words emphatic. "It's okay, Charity. You're allowed to feel whatever it is you're feeling. I shouldn't have to tell you that."

No, he shouldn't have to tell her that...but it was nice to hear it nonetheless.

She sucked in a deep, messy breath and laughed self-consciously at the wet sound. She swiped at her damp cheeks with the back of her wrist, and when she opened her eyes, Miles had his eyes on Stormy, clearly giving Charity the privacy she needed to gather her composure.

She looked at the table and saw a monogrammed blue handkerchief neatly placed beside her plate. She smiled and traced the letters with a shaky index finger.

MHH

It was such a quaint custom, to carry a monogrammed handkerchief, but one that suited Miles to a T. She lifted the expensive linen square and dabbed at her cheeks, before—cringing at the necessity of the action—blowing her nose heartily.

"Thank you," she said, and he lifted his gaze back to hers. She grimaced at the sodden handkerchief and sighed. "I hope you weren't expecting this back right away."

He started to say something but Estie came shuffling around the corner. She fussed happily, praising them for *mostly* eating all of their food before clearing away their plates and promising to return with their coffee and cake.

"On second thought, Estie, let's change the coffee to a nice strong pot of tea," he instructed the woman. The demand made Charity smile. She knew why he had ordered it.

She had noticed that about Miles Hollingsworth before. Tea was his remedy for everything. From a hangover to a broken heart. She had often seen him administer it to his distraught siblings. His demeanor brisk and efficient, but his eyes concerned.

She had always considered it a sweet quirk in an otherwise aloof character.

Estie nodded, and they watched her depart.

"I don't think she has just the one toy boy, she probably has a guy in every village from here to Cape Town," Charity said on a wobbly voice, keen to continue their game.

Miles smiled, his eyes and his expression inscrutable again. He looked more like the Miles Hollingsworth she had known these last three years. A little grim and a lot unapproachable, and Charity regretted the loss of the man who had been so kind moments ago.

"*I* think she met the man of her dreams when she was in high school," Miles said after a long silence. "She married him just after university, and they have lived a long and wonderful life together. They have four children, twelve grandchildren, and three great grandchildren. And every evening they sit in their rocking chairs, hold hands, and watch the sun set. They talk about their day, the people they saw, and the things they did."

"That's very..." Charity struggled to find the right word and finally settled on, "romantic."

"I can be romantic," he said, but the contrast between the words and his grim voice and expression was frankly ludicrous.

"Can you?"

He sighed, the sound was heavy and despondent.

"Are you okay?" he asked, still in that fierce voice.

"Yes. Thank you."

"I'm sorry. I shouldn't have pried. Into your marriage, I mean."

"You didn't. It was just a question. And most people would answer it without all the drama."

"You're not most people."

"No. I'm a total drama queen. As you just discovered."

"I don't suppose you want to tell me about it. About him."

His face was stark, all angles and planes in the lengthening late afternoon shadows, and it gave him a vaguely sinister look. She smiled bittersweetly and, before she could overthink it, she reached across the table and stroked the bristled, sharp edge of his jaw.

"I feel...we're..." She shook her head, trying to find a way to verbalize how she was feeling without adding to the confusion of what was happening, or not happening, between them. "I don't know what's going on here. With us. I work for you. And the thought of confiding something so highly personal to you, when I haven't even told my family or friends about it, feels—I don't know. I don't know how it feels."

"Why did you hate him?"

She hesitated, not sure if she should answer. Not after what she had just said. But in the end, the need to confide in someone after so long overwhelmed all else. "He was a *monster*."

"And why didn't you confide in your family and friends?"

"Because everybody loved that monster. They thought he was a saint. Especially for marrying someone like me. I was high maintenance, you see? Wild and carefree. While Blaine was patient and kind. Exactly the man my family thought I needed. The kind of man *I* thought I needed."

He was distracted from his questions when Estie returned with a sunny smile on her face.

She deposited their desserts and tea on the table and offered Stormy a dog biscuit and an ear scratch.

Charity determinedly changed the subject to more neutral topics after that, delving into the limited and outdated town gossip she knew.

He allowed the subject change with nothing but a raised brow. He didn't seem at all interested in the subject matter but nonetheless listened attentively and kept her going with the occasional encouraging grunt, while he dove into his cake.

They headed home soon afterward, and they both determinedly kept the limited conversation impersonal for the rest of the afternoon.

Chapter Nine

Miles was mentally, physically and emotionally drained after the day out. Despite their conversations and confidences of the day, Charity Cole still remained a mystery to him.

He felt like he was on the cusp of finding the key to decrypting the enigma that was his lovely housekeeper. But he had to tread carefully, she appeared to have been badly hurt by her husband, and Miles didn't want to add to that damage.

He should leave her alone, and they should return to their respective neutral corners. But he found himself unable to stop thinking about her, about the indescribable vulnerability and pain that he had seen on her face when she had spoken of her dead husband.

She had tried so hard to hide it from him, but it had been there; between each labored breath, and in every tightly restrained movement of her body. He wasn't sure how her husband had hurt her but his initial instinct had been that the bastard had cheated on her. And he couldn't fathom how any man could treat a woman so poorly. His relationships—for lack of a better word—were usually only physical...but they were always monogamous. He believed that the woman he was sharing a bed with deserved to be treated with respect for however long their agreement lasted. That meant no fucking around. And he expected the same consideration from her.

He couldn't even *imagine* cheating on a spouse. Someone you had promised to love and cherish above all others.

He stood beneath a hot shower for ages washing the day off and reflecting on the conversations he'd had with Charity. She was easy to talk with. He rarely confided in people, and he had exposed fragments of himself to her that he wouldn't normally share with anyone else. Not even his family. She was the only one who now knew about his obsession with fantasy sagas. He cringed as he recalled the way he had enthused about his current read, but she had seemed interested and even entertained.

Admitting how ill he had been was a first as well. He had brushed it off with family and colleagues and had dismissed the seriousness of his condition even when *he* knew that they knew he wasn't being quite truthful. They had been happy to allow the lie, until he had gotten too ill for anyone to ignore.

But he hadn't even considered dissembling like that with Charity.

He didn't know what it meant, all he knew was that he wanted to explore this attraction between them even further. But he was questioning the wisdom of doing so.

Beyond the obvious, he had no real idea what he wanted from her. She rang all the right physical bells in him. He was attracted to her, he wanted to touch her and stroke her and pleasure her. And he wanted her to want the same from him. But it hardly seemed fair to act on that when she was the one taking all the risks. He knew that she'd worry about her job, and naturally there was always the fear of emotional and physical dependency. She had so much more to lose than he did.

And he wasn't certain how any sexual relationship between them would be structured. He usually offered his partners an arrangement of mutual, no strings pleasure for as long as both parties required it. His only caveats being exclusivity and a clean bill of health. While he had found such understandings perfectly suitable before, he now wondered if Charity would consider a similar offer crass and insulting.

It was best to step away from this and stop seeking her out. He had unfairly exposed the disguise that she had hidden behind for so many years. Mrs. Cole existed for a reason, and by stripping her of that armor, he left her open to who knows what kind of pain.

Unless he was willing to shoulder that burden with her, he should leave her alone. Allow her to be Mrs. Cole and leave Charity for some other man to discover.

It was the right thing to do. He knew that.

Still...despite that resolve—after his shower, when he returned to his room to find Charity timidly stepping across the threshold of his bedroom door, common sense beat a hasty retreat. And all he could do was stare in shock at the very welcome intrusion.

She froze when she spotted him and a dull red flush started at her throat and crept upwards until it reached her cheeks. She took a startled step backward, stumbling as she hit the door, which swung shut with a quiet click.

Leaving them alone...in a closed room.

She looked confused, torn between fleeing and standing her ground.

"Uhm...Stormy brought..." She didn't complete the sentence, instead lifting the item clutched in her hand for him to see.

A lone sock.

His eyes dropped to her feet, looking for his larcenous dog, but she was nowhere to be seen.

Charity seemed to know exactly who he was looking for. "She passed out on my sofa."

His gaze travelled back to her face, noting that she had changed into her horrid Mrs. Cole uniform, and he bit back a growl of frustration. Desperate to tear the hideous clothes off her.

His hands fisted at his sides and he fought the impulse to say something about it.

"I-I'll just put this..." She ventured into his room, her movements slow and tentative. A few tiny steps took her to the bed.

"You said that you usually wait until I take Stormy for her walk before bringing the loot back." He recalled, and she froze in the act of replacing the sock beside its mate. Her hand tightened fractionally around the tube, but she kept her gaze averted while her flush deepened.

"I thought you would need..."

"Why are you really here?" he interrupted her, his voice hoarse with suppressed desire. He wanted her to admit that this was a ruse, that she had known he would be in the shower, that she had hoped to catch him in nothing but a towel...Jesus, he wanted her to admit it so damned badly. Because then they could *finally* do something about this growing sexual tension between them.

She licked her lips, and he shuddered at the sight of that pink tongue, gooseflesh breaking out on his wet, naked skin. His dick responded, tenting the towel knotted around his waist.

She appeared to be aware of the movement beneath the towel, and her eyes darted down nervously before leaping back up to remain fixed on his Adam's apple. The outstretched hand still clutching the sock began to tremble violently.

"Do you want to touch me, Charity?" he asked in a barely audible whisper, and she swallowed, the click of her throat as loud as a gunshot in the quiet room.

Her gaze met his: large, liquid, and filled with longing.

Her head moved. A barely perceptible nod.

"Say it, please." He could hear the strain in his voice as the air in his lungs thickened. The deep, heavy saw of his breath came faster as he fought to remain composed.

"I want to touch you...Miles," she admitted, and he swallowed back a groan as his cock swelled to painful proportions.

"Come here," he invited, holding out a trembling hand to her, and she closed the gap between them with agonizing slowness. She reached out and the sock tumbled—forgotten—from her hand as it opened to take his.

That first touch was like a jolt of electricity through his entire body. He sizzled with awareness of her. Of her closeness, of her soft skin against his, of the flowery scent of her ruthlessly bound hair.

He guided her captive hand to his chest, certain she could feel the frantic, heavy beat of his heart as it tried to hammer its way right into her palm.

"I'm all yours."

THREE WORDS. Small, uncomplicated words.

I'm all yours.

Tiny words that promised complete sovereignty over the hot, smooth skin beneath her palm, and ownership of his magnificent body.

It was a freedom that Charity had never dreamed he would

afford her. A privilege which hadn't been offered to her in so long that she wasn't certain what to do with it now...all she could do was act on instinct, desire, and need.

Her hand smoothed its way over the still damp expanse of his chest. Silky hair attractively dusted across his pecs, darkened and thickened as it followed a trail down the center of his chest, along the shallow valley between his abs and then spread to his flat stomach around his indented belly button.

His muscles spasmed and bunched beneath her tentative touch, and he bit back an anguished groan when she swept her hand back up, just missing his tight nipple on the way to his shoulder, where she wrapped her palm around that hard, muscled curve and squeezed gently.

He felt so wonderful. All smooth, tensile, and repressed strength.

She shifted closer until they were almost chest to chest; an echo of their pseudo-embrace that night at the pool...So close that she could feel the warmth of her own breath as it bloomed against the skin of his throat. All she had to do was be brave and bridge the virtually non-existent gap between them.

But she wasn't certain she had any courage left. Not after the day she'd had. Joining him on his trip to Klein Bekkie, kissing him on the beach, and even telling him about Blaine. And now *this*; coming to his room, when she had known that it would lead to so much more.

Be brave. Her new mantra. Her prayer. Her wish...

She could be brave. She *was* brave.

Her lips touched his clean, damp, *hot* skin. Softened and blossomed against it.

He groaned and the soft, deep rumble reverberated through her chest and trembled down her spine until her legs liquefied, and her free hand moved up to his other shoulder for support.

Her lips trailed up beneath the firm ledge of his jaw, and she was both disappointed and gratified to find that he had shaved. She missed the pirate, but she welcomed back the attractive, urbane man she had initially found herself drawn to.

He still hadn't moved, and she wasn't quite sure what she would do if—*when*—he did. Bravery was one thing when it wasn't tested...but the moment he took the initiative from her; she *would* find herself tested. Still, expecting him not to move while she had her wicked way with him wasn't practical, and it wasn't what she wanted.

But what she wanted terrified her.

She—*very* slowly, as if she were handling a wild animal—wrapped her arms around his neck and finally found his mouth. For the first time since he had so generously offered his body to her, he moved; bending his neck to allow her easy access to his mouth. She traced the outline of those sensuous, wicked lips with her tongue, before softly planting her mouth on his.

This kiss was as timid as the one on the beach and, while she was eager to deepen it, to explore him more fully, she was petrified of unleashing something in him. Something wild and uncontrollable. It was an unfair and unfounded fear. She knew that...

Miles was not Blaine.

She had never met a more controlled man than Miles. And the iron clad command he appeared to have over his emotions and his responses, *should* make her feel safe. But self-governance was one thing when you were dealing with your family, your staff, or business. However, things could get messy when sex was involved.

"Get out of your head, Charity. Stay in this moment. With me." His gruff voice startled her. She opened her eyes and tilted back her head to stare at him. His gray eyes were warm and accepting. She was startled to realize that she had frozen with her arms still wrapped around his neck. The kiss that she had initiated now dead on their lips, while she wallowed in self-pity and fear.

"I'm sorry," she whispered, hearing despair quivering in the words.

"Don't be," he said. "You have nothing to be sorry for. Do you want to stop?"

She reflected on the question. Then considered how wonderful it felt to be plastered against his hot, hard body. Contemplated how glorious his erection felt cradled against her subtly rocking pelvis.

She brought her hands to his face, palming his lean cheeks, and smiled at him.

Did she want to stop?

She planted her open mouth over his and proceeded to show him exactly how much—no, how *little*—the thought of stopping and backing away from him appealed to her.

At last he moved, his arms wrapped around her back, and he held her close as he deepened the kiss. Adding the dimension that was missing before. This was no longer a solo endeavor, he was fully on board and very capably demonstrating how much better a kiss could be when both participants shared equal amounts of themselves.

His tongue welcomed hers into his mouth, before following it back into hers. The thrust and parry, the heat and intensity of the kiss set her nerve endings aflame, and Charity moaned as she pushed herself even closer to him.

She wanted more.

She hadn't expected to want so much more, in so short a time.

One of his hands swept over her back to the nape of her neck, and he tenderly smoothed his palm over the bare skin he found there. Charity shuddered at the contact, but his hand moved on all too quickly. He clearly had a goal in mind, and when he found the bun secured at the back of her head, she knew exactly what he wanted. She left him to explore there while she did a little of her own stroking and petting.

One of her hands found the hard curve of his butt while the other discovered the drying silk of his thick hair.

Her breasts felt swollen and tight in their confining bra, and she ached for him to release them, to touch them and fondle them. She longed to feel his hot, wet mouth on the swollen peaks. She released her grip on his tight behind, and groped for the hand he had on her back. It felt large and capable in hers, and she shuddered in anticipation as she imagined how that rough skin would feel on her nipples.

His breath snagged when she moved his touch to her torso, and he understood what she needed from him. With his mouth still on hers, and his other hand busily tugging pins from her hair, he yanked her blouse out of her skirt's waistband. She made an embarrassingly throaty sound of pleasure at the first touch of that roughened palm on her naked, sensitive skin and he chuckled.

The masculine sound was laden with satisfaction and a little smugness. But she found she didn't mind it, not when he was violently trembling in her arms, and certainly *not* when he was so insistently and helplessly thrusting himself against her.

No. She felt more than a little smug herself.

He finally achieved the goal he had been working toward for so long as the tightly anchored bun at the nape of her neck loosened and tumbled. Taking her inhibitions along with it. His towel was gone, fallen to the floor after she had tugged it away. Now he stood, naked and magnificent before her. She shifted her mouth from his to stare at all that glorious nudity...taking a moment to catch her breath and revel in the perfection of his sinewy, beautiful body.

His penis arched and throbbed against his flat belly, and she stared at it in fascination, part of her wanting it desperately, and the other part wanting to flee from him in irrational terror. He hadn't done a single thing to make her fear him. That was her own baggage weighing down the moment.

His hand slid out from beneath her blouse and he cupped her face, lifting her head until she was looking at him.

"You still okay?" he asked, his voice calm and level...despite his breathlessness.

"What if I'm not?"

"Then you're not and we stop."

"I want...I want..." she paused and frowned, not entirely certain what she wanted.

"Tell me. And I'll do everything in my power to make sure you get it."

Her eyes misted, and she blinked rapidly, determined not to cry. But it was hard not to in the face of such a selfless and sweet comment.

"Can you—"

His eyes were patient as he waited for her to complete the sentence. Because of that patience, and since the face she was staring into was so gorgeous in its stark severity and nothing at all like the monstrously beautiful face she had once so desperately feared, she sucked in a breath and gave him the selfish truth. Because she knew he would not punish her for it.

"Can you make me come? I want an orgasm."

Despite the trust she had placed in him in that moment, she still braced herself...fearing the worst, expecting the best. And she was rewarded with a rusty chuckle.

"Can I? Sweetheart, next time make it a real challenge."

She laughed, her relief effervescing through the sound. "Arrogant."

"Indubitably," he agreed with a grin and dipped his head to kiss her.

Hard, hot, fast...before he gentled the caress and worshipped her with his mouth and tongue. He led her to the bed, sat, and tugged her down beside him to continue his sensual onslaught. His hands busily unbuttoned her blouse and shoved it aside. The sexy sound of satisfaction he made when he first spotted the delicate lacy bra, sent gooseflesh rippling along her arms.

"Lovely," he muttered, his mouth dropping to one of the small mounds and planting kisses along the scalloped edge of the bra. His teeth gently closed around the hard, straining bud and he gave her a nip through the lace but closed his hot mouth over the aching peak before she could even register the sting.

Her back arched as she attempted to push herself nearer to him, so close to coming from just this touch that she wasn't sure how long she would last. He dragged the cup down with his teeth and suckled her again with a hungry groan of pleasure.

Charity's breath caught and released on a long moan. Her fingers were fisted in his hair as she held him close.

He turned his attention to the other peak, gifting it with the same lavish treatment. She was dimly aware of being shifted to her back while he worked at her breasts. By the time he finally lifted his head, he was cradled between her spread thighs, her blouse was completely undone, and her skirt was hiked up around her hips. His position allowed him to saw the ridge of his erection against her furrow through the damp silk of her panties.

His weight on top of her felt...confining, and while Charity fought to stay in the moment, she began to feel claustrophobic. Her quickening breath had nothing to do with the desire she had relished moments before and everything to do with how trapped she now felt.

He lifted his head from her breasts with a smile, and his eyes darkened when he appeared to recognize that she was no longer enjoying herself.

"Not a fan of missionary, I take it," he muttered, his voice cracking as he attempted to regulate his breathing. Before she could respond, or descend into a full-fledged panic attack. Before she could so much as blink...he reversed their positions until she was straddling him with her breasts spilling over the top of her bra and into his waiting hands. Her mound was now resting on top of his big, bold cock.

She sucked in a shocked breath, and her hands dropped to his chest for balance. Her hair tumbled around them, a dark curtain cutting them off from the world.

"You're so beautiful," he whispered, his voice reverent.

"So are you." She heard the reverence echoed in her shaky voice.

His hands went to play with her breasts and he lifted his head to kiss her again. He bent his knees and thrust up against her, the tip of his penis stimulating her overly sensitive clit and she whimpered helplessly at the sensation.

To her eternal regret, one of his hands slid away from her breasts, but that regret was fleeting when he felt his way down to her hip. His deft fingers slid beneath the waistband of her panties before circling around to grab a generous handful of her butt. He squeezed her flesh for a moment and guided her movements until she found the rhythm she needed. His intrepid hand glided farther down until it found the tight, slick entrance to her clenching channel. Charity shuddered when he slid one, long thick finger inside and she lost her rhythm for a second.

"Keep going, sweetheart," he urged, his voice strained.

A second finger found its way into her spasming pussy, and Charity sobbed. She couldn't remember anything feeling so all-consumingly good before.

She felt wonderful. Alive...vibrant, young, whole, and so powerful.

"Oh. *Oh.* Oh my *God*!" She was dimly aware of her nails digging into his chest as she thrust against him. Grinding on his cock, impaling herself on his fingers and finally...*finally* coming. Hard. Almost painfully.

And so damned spectacularly.

She was dimly aware of *his* voice.

Miles.

He was speaking quietly, articulating gentle assurances. Stroking her and guiding her back to the present with him.

He pulled her to his chest and wrapped his long, hard arms around her. She immediately felt warm and secure.

And cherished.

He planted sweet kisses on her damp forehead, and his hands burrowed beneath her blouse to caress her back—sweeping up and down the sweat dampened expanse in soothing strokes.

"You're still hard," she observed after a few minutes, and his penis jerked, apparently happy to be acknowledged.

"You asked for an orgasm, I believe that's exactly what I delivered."

"But I thought that we would both..." Her voice trailed off in confusion.

"I'm fine. This was about what you needed."

"Thank you," she mumbled. A little staggered by his incredible unselfishness. She hadn't expected him to deny his own gratification.

"Oh, Christ. It was my definite pleasure, Charity. Anytime you need an encore, I'll be right here."

She didn't reply. Instead, she snuggled even closer, loving the way he smelled. Warm and woodsy after his shower, with the musk of sex adding that extra layer of delicious sensuality.

She must have dozed because when she startled awake what felt like seconds later, the room was oppressively dark. And she couldn't move. Her arms were confined, her legs were entangled in something. Not the bedsheets; this was heavier, warmer...

Alive.

A man's legs.

She stifled a scream and kicked at the legs as she frenetically fought her way out of his hold.

She irrationally wondered how he had found her when he was dead.

Was she dead too? Had he killed her in those final, frantic moments? Was she doomed to forever be hunted by him in the afterlife?

"Charity, it's okay. It's Miles. You're fine. You're safe..."

The words registered and the voice—curt, controlled...*concerned*—registered. But she could not defeat the asphyxiating anxiety until she was out of his hold and off the bed. She wriggled away from him until she ran out of mattress and tumbled; landing on the hardwood floor with a thump.

The room flooded with light seconds later.

"Fuck. Are you okay?" Miles's head appeared over the edge of the mattress, and Charity blinked up at him in shocked confusion and dawning mortification.

"I-I'm sorry. I had a..."

"It's okay." The ice was gone from his voice. Instead, he sounded almost eerily calm.

The laugh that burst from her lips had a hysterical edge to it.

"You're always saying that," she pointed out. "Telling me it's okay."

She shoved her stupidly long hair out of her face, irritated when she tried to push herself to her feet only to trap her hair beneath her hands.

"It's not okay. It's not. *I'm* not." She fought her way through the dark, all-encompassing veil of her hair and surged to her feet, belatedly recognizing that her blouse was undone and her bra was sagging and she was in all kinds of disarray.

She tugged everything back in place with a humiliated moan, and Miles slowly moved to the center of the king-sized bed, propping himself up against the headboard, and dragging a sheet over his nudity.

"You're not what?" he asked. And she sobbed, folding her arms protectively over her chest to keep her ripped blouse in place.

"I'm not okay," she admitted, the words tumbling out before she could bite them back. It was the first time she had acknowledged as much...even to herself, and she took a moment to mull over the confession in wonder.

Miles shoved a hand through his hair and shook his head. "No. You're not okay, Charity. And I probably shouldn't have allowed what happened between us to go as far as it did."

"I wanted it."

He sighed, the soft sound was laden with resignation and despair.

"I did too but..."

"It's complicated," she finished for him, and he scrubbed his hands over his face and nodded.

"I know it's not my place to say but sweetheart, I mean I don't know you very well, but it seems that the fucker you were married to did a real number on you. I'm not sure exactly what went down but maybe you need...I don't know? Help? Counseling?"

"I'm sorry...this was supposed to be fun. And I freaked out and ruined it."

"This was always going to be messy and intense while we attempt to figure out what the fuck is going on between us."

"It would probably be best if we forgot this happened and continued on as usual," she suggested reluctantly.

"Undoubtedly." His expression inscrutable, and she chewed on her lower lip while she tried to figure out what he was thinking.

For a long moment that veneer of implacability did not shift from his face, but then the corners of his lips lifted wryly. "But since it's going to be difficult as hell to do that, I say we soldier on."

"What *precisely* does that mean."

"What would you like it to mean?"

She huffed irritably and fixed her best glower on him. "And you said *I* enjoy being an enigma?"

He full on grinned at her, and she shook her head, before sitting on the bed beside him.

"I'm probably going to resign," she informed him, crossing her outstretched legs and enjoying the fact that they were almost as long as his.

"You don't have to do that."

"I do. I've been hiding here. If nothing else this thing

between us has shown me that I'm ready to join the world again. Meet people."

"Meet men you mean?" he corrected her sourly, and she turned her head to stare at his implacable profile.

"Well, yes. I suppose I do. Eventually. After this...After us."

He sighed again and reached out to tuck his palm around the nape of her neck. He tugged her toward him, and she made a soft, contented sound in the back of her throat. She dropped her head to his shoulder and snuggled close. This was exactly where she wanted to be right now.

He released her nape and curved his arm around her slender shoulders. His fingers toyed with a strand of her hair.

"Thank you for coming to me tonight."

She smiled at the words. "Thank you for helping me come tonight."

He snort-laughed at that.

"Want to fool around some more?" He dropped the question into her ear. His voice wicked and dark.

She giggled and was amazed that the carefree sound had come from her. "How about I give *you* an orgasm this time?"

"How about we make it one each?"

"You're so competitive," she complained and hiked her skirt to straddle his lap.

"Only way I know how to be," he retorted, framing her face with his palms to give her a long, drugging kiss.

By the time he relinquished her lips, Charity had lost all semblance of time and place. And when he removed her ruined blouse, she unthinkingly allowed him to manipulate her arms through the sleeves.

It was only when he was smoothing his hands up her arms that she started thinking clearly again, and by then it was too late, his left hand had frozen halfway up her right forearm. His brow lowered as his fingers traced the scars he found there, trying to make sense of them.

"What—?"

She didn't allow him to complete the question. Instead, she tore her arm from his grasp and leaped from the bed in a panic. She was so stupid. Why did she think she could do this? There were too many secrets that she had kept for too long. Secrets trapped in her heart and memory and scattered all over her body. Getting intimate with any man required revealing some of those secrets. The physical ones if not the psychological and emotional ones.

And she now knew that she wasn't ready for that.

She had her hand secured over the spot he had unwittingly stumbled upon, while she stared at him in panic and she tried to figure out how to get away from him without exposing even more of her broken self.

He had followed her off the bed and now stood in front of her, unashamedly naked. *His* body so flawless he didn't have to hide a single part of himself.

"I changed my mind." The words tumbled over each other in her haste to get them out. She wanted them to disgust him enough to give up on her and on this madness between them.

"Oh?" His tone of voice was menacing and nothing like she'd ever heard him use before. It scared her, and she hated that anything about him could frighten her. "Why? Because I found the cigarette burns on your arm?"

"They're...they're not..."

"Charity, I know what they are."

"H-how?"

"A girl I went to university with used to self-harm...the scars are very distinctive. How did you get those? Did you do that to yourself?"

He reached for her arm, and she flinched violently, jumping away from him like a terrified rabbit.

His jaw clenched, and his face whitened. He lowered his arm. The movement was slow and deliberate.

He *knew*. How could he not know? When she had cowered from his touch like a whipped dog?

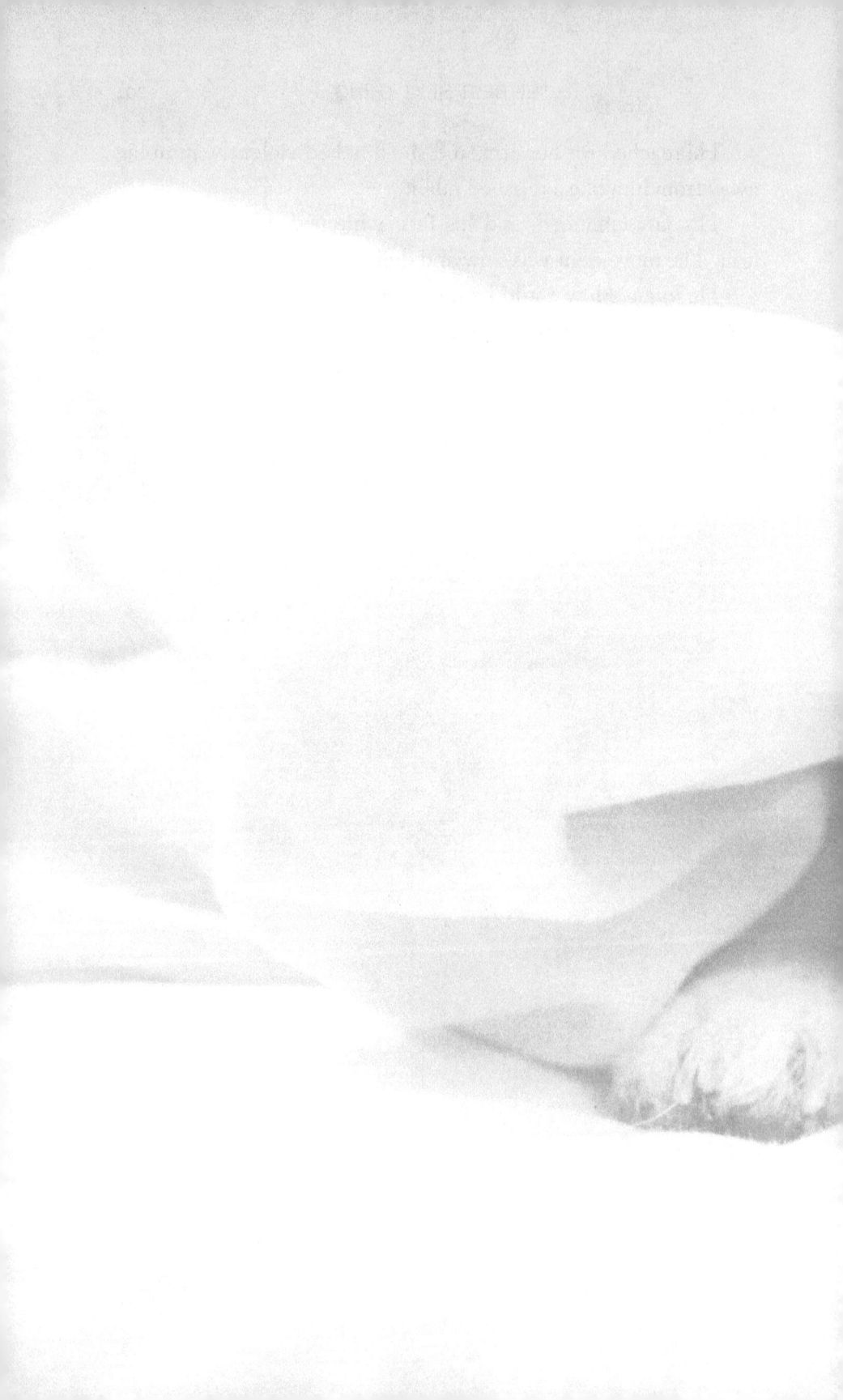

Chapter Ten

Miles wanted to hurt someone. Preferably the fucker who had marked Charity. He wanted to tear *that* bastard limb from limb. But he couldn't, because the monster who had taken a lit cigarette to her soft skin and *burned* her was far beyond his reach.

Miles's stomach twisted with revulsion at the thought of the pain she must have endured. But he swallowed back the nausea churning in his gut and focused on the wounded, vulnerable woman in front of him.

He hated that she appeared afraid of him. The expression of absolute terror on that lovely face made him want to do violence, but he knew that he couldn't allow her to see that. Not in in her current fragile state.

She had fucking *flinched* from his touch. As if he would hurt her. As if he would physically hurt *any* woman. But he couldn't be offended or wounded by that. She needed patience. Understanding.

Everything Miles was not.

"May I..." his voice was thick, and he cleared his throat before continuing. "May I see?"

She didn't respond, keeping her hand clamped protectively over her arm while she watched him through her long fall of hair. She looked feral, half crouched in a defensive stance while she eyed his every move warily.

"Why?" The word floated between them, soft and light as butterfly wings.

"It's patterned, isn't it?"

"It's ugly."

"*Nothing* about you is ugly." The hoarse vehemence in his voice startled him, and he took a moment to compose himself before continuing. "Absolutely nothing."

She never took her eyes from his face but she did stand up straighter; some of that familiar pride returning to her posture. She hesitated for a moment longer before lifting her chin and defiantly thrusting her arm out for him to see.

This time he was the one who wavered, before ever so slowly reaching out to tenderly grasp her slender wrist. He turned her arm until the delicate underside was exposed to him and then valiantly fought back a surge of fury so fucking hot it actually blinded him for a second.

The small round burns were pink and shiny—obviously quite old by now—and neatly arranged in a circle.

Inside the circle—

Miles blinked back the scalding moisture that pooled in his eyes and gritted his teeth against the snarl he could feel forming in his throat. Monster was too kind a word for the *thing* who had done this to her. There were no adjectives to describe anyone who could mark, demean and hurt another human being in this way.

He traced the obscene pattern with his trembling forefinger.

He hated knowing how much she must have cried and writhed and pleaded, while this less than human cocksucker had burned a crude smiley face into her skin.

He lifted her arm and unthinkingly kissed the scars there. He didn't know how to deal with this, and he was absolutely certain that a man like him...irascible, blunt, and lacking in finesse would do more harm than good in a situation like this.

"I'm glad he's dead." His voice trembled with suppressed violence. "But part of me wishes he were still alive so that I could hunt him down and *end* him for doing this to you. For hurting you."

He kept his gaze diverted, even though he could feel her keen stare on his profile.

"Don't you want to know why he did it?" she asked in the smallest of voices, and the question succeeded in whipping his head around so that he could meet her eyes incredulously.

"*Why*? It doesn't matter *why* he did it. Nothing you said or did could in any way justify this-this...atrocity."

"H-he said I didn't smile enough, that his parishioners would start to wonder why he had taken such a miserable bitch as a wife. So, he gave me a little reminder to k-keep smiling."

NOW YOU'LL ALWAYS REMEMBER to smile, won't you, Cherry?

Charity gritted her teeth against the memory of Blaine's refined voice. How he had enjoyed hurting her like that. He had straddled her chest and pinned her arm down, using his superior strength to keep her helpless and subdued. She had barely registered the agonizing pain, shock and adrenaline shielding her from the worst of it. But seeing it afterward; she shuddered at the recollection. In a marriage filled with degradation after degradation, somehow, this had felt like the worst of it. This *brand* had been exactly what he had wanted it to be. A mark of complete and utter ownership.

It had obliterated the last remnants of the old, carefree Charity. After that she had been Blaine's creature. Humiliated and terrified of doing or saying the wrong thing. Of setting him off. Because his loss of temper and control had *always* been her fault. For so long, she had truly believed that. And his parents—his *mother*—had perpetuated that lie.

Blaine's a good, kind man. You bring out the worst in him. Maybe if you'd stop making him so *angry, Charity. If you were more aware of his needs.*

"Hey," Miles's assertive voice forced its way into the unwelcome recollections, drowning out her former mother-in-law's pseudo-sympathetic advice. His touch was gentle as he cupped her jaw and lifted her face until she met his eyes. "There you are. Don't go back to that dark place, Charity. Okay?"

"You're still naked." It was the first thing she could think of to say, and he smiled. Not one of the warm, generous smiles she was borderline addicted to, but a polite parting of his lips.

She didn't like it, but she appreciated the effort.

"And you're still topless," he pointed out.

She gasped and crossed her arms over her chest.

"Why don't you grab a shower?" he suggested. "I'll fix dinner tonight."

"You *will*?" She couldn't quite contain her skepticism and he smiled again. This time it was a warmer and more like the ones she was growing so dangerously dependent on.

"This I have to see." It was a weak attempt at levity after the intensity of the last half hour, but his smile deepened.

"Wiseass. Prepare to be awed by my culinary prowess. And —" he stopped abruptly, and his eyes widened as he seemed to realize something. "*Fuck*, Stormy must be starving."

He strode to the door and jerked it open to find Stormy sitting in the hallway. The dog got up, shook herself, and wagged her tail before trotting into the room and climbing into her basket. She turned a few times before snuggling down with a contented sigh. Miles watched her with some consternation on his face, apparently having expected more fanfare or fuss from the pup.

Charity smiled, the sight of the dog alleviating some of her anxiety and tension.

"I'll grab that shower," she mumbled, and left the room. She was already out in the hallway when his voice stopped her.

"Charity?" She still loved the sound of her name on his lips. She smiled quizzically, wondering why he had halted her progress. But he didn't return the smile. Instead, he stared at her with an intensity that should have unsettled her.

But didn't.

"Yes?"

"You're a strong and capable woman and more than able to physically kick my arse any fucking time you damned well please," he said, his words concise, and his voice no-nonsense. "But I will never, *ever*, give you any cause to defend yourself against me."

She gulped, and her eyes flooded at the unexpectedness of the vow.

"I know that, Miles," she whispered, unable to control the wobble in her voice. "I *know* that. But...it's still good to hear it."

CHARITY WAS busy repinning her hair when her phone buzzed. She dropped her arms in frustration, allowing the mass of hair to tumble down again and reached for the phone, expecting to find a message from Faith.

> MILES
> Meet me in the den. Dress comfortably. Mrs. Cole's services not required. Leave her behind.

She grinned, feeling like a teenager preparing for her first date. It was unbelievable how much their relationship had altered in the last twenty-four hours.

The last text exchange between them just above this newest message, dated a year and a half ago, was ample testament to that change:

> MILES
> Dinner for eight tonight. Formal. 6pm.

> CHARITY
> Very well, sir. Any special dietrary requirements?

> MILES
> None.

Dull, curt, and stiff. Those three words pretty much

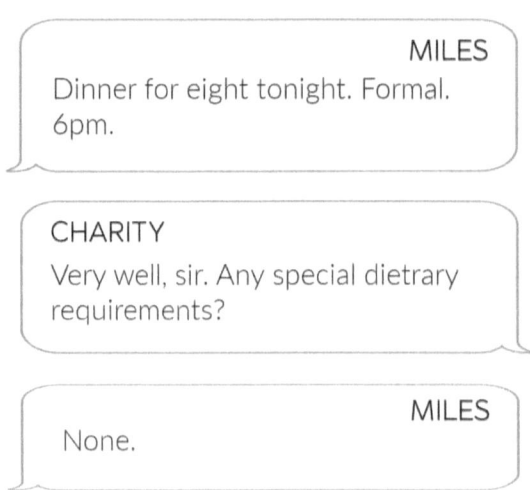

described their relationship before now. They had spoken only when absolutely necessary.

The smile fell from her lips as she continued to stare at the screen. This was so confusing. She wasn't sure how she felt about anything right now.

All she knew was that she wanted to spend time with him. Wanted to talk with him, laugh with him, play with him...love with him. If she could even remember how to do any of those things. It had been so long since she'd been just *normal.*

Well, like the saying went: *Every journey begins with a single step...*

She inhaled deeply, held the breath for a beat and then released it on a slow controlled sigh. And took that step.

CHARITY
Dress "comfortably"? Define "comfortably"

Charity stared at the words she couldn't quite believe she had typed.

And chuckled when the response drifted onto her screen a second later:

MILES
Adverb: comfortably - in a physically relaxed way that is free from contstraint

Wiseass. She laughed again and shook her head.

CHARITY
Fine. No bra then.

She sent the response before she could overthink it and regretted it an instant later. Especially when he took absolute ages to reply. She worried her lower lip with her teeth and watched the three dots appear and reappear endlessly as he formulated his response.

MILES
You're driving me a little crazy, Mrs Cole

Charity grinned at that and instantly replied:

CHARITY
As per your request, Mrs. Cole has taken the evening off, you're stuck with Charity tonight.

MILES
Thank fuck for that. Get over here ASAP! The dinner I slaved over is getting cold.

Despite the playful tone of their text messages, or maybe because of it, Charity still hesitated outside the den ten minutes later. The door to the cozy room was shut, and she wiped her sweaty palms on the seat of her slouchy sweatpants before curling one of them into a fist and tentatively knocking on the door.

"Why are you knocking?" The impatience in that masculine voice was evident even through the thick wood. Charity rolled her head and shook her arms like a boxer before entering the ring, attempting to alleviate some of her nervousness.

She curled her hand around the doorknob only to have it unceremoniously yanked from her hand as the door swung inward.

"There's no need for you to knock, Charity. This is more your home than mine."

A polite fiction that she accepted with nothing but a tight smile. After the flirty texts, she was disappointed with the way this was starting. Disappointed in herself for not being more confident.

But then he smiled and all of her disappointment went flying out the window. He just looked so happy to see her.

He stepped aside and ushered her into the den with a bow, and she gasped when she saw what he had done. The entire room was glowing with soft candlelight. Lit candles of all shapes and sizes adorned just about every flat surface. He had scattered fat, fluffy pillows on the carpeted floor around the coffee table. A large silver cloche sat atop the table, accompanied by two empty, long-stemmed wineglasses, and a couple of delicate porcelain plates. A single protea, likely from the garden, shoved into a plastic water bottle took pride of place in the center of the table.

He even had a fire merrily crackling away in the massive hearth and some light jazz playing in the background

"Miles, this is..." She shook her head as words escaped her.

"You look gorgeous," he said, and she laughed at the extravagant lie. She was wearing pink sweatpants, a hoodie, thick socks, and no shoes. She didn't have on a lick of makeup, and her hair was tied back in a loose French braid. But her laughter died when his lingering gaze told her that the compliment was sincere.

She cleared her throat and smiled when she took in the way he was attired. They were practically matching, he was in gray sweatpants, a form fitting white T-shirt that emphasized his chest and biceps impressively and no shoes or socks. She loved the sight of his sexy bare feet.

"Where's Stormy?" she asked, thinking it prudent to distract both of them. At this rate, they wouldn't get through dinner without jumping each other's bones.

"Napping," he said, and nodded toward the crate in the corner. The crate was usually kept in his bedroom, and she frowned at the unfamiliar sight of it in the den. His next words cleared up her confusion and melted her heart, "I didn't want her to feel left out or alone, so I thought she could snooze in here while we have our dinner."

"That doesn't help with separation anxiety, you know?" she felt obligated to point out, and he grimaced.

"I know. But she looked so sad when she knew I was going to leave the room and..."

"Miles," Charity interrupted him and lay a tentative hand on his bare arm. "I think *you're* the one with separation anxiety."

Her words made him laugh as she had intended them to, but she couldn't bring herself to remove her hand from his arm. Instead, her palm slid to his and, he entwined his fingers with hers.

"You're right. It's something I need to work on. Tomorrow. For tonight she's fine. She's had her dinner, her toilet break, and she's snuggled up with her heated beanbag, fast asleep. I'd hate to disturb her."

Charity angled her body toward his and cupped his jaw with her free hand.

"You're such a softie," she teased, and he lifted her captured hand to his lips to kiss her knuckles.

"Sit down," he urged, tugging her toward the coffee table. They sank onto the heap of cushions.

Her eyes did another awed tour of the room, "You've done so much work."

"I knew you'd appreciate my paltry attempts at power conservation," he said, with a cheeky wink and she laughed.

"It would have been even more appreciated when we were running on a generator, but thank you nonetheless."

He grinned unrepentantly and released her hand to gesture toward the cloche.

"You hungry?"

"A little."

"Good, because I've prepared a feast."

Charity tilted her head and stared at the cloche and then glanced around the room to see if he had any other containers stashed away. But nope...it was just this one, lonely cloche. She couldn't imagine it containing anything remotely feast like.

"Okay, close your eyes," he instructed her, and she blinked. Not certain she had heard him correctly.

"What?"

"Close your eyes."

"You're making quite the production out of this, aren't you?"

"This used to be Hughie and Vicki's favorite meal when they were kids. I'm the only one who could make it exactly how they liked it."

She sighed and covered her face with both hands.

"No peeking."

"Oh my God, I had no idea you had such a flair for the dramatic."

She heard the faint metal on metal *ping* as he lifted the lid.

"Don't look until I tell you to," he said. And she sighed in fake vexation. Truthfully, she was enjoying every moment of this. There was a slosh of liquid, and she assumed he was filling up the wineglasses.

"Okay, three, two...two and a ha—"

"*Miles*!" Her voice was shaking with suppressed laughter as she tried, but failed, to sound exasperated. She was delighted by this unexpectedly whimsical side of him.

"Spoilsport! Fine. Open your eyes."

She lowered her hands and opened her eyes and then stared, uncomprehendingly, at the...*feast*(?) in front of her.

A precarious pyramid of sandwiches, each a neatly sliced triangle, stacked one on top of the other.

"Sandwiches?" Her voice was faint, and she cleared her throat and looked up to meet his expectant gaze.

"Not just any old sandwiches," he stated proudly. "These are peanut butter, strawberry jam, and banana sandwiches."

"Oh." She shifted her focus to the wineglasses, and her lips twitched. Each expensive, handcrafted crystal glass was filled to the brim with milk.

"Tuck in," he invited, and stacked a few sandwiches onto his plate. Charity took a couple of slices and sat back, folding her legs crosswise before taking a hearty bite from the generously filled sandwich.

The flavors sang on her tongue, reminding her of her carefree childhood. So much nostalgia in just one bite.

She grinned at him, certain her delight must be plain to see.

"This is so good," she enthused around a mouthful of bread. The peanut butter stuck to the roof of her mouth and teeth, and she didn't even care. Instead, she washed it down with some milk and went in for another bite.

He grinned at her. She laughed and impulsively reached across the table to thumb a smudge of jam away from the corner of his mouth. He turned his head to flick the jam off her thumb with the tip of his tongue.

The casual intimacy of their actions astonished her. Even more astounding? The fact that she didn't mind it at all. She withdrew her hand and, holding his gaze hostage, deliberately sucked the thumb he had just licked into her mouth. His breath caught, and his eyes sparked, then darkened to almost black.

"These are seriously amazing," she said, her voice embarrassingly throaty after their sexy interplay. "Takes me back to my childhood. Although my mother never added banana. I don't know why not. It adds so much flavor."

"Like I said, I used to make these for Hughie and Vicki. I use a different knife for each spread, and they have to cover the entire surface of the slice. Corner to corner." He grinned wryly, flashing her that adorable dimple. "You may have noticed that Hugh is a little particular."

She raised her brows at that understatement.

"He has OCD, right?" She instantly regretted the question. Mrs. Cole's reticence was so ingrained that it felt improper asking him such a personal question.

Miles didn't seem to mind though. Instead, he nodded and took a swig of milk before talking again.

"Yes. It went untreated for much too long. None of his teachers picked up on it. Or maybe they just ignored it. He was ten before I dragged my mum and Hughie to a clinic and demanded to see a child psychiatrist. Mum had been working such long hours she was happy to just avoid the issue. He was healthy and happy for the most part, but she didn't see the quirks and didn't recognize how much they were holding him back. He was being bullied at school because of it and then later, because he was gay. I always knew he was gay, I think before Hugh knew. And it was confusing and distressing for him to be called names he barely understood. It pissed me the hell off that he wasn't allowed to discover his sexuality in his own time. Kids can be fucking arseholes at times. Anyway, the lack of control at school fed his obsessive-compulsive tendencies.

"When he was younger—it's not as bad now—he also suffered from something called *brumotactillophobia*. Which means he had aversion to his food touching. It took a long time to get him to accept a sandwich like this. With everything smooshed together so haphazardly. But money was tight, and we had to make do with what we had. These were a cheap, tasty meal so Hugh and I sat down one day and discussed how we could make this work for him. Different knives for each spread, no messy oozing on the sides—let me tell you, that's fucking hard to avoid—the banana slices have to be perfectly uniform, nine on each sandwich and arranged in three rows of three. And of course, they have to be sliced into perfectly even triangles. With three whole and three perfectly halved banana slices on each side.

"I've never gotten out of the habit of preparing these sandwiches to Hugh's exact preference. Even though I can't remember the last time I made these for him. They bring back some pretty great memories though."

"You and your siblings are so close," Charity said, touched by the story and what it said about the man sitting across from her.

"I don't think we are," he responded with a nonchalant lift of his shoulders. "Hugh and Vicki are tight, they share a flat and talk all the time. I fed them, dressed them, disciplined them, helped them with their homework and school projects. I think they find it hard to think of me as a big brother when I was more of a parental figure than our mum. Don't get me wrong, she tried her best, but she had her hands full keeping food on the table and a roof over our heads. Looking out for the little ones was the least I could do for her."

"But...who looked out for you?" she asked, her voice tentative. The question seemed to flummox him, and he stared at her for a long moment as if he couldn't quite fathom the meaning behind her words.

"I didn't need..."

"You were *eleven*," she interrupted.

"I was old for my age. By that time, I'd already spent a year taking care of my terminally ill father, while helping mum with the kids."

That was *heartbreaking*. He had never had a childhood. And as far as she could tell he rarely allowed himself time to let loose now either.

"What do you do for fun?"

"Fun?"

"You know, *fun*. Something you do for the sheer enjoyment of it."

"I have my audiobooks. And I like to hike. And the thrill of a new acquisition can't be beaten."

"When did you start listening to your fantasy books?"

"I used to read them when I was a kid. But as I got older, I got busier and I didn't have much time for reading. About eight years ago, I happened to see a commercial for my favorite author's new book. When I saw it was available on audiobook, I didn't hesitate. I haven't looked back since."

"Why fantasy?"

"You're full of questions tonight," he said, with a tiny smile, taking a nibble from his fourth sandwich. Charity was still on her second.

"Just interested."

"Why do *you* think I love fantasy novels?"

"Because it was so very distant and different from your reality?"

He didn't reply but his smile widened.

They were both silent for a few moments as they polished off a few more sandwiches.

"I think you underestimate the strength of your relationship with your siblings," she said, and he lifted a quizzical eyebrow.

"Why do you say that?"

"I've seen the way they vie for your attention, and constantly try to include you in their activities. I always thought you were just being a total douche when you'd brush them off and sit in your corner with your headphones. I assumed you were working and didn't have the time or patience to spend time with them."

"No...I..." His voice trailed off, and his brow puckered into a formidable frown. One that would have had her running scared a week ago. "I was listening to my books. Not working...I always thought they were just inviting me along because they felt they had to. I'm not exactly Mr. Hip and Cool."

She chuckled. "The fact that you used the words 'hip' and 'cool' kind of highlights the point you were making about being neither of those things. They weren't inviting you out of some sense of duty. They always looked so crestfallen whenever you rejected their invitations."

"I wasn't rejecting them," he denied, his voice heating defensively.

"I'm just telling you how it looked to me. And possibly to them?"

"Fuck." The word was rife with remorse, self-recrimination and frustration.

Feeling terrible for pointing out what had seemed so obvious to her, Charity covered his hand on the table with her own and squeezed reassuringly. She didn't speak, lending silent support because she could sense that he needed that more than any words.

He flashed her a tight smile that didn't quite reach his eyes.

"I sometimes—" He stopped and cleared the gruffness from his throat. "I'm not always great around people. Not even my own family. When I was a kid, I kept my emotions under lock and key. My mother did so much for us, she didn't need to be burdened with my fears and frustrations. Not when she had so much to deal with already. Work, Hugh's needs, and then Vicki started acting out when she was older. She needed to be able to depend on me, you know?"

"I know."

"I was old enough to understand what it would mean for us if she lost any of her jobs and couldn't make the rent. We'd all be out on the streets, or worse, the kids and I would have been taken from her." Charity found it telling how he often referred to his siblings, but not himself, as kids. He really had been old before his time and she found that knowledge more than a little tragic.

"She has no idea," he continued, unaware of her troubled thoughts. "That I know how many nights she came home and locked herself in the bathroom and cried. I didn't want her to have to worry about what was happening at home with the kids. I strove to be dependable. Took care of the little ones, got good grades, even though it meant staying up till the early hours studying. I promised myself that one day I'd be successful and my mother would never have to work or worry again."

"You were. So why don't you cut yourself some slack once in a while, Miles?"

"I'm afraid..." His voice faded as if he was having second thoughts about what he had been about to say.

"Of?" she prompted him.

"I'm afraid that if I stand still or stop for too long, I'll lose everything I've built. And I won't be able to take care of them anymore."

"Do they still *need* you to take care of them?"

His forehead puckered, and he shook his head abruptly.

"I'm sorry, I've been banging on about this for way too long. This was supposed to be a relaxing evening. Tell me about you." He looked troubled for a second before adding, awkwardly, "You, *before* everything."

"Before my marriage you mean?" she asked frankly.

"I didn't think you'd want to discuss that with me now. Or ever. I mean, it's up to you if you...*shit*. Sorry, I told you I'm no good at this."

"At what?"

"Conversation. Seriously, I'm best in front of a computer, figuring out ways to acquire the companies I want. Working out if they're worth salvaging or just hacking into pieces and selling off. I'm great with numbers, legalese, seeing the bigger picture. But I leave the interpersonal stuff to my right-hand man, Bryan. I am truly abysmal at peopling."

She laughed at that.

"You're doing fine. I have only one sister. Older. Her name is Faith. She has this gorgeous little girl, Grace." She stopped, finding it harder than she had expected to talk about them. Especially when the pang of yearning and loss in her heart intensified at the thought of them.

"How old is Grace?" His voice was quiet, soothing and

perfectly pitched to get her talking again. And he said he was bad at "peopling". He didn't seem to know himself very well.

"Five," she replied, setting aside her half-eaten sandwich and drinking down the last of her milk. "Uh, nearly six. It's her birthday in a couple of weeks' time."

"That's a great age," he said, with a smile. "She irritated the ever loving shit out of me at the time, but when I think back now, Vicki was an adorable six-year-old. With her curly mop of black hair and her irrepressible smile and constant questions. She had such a thirst for knowledge. Still does actually. What is Grace like?"

"I haven't seen her in a while. Not since she was three. I mean we skype but...that's not the same is it? She doesn't have the patience to sit and talk to this stranger on the computer. She knows me, but, not really."

"Do you have any pictures?"

She nodded and reached into the front pouch of her hoodie for her phone. She didn't even know why she had it on her, she rarely received any calls or messages.

She flicked through her photo album and found a picture of her niece. Grace was wearing a pink tutu, fairy wings, and mismatched Wellingtons. She was grinning widely at whomever was taking the picture.

She silently handed the phone to Miles, who took it without comment. He flipped it around and stared at the picture with a frown of concentration.

"She's pretty cute," he said, flashing Charity a grin. "She has your eyes."

"We all have my mom's coloring; her mother—our *ouma*—was a mixed-race woman from the Cape Flats. And our *oupa* was a second-generation Lebanese man. Faith and I inherited our dad's height. But his blond hair and hazel eyes didn't stand a chance against our mom's dominant genes." She smiled fondly as she thought of her parents. She missed them so much, and it felt wonderful to talk about them. "Because they faced so much discrimination after their marriage during the later apartheid era, they moved to Canada for a few years. But they returned just before the first democratic election. I was about four when we moved back. Faith was two. I have only the vaguest recollection of it."

"Have you seen *any* of your family in the last three years?" he asked, after handing her phone back.

Charity swallowed and ran a finger over her niece's image.

"No. I speak with them, FaceTime sometimes...Faith wants me to come to Gracie's sixth birthday party."

"You should go."

"I can't."

"Charity..."

"Miles we've known each other for about a minute," she pointed out shortly, pocketing her phone, before levelling a blistering glare at him. "You don't get to have an opinion about this, okay?"

Chapter Eleven

"I'm sorry."

His softly spoken apology took the wind out of her sails and robbed her of the fuel she needed to stoke her fiery indignation. She sagged and buried her face in her palms taking a moment to compose herself.

He didn't say another word, merely sat quietly and waited for her to speak.

"No. I'm the one who's sorry, Miles." She dropped her hands and met his eyes. "I shouldn't have snapped at you. I get a little defensive. My family has been so hurt and confused by all of this. But I find it hard to be around them and their sympathy. They think I'm grieving for him. And how do I explain to them that I would never mourn him, that I don't miss him, and that I'm so damned grateful to be free of him?"

She made a despairing sound and wiped at her wet eyes.

"I didn't want to talk about him tonight. I don't want to talk about him *ever*."

He was silent for a long, long moment after her outburst, but when he eventually spoke, the words emerged slowly. As if he were weighing every syllable for fear saying the wrong thing. "I think...and I'm not an expert. And I *know* it's none of my business. But I think that perhaps if you *did* speak of him, to someone—anyone—it would help you find some clarity and possibly some closure. Or at the *very* least it'll start the healing process on the still festering wound that was your marriage."

"Speak to *you*, you mean?"

"No, sweetheart." His voice was so painfully gentle it just about broke her heart. "You don't have to tell me anything. But you *do* have to tell someone. If not your parents or your sister, then a therapist."

"I think for me, the worst of it all, was that he stripped me of my self-worth, my self-confidence, my dignity...and I *allowed* it."

"Charity you've clearly lived through, and *survived,* hell. I can tell you that I think you're an amazing woman. The strongest, most capable, and interesting woman I've ever met. But until you look in a mirror and believe those things about yourself, my words are meaningless. And because that fucking bastard has controlled your life for so long, I know how hard it must be for you to do so. You're the only one now who can take that power away from him."

Tears had been silently streaming from her eyes throughout his little speech. Logically and emotionally, she knew that his words were true. But Blaine had kept her imprisoned in a cage of fear and intimidation for so long, that even now, *years* after the door had been left open and unlocked, she was too terrified to step foot outside of those familiar confines.

She had fled, sure, but she had taken her cozy cage with her. She had painted it, decorated it, and deceived herself into believing that the bars weren't there. Fooled herself into thinking that she was free. But she wasn't. She was still in the cage Blaine had put her in.

And she was only now beginning to recognize that fact.

She had allowed her parents, her sister, the people who *loved* her, to mourn her abuser. As if he warranted that consideration. As if he was worth a single one of their tears. She had permitted *his* parents to silence her with their stoic disappointment in her. The oh-so-subtle jabs that perhaps he wouldn't have killed himself if she had only been a better, more loving wife, had been a different kind of abuse.

He did not deserve to live on fondly in people's memories.

He deserved to be known as the hideous, repulsive monster who had raped her and beaten her almost daily.

She was shaking. Violently. She became aware of it when she heard her teeth chattering.

"W-why are you so invested in this?" she asked him, her voice unsteady. "This isn't fun, or flirty or anything close to a holiday romance. You should be running in the opposite direction and avoiding me like the plague after what you've learned about my marriage."

"Give it time." The words were placid, his smile soothing. "There's always tomorrow."

"Always tomorrow for what?" she asked blankly.

He responded, still in a ridiculously serene voice. "Running scared and avoiding you like the plague."

His words coaxed a reluctant laugh from her and he reached for a napkin and gently dabbed the moisture from her face.

She took the napkin from him and gave her nose a good blow before speaking again. "I'm serious, Miles. I'm clearly a mess. This thing between us isn't developed or strong enough for you to stick around for this crap."

"Charity, I didn't come here looking for a holiday romance.

I'm here to hide from the world while I recover from a debilitating illness. I wasn't expecting to find you here."

"Of course, you were."

"Don't be pedantic, Charity," he chastised without heat. "You know what I mean. I admit that at first, I did consider you an intriguing mystery that had to be solved. It was that fucking power outage. I was bored out of my mind. You and Stormy were the only diversions around. And *she* sleeps eighteen hours a day. But after that night at the pool...things changed. I was still interested but on a more, shall we say, *personal* level."

"You wanted to shag me you mean?"

"So bloody desperately. I mean, there was sexual interest before that. But mere twinges compared to how much I wanted you after that night."

"This is a lot of baggage to tolerate for a little nookie," she pointed out acerbically, and he gave her a lazy smile.

"While I may feel like a perpetually horny teenage boy around you, Charity, I am *not* an adolescent. And I do have a modicum of hard-earned control over my hormones and base desires. Look, what I'm trying to say is that there's no one else here for us right now. So why don't we each be what the other needs us to be."

"And what do you need me to be?" she asked in frustrated confusion. "A sexual partner?"

"No. Not because I don't want it but because it's probably not what *you* need right now. And that means it's off the table."

"So, what do you think I need right now?"

"The same thing I need...A friend."

A friend? How...*novel.* And yet the notion of having someone in her corner, someone to confide in, spend time and laugh with, after so many years alone was incredibly appealing.

"And you can switch off the sexual thing? Just like that? Why would you even want to? What if *I* don't want you to?"

"I can't switch it off. I'm not. It's on the back burner for now. It'll happen or not. Either way, I'd like for us to be friends. In fact, I do believe we're well on our way to establishing a friendship already."

"I *really* liked what we did earlier though. In your room."

He groaned before slanting her a heated look. "I did too."

"I like the idea of having a friend, Miles. But I like the idea of having a lover just as much."

She watched his throat move as he swallowed.

"I do too."

"Blaine took so many decisions from me. How I should dress, who I should speak with, where I could go...when, where, how we had sex. It's been so long since I had a choice. And right now, I need a friend...but I would also like a lover."

"You can have both, Charity. I just don't think we have to rush into anything."

"What about friends with PG-13 benefits?"

He placed his hand, palm up, on the coffee table between them. She smiled, and without hesitation, put her hand in his. His fingers curled around hers.

"You mean some handholding, closed mouth kisses, and hot fumbling through our clothes? Count me in. I'm awkward as hell anyway. This would be right in my wheelhouse."

She laughed at his words and squeezed his hand, before impulsively telling him, "I really, *really* like you Mr. Hollingsworth."

"Well, hell, Mrs. Cole...the feeling is entirely mutual. Now come over here and give me a friendly cuddle." He tugged her to his side of the table, and she happily burrowed under his arm and snuggled against his side.

"Tell me what happened when Willow Cedarian took Delonix to the Fire Maester for his Draegus Fleshing Day," she invited, and his chest rumbled when he chuckled.

"Don't get me started," he warned. "You know what happened the last time I talked about this stuff."

"I like listening."

"You can borrow my audiobooks," he offered magnanimously, and she smiled before lifting her head to look at him.

"I like listening to *you*, Miles."

He flushed and cleared his throat before nodding. He leaned back against the sofa and started to talk.

Charity nestled closer, loving the hardness of his body against hers and how the wonderful scent of his cologne blended with his natural musk. She soon lost herself in the gentle cadence of his gruff voice, unable to remember the last time she had felt safer or more content.

His voice had gone hoarse by the time he realized that she had fallen asleep. Miles would have been offended, if not for the fact that he had been speaking for nearly half an hour before she had gone quiet. She had kept him talking with interested questions, clearly paying attention to the story. Her undivided attention had been gratifying. Aside from business, where people *had* to hang onto his every word, he couldn't remember anyone being so genuinely interested in anything he had to say before. Because of his wealth and influence, the more sycophantic people who tried to befriend him, or curry favor with him, merely *pretended* interest in his conversation and opinions. But Miles always knew when someone was stringing him along for a potential payday. And since that was just about everybody he met, it made it easy for him to keep everyone, other than his family and a few close friends, at a distance.

Charity was different. She was so damned genuine in everything she said and felt. But so hideously damaged by the one person she should have been able to trust above all others, that Miles knew he had to put her wants and needs above anything he was feeling.

He wanted her, with more urgency and desperation than he could ever recall wanting a woman before. Usually, when he found himself physically attracted to someone, it was nothing more than an itch that required scratching. And sometimes, if he ignored it long enough, the itch would simply go away.

But this desire he had for Charity was so much more complex than anything he had experienced before. It wasn't just physical. He *liked* her. He liked being around her and talking with her, and he was interested in what she was thinking and feeling. She made him laugh, often without intending to. And today, after he had learned of what she had endured at the hands of her husband, she had damned near made him cry.

He wanted her, desperately, fucking passionately but until *she* was ready he, Miles Henry Hollingsworth—a man accustomed to taking whatever he damned well pleased whenever he damned well wanted—would wait.

"Charity," he whispered, dropping a kiss on top of her drooping head. "Hey, come on, sweetheart. It's bedtime."

She groaned in protest and nuzzled closer and then, as consciousness gradually returned, she became more and more tense. She slowly, inch by painstaking inch, moved away from him. As if she were afraid of making any sudden movements.

He remained relaxed, not wanting to spook her. Giving her the time to decide how she wanted to react to the situation.

She pushed a loose strand of hair from her face and offered him a tentative smile. "I'm sorry, I didn't mean to doze off. I must have been more tired than I realized. And you have a very soothing voice."

He chuckled. "That's the first time anyone has ever said that to me. Not sure how I feel about that. I like having my minions cower in terror at the mere sound of my voice."

"I doubt that happens very often."

"Why don't you head to bed? I have to let Stormy out. I'll see you in the morning, okay?"

He pushed to his feet and offered a hand to help her up. She took it without hesitation, and when she was standing upright, she leaned in and lifted her face to his.

His breath caught in his chest and remained there when she went onto her toes and gifted him with a sweet, lingering kiss.

"Thank you for today, Miles. It meant so much."

He palmed the side of her face and, for the first time, initiated a kiss. The embrace was tentative at first, as he tested her receptiveness, but when she opened her mouth to his tongue, he grew bolder and asked her for more than she had previously given him. More heat, more passion, and so much more hunger.

She groaned and encircled her arms around his neck. She undulated against him, a slow roll of her body against his, the sensuous movement seemed unintentional, but it set his every nerve ending alight and had a very predictable effect on his half-mast cock. He went hard as an iron spike, and the way she was grinding herself against him, he knew she had to feel it.

His captured her still slowly rolling hips in his palms and stopped the movement, but she made a sound of protest.

He lifted his mouth from hers, and she cried out in frustration.

"PG-13 remember?" he reminded. Speaking between harsh,

gasping breaths was difficult, but he managed to get the words out coherently enough.

Her cheeks were flushed, her hair a mess and her lips swollen. She looked fucking irresistible and it took more willpower than he knew he possessed to step away from her.

She looked so bereft by the movement that for a second, he considered throwing caution to the wind and taking her back in his arms. But before he could act on that impulse, the glaze in her eyes faded and she nodded shakily.

He knew he had made the right call when she folded her arms defensively across her chest. Her walls firmly back in place.

"I should tidy up," she said, her voice throaty and sexy.

"No, that's fine. I'll do it."

"It's my job," she reminded him frostily, and he winced. Right...those walls were being heavily fortified if Mrs. Cole felt the need to assert herself in this moment.

"Nah, that's Mrs. Cole's job, and she's not here tonight, remember?"

"God, you make me sound like I have multiple personality disorder," she said with an impatient huff. "Rest assured, Mrs. Cole and I are the same person."

"I know...but I also know you wear the persona like an armor. You don't have to with me."

"It's a professional identity. Not a persona."

Miles disagreed with that. Mrs. Cole was a disguise plain and simple. But he didn't argue. Choosing instead to say, "But you were here in your personal capacity tonight, Charity. As my friend. Not my employee."

"It's just a few plates, Miles," she said, her voice softening.

"I know, which is why I'm perfectly capable of cleaning them up myself."

She sighed, and the starch went out of her shoulders.

"I'm sorry, you're right. I...goodnight, Miles."

She left before he had a chance to return the greeting. Miles heaved a deep sigh and scrubbed a hand over his face.

He was still hard and wanting and dreaded the prospect of yet another cold shower before bed tonight. It had been a kiss. A tame kiss with a little grinding thrown into the mix. He had done more risqué things when he had been a fumbling adolescent with his first girlfriend. His over-the-top reaction to a bit of light petting was rather embarrassing.

He shook his head and moved to open Stormy's crate. This was going to be a lot more difficult than he had first imagined.

"You're up early," Charity observed when Miles and Stormy joined her in the kitchen the following morning.

"I was hoping to get to the kitchen before you and start breakfast." He was a little peeved that she had beaten him to it. He had waited for her to go jogging as usual, figuring he could get breakfast started while she was out. But of course, today of all days, she broke routine and didn't go running.

"You'd have to get up pretty early in the morning to beat me to the kitchen, sir," she said archly, and he glared at her.

"I *did*. And yet here you are."

She smiled. A wicked grin that set off a naughty twinkle in her eyes. "Then it clearly wasn't early enough."

He gave her an aggrieved look, not because he felt aggrieved, but because she seemed to be enjoying his feigned disgruntlement so much.

"Well, can I make myself useful in any way?"

"Feed Stormy," she instructed him, looking at the dog who was dancing around their feet.

He immediately moved to obey, grabbing the Stormy's bowl and measuring out a portion of kibble for her. Task done, he was back at the island in under two minutes to watch her whisk eggs.

"What else can I do? Should I get the coffee on?"

"Done. In fact, why don't you grab a cup and have a seat? Breakfast will be served in a few minutes."

"I could put some bread in the toaster."

"Toasting as we speak."

"Should I fry up some bacon?"

"Use your nose," she said, with a soft laugh, and he inhaled deeply, absently noting that there was barely a twinge in his chest anymore. The smell of bacon permeated the air, making his mouth water and his stomach growl. A quick glance confirmed that it was grilling in the eye level oven.

"Well, what can I do?" he asked, now feeling genuinely aggrieved. And more than a little useless.

She stopped whisking and scrunched her nose, before leaning toward him across the island.

"You can..." she began, and he edged closer, keen to hear how he could help. "Kiss me good morning?"

His breath caught, and his eyes dropped to her lush lips. His throat went dry, and he swallowed in an attempt to moisten it.

"Mrs. Cole," he whispered, his voice hoarse with unabashed lust. "You *do* shock me."

"Good. As long as I don't bore you."

"Never that," he denied. They were so close his nose nuzzled against hers. He canted his head to the side, never taking his eyes from hers, and captured her lips with his.

Another soft kiss, but he put all the yearning and desire he felt for her in the tender caress. When he released her mouth after one last, decadent nip of her lower lip, and lifted his head, her eyes were screwed shut, and her mouth still pursed as if she were waiting for more.

"Good morning." His voice was filled with gravel, and he cleared his throat self-consciously. Her eyes fluttered open, and she smiled at him. A sweet smile. One that lacked any artifice or reservation whatsoever.

"Morning."

She was wearing her Mrs. Cole disguise, but her hair was different. Still up in a bun, it looked softer, less severe than usual. With wispy tendrils framing her face. And if he wasn't mistaken, she had on some eyeliner and lip gloss as well.

He sat on one of the high bar stools at the island, rested his elbows on the marble surface and his chin in his palms. Settling in to watch her work.

"Tell me," he invited, while she poured the whisked eggs into a skillet. "Is there some kind of uniform clause in your contract that I'm unaware of?"

She wiped her hands on a tea towel and shifted her body so that she could keep an eye on the skillet and converse with him.

"No," she replied, giving the eggs a stir. "But considering the nature of my job, I thought it was appropriate to dress the part."

He supposed that made sense. He didn't like it, but he knew saying as much would probably not be very well-received. He couldn't dictate what she wore, it was up to her to decide when she wanted to relinquish her armor.

That didn't mean he couldn't give her his opinion on her choice in garb though. "Great. As long as I wasn't the one who unconsciously approved some draconian rule that dictated you had to dress like a seventeenth century governess."

She made a choking sound, and her eyebrows shot to her hairline.

"It's *not* that bad."

"No, it's worse. More like a workhouse schoolmarm."

She couldn't maintain her outrage, and a giggle escaped at those words.

"What did you do before your marriage?" He didn't know where the question came from, but he instantly regretted it when it wiped the smile from her face.

"Not workhouse schoolmarming, that's for sure," she said, in a weak attempt at levity, and he forced a smile. She cleared her throat and removed the eggs from the stove and scraped them onto two plates. She set the plates aside and opened the oven to retrieve the bacon.

Miles didn't push her for an answer, instead, he got up and poured a couple of mugs of coffee. He was happily surprised when she transported both plates to the banquette and placed them on the table. This would be the first time since his arrival that she joined him for breakfast.

She added a bowl of mushrooms and a plate of grilled tomatoes to the table and sat down.

"How do you take your coffee?" he asked.

"Black, one sugar."

He joined her at the table and grinned when he saw the spread she had laid out. "This looks amazing."

"I've been wondering what triggered your sudden aversion toward boiled eggs."

"I've had the same thing for breakfast for fourteen years," he muttered, spearing his fork into the fluffy eggs. "I didn't see the point in having anything different. I'm a creature of habit. Some would call me boring, I suppose."

"Some?" she repeated. "Like who?"

"Vicki has called me stuffy a few times. Hugh has accused me of lacking imagination. One of my...uh, intimate acquaintances flat out told me the sex was great, but the conversation abysmal. Those are all fair comments."

"No, they're not." He quite enjoyed how affronted she appeared on his behalf. "They're totally wrong. Well, in Vicki's case, you're her big brother, you raised her, I'm afraid being called stuffy comes with the territory. And why would Hugh accuse you of lacking imagination when you love fantasy novels so much? It seems like a complete contradiction."

"Well, nobody else actually knows about the fantasy novels. They all think I'm listening to economic podcasts. I've never seen fit to correct them."

"That's a big chunk of yourself to withhold from your family, Miles."

"It's personal," he felt compelled to defend himself.

"It's your family." Considering the huge secrets she was keeping from her family, she should be the last to criticize. She seemed to grasp the innate hypocrisy of her words at the same time he did and went bright red before continuing. "And as for that *intimate acquaintance*...wait, you mean lover, right? Why would you call her a mere acquaintance?"

"The word lover implies more than just sex, it indicates a depth of feeling that has never been present in my interactions with my sexual partners."

She stared at him silently for a long, awkward moment, and he nearly gave in to the urge to tell her that *she* would be different. Not a mere acquaintance but so much more than that.

Fortunately, she spoke before he could say something truly cringeworthy. "Well, this *acquaintance* sounds like a dumbass."

"She holds a doctorate in nuclear physics," he said, keeping his voice grave, even though he felt like grinning like an idiot at her vehement defense of him.

"Nuclear physics? Okay, a brainy dumbass then. I may not

be a nuclear physicist or anything, so maybe it won't mean much, but *I* don't find your conversation abysmal at all. I think you're a very interesting man."

He coughed to cover up a chuckle and stared hard at his plate, before nodding gravely. "It means a hell of a lot, thank you. Anyway, as I was saying...I'm a creature of habit. I don't have a very adventurous palate. I know what I like, so I stick with it. No chance of disappointment that way. I take very few personal risks. And even less risks in business.

"I think that's why Hugh accused me of lacking imagination. He's been pushing me to make riskier moves, gamble as it were. But I hate making reckless decisions with my business. Yes, taking a gamble can pay off in spades. But we don't have to take stupid risks, we're doing fine. I dislike the notion of failure, of losing money. That's not how I'm made. My acquisitions may be boring and safe...but they keep my company in the black. If something works for me, I stick with it."

"If that's the case, why the sudden change in diet?"

He shoveled down another forkful of eggs and washed it down with coffee.

"I don't know," he admitted ruefully. "I looked at my breakfast that day and decided that I wanted something different. I've considered the fact that it may be because of the near-death thing."

"Could *all* of this be because of the near-death thing?" The question disconcerted him and he stared at her troubled expression for a long moment as he tried to figure out exactly what she meant by it.

"All of what?"

"Stormy. Your sudden interest in me. It all seems uncharacteristic."

"Charity, you know as much about my character as I do about yours. Which is to say, not much."

Charity considered that gentle rebuke and assessed the unperturbed expression on that very attractive face.

"I fell for Stormy the second I saw her standing in that doorway. Bedraggled, wet, shivering and so terrified."

Charity watched him slant an affectionate look at his napping dog. The question that popped out of her mouth next came from nowhere and shocked the ever-loving hell out of her. "And me?"

But he didn't miss a beat. He diverted that affectionate look to her, and his lips parted in a soft smile. "You? I haven't fallen for you...*yet*."

She didn't know how to respond to that. What the hell did one say to something like that anyway?

He didn't seem to expect a response, instead he continued, "But like I told you before, you intrigue the hell out of me, Charity. On so very many levels."

She chose not to respond to that and waved her fork at his plate. "Eat your food, it's getting cold."

"Yes, ma'am."

The rest of the meal passed without further awkwardness and afterward, Miles attempted to help her clean up.

"Oh my God, *what* are you doing?" Charity snapped in exasperation when she walked into him a third time. He kept getting underfoot.

"Trying to help," he muttered, looking sheepish.

"This again," she muttered beneath her breath. Doing her utmost not to roll her eyes. "Are you getting paid to do this?" Her pointed question made him wince but he didn't reply. "Well, *I* am. And I have a system. If you want to help, take your dog for a walk and leave me to do this."

"It's pouring," he pointed out sullenly, and she glanced out the window to confirm. It was a hard drizzle at best, but since the man was recovering from an illness, he probably shouldn't be out in it.

"Okay, fine. Sit over there and just...stay out of the way." She pointed toward the banquette, and he slanted her a grin.

"Oh no, *not* the naughty corner, Mrs. Cole! I promise to be a good boy from now on."

The words startled a laugh from her. "Okay, I suppose I sounded a little like that workhouse schoolmarm just then."

"A tad," he agreed, pouring the dregs of coffee from the machine before doing as he was told and taking a seat at the banquette. He dug his phone out of his jeans pocket and started tapping away.

Charity left him to it and continued with her work. It was surprisingly companionable, having him sit there while she went about her chores, and Charity found herself watching him often while she rinsed dishes for stacking in the dishwasher. His hair was a mess, he had once again neglected to shave, and his expensive polo shirt had a ketchup stain on the chest.

He looked sexily mussed, and she found it *so* appealing.

"Hey, George." Her head whipped up at the sound of his voice, and for a second, she was confused, and glanced around the kitchen for George. But she soon realized that Miles was on the phone with the man. "I need a ride into town. Are you available? Yeah? Around three. Thank you, see you then."

He disconnected the call and went back to texting.

Curious and frustrated when he didn't seen fit to immediately tell her what the call was about, Charity couldn't stop herself from asking, "Where are you off to?"

"Hmm?" He looked up absently, and his eyes cleared when he registered the question. "Oh. I thought I'd look into that puppy socialization class Brand spoke of yesterday. The vet has an app that allows you to reserve a slot."

"Why call George? You're capable of driving a short distance like that yourself."

He looked abashed, and when he spoke, the words were almost reluctantly conceded. "I pay George a retainer, but he earns something extra every time he has to drive us somewhere when we're on vacation. And I figured with a grandchild on the way..."

He shrugged, allowing her to fill in the rest herself.

"Oh." Her heart turned to mush. How incredibly sweet. "That's so nice of you."

The tips of his ears turned pink, and he lifted his shoulders in a small awkward movement.

"It's a small thing. And George is a good guy." His voice was gruff, and he refused to meet her eyes.

"You're the good guy," she whispered, still astonished that she had she not recognized that fact before now. How had she always assumed that this gentle, considerate, kind man was cold and unlikable?

She was once again struck by the differences between him and Blaine. Her dead husband had lauded his good deeds over the rest of the world. He had frequently managed to casually drop his latest act of charity into random conversation and then feigned humility when people sang his praises.

Oh, it was nothing. I don't seek acclaim for doing the Lord's work.

Ugh.

Miles sought no such accolades, he was inherently kind. He cared about his family, those who worked for him or depended on him and he expected nothing in return. In fact, he seemed downright embarrassed that he had even mentioned it to her.

"I think I'll come to town with you, I haven't been to my self-defense class in a while and they have a session this afternoon."

"Sounds good." He graced her with a smile, and she went back to loading the dishwasher, wondering why the hell she felt so excited at the prospect of just being in the same vehicle with him. It wasn't like they would be spending the afternoon together or anything.

Chapter Twelve

Charity was enjoying her sparring session with Greyson Chapman. When she had first started this class, the mere thought of allowing a man to lay hands on her with anything resembling violent intentions had been terrifying. But Sam Brand had been so professional and impersonal, and so *obviously* in control of his every action, that it hadn't taken long for her to relax in his presence.

It had soon become apparent that the handling and grabbing and pushing were very different from anything she had experienced with Blaine. Brand had no intention of hurting her, there was no extreme emotion attached to his movements. He felt no malice, or love, or hatred toward her. All he wanted to do was instruct her. And to instruct her, he had to touch her in ways that she had initially found uncomfortable.

He was an observant man and she knew that he, and possibly Greyson, were probably more aware of her background than she was comfortable with. But neither man had ever said a thing about it to her. Instead, they continued to train her to the best of their abilities. They tailor-made each woman's training exercises to her fitness level and what she hoped to achieve. Charity hadn't been very forthcoming about her goals other than stating a need to "feel safe," and Brand had focused a great deal of her instruction on deflecting punches and wrestling her way out from beneath an opponent. And once she had mastered those, he had started teaching her how to fight back. But they didn't only concentrate on the physical in these sessions—they had helped rebuild her mental, as well as emotional strength and had boosted her self-confidence and self-belief. And somewhere along the line that fear of being around these big, muscular men had faded.

She did not feel as comfortable around them as she now did with Miles, but she wasn't afraid of them. They had helped her find an inner strength she had forgotten she possessed, and she valued these classes because of that.

Greyson swung at her, and she deftly sidestepped his punch and used his own momentum against him, utilizing her speed and smaller size to duck beneath his arm and flip him over her shoulder. He wound up on his back, her knee on his chest, and his arm twisted in her grip.

There was a smattering of cheers and applause at the move, and Greyson writhed for a moment before swearing. "*Shit*!"

He thumped the mat with his free hand, and she grinned and released her grip on his arm, offering her hand in assistance instead. He gave her a rueful glower and took her hand, before leaping nimbly to his feet.

"You had to toss me on my butt for my wife and daughter to see, didn't you? Not cool, Cole!"

She wrinkled her nose ruefully and tossed him a towel.

"Sorry about that, but you taught me to exploit all weaknesses. It's not my fault you were showing off because you knew

Olivia was watching." She glanced over at the mommy and baby yoga group on the community center stage, and sure enough, Greyson's tall, stunning wife—baby in arms—appeared to be laughing at her husband's ignominious defeat. The woman spotted Charity watching and waved at her.

Charity didn't know Olivia Chapman very well. She had seen her in passing a few times and had had an awkward introductory chat with her one Sunday afternoon when she had run into the couple on the Boulevard. Greyson's wife was the head chef at the recently revamped eatery in town. This was the first time Charity had seen her at the Wednesday baby yoga class. She remembered Greyson mentioning that they usually came to the Monday morning sessions.

She returned the woman's smile uncertainly and went back to dabbing the perspiration off her brow and neck. Greyson excused himself and jogged lithely over to the stage to have a chat with his wife. Charity watched as the woman handed their daughter to him and gracefully dismounted the stage to give her husband a laughing hug and kiss. Greyson put the toddler down and kept an indulgent eye on her while she tottered from person to person for high fives.

Feeling an unexpected pang of envy at their intimate family moment, Charity swept her gaze around the busy community center. Their training hour was nearly up, and Sam was wrapping up some basics with the beginners, a motley mix of teens and elderly ladies. The senior knitting group was gathered in a gossipy semi-circle, busily knitting squares for a quilt that would be raffled off at the upcoming winter cheese festival. It would be the very first time Riversend hosted the popular event and everybody was excited and determined to keep the lucrative annual festival in their town.

Sam often joined the knitters for a gossip. He really loved

those old girls, shamelessly flirting with them and teasing them. It was one of the first things that had made her relax around him, how kind he was to those sweet ladies.

Her eyes continued her scan of the room. Because the schools had just closed for their mid-winter break, the community center was more crowded than usual. A group of teens was gathered in the furthest corner of the large space. They didn't appear to have any kind of adult supervision...and all they were currently doing was being rowdy and talking over one another.

Charity watched as one of the girls, smaller than the rest, tried to get them organized. She knew the girl was related to the McGregors in some way, but because Charity kept herself separate from everyone else, she hadn't gotten the specifics of that relationship. The girl was pretty and looked around seventeen, curly hair, golden brown skin, and very petite. She was waving her arms frantically but no one was paying any attention to her.

Charity slung her towel around her neck and made her way to the group. Uncharacteristically curious to find out what was happening.

"Hi, Mz. Cole," one of the kids called as she got closer, and Charity nearly stumbled. Okay, so even the teens knew her name in this town. She couldn't recall ever speaking to a single kid during her entire time here, so having an adolescent casually greet her as if he saw her every day was disconcerting to say the least.

That greeting was followed by several others, and Charity nodded awkwardly in return. "Hey guys, what are you up to?"

"We're trying to choreograph a dance for the cheese festival," the girl, who had so futilely been attempting to get them organized, stated. Small for her age, freckled, with that curly mop of hair and wearing oversized dungarees, she was pretty darned cute. She had green eyes that were a striking contrast against her dewy brown skin.

"Only we don't know what we're doing," one of the boys piped up.

"I know what we're doing, Jason," the girl retorted. "You guys just won't listen."

"I say we do hip hop," one of the other young men said with a wicked grin, before grabbing his trousers at the crotch and wriggling his hips. Charity wasn't sure if his intention was to be sexy or lewd, but she thought he looked like a little boy who desperately needed the restroom. The rest of the boys laughed and the girls looked completely grossed out. "Whaddya think, Charlie?"

"No," the girl in the dungarees, Charlie, said flatly. "We're doing a *gwara gwara* dance to a techno beat. But you haven't got the skills for that, Sinclair, so you can stand in the back where no one can see you and feel up your own dick like a total loser."

The other kids sniggered at that, and Sinclair, a tall, floppy-haired, handsome bruiser of a boy, glowered mutely at Charlie.

"So, what's this dance you're talking about?" Charity asked, hoping to defuse the tension between the two.

"Oh, you move your arm like this and then your leg picks up the rhythm and you just..." The girl proceeded to demonstrate, and Charity stood gaping while she took off in a rolling, energetic dance that seemed to require a lot of leg strength and stamina. It was amazing how one of her legs would move with seeming complete independence from the rest of her body, before the rest of her limbs joined in. Charity was awestruck by her flexibility and talent. The other kids whooped and clapped and soon most of the them were joining in.

Charity laughed, genuinely impressed and clapped when they stopped and grinned at her.

"I'm sure it'll be fantastic by the time you have it properly choreographed," she encouraged them.

"Try it, Mz. Cole," one of the boys challenged, and Charity laughed again.

"Oh no. I don't think so."

They cajoled and pleaded but Charity held firm.

"Hey guys," Sinclair—he of crotch grabbing infamy—called from the back of the group, clearly not liking it when the attention was off him for too long. "We can add some tricks like this into the routine..."

He climbed onto a wobbly looking chair while he was talking, and Charity's eyes widened in horror when she understood his intention. She lifted her hand in protest, wanting to physically stop him from doing what she knew he was going to do. But she was too far away from him.

"No *don't—*" But her sharp cry fell on deaf ears, and the damned fool boy attempted a backflip off the chair and landed awkwardly on his extended damned fool arm.

He screamed in agony, and Charity winced as she dashed toward him. He was writhing on the floor. His friends already clustered around him watched in helpless, horrified silence as he hugged his arm to his body and tears of pain streamed down his red face.

Charity went into autopilot. She was dimly aware of others rushing toward the injured boy, but she was there first, her eyes assessing the damage with a professionalism she had believed long lost before this moment.

"Sinclair!" She used her firmest voice to get his attention. Probably one Miles would have deemed schoolmarmish. He blinked up at her through his tears, looking shaken and shocked. Charlie was on her knees beside him, and Charity flanked him on the other side, also kneeling next to him.

Charity continued to speak with what she hoped was reassuring authority, keeping her voice calm and level. "Sinclair, I know you're in pain, but I need you to let me look at it, okay? I promise I won't hurt you."

Charlie gently pried his uninjured hand away from his arm and held it in one of hers.

"It's okay, Sin," the girl whispered. "Let Mz. Cole look at it. She knows what she's doing."

Charlie had no way of knowing if that was true, but the absolute trust in both adolescents' eyes was staggering and brought a lump to Charity's throat.

She blinked, telling herself not to be a sentimental ninny and diverted her attention to the boy.

"Can you tell me how you are, sweetheart?" she asked, assessing his ABC's.

"My arm hurts!" His breathing while fast, was within normal range, and did not appear to be impaired.

She gingerly lifted his right hand, quickly evaluating the temperature and coloration, before checking his radial pulse. It was elevated, probably from the shock and pain, but there did not appear to be any immediate signs of vascular damage or impaired circulation.

"I'm going to have to examine it, to see if it's broken. I won't do anything that makes you more uncomfortable, but I have to see if we need to immobilize it before the ambulance gets here."

That reminded her.

"Hey, did someone call an ambulance?" She looked up and realized that everybody was crowded around them in silent concern. Greyson was clutching a first aid kit, Sam was on his phone, and he nodded in response to her question.

And Miles...*Miles* was here. Hovering close by and silently watching through narrowed eyes. Why was he here? Shouldn't he be at puppy school or whatever it was called?

She shook herself, she couldn't allow herself to be distracted by him right now, the boy needed her.

She ran expert hands over Sinclair's arm. It had been a while since she had done this, but the steps were comfortingly familiar, and she knew exactly what she was doing. The boy was tense and trembling, and clearly expecting more pain from her touch.

"Can you tell me exactly where it hurts?"

"My sh-shoulder, M-Miss."

Miss. As if she were one of his teachers. So polite, despite his pain. She wouldn't have pegged him as a gentleman. Not after the crude first impression he had made. Her hands lightly skimmed up to his shoulder, and she made a soft sound of affirmation beneath her breath, when her touch confirmed what her eyes had already told her. Anterior dislocation of the right shoulder.

"You've dislocated it. I don't think you've broken anything and there doesn't appear to be any nerve damage. Don't worry, the doctors will manipulate it back into place when you get to the emergency room."

Ordinarily, Charity would have popped it back herself, but with this many eyes on her, she knew it would raise more questions than she was ready to answer.

"Will it hurt, Miss?" Sinclair's lovely blue gaze pleaded mutely with her to say it wouldn't. It was sweet how he had regressed to an insecure little boy, looking for reassurance from someone in perceived authority.

She smiled at him. "It's nothing like you've seen on television. They have to X-ray your arm to be sure nothing's broken, and if it's all fine, they'll give you something for the pain and ease it back into place as carefully as possible. You'll have to rest it for a few weeks and after that you'll be right as rain. With a cool story to tell your buddies."

"Don't think so, Miss. They all saw m-me jump off the chair like a twat—" He winced. "Sorry, Miss, I shouldn't have used that w-word, but..."

"That's okay, you get a pass right now, because you're in pain." She looked at the tall, grim man silently holding the first aid kit and gestured toward it. "Greyson, could I have that, please?"

He handed it over, and she opened the box to see if it contained anything she could use to make Sinclair more comfortable.

"Aah, here we go," she said, with a satisfied grunt, removing a sling from its sterilized packaging. "Let's immobilize this arm until the paramedics get here."

She helped him ease his arm into the sling, keeping his movements small and excruciatingly slow.

She had just finished when the EMTs slammed into the community center.

"You'll be fine," she reassured the young man, who was still desperately hanging onto Charlie's hand. She stepped away and allowed the EMTs to take over and watched as the boy was ministered to and lifted onto a gurney, before being bustled out of the community center. Charlie was still by his side, and the other teens trailed behind them shouting out words of encouragement.

All other activities had pretty much ceased during the emergency, and to her extreme chagrin, Charity found herself surrounded by people who wanted to thank her and pat her on her back. Happily, everybody soon dissipated into smaller groups, still talking excitably while packing up their things.

She picked up her towel from where she had dropped it on

the floor and, on extremely reluctant feet, made her way to where Miles was now chatting with Sam and Greyson.

Greyson's face lit up in a rare grin.

"That was pretty goddamned impressive, Cole," he said. High praise indeed from the usually aloof man.

"*Very*," Sam concurred. "You a moonlight as a doctor or something?"

"Or something." She shrugged nonchalantly. Sam and Greyson were both discreet enough to drop the subject when they sensed someone didn't want to talk about something. She turned her attention to Miles, who still hadn't spoken. "Uh... ready to go? Is Stormy in the car?"

"I told George to take her home."

The statement confused her. "But...what about us?"

"He took an Uber. He'll feed Stormy and make sure she's settled for the evening and then come back in his own car. I'll drive us home later. I thought we could grab something to eat."

"I'm hardly dressed to eat out," she pointed out beneath her breath, casting a self-conscious glance at the two other men. They were both feigning avid interest in the walls and floors... the ceiling. Seriously, their eavesdropping would be less overt if they just pretended to chat with each other.

"You look great," Miles said, giving her an appreciative once-over. Her abruptly sweaty palms and elevated breathing had *very* little to do with the extreme tension of the last twenty minutes and everything to do with the sensual light in his eyes. God, that look should be outlawed.

She gathered her scattered thoughts enough to protest, "I'm definitely not fit to eat out in public after my earlier workout."

"Well, why not join Lia and me for dinner tonight then?" Sam chimed in, proving that he'd totally and unashamedly been listening in on their conversation. "You don't have to dress up to hang out with us."

"You can't just invite us without clearing it with your fiancée," Charity said, appalled. Definitely not wanting to do that. A restaurant would be preferable to the intimacy of a couples' dinner.

"Hey, sunshine!" Sam's voice traveled above the noise of the still babbling people—clearly this had been more excitement than they had seen in a while—and caught the attention of the slender, pretty woman in yoga pants and a sports tank. She had been instructing the mommy and baby yoga class and was chatting with a few of the lingering moms. Lia MacGregor gave her fiancé an exasperated look, clearly not impressed with the shouting.

"Can Miles and Charity come to dinner tonight?"

She flashed him a smile and thumbs up before continuing her chat with the women.

"See? It's fine," Sam said, with a grin. "Let me stow the equipment, and you guys can follow us home."

"You sure it's okay?" Miles asked.

"Yeah, we could *braai* or something. That way Lia won't have to do too much. You and Clara want to join us, Grey?"

"I don't think so. She's cutting a molar and a bit moody. She won't be good company." Clara was his eighteen-month-old daughter, and he watched her every night while his wife was at the restaurant. "And my brother is popping over for a couple of brews and some pool. Rain check? Maybe on a weekend sometime when Olivia is off?"

"Sounds good."

Sam and Grey excused themselves to stow the equipment, leaving Charity to glare at Miles, who was still giving her a leisurely once over.

"This is going to be uncomfortable," Charity pointed out, from between gritted teeth and that drew his wandering gaze up to her face.

"Why do you say that?"

"Miles, I'm your *housekeeper*. I shouldn't be having dinner with you and your peers."

"Well," he said, shoving his balled fists into his trouser pockets, ruining the cut of the well-fitted slacks. "That's some medieval bullshit right there. Stop being such a snob."

"But this is really weird, they know I work for you."

"Technically, Brand works for me too," he said, with frustrating male logic.

"That's different."

"How?"

"It just is."

"Brand and Lia are *your* friends, I'm the interloper."

"Oh my God, that's so untrue. I barely know her." Charity moved until her body was brushing against his and breathed the urgent whisper directly into his ear. Brand was returning, and she didn't want him to hear her words.

She instantly regretted the move, when Miles hooked his arm around her waist to keep her in position. He turned his head until his mouth was right beside her ear, and his whispered response feathered against her sensitive skin and ruffled the fine hairs at her temple. "Well, then it's high time you get to know her."

"*Why?*" she fired back indignantly.

"Why not?" This time the infuriating practicality left her mute. Because she honestly had no answer to that question.

He grinned and planted a quick kiss on her nose before relinquishing his hold on her waist.

"We're in this together, you know how awful I am with

people." He kept saying that, but Charity had thus far seen little evidence of his so-called ineptitude with people. "And I'm counting on you to stop me from making an arse of myself."

Charity sighed huffily and pasted a smile on her face, mentally preparing herself for a long evening of painful small talk.

"I'M so happy that you decided to join us for dinner tonight, Charity," Lia said, her sincerity evident in the warmth of her voice. The women were in the kitchen preparing some salads to accompany the barbecued meat that the men were grilling on the patio. A task that Charity did *not* envy in the icy temperatures. The kindergarten teacher was still in her yoga gear, her dark hair up in a high ponytail. It made Charity—in her sweats and with her hair tied back in a messy bun—feel less gross.

"Thank you for the invitation. I hope it's not too much of an inconvenience," she murmured politely, and Lia smiled brightly.

"Are you joking? Myself and a few others have been wanting to invite you to hang out for absolute ages, but Sam advised us to back off because you're shy and he suggested easing you in to the idea first. I didn't think his idea of 'easing' you into it would take literal years."

"I may have been a little reclusive." Charity was pleasantly blown away by the knowledge that Sam Brand had kept the over eager citizens of Riversend—including his own fiancée—at bay. It confirmed the suspicion that he was more aware of Charity's background than she had wanted anyone to be.

Lia handed her a cucumber and knife. "Slice this, will you? There's nothing wrong with keeping to yourself, but if you want a friend, or friends, there are so many of us who would *love* to get to know you."

"I know." Charity shot the other woman a quick smile, before refocusing on her assigned task. "I'm not really shy. But Sam was right to a certain extent…I wasn't ready to be around people."

Lia pursed her lips as she considered Charity's words and then nodded.

"Fair enough. And do you think you're ready now?"

"Maybe." For some reason, despite there being absolutely no pressure or judgment from the other woman, or perhaps because of it, she felt compelled to explain herself more. "My husband died a couple of weeks before I moved here three years ago."

"I'm sorry."

"Don't be." The words were out before she could stop them. But the ones that followed were voluntarily offered. "He wasn't a good man. And I didn't want to watch my family mourn him."

It was getting easier to admit that. Lia nodded again.

"I'm sorry that was intense, wasn't it?" Charity said with a grimace, and the other woman squeezed her forearm reassuringly.

"I get it. I was engaged to a complete a-hole a few years ago. Possibly a different kind of jerk to your husband, but he wasn't a good man either."

The lack of probing questions and the unflinching acceptance of Charity's claim that her husband had been a bad man was humbling to say the least, and strengthened her resolve to tell her family of everything she had endured at Blaine's hands. If a complete stranger could be so accepting of her truth, then she owed the same opportunity to the people who loved her.

She cleared her throat and searched for a way to change the subject. "So how long have you and Sam been engaged?"

"A couple of years. He's been pushing to get married, but I'm happy for now. We love each other, there's no rush. And what's going on between you and Miles?"

Charity felt her face going red and nearly choked on the slice of cucumber she had popped into her mouth a second before.

"N-nothing," she managed, once she had regulated her breathing. "He's my boss."

"He clearly wants to be more. You should have seen the way he stared at you when you were talking with the kids, right before the accident."

Charity wanted to probe, she was keen to know *exactly* how Miles had been staring at her, but her natural reticence stayed her tongue, and Lia grinned knowingly.

"I mean, I thought the way Sam looks at me is intense, but wow. I'm surprised you don't have scorch marks up and down your body because it was *haaaaawt*."

"We've grown closer these last few weeks." Charity was horrified to find herself divulging so much private information, but Lia was so easy to talk to. Or maybe it was because it had been way too long since Charity had had anything resembling a female friend to confide in.

"Good for you."

"Don't you think it's a little...inappropriate? I'm his housekeeper."

"Please, most wives and live-in girlfriends are unpaid housekeepers. Kudos to you for making a living out of it. Does the situation *feel* inappropriate?"

"I feel like it should."

"But does it?"

"Not really. I've worked for him for three years and never thought of him in that way...until one day I did."

"And do you feel taken advantage of?"

"Far from it."

"Then I think you should give yourself permission to enjoy it. To enjoy *him*."

Charity wasn't quite sure what to say in response to that and appearing to understand her discomfort, Lia changed the subject. "So, you were pretty phenomenal back there. With the boy. You handled it almost...professionally?"

Not an ideal shift in topics. Charity could tell from the upward lilt in her voice that Lia, like so many other people present at the community center today, was going to be even more curious about Charity and her background now. In fact, she was surprised it had taken the woman this long to bring it up.

"It was basic first aid," she dismissed. Hoping that would be the end of it.

"Are you talking about that business with Sinclair Ross?" Sam's voice intruded, as the two men entered the kitchen through the backdoor with Trevor, Sam's ever-present shadow, trailing behind them. Sam was carrying a tray of cooked meat, and Miles was clutching a couple of beer bottles.

"Yes, I was just telling Charity how wonderfully she dealt with the situation."

"I was just trying to keep him calm," Charity deflected. "He was terrified and in pain...and I dare say, a little embarrassed. He's an attention hog, but that wasn't exactly the kind of attention he was looking for."

Sam laughed at her statement. "Oh, it got him the attention he wanted alright."

"What do you mean?"

"That dumb kid wanted only one person's eyes on him, and in the end, he had her undivided attention. Dislocated shoulder or not, I'm thinking he's not feeling too badly right now."

Charity's eyes widened as she gleaned his meaning, and she chuckled as well. Of course! That made so much sense.

"Oh, my goodness!" she exclaimed, feeling silly for not realizing it herself. "He has a crush on Charlie."

"Major one, poor bastard. He's in for a tough time with her brothers."

"How many brothers?" Miles asked..

"Just two. You know Mason, my former business partner. But I don't think you've met his brother, a big taciturn guy named Spencer. They're married to Lia's sisters. And they'll eat that poor kid for breakfast." Sam put the tray of meat on the kitchen counter. He then made a beeline for Lia and wrapped his free arm around her slender waist.

"Hey there, sunshine, did you miss me?"

"While you were *miles* away on the patio, tending the fire?" She laughed, raising her hand to cup his jaw. "Of course, I did."

He nuzzled her neck, and she playfully pushed him away.

"You smell like smoke and sweat," she protested, wrinkling her nose.

"Like a manly man, you mean?"

Charity watched them lightheartedly bicker, grateful that their interest had shifted from her. She sneaked a glance at the silent man who had come to stand beside her at the kitchen counter. He wasn't watching the playful couple, instead his eyes were trained on her face. He smiled lazily when he recognized that he'd been caught staring, but did nothing to disguise the smoldering intent in his gaze.

Lia was right. Charity's every nerve ending felt scorched by that penetrating stare. She felt stripped naked, vulnerable, and on edge. Her skin was too tight for her body, her nipples were hard, painful points, and her knees threatened to give way. She fought to control her breathing, a little embarrassed—and a lot exhilarated—by how quickly a single look could turn her on. She already knew how fast he could make her come, but she was starting to wonder exactly what else he could do with his body, hands, and mouth.

She took a fortifying gulp from her glass of red wine.

This was going to be a draining evening.

It started innocently enough. They were having a perfectly civilized, adult evening. The conversation had been pleasant, the food good...and Charity was surprised to recognize that she was enjoying herself.

Until Sam produced the deck of cards. Miles, who had been reclining on the love seat next to Charity, his arm stretched out behind her and his hand idly playing with the loose strands of her hair in the nape of her neck, sat upright in an instant at the sight of the cards. He rubbed his hands together, in a gesture that could only be described as gleeful and grinned wickedly.

"Oh hell, yes. I'm a legendary Uno player."

"Please, you haven't played until you've been stuck with a squad of bored, soldiers waiting to go on a covert op. We would do anything to alleviate the tedium and tension. This game was our number one boredom buster. It got fucking cutthroat..."

"Sam," Lia rolled her eyes with a sigh. "Language."

"Sorry. Forgot myself. It got darned fucking cutthroat."

Charity choked on her wine, before hooting with laughter, and Lia palmed her face in exasperation.

"We're talking about edgy, highly trained, SAS men, with itchy trigger fingers...all of that pent-up aggression and frustration had to go somewhere. We got really good at this game really fast."

"Well, I had equally cutthroat competitors. It was my siblings' favorite school holiday pastime growing up. You ever try playing this game with a ten and twelve-year-old? I assure you, your SAS buddies would cower in terror."

"I've never played this game before," Charity ventured, and they all three turned to gape at her in shock. She flushed and felt immediately self-conscious. Truthfully, her parents and Faith had probably played it often, but a game like this would have seemed much too tame for her younger self. If it wasn't physical and didn't contain some element of danger, it just wouldn't have interested her. Even as a child, Charity had always been outside, on her bike, board, or blades. Card or board games could never hold her interest for long.

But now, the idea of a fun activity that didn't involve any kind of risk to her physical well-being, was highly appealing.

"Uh...it's pretty easy," Lia said, after a beat. "It's fun. A little juvenile, we like to pretend that we keep it around for when Charlie comes to visit, but truthfully, my sisters, their husbands, and Sam and I play it without Charlie more often than not."

WHAT FOLLOWED WAS two hours of competitive and hilarious backstabbing, laughter and fabricated drama. Charity honestly could not remember the last time she had enjoyed herself more. Miles and Sam were so focused on taking each other out, that the women snuck in more than a few victories. Leading to a catastrophic "team up" between the guys in a bid to take out the "female threat". That didn't end well, with the uneasy armistice between them failing after just one round.

"Why the hell did you throw down a wild card on me?" Miles seethed, two rounds later. "You should have kept it for her. You had her dead to rights."

"Are you still on about that? She's the woman I love and want to have babies with someday, I couldn't do that to her. She's a delicate, fragile flower and...Lia, what the fuck?"

The last as Lia smugly and triumphantly threw down a draw four wild card, while stating, "Uno. Blue, please."

He drew his four penalty cards, grumbling bad temperedly while he did so, and Lia happily put down her winning card on her next turn.

She stretched and yawned immediately afterward, "That's it for me, I like to end things on a victorious note."

"Your fragile flower is more than a little bloodthirsty, Brand," Miles pointed out grimly, and Lia laughed. A sweet fairy-like sound that was completely at odds with the slightly evil grin she leveled on them.

"Oh, while you honed your questionable skills playing with your younger siblings, Miles, and Sam was grunting and growling away with his SAS buddies, *I* cut my teeth playing this game with the most ruthless and villainous of all competitors...*sisters*. Trust me, you do *not* want to play this game with them. Now would anybody like some coffee or tea?"

Miles glanced at Charity with an enquiring tilt to his head, and she lifted her shoulders slightly, leaving the decision up to him.

"It's getting late," he said. "I think it's time we head home."

Charity pushed to her feet when he did, and Lia and Sam walked them to the door. While the men continued their banter, Charity turned to Lia and gave her an impulsive hug.

"Thank you, I had a wonderful time."

"I'm so happy you joined us tonight. Why don't we have lunch on Friday, if you're free? I'm at loose ends during the day because of the school vacation and would love the company."

"That would be nice. Thank you."

"No. Thank *you.* It gives me an excuse to get out of the house."

Charity was sure that Lia had no end of friends and family who would happily have lunch with her and was under no illusion as to who was doing whom the favor. But it was kind of her to pretend.

They didn't linger much longer after that and were soon in the SUV on their way home.

Chapter Thirteen

"Thank you," Charity murmured, after a lengthy, comfortable silence. Miles shifted his attention from the road for a second to look at her.

"For?"

"That was the most fun I've had with both feet on the ground in I don't know how long."

"You know that that statement is going to need a shit ton more elaboration, right?" he deadpanned, and she laughed.

"Before my marriage, while I was a student, I was into just about anything that involved height, flight and/or freefalling. You named it, I tried it. It started with paragliding, then parasailing, kitesurfing, hang gliding, parachuting...I loved the rush of it. The freedom. There's nothing quite like it. My parents—both of whom are very levelheaded and practical people—thought I was crazy, of course." She could hear the affectionate exasperation in her voice as she recalled their hand-wringing concern. "They were so terrified that I would get myself killed. But I was always scrupulously careful. I tripled checked my equipment. I was a thrill seeker. Not suicidal. And no matter how much I told them that what I was doing was perfectly safe, they never quite believed me.

"They were so relieved when Blaine and I got serious. They had always liked him. And knew that he would keep me grounded, both literally and figuratively." She laughed. But the sound was filled with bitterness. "Little did they know that marrying Blaine would be the most dangerous thing I'd ever do."

She shook her head to drag herself out of the funk that had settled over her.

"Uhm. So, yes...my younger self, the idea of an evening of conversation and Uno would have seemed utterly unappealing. But I loved it. So, thank you."

"Do you miss that thrill?" he asked, not quite concealing a shudder. "Of throwing yourself out of planes, or off cliffs?"

She considered the question, staring unseeingly out into the dark night.

"No. I was always looking for that extra *something* to make me feel more alive. But after marrying Blaine, there was no longer any need for that affirmation. Not when I was living in a constant state of terror and hypervigilance. Marriage to Blaine permanently eradicated the thrill-seeking young woman I had once been. The first time he..." She paused not sure how much to tell him.

He seemed to sense the reason for her hesitation. "I want to know, Charity."

She wavered a moment longer, before deciding to take him at his word.

"The first time he hit me was on our wedding night. The first of many punishments. Only he called them *lessons*. Lessons on how to be a good wife. The cigarette burns were to remind me to smile. A pastor's wife has to be approachable you see?

And an unsmiling, sad-eyed wife, made parishioners uncomfortable."

"*Jesus.*" The softly hissed word was barely audible above the engine.

Charity found the near darkness in the SUV comforting. Being unable to see his reaction to her words allowed her to speak freely. It permitted her to say things she would have hesitated to tell him in any other setting. There was anonymity in the dark. Anonymity and security. She imagined this was what a confessional felt like.

"Jesus had nothing to do with it. Blaine was the devil, a wolf in sheep's clothing. A failed human who had no business preaching to others.

"As I was saying, the first time it happened was on our wedding night. We'd waited, on his insistence, we'd waited to have sex. He said it would be more special that way. I was stupidly in love with the wonderful, caring man I thought he was. And I thought he was being romantic. And that he meant for our first time together to wipe the slate clean for both of us, so to speak. I knew he wasn't a virgin or anything. He'd blatantly admitted to being weak—his word—with his former long-term partners. I didn't care, we'd both had other relationships before we started dating each other. I had a healthy sex drive, I *liked* sex. And I admit, I found the idea of waiting erotic. The thought of all those pent-up desires being unleashed on our wedding night was a powerful incentive to just go along with it.

"But after the sex, as I was getting up to go to the bathroom, he made a comment about his little Cherry—my family's nickname for me—not being so cherry after all. I laughed it off. And said something silly in response. I went to the bathroom and when I came out, he..." she paused and swallowed thickly. Flinching away from the memory.

You think it's fucking funny? You're my wife, there are expectations. You never told me you were a whore!

"I was so shocked," she whispered, after repeating Blaine's words verbatim. "Not just because of what he was saying but because of the language he had used. I mean, I could swear like a trooper, but after Blaine and I got serious, I toned it down because he was such a boy scout, you know? *Darn* and *shucks* and *gee whiz*, that kind of thing. Hearing that kind of language from him threw me for a loop. I think I must have done something... laughed maybe. I don't know. *Something*."

"YOU BITCH, you fucking cheap little cunt! What's so funny?" His voice increased in volume. It was shrill, and high, and almost feminine in pitch.

Something struck her. Hard. And her legs gave way, the shock more than the pain stealing the support out from beneath her. She was on the floor, staring up at the man looming above her.

"I fell." Her words were filled with astonishment. He leaned toward her, and she gratefully reached for his hand. She wasn't sure how she wound up on the floor, but despite his unfathomable fury, her beloved Blaine was there to help her up.

Only...instead of helping, he balled his hand into a fist and slammed it into her stomach. She doubled over in agony and fought to breathe.

He grabbed a fistful of her hair, and she futilely batted away his arm in an attempt to get him to release his painful, punishing grip. Her feeble efforts were no match for him. He yanked her to her feet by her hair, slammed her into the wall and held her there, while his other hand closed around her neck and squeezed.

Slowly and purposefully.

Breathing became an impossibility.

Her eyes were wide, panicked and glazed with terrified tears. She stared into his face, searching for the loving man she had married just that afternoon. But she was unable to find him in the features of this hateful, terrifying stranger who now had her helplessly pinned against the wall.

He was screaming at her. Saying horrible things. Calling her despicable names, while his hand continued to tighten around her throat. Black dots swirled in front of her eyes, until his face was obscured by them. His voice was fading...

She was dying. She was sure of it. And that absolute certainty terrified her.

But he released her abruptly and stepped away from her. Without his support, she slid down the wall and collapsed into a limp heap on the floor.

Seconds later, he was on the floor beside her. Crying with her, holding her, apologizing. Begging her to forgive him.

"I PLAYED it over and over in my mind afterward," Charity's voice was barely a whisper in the dark, and she wasn't sure if Miles could hear her. "What did I do to set him off? What did I say?"

"He was going to do whatever the hell he was going to do, Charity. Regardless of your actions and words," Mile's harsh voice startled her out of her safe confessional and yanked her back to the present.

"He said he was sorry." Charity's voice was thick with tears. She was dimly aware that Miles's free hand was tightly latched onto hers. "Said that he had been *so* very disappointed to discover that he wasn't my first, and he hated how I had dismissed and mocked that disappointment. My tone of voice had just *triggered* something inside of him. I would later understand that it was a pattern with him. I suppose it's a pattern with most abusers. He'd apologize profusely while reinforcing that it was actually my fault he had reacted the way he had. He was so *so* sorry but, I shouldn't have done this, or said that, or worn whatever."

She became aware that the SUV was no longer moving and looked up in surprise.

"Oh. We're home."

"Yes. For several minutes now." His voice was quiet, as if he were afraid of startling her.

Charity cleared her throat self-consciously and tugged against his grip on her hand. He released his hold on her immediately.

"I need a shower. I'll see you in the morning. Thank you again, for a lovely evening."

MILES DISLIKED the distance and formality in her voice and demeanor but he understood her need for space. Listening to her soft, almost dispassionate, recounting of such a harrowing example of abuse—the first of many such incidents—had been absolutely heartbreaking. He had hated hearing about it, had wanted to plead with her to stop...but he had also recognized that he was probably the only person that she had ever told.

That trust meant everything to him. It felt sacred and he would be damned if he would flinch away from it just because he felt fucking physically ill to hear her speak of her trauma.

But she had *lived* through that nightmare. The least Miles could do was listen.

She was out of the SUV and halfway up the basement stairs before he could say another word. She opened the door, and paused...but didn't look back. Instead, she straightened her shoulders and disappeared from view.

Only when she was gone did he allow himself to react. He had both hands firmly locked around the steering wheel his grip so tight, his knuckles were white and his palms were starting to hurt. He inhaled, filling his lungs to capacity and holding the air for a long moment before releasing. The sound that emerged from the back of his throat, riding the exhalation, was low, feral... unrecognizably harsh.

He wanted to hold her. Wrap his arms around her and cocoon her from the world. He wanted to kiss her, hug her, love her until all she could see and feel and taste was him. Until he could obliterate what that fucker had done to her from her memories. He would happily give up all his wealth to erase the pain she had suffered. Every bruise, broken bone, burn, bite... and whatever the fuck else that sadistic monster had done to her. He wanted it gone. He wanted to do that for her.

But he couldn't.

And for the first time in a very long while, Miles felt helpless.

SHE WENT rigid when she sensed him in the shadows. Terrified of what he would do. He walked toward her, a shadow figure...large, looming, and menacing. The closer he came, the less of him she could see. His face obscured by the bright light streaming from behind him.

He spoke...

"Charity."

...And the strength deserted her limbs. It took her forever to fall but his arms closed around her. Stopping the descent and saving her from harm.

She stared up into that face but it remained obscured by the shadows. She could see only suggestions of shapes, the glint of his eyes, the curve of his mouth. And yet...

This no longer felt menacing.

She lifted a wondering hand to his lean cheek. "You're here."

"Always."

His mouth met hers, and she sighed, welcoming the familiar taste of him. The kiss consumed her, inflamed her, awoke every sense, and she curved herself into his hard body. Wanting it. Wanting him.

He lay her down, and suddenly he was on her, in her...thrusting, demanding, taking, and giving.

She raced toward her climax. A little shocked by how fast this was happening.

She was nearly there. On the verge...

"Miles..."

Charity woke with his name on her lips. She sat up with a gasp, her heart racing, her entire body humming. She was wet, aching, and empty.

"Oh my *God*."

She covered her face and groaned.

She had expected dreams after reliving her wedding night earlier. Expected to find Blaine haunting her nightmares, as he always did.

Instead...she had found Miles. And safety.

She flattened a hand against her chest, trying to ease the frantic fluttering of her heart. Her nipples were hard as coal, her femininity hot, wet, and swollen. Her nerve endings felt scraped by pure fire.

She palmed a straining breast and thumbed her nipple and gasped at the sensation the light friction sent arrowing straight to her aching pussy.

She cupped herself down there...then stroked.

But it wasn't enough.

STORMY's soft *woof* coerced Miles out of a restless sleep. He blinked into the darkness, disoriented, not sure why the dog had barked.

Until he saw the dark shape hovering beside his bed. Despite the lack of light, he recognized the tall, slender figure instantly.

"Charity?"

She didn't reply, but lifted the covers and slid into bed beside him. He sucked in a shocked breath when she curved herself around him, her cold, bare skin sending gooseflesh down his spine.

She didn't seem to be dressed in much, a tank top and panties, maybe. Or possibly a pair of very short shorts. He was near naked himself, wearing only a pair of low riding boxer briefs, and he was *excruciatingly* aware of every inch of her gorgeous body pressed up against his. But, despite all of that tempting lush flesh within stroking distance, he refused to allow his hands to go roaming.

"What's wrong?" his voice sounded croaky and still heavily dusted with sleep. "Did you have a nightmare, sweetheart?"

She had squeezed herself into all his empty spaces, filling the gaps he hadn't even known were there, with her body and her presence. Her chest to his chest, torso to torso, pelvis to pelvis, her long, silky legs were entwined with his...her mouth was so close he could taste her sweet breath on his tongue. The heat generated between their bodies was off the charts, but he wasn't sure what she wanted of him. She had to know what this was doing to him.

It was becoming increasingly hard to ignore the very large erection in the room. The one making its insistent, throbbing presence known, sandwiched as it was between his abdomen and hers.

"Charity." He didn't know what he wanted to say, only that he needed to say it. "What—"

Her mouth closed over his, cutting him off, leaving him in no doubt as to what she wanted. He groaned when her tongue flitted along the seam of his lips, eroding his self-control. Before he could open for her, he needed to know that she was really fine. That this wasn't her seeking comfort after a nightmare.

He reluctantly pulled his head back and opened his eyes. The only light in the room was spilling in from the hallway through the door that she had left ajar, and he could barely make out her features.

"Are you sure you want this?"

"Yes," she moaned. "I want this. Please, Miles."

Her hand slid between their bodies and found his straining length. He hissed at the contact and arched into her touch.

He claimed her lips with his own, inserting every ounce of passion and desire he felt for her into the caress. His tongue requested, and was permitted, entry into her soft, hot mouth and he groaned when her own tongue eagerly met his.

He fisted her unbound hair, glorying in the silken slipperiness of it, and pulled her closer to deepen the kiss. He wanted her to feel his desperation, his yearning, and the absolute pleasure he was taking in being with her like this.

His kiss was everything, it transported her higher than any of her thrill-seeking adventures had ever taken her, above the clouds and into the heavens. Charity was lost in it. Lost in his taste and scent...

His hands had left her hair to explore the bare, sensitive skin of her upper arms and shoulders. A stroke here and a caress there. Not enough to be satisfying but just enough to tease, torment, and titillate. He eased her onto her back and settled between her spread thighs, his thick shaft, riding the furrow between her legs. He lifted his head, relinquishing her lips to peer down at her, the gloom making it hard to gauge what he was thinking.

"Is this okay?" he asked gruffly.

Charity reached around to grab his tight butt with both her hands and ground herself against his hard cock, wanting him to know exactly how okay it was. Wanting to reassure him—and her—that she wouldn't react the same way she had last time they had found themselves in this same position. Eager for him to know that she trusted him, and that she loved having his weight on top of her.

He groaned at the hot friction she generated between his shaft and her damp, eager womanhood.

"You're killing me," he said, on a gasp of pure pleasure.

"Only a little," she promised him.

He laughed huskily and dipped his head to trace his lips to the cove of her neck, unerringly finding all her most sensitive spots. It was as if he had a map of all her erogenous zones because he found, and lingered at, each and every one of them. Flipping switches, turning dials and adjusting signals, until he had her humming at exactly the right frequency.

By the time he eventually got to her nipples, she was writhing in the best kind of agony, beyond ready to take that next step with him.

But he had other plans. Plans that did not yet involve taking next steps...plans that meant he would linger at the crests of her breasts *forever*. He suckled, licked, nibbled, came perilously close to biting...but *would not* move on from there.

"Oh please. Oh *please*, Miles. More. I need more." Her words emerged on gasps as she fought for breath and writhed restlessly beneath him. She planted her feet on the mattress and unabashedly thrust against his hardness...eager for the column of flesh he was so selfishly withholding from her.

"Soon, sweetheart..." he whispered. His hot breath washed over one tightly furled nipple and sensitized the flesh beyond bearing. "I promise."

No longer content with being the passive recipient of so much sensual torment, Charity decided to spur him into action by beginning her own erotic onslaught. She ran her hands over his back and chest, testing the firmness of those muscles beneath all that gloriously smooth skin. He was stronger than the last time they had been together like this. But it didn't frighten her. Because she knew that he was keeping all of that strength leashed just for her. There was something so damned sexy about that.

She trusted that he would never do anything to hurt her and that knowledge, that trust that he had fought so hard to win, was so much hotter than anything else he had done in bed with her so far.

Her palms slid down his slick chest, exploring the hard

points of his nipples, playing there for a moment, until he groaned and lifted his mouth from where he had been nibbling at the crease of one of her aureoles.

Once she was sure she had his attention, she deliberately left his chest and smoothed her way down over rock hard abs, to his pelvis and finally to the plump head of his cock, which had escaped the confines of his briefs.

He inhaled sharply, and his stomach muscles jumped at the contact.

"Charity. Wait..." She disregarded the urgency in his grating voice and happily pushed down his briefs until she had both hands wrapped around his pulsating hotness. "Oh *fuck*, sweet-heart. That feels good."

"Kiss me." She punctuated her demand with a long, sultry stroke of his cock, and he instantly complied, helplessly thrusting into the channel she had created with her tightly curled hands.

He lifted his head and stared fiercely into her face while he continued to stroke himself in her snug hold.

The sprinkling of hair on his chest rasped the aching peaks of the nipples he had left exposed above the top of her tank. And this time she was the one who groaned.

"I want you, Miles. Inside of me. Now!" She remembered her manners enough to add, "please."

He chuckled, the sound rusty, and pushed himself up until he was kneeling between her thighs. He tugged at her tank top, and she arched her back and raised her arms, assisting him in the removal of the superfluous item of clothing. He tossed it over his shoulder and made a soft sound of satisfaction as he stared at her near naked body, his pleasure evident even in the limited light.

Her hand was still on his cock, and she gave it a tug to keep him on task. He leaned over her, reaching for one of the bedside stands.

"Wrong side," Charity told him. "They're in the other stand."

He shifted his weight toward the other side, tugged open the drawer and pulled a condom from the box she always kept in stock for him. His hands were shaking and he had to use his teeth to rip the foil package open.

She took the sheath from him and rolled it down his eager length, prolonging the task because she enjoyed the way his back arched and his head flew back in reaction to her leisurely pumping motion.

God, he was magnificent.

He kissed her again. His mouth hot and voracious.

He tugged her panties down to her hips and made a frustrated sound when it wouldn't move any farther. Charity reluctantly relinquished her hold on his penis and helped him with the urgent removal of their underwear.

Seconds later his lips were on hers, his cock poised for entry, while he was braced on his elbows with his tight, hard body trembling above hers. His damp hair framed his face and that, combined with the intensity in that steel gray gaze, made him look feral. His eyes were laser focused on her face, watching her every reaction as he slowly pushed his way inside.

Oh God! He felt amazing...thick, hard, hitting all the right spots with his smooth, expert entry. He levered himself to his knees, her thighs and butt propped up by his well-muscled thighs. He flicked the bedside light on, flooding the room with warm light and stared at her for a long, appreciative moment. He grinned wickedly before bringing one of his long, elegant thumbs to his mouth and slowly and oh-so-fucking sexily sucking it into his mouth, getting it good and wet. He gave it one last lick for good measure, his tongue lapping the digit with quite thorough deliberation.

He winked at her, and insinuated his hand down to where his body so perfectly slotted in hers and that wet thumb found her clit with unerring accuracy.

She moaned at the touch, and her back bowed as she struggled to get closer to that subtle touch.

"More, more...please. More!" He increased the pressure, flicking her clit in time with his strokes, light rhythmic butterfly taps on the sensitive bud that felt beyond description. Combined with the slide of his generous cock, it was swiftly driving her toward the orgasm she craved.

"Don't stop!" Her voice was a high-pitched, frustrated entreaty when his thrusts slowed. "Don't stop! Please don't stop, Miles."

"Ssh," he soothed, and kissed her gently to silence her pleas. He grabbed her hips and held her firm, while he flipped himself around until he was on his back, and she was straddling him. Open, naked, knees braced on the bed. He had done it so smoothly they hadn't even disconnected. His presence inside of her took on a different, deeper dimension, and she gasped at how full she felt.

His thumb went back to her clit, and he stroked her again, but he had stopped thrusting, and she glared into his imperfectly beautiful face. His damp hair was haloed on the white pillow around his head, sweat gleamed on his forehead...He had never looked more gorgeous. Her hands were flat on his chest and she gave him a shove.

"What's wrong?" he asked huskily.

"Why'd you stop? I told you not to stop."

"Thought I'd let you set the pace, that way I wouldn't get it wrong," he was breathless and struggling to talk but his meaning was clear.

"*Oh.*"

"Come on, sweetheart," he encouraged, his other hand creeping around to her butt and squeezing. "Show me what you want."

She moved, slowly at first, her spine arched, head back as her hips rolled against his. Her internal muscles rhythmically stroked that proud column of hard flesh and her clitoris bounced against his thumb. His muscles were taut beneath her hands, the cords in his neck stood out in stark relief, and his teeth were clenched. Miles was starting to huff, great, gulping breaths sawing in and out of his chest, bringing to mind a thoroughbred stallion halfway through a bracing sprint.

She found the rhythm she liked; fast and hard. She controlled the depth of his thrusts so that every second stroke hit her right where she most needed it until her internal pleasure and pressure were equal to the external, where his thumb still teased and tormented her.

She couldn't last much longer at this pace, and when his left hand strayed from her bottom and found one of her straining nipples, she careened off the tracks and slammed straight into a massive orgasm.

Her nails dug into his chest, her thrusts lost coordination, and she clenched around his penis, spasming frantically as she milked him to intensify her own pleasure. Charity was vaguely aware of him jerking beneath her, his hands were on her hips, as he tried to control her movements, but she was a living flame... burning out of control.

Untamable, unstoppable, and uncontrollable.

Her movements finally slowed down, her inner muscles relaxed and relinquished their fierce grip on his rigid cock. Where before she had been flame, she was now liquid, and she melted onto his chest with a happy sigh. Her unbound hair blanketed them, and her cheek found a home right beside his frantically thumping heart.

She was only peripherally aware of him removing the condom and setting it aside. He did so without shifting her from his chest, and once he had completed the task, he wrapped his arms around her relaxed body and held her close.

They lay like that for a long while, and Charity was on the verge of dozing off, when a soft rumbling chuckle jerked her out of her somnolence.

"Whaz funny?" she asked, too lazy to bother lifting her head.

"When you came...you cried out and Stormy h-howled," he explained, his voice wobbling at the recollection. "I was too preoccupied in that moment to pay much attention to it. But I just remembered."

She lifted her head to stare at Stormy's crate. The dog had settled down again and was snuggled around her heated bean bag fast asleep.

"We must have frightened her," she whispered, not wanting to disturb the pup.

"I think she was just confused," Miles said, one hand idly stroking her hair, while the other played with the fingers of her hand on his chest beside her face.

His index finger traced the band she had on her ring finger. She sensed his curiosity but waited for him to ask.

She didn't have to wait long. "Why do you wear this?"

"It's not Blaine's," she told him, hooking her own index finger around his and holding it captive. He didn't seem to mind and left his hand where it was. "I donated everything Blaine ever gave me, wedding ring included, to a shelter for abused women. I tossed in the car for good measure. I *did* keep most of the money from the estate, in case of emergency, but I haven't had reason to use it yet.

"I wear this ring because I thought it would keep questions at bay. I knew people would correctly assume I was widowed—divorcees rarely continue wearing their wedding bands—and be reluctant to ask me about what happened to my husband."

"How much longer do you think you'll stay here?" The question was unexpected but valid. They both knew she couldn't, wouldn't...*shouldn't* stay here for much longer. This place had been her escape for much too long, and she needed to find her way back to home and family.

"I think..." she paused, her index finger idly picking and playing with his. "This will probably be your last Garden Route break with Mrs. Cole running your holiday household."

"I'm going to miss her. She is extremely efficient."

"I took what *he* taught me and used it to my advantage," she explained.

"What do you mean?"

"I had to be the perfect housewife, well organized, everything in its place, everything on a schedule. Any deviation from what he wanted would result in a *lesson*." He tensed beneath her, but she wasn't going to let Blaine ruin this moment and she tugged his index finger to her mouth and dropped a playful kiss on its tip. "Anyway, when the opportunity to work here presented itself, I knew enough about efficient household management to fake it till I made it. But, it's time to go back to my real life. To pick up the threads that I dropped or lost along the way. I was twenty-four when I married Blaine. I'd just finished my Masters of Technology in Chiropractic and..."

"Wait. Hold on," he lifted his head to peer into her face. "What? You're a chiropractor?"

"Yes. But I've never practiced on anybody outside of the university clinic. I married straight out of university, and even though I went into marriage with Blaine thinking I'd set up shop after a year or so of wedded bliss, he needed to have control over every aspect of my life. And allowing me to have a career would have afforded me a measure of independence that he did not want me to have. I was young and stupid and, after a while, much too terrified of him to defy him."

"You're a chiropractor? A fucking *doctor*? And you're working as my housekeeper?"

"I mean, some would argue chiropractors don't hold medical degrees so they're not technically doctors."

"You fix people's bones," he rejoined. "You're a doctor."

"That's oversimplifying it. Anyway, I think what I'm trying to say is that my resignation will probably be effective as of the day your stay here ends."

"Will you go back to it? Chiropracting, I mean? Can you? After what? Six years of not practicing? Is that allowed?"

"Despite my fear of the repercussions, I *did* hang on to my practice number. It meant attending seminars and at least one conference while we were married. I lied to Blaine about where I was going on those days. And the conference I managed to attend was within driving distance, and happily fell on a weekend Blaine was away on a fishing trip with the church youth.

"The prospect of being caught in that lie was terrifying, but absolutely worth the risk. I fought hard to hang on to that number and everything it represents. Blaine controlled so many aspects of my life...but that was the one part of me I wouldn't let him have. I've remained up-to-date on techniques and the latest innovations. And I've also been studying for a clinical competency test. I don't know when, or if, I'll take it... but I've been studying for the last year. The exam will test my knowledge and suitability to practice after such a long absence from the field."

He didn't say anything, and she propped her chin onto her

hand to better see his face. His expression was inscrutable, and he remained mute for a moment while he stared fiercely into her eyes.

"You're so fucking brave. And so incredibly beautiful," he murmured, his face softening as he tugged her up for a sweet kiss. Not saying anything further about what had basically amounted to a verbal resignation.

They lay like that for a while, her head on his chest, his hands stroking her back.

"Do you need to take a nap or grab something to drink?" The question came some minutes later. "Perhaps have a snack? Or are you ready for round two?"

His accelerated breathing made a liar out of that insouciant drawl.

She laughed and dragged a thigh over the erection that had not quite waned since "round one". "I probably won't fade away from hunger or thirst just yet. So why don't we do something about this chronic swelling you have over here, sir?"

He chuckled and covered her lips with his. And for the next forty-five minutes all talk of a serious nature was suspended.

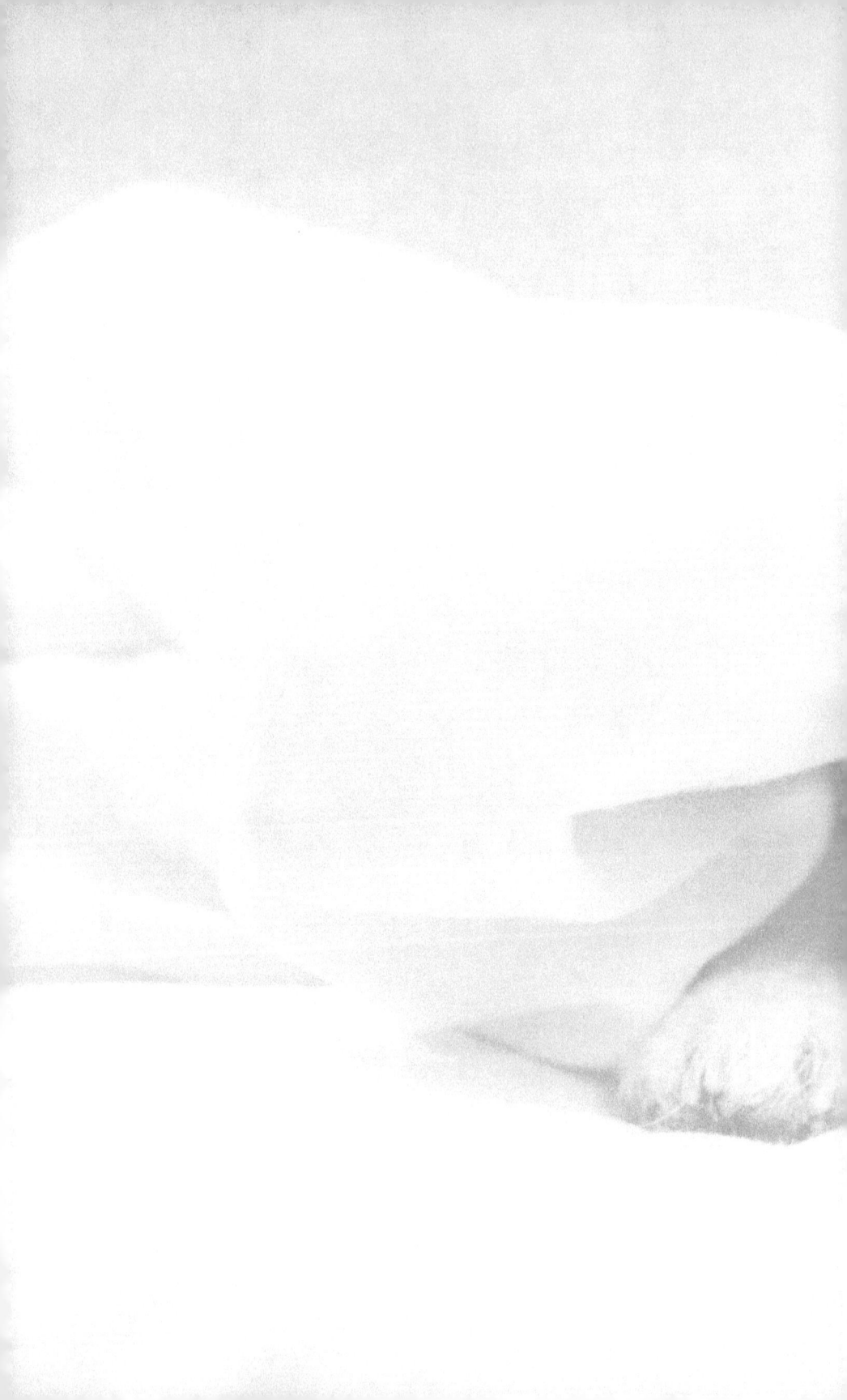

Chapter Fourteen

"Do you have to leave?"

"You sound like a sulky little boy," Charity teased, and then automatically tensed. Sometimes, it crept up on her, that instinct for self-preservation. The feeling of unease that never quite left her. The lizard brain that reminded her that teasing a man could result in swift and violent backlash.

But this particular man laughed, his eyes wrinkling attractively at the corners. "I know. Sulky and selfish, yeah? I've had you to myself for the last two days. I'm sure you must be bored out of your mind by now. You definitely need to go out and have some gal pal fun."

Her instances of fear and hypervigilance were decreasing by the day. Because of Miles's good-natured responses to statements from her that would have resulted in swift and violent reprisals from Blaine.

"You know you don't bore me, Miles."

No. He charmed, seduced, challenged, and interested her.

But he definitely did not bore her. The last couple of days had been filled with fantastic sex, sure. But she had also laughed with him, played with him, walked, swam, and talked with him. She had fallen in like with him a while ago…but that like was deepening, becoming less tenuous and more substantial.

And that scared her, because she didn't *want* to want more from him. This was enough.

But it was starting to feel like too little.

She was relieved that she had committed to spending the afternoon with Lia McGregor today. It would afford her some much needed breathing room. Time to think, regroup, figure out what her next move should be. Being around Miles twenty-four seven was clouding her judgment. She needed to find some clarity, and she could only do that when he wasn't around to distract her with his body, or his wicked sense of humor, his big sexy brain, and his kind, generous nature.

It was ridiculous how much Miles missed Charity after she left for her lunch with Lia McGregor. He pottered around the house, took Stormy for a walk, and texted his mother and sister. He had also contacted both Hugh and Bryan and badgered them into giving him updates on a couple of contract negotiations he had been working on before getting ill.

But that barely ate into his time without Charity. The house smelled like her. He loved that he could go into any room and find a lingering trace of her subtle perfume.

These last two days had been amazing. And he was already dreading the day he would have to say goodbye to her permanently.

He was sitting in the solarium, his laptop open on the coffee table in front of him and impulsively called up his rarely used Facebook account. He had four friends, his family and Bryan, and a few hundred friend requests. The only pictures of himself on the page were ones added by Hugh and Vicki. Photos he hadn't even known existed. He glared at one taken of him at that very house, headphones over his ears, while he stood on the dock, hands in his trouser pockets, staring sullenly out at the lake.

He looked like a miserable tosser.

In fact, he looked like a moody bastard in most of their vacation photos. His expressions ranged from mildly exasperated, to bored, to fully pissed off.

Jesus. He was amazed they continued trying to include him in anything. He would have written himself off as a lost cause years ago if the positions had been reversed.

But he wasn't on Facebook to contemplate his failings as an older brother. He typed the name *Charity Cole* into the search bar, but all it yielded was a handful of Charity Coles who were decidedly *not* his Charity.

He tried *Blane Cole* next. No one who seemed to be the douchebag he was searching for. Then *Blaine Cole*...more smiling faces. But he didn't think any of them were the bastard.

He rubbed his chin, absently noting the need for a shave, before minimizing Facebook and opening a Google search page.

He could call his attorney and ask who had recommended Charity for the job, but this search already felt like a major intrusion into her privacy.

This time he went broader with his search parameters, typing in *Pastor Blaine* and *Charity* and *Cole* to see what would come up.

Bingo!

Several news articles, from just over three years ago.

Miles clicked on the top article, *Popular Minister Takes Own Life*. Below the headline was a wedding picture of a beaming Charity and a good looking arsehole in a tux.

Miles stared at the picture for a long while. She looked so young and happy. Her hair was much shorter. A sleek, chin length bob. Her smile was all sunshine and joy and rainbows. Miles had never seen that particular smile on her. And he wondered if it was gone forever.

A tragic loss if it was. And yet another reason to hate the fucker in the picture next to her. He had violently stolen that joy from her.

Miles scrubbed a hand over his face and took a bracing breath before reading.

Blaine and Charity *Davenport*.

She had changed her name. Likely reverted back to her maiden name. Who could blame her? She hadn't wanted to keep anything of his. Not his ring and—apparently—not his name.

The details of the story made him sick to his stomach. The bastard had shot himself. While Charity had been asleep in bed beside him. No reason for the suicide was given. A police statement that the circumstances of his death had been deemed "not suspicious" and "self-inflicted" had been swiftly issued. The article ended with glowing avowals from "parishioners" and "friends" about how *wonderful* and *caring* and *kind* he had been. *So selfless. Always putting others first.* People were described as being "heartbroken" at the loss.

Too many not-so-subtle inferences that perhaps his marriage hadn't been as happy as it had appeared on the surface. The wording implying that his wife hadn't been as supportive of his work as perhaps she should have been.

Fuckers! No wonder she had fled.

The article ended with the family's plea for privacy during "this difficult time".

He read a few more articles. They were all pretty similar. There was a glowing obituary. Funeral notice and then interest in the story had tapered off.

Armed with a name, Miles headed back to Facebook. And this time immediately found the bastard's page. It was open to the public and in memoriam. There were posts as recent as three days ago, stating how much his parishioners and family and community still loved and missed him.

Miles wanted to puke, reading about this *wonderful, amazing* wife beating motherfucker. He had seen all the faded scars on Charity's body. Some she had happily explained. Childhood accidents, a bad hang gliding landing, rollerblades, ice skating, cycling. Tales of an active, adventurous girl and young woman. Others—far too fucking many of them—she had clammed up about. And he knew that those had come from Blaine. Burns, cuts, the scar on her forehead, and a small, oddly shaped crater on her thigh.

He didn't want to hear about them, but at the same time he wanted to know. Needed her to share these war stories with him. Even though he didn't want them in his mind or memories.

He found himself occupying a conflicting emotional space, and he wasn't sure how to deal with it.

He sighed deeply as he scrolled through Blaine Davenport's pictures.

He had been a tall, handsome, sandy haired man, with a blindingly perfect smile. Miles could see how this golden pretty boy could charm those around him. Beguile them. Deceive them into thinking he was an actual human being instead of a total fucking monster.

Miles paid particular attention to Charity in the pictures

and he couldn't understand how no one had seen how unhappy she had been. She always had a smile pasted on her face. One that never reached her eyes. Nothing at all like the wedding picture. Her smiles after her wedding had been fake, forced...and so sad, it just about broke Miles's heart to see them.

How had her family, her friends...people who had known her for years, not seen this transformation? When it was as clear as day to him?

The long sleeves, the high-necked blouses, the neckerchiefs. All perfectly respectable for a pastor's wife, but Miles knew what they were hiding.

He made a distressed sound, and Stormy's head lifted from where it had been planted on his thigh. He stroked her ears, needing the contact and comfort.

He went through Blaine's "friend" list and found a name that rang a bell.

Faith Culpepper. The accompanying picture of a smiling woman hugging a familiar looking little girl confirmed that it was Charity's sister.

Miles stared at the profile picture for a long time, telling himself it was none of his business. He should stay out of it. Just enjoy his time with Charity and eventually move on.

He opened up a direct message and stared at the blank page for a while. They weren't friends, odds were she probably wouldn't even see the message. And if she didn't reply then that was fine. He wouldn't pursue this any further.

Fuck.

His fingers restlessly tapped the glass-topped coffee table as he continued to stare at the page. Charity could well hate him for this.

Eventually, as if by their own volition his hands lifted and his fingertips splayed on the keyboard.

Good morning. My name is Miles Hollingsworth...

THE HOUSE WAS quiet when Charity arrived back after five that evening. She was so late. It was just supposed to be lunch, and Miles would have expected her back hours ago.

Her stomach was in knots as she cautiously made her way to the kitchen. She didn't know why she was so nervous...so *afraid.*

This was Miles.

Miles wouldn't hurt her. He didn't want to control her. Or own her. And just because they were now lovers didn't mean she owed him any explanations as to her whereabouts.

She told herself all of that, and still her dread would not dissipate. And every hesitant step farther into the quiet house, deepened her anxiety.

"Miles?" No response.

Well, no human response...she heard the scrabble of claws on the wooden floors as Stormy dashed from the direction of the living room into the kitchen. The dog danced and twirled happily, huffing and whining in excitement as she greeted Charity.

"Hey girl, did you miss me?" she asked, bending at the waist to pat the pup's head.

"She did." Miles's voice startled her, and she looked up to find him standing in the kitchen doorway. "We both did."

"Uh...I'm sorry I'm late." Charity could have kicked herself. It hadn't been her intention to apologize. It was an unfortunate instinctive response she had to work on getting rid of.

His eyes reflected confusion.

"I wasn't aware that there was a time limit on your afternoon out," he said, and then smiled. His eyes took on an appreciative glint as he assessed her appearance. "But it's evident you've been quite busy."

One of her hands self-consciously went up to her newly shorn hair, and she straightened slowly. Lia had offered to accompany her to a salon after Charity had tentatively mentioned wanting a haircut. The drastic new style had been an impulse. She had stared blankly at herself in the mirror, while the stylist had enthused about the length and texture of her hair. Barely recognizing the woman hidden beneath all of that hair and the words had been out before she could stop them.

Cut it all off.

She had just about broken the stylist's heart. But once she had spoken the words, Charity had been determined to follow through. She had happily donated her two-foot-long fall of hair to CANSA.

Her hair hadn't seen a pair of scissors in three years, and before that, it had been kept in a strictly jaw-length bob...as per Blaine's preference. The change now was drastic. And defiant. Her nearly waist-length hair had been shorn into a soft, pixie cut. Charity had never had her hair this short before but she liked how light and airy it felt.

But despite all that earlier certainty and determination, she now anxiously watched Miles for his reaction. Not because she needed his validation, but because of the other thing. The irrational fear that he would lash out because of a very personal decision she had made about her image. She knew that he loved her long hair, he had told her often enough. And her entire body was stiff with tension as she watched his every move, ready to bolt if he so much as...

"God, you look gorgeous." His words brought her panicked thoughts to a grinding halt. He didn't seem to notice her tension, instead his gaze was still focused on her hair. "It's a big change, but it does fantastic things for your bone structure and eyes. Then again, you could shave your head and still look lovely."

Charity swallowed thickly. Berating herself for being surprised by his words. He wasn't anything like Blaine. She wasn't making the same mistakes with the same awful kinds of men.

"Shaving my head would be drastic," she forced herself to say, struggling to insert some levity into her strained voice. "Although, going from nearly two feet of hair to barely two inches is pretty extreme in itself, I suppose."

He laughed and she relaxed even more.

"What did you two get up to while I was gone?" she asked. She bent at the waist to rub Stormy's head again, grateful to have the dog there to offer some distraction.

"We went for a short run on the shore—" He held up a palm when she opened her mouth to chastise him for that. "I paced myself and didn't overdo it. But I've got to say...I've pretty much recovered most of my stamina...thanks to you."

He chuckled when she blushed and continued. "I also texted my sister and mother. I then called Bryan, as well as Hugh, and convinced them to give me a proper business update. Without tennis or golf anecdotes to bore me into hanging up. It seems that everything is going swimmingly without me. And, finally, I caught up on my audiobook."

"Oh? Did Willow and Delonix finish the second trials?"

"Not yet."

"I'll expect an update later."

"Of course."

"Have you eaten? You must be starving."

"I ate. A cheese sandwich. I'm not completely helpless you

know," he said, with a grin, stepping toward her and winding an arm around her waist.

Her weird earlier mood had dissipated beneath their banter, and she barely tensed at the gesture. She hoped the instinctive initial reaction was small enough for him not to notice.

He gave her a quick kiss.

"I missed you."

She twined her arms around his neck and reciprocated his next kiss with a lot more enthusiasm.

"I barely thought of you," she lied breathlessly after the kiss ended, and he laughed.

"Good. That must mean you had fun."

"I did."

He still had his arms loosely looped around her waist and she tightened hers around his neck, getting comfortable as she told him about her afternoon. "Lia's sister Daff Carlisle, and her, Daff's, five-month-old baby, Connor, joined us for lunch. We were talking about makeovers for some reason and I mentioned needing a haircut. Lia convinced me to get one today, before I chickened out. I never could resist a dare."

"No? Well then...I dare you to give me another kiss and see what happens."

"Oh, I already know what'll happen," she countered with a laugh, before giving him a light, teasing kiss. "And that's not much of a dare, really."

"Well then, I dare you to..." he paused and seemed to consider his options, his eyes taking a lazy meander over her face and lingering on her lips. His breathing sped up, and she could feel his heart racing against her chest. "Take off your panties."

Her lips parted in a slow grin, and she unwound her arms from around his neck and hiked up the skirt of her knee length dress. Maintaining eye contact, she hooked her fingers in the sides of her bikini panties and slid them down, deliberately brushing her abdomen against his lengthening hardness as she shimmied out of the scrap of fabric. She slipped off her pumps and stepped out of the silky, white panties.

"Yet another easy dare," she taunted him, her own voice husky and breathless.

"Well then," he muttered, clearly trying very hard to keep it together. "Why don't you show me how it's done?"

She gave him a long, searching look. The inflexible ridge of his penis was an insistent presence between them, his hair was mussed, his eyes glazed, and he was starting to pant. She wasn't much better off. Her nipples were so hard, she wondered they didn't make dents in his chest. She was soaking wet and more than ready for him. She was still shocked by how fast this man could turn her on. Every single time. All it took was a look, or a word, and she was ready to climb all over him.

Their chemistry was mind-boggling.

"I dare you..." She hesitated and licked her lips as she considered her options. Her gaze dropped to where Stormy was staring up at them, her head tilted in confusion and she chuckled.

"Go to bed, Stormy," she commanded the pup, and the dog whined unhappily. "Go on. Good girl."

Stormy whined again. She turned away despondently and trudged out of the kitchen.

"Charity, focus," Miles sounded equal parts amused and exasperated, and Charity buried her fingers in his hair and dragged his head down until his lips were a hairsbreadth from hers.

"I dare you to get on your knees and make me come with your tongue. In under two minutes."

"Two minutes? I'll get it done in a minute."

"You turned my dare into a bet," she protested.

"Whatever. I'm going win it."

He sank to his knees in front of her, lifted her skirt, palmed one of her thighs, and unceremoniously hitched it over his shoulder. The move allowed him easier access to the aching heat between her legs. In an attempt to maintain her balance, she planted her hands on the kitchen sink behind her.

He was hidden beneath her skirt, and she couldn't see what he was doing, but *oh God* could she feel it. He used his thumbs to part her folds, and she shuddered at the first touch of his tongue on her rigid, throbbing clit.

Charity's head fell back, and her pelvis tilted forward.

She heard him swearing shakily before he went to work.

"Oh, *oh*! Oh, yes. Miles. Right there. Right..." She had never been very vocal during sex but for some reason she always found herself encouraging him, talking to him, telling him what she liked. How she liked it.

He lapped at her, like a cat drinking up the richest cream. And it was heavenly.

He won the bet, because after a few strokes of his tongue, she was on the verge...and when he clamped his lips over her aching bud and sucked, she was wrecked.

She was still spasming violently when he got up and hastily undid his trousers to release himself.

Soon her butt was braced on the edge of the sink, and her legs were wrapped around his waist while he pounded into her. She came again, and then again...and was on the verge of a fourth climax when he swore.

"What?"

"I'm sorry, I forgot the condom." He withdrew and gripped himself tightly as he tried to stave off his orgasm.

Charity didn't think about it. She was on her knees and had

him in her mouth before either of them could take another breath.

"*Fuck*!" He cupped her head, and she lifted her eyes to stare into his straining face. "Jesus. I can't...Charity. I can't..."

She smiled at him around his length before closing her eyes and sucking him deeply into her mouth and down her throat. She relished the salty sweet taste of him, the size of him...one of her hands crept up to the rigid muscles of his abdomen and the other cupped the smooth, heavy sac at the base of his penis.

He groaned. The sound was long and low and helpless. And, knowing she had him right on the verge, she withdrew until she had only the tip of him in her mouth and scraped at the sensitive underside of his glans with her teeth.

He muffled a cry and came. Copiously, almost violently. His entire body remained in spasm while he emptied himself into her mouth.

And Charity, who had pretty much despised this act during her marriage, moved a hand to the sensitive, throbbing spot between her legs and strummed herself to completion.

She wasn't sure how it happened, but they wound up sitting side by side on the floor, backs braced against the dishwasher. His arm was curled around her shoulders, and her head was slumped on his still heaving chest.

"That was fucking phenomenal," he said.

"It truly was. And well done on winning the bet."

He chuckled, sounding drained.

"Thank you, Mrs. Cole. I do strive to please." He paused for a beat before adding, "Well...I guess that takes care of dinner for both of us."

Charity choked. She lifted her head to stare at him incredulously and burst into laughter.

He grinned and then began to chuckle and before long he,

too, was laughing helplessly. His rich, deep guffaws a masculine counterpart to her girlish, carefree giggles.

And in that moment of sheer unbridled joy...Charity fell hopelessly, helplessly, head over heels in love with him.

And that terrified her because she didn't want to love anyone. Not now. Possibly not ever.

Not while she was still the wrecked woman of Blaine's creation.

"CAN you tell me about the day he died?"

The words were quiet and fell like unwelcome stones into the cold, silent darkness of night. Charity and Miles were cuddled up on the love seat on the patio, warm and toasty beneath the patio heater. Stormy was curled up on Miles's lap, and they were all bundled beneath a blanket and staring out at the dark, still lake.

They were sipping hot chocolate and after a lively debate about the potential direction of the *Terra Arbor Chronicles,* talk had drifted to Miles's telephone conversations with Vicki and his mother that afternoon. After which they had lapsed into a comfortable silence.

Until now.

Her brow furrowed as she watched the lights from the dock ripple on the surface of the black water. She didn't want to think about that night. Not while she was warm and safe and happy.

"Why do you want to know?"

She felt his throat move beneath her head as he swallowed heavily.

"I looked him up. I'm sorry. I know it was an unforgivable

intrusion but I wanted to find out more and I know it was wrong but..." His voice tapered off, and Charity silently mulled over his disjointed confession. She wasn't sure how she felt about him prying into her private business, but he already knew more about her than anybody else, and she found that she didn't mind as much as she thought she would.

Instead, she was curious about what he had found. She had never read any of the news articles, or the sympathy posts on social media, not even the cards that a few—*very* few—of his parishioners had sent to her. "Looked him up how?"

"The Internet. It wasn't easy. I thought his last name was Cole."

"I didn't want his name. I reverted to my maiden name when I took this job."

"He killed himself? I was surprised by that. Everything you told me about him indicated toward some type of narcissist. A man who valued his own life above all else."

"He was...he did."

Tonight's the night you die, Charity.

She shuddered violently, and Miles's arm tightened around her shoulders.

"You don't have to tell me about it. Okay? I'm so sorry for snooping. I just wanted to understand you better."

"I think..." Her voice was hoarse, and she paused to clear her throat before continuing. "He thought I was dead. He thought he'd killed me. He nearly did. He meant to, he told me I was going to die. And then he held me down and covered my face with a pillow. But I passed out, and he stopped before the job was fully done. I can only speculate as to what happened after that. I think he panicked. He wrote a bullshit note about not wanting to live without me, lay down beside me and blew his brains out."

She woke up covered in blood. So much blood! Was she bleeding? He didn't usually make her bleed...

"There was so much blood," she recalled distantly. The memory still had the power to make her shudder. "At first I thought it was mine. I believed he had cut me while I was unconscious. And I was terrified, I thought I was bleeding to death."

Miles was shaking, she could feel the violent trembling of his body beside hers and patted his knee reassuringly. This wasn't easy to talk about, and for a decent, kind man like Miles, it couldn't be very easy to hear either.

But he had wanted to know. And this was the bitter unvarnished truth. The ugliness that simmered beneath her surface.

She could hear his breath stuttering in and out of his chest. It sounded painful and uneven. Like sobs, and she lifted her gaze to his face. The heater provided dim illumination, and she could see the gleam of his eyes as he met her stare.

He hugged her closer. "I wish I'd met you sooner. Before you'd met *him*. I would have swept you off your feet. I would have loved and cherished you and kept you away from that fucking monster."

She lifted her free hand to his cheek, warmed that he cared enough to be so deeply affected by something that had happened to her so very long ago.

"That would have been difficult. I grew up with him, you see? Went to school with him. And in my twenties, I fell in love with the kind and generous man he had pretended to be. But, thank you. For saying that. It means a lot."

"Not enough though," he whispered. "Nowhere near enough. You have no idea how helpless and frustrated I feel. How much I want to make this right for you."

"I don't need you to make things *right* for me, Miles. Or to feel helpless and frustrated on my behalf. It's not your place and it's not what I want from you. What I *do* need from you..." She paused and smiled, even though she knew he could not see it. "I'm getting it already. And it's enough for right now."

But it wasn't enough for Miles. He wanted this thing between them to be more and mean more. He wanted to take on the world for her. Wanted to show her how precious she was to him. Wanted her to see how much she amazed him, awed him, and impressed him.

He wanted a future with her. More than a future.

He wanted forever with her.

Yet every day brought them a step closer to the inevitable end of their affair.

And it was going to break his fucking heart to say goodbye to her.

"He wanted a baby."

Her words surprised him. He hadn't expected her to continue, and the dullness in her voice filled him with dread. He wasn't sure he wanted to hear this. But he had invited the confidences and that meant listening to whatever she had to tell him. "Almost from the very beginning. But as you can imagine, I was hesitant. I didn't want to bring a baby into that environment. I wasn't even sure if pregnancy would have served as a deterrent to the abuse. I had a brief moment of weakness where I selfishly considered it. I fantasized that maybe a baby would miraculously fix what was wrong, and Blaine would go from this abusive monster to a loving husband and father.

"I came to my senses pretty quickly. I knew a baby would make it worse. Either he'd hurt the baby, or use it as leverage against me. And I didn't want any child of mine to grow up in a toxic environment like that."

Another long pause.

"I suppose you're wondering why I stayed with him?"

"I'm not," he replied truthfully. The thought hadn't occurred to him. He was aware of how manipulative abusers could be. The absolute control they held over their victims.

"I was afraid of what he'd do to me if I tried to leave."

"You don't have to explain, Charity. I get it."

"How are you so understanding?"

"I understand how abusive emotional manipulation works, Charity. I may not have experienced it firsthand, or even witnessed it, but the mechanics are pretty straightforward." He played the words back in his own mind and grimaced at the dry logic of his statement. Nothing in his voice or in his words betrayed the extreme, gut-wrenching emotional wringer her descriptions of life with Blaine Davenport put him through.

Her heard her swallow. He blindly reached for her hand in the darkness, and she latched on tightly when he found it.

"He was a by the book abuser, so to speak. First made me doubt myself, made me believe that somehow if I just tweaked little things about myself, I'd be what he wanted me to be, and he wouldn't have to punish me any longer. By the time I realized *that* wasn't going to happen I was a year into the marriage and that was when he convinced me that no one would believe me if I told."

She laughed. A bitter, joyless sound that tore at his heart. "By the third year it was clear that he just plain enjoyed hurting me. And controlling me. There was no more pretense between us, he had resorted to threats. He'd kill me if I tried to leave. He'd hurt Gracie. Faith. Anybody that I loved. And he was so evil and twisted I absolutely believed that he would.

"And through it all he kept trying for a baby. Every month when my period arrived like clockwork, he'd *punish* me. It was my fault. I was worthless, pathetic, dried up...I honestly hoped his desire for a child, and my apparent inability to give him one would drive him to divorce me. But he was obsessed with me. Or as he put it, he *loved* me too much to let me go. He'd kill me before releasing me. Die rather than lose me."

"Did you get pregnant?"

"No. Because he was right, it *was* my fault I never got pregnant. For the first two months of our marriage I was sneakily taking the pill. But when he started to suspect something was up, I was forced to flush them. I got an implant instead. Under an old scar so that he wouldn't feel it. It was the one thing he wanted above all else, and the only thing left to me that I had any control over. I knew that if he discovered what I'd done he'd kill me."

The risk she had taken by using something as fundamental to her rights as birth control was staggering. And the sheer courage of her actions stole his breath away.

"And then, one day, my luck ran out...he saw the renewal notice on my phone..."

Tonight's the night you die, Charity.

The words played themselves out over and over again in her nightmares. The fury in his face. The absolute fear and dread in the pit of her stomach. The certainty that her last breath was mere minutes away.

. . .

The cold, flat fury in Blaine's eyes was more than enough to send her scampering for the dubious safety of the bedroom. But he beat her to the door, grabbed her elbow, and flung her onto the bed.

Before she could scramble away he was on top of her, straddling her.

"Please. Please Blaine! I can explain. I'm sorry. I can explain. Please don't hurt me. I'm sorry."

The words were a breathless, panicked jumble. But he didn't seem to hear them. He wrapped his hands around her neck and lowered his face until she could feel his breath on her skin. His mouth opened, and his teeth gently closed over her cheek. She heard the involuntary mewling in her throat. Her body was stiff as a board as she waited for him to bite down. To rip, tear...maim. Destroy.

He would. He wanted to. She knew it. She had seen it in his eyes, sensed it in the leashed fury of his movements. He was going to kill her. But first he would hurt her. He would make her regret defying him.

She thought of her parents, of Faith. Of the beautiful niece she would never see grow up. She regretted the life that she could have lived, the love she should have found...She didn't want it to end. Not now. Not like this.

She managed to get both hands between their bodies, braced her palms against his chest, and shoved him as hard as she could. The move surprised him, and he reared up. She used his momentary confusion to try and wriggle out from beneath him.

But he recovered too quickly. Compressing his thighs over hers to prevent her from getting away, his hands clamped around her neck.

"Let go of me!" she demanded of him. Tears seeped down her face and soaked into the pillow beneath her head. He had an erec-

tion. He always had an erection when he hurt her. And she hated it! Hated *him.*

"You stole from me, Charity," he said, from between gritted teeth. "You stole my child from me."

"F-fuck you, Blaine!" She hurled at him, finding her voice, her defiance, her bravery now. When it was too late. "I stole nothing from you. I would die before I give you a child."

He reached for a pillow, and the last thing she saw, before he covered her face with it, was his lips parting on a thin, menacing smile.

The shroud of darkness was accompanied by the terrifying sensation of being smothered. Each excruciating exhalation left her with even less air in her lungs. And while she fought to breathe, he was right there, intimately close...applying ever more pressure.

"Oh, don't worry, my love. I can promise you this...Tonight's the night you die, Charity."

She gasped and redoubled her efforts, seeing the absolute truth in his eyes.

"I FOUGHT HIM SO HARD. I knew he meant what he'd said." Her cheeks were wet, and she wiped the moisture from them with her sleeve. "And I didn't want to die. I was so desperate to live. But in the end, he was too strong for me. He didn't even hurt me. Didn't hit me. Or bruise me or bite me. He knew exactly what he was doing and that meant leaving no questionable marks on me for the police to investigate. He left a half empty bottle of pills next to the bed. I think he wanted people to assume that I'd committed suicide and that, devoted to the end, he had taken his own life because he couldn't live without me. It wasn't entirely rational, an autopsy would have revealed the truth. But he was beyond reason at that point. I have no idea how he had missed the fact that I was still breathing...but I'm eternally grateful that he did."

Mile's breathing was ragged, his hand had long since dropped from hers. She could feel the tautness in his body, and she tensed in reaction to it.

"I-I..." He couldn't seem to find the words he needed to complete that thought, and Charity turned her head to look at him. She couldn't see much more than his harsh profile as he stared out into the blackness.

"Miles..."

He shook his head and interrupted her. "I'm sorry, Charity. I-I just need a moment. It's...I—"

He surged to his feet and scooped Stormy from his lap in one motion.

"Just..." He handed the dog to her and didn't finish his thought, instead he stalked away and slammed into the house. Charity hugged the trembling dog close and contemplated the closed patio door for a long moment, before getting up and following him inside. She put Stormy down, and the dog scrabbled off toward Miles's bedroom.

Charity hesitated for a moment and slowly followed Stormy down the darkened hallway to his room.

She found him in the en suite, hands braced on the sink, head bowed, and shoulders shaking.

"Miles?" Her voice was low, questioning. But he kept his stare directed at the porcelain sink.

She lay a tentative hand on his shoulder. His whole body was vibrating with suppressed emotion.

"I'm sorry," she whispered. He made a soft, anguished sound

in the back of his throat and lifted his eyes to meet hers. The expression in them staggered her. He looked wrecked and, as she watched, that harsh, masculine face dissolved into absolute despair. *Tears* welled up in his beautiful eyes, reddening the whites and spiking his lashes. Charity could tell from the brutally clenched jaw, the gritted teeth, and muscle jumping in his temple, how hard he was struggling to keep those tears at bay...But he lost that valiant fight when she palmed his taut jaw. His reactionary flinch from her touch, dislodged the fiercely battled tears and sent them streaking down his lean cheeks.

"*Fuck*," he groaned, and leaned into her touch, reaching up to capture her hand against his face. "I'm sorry. I didn't want to upset you. I didn't want to make this about me. But fuck, Charity, it kills me to hear what he did to you."

"I know."

"I feel violent. Furious...and I don't want to scare you."

"You never could."

She stepped closer, and he enfolded her in his arms, wrapping himself around her, making her feel safe and protected.

"You don't scare me, Miles. Because I know you won't hurt me."

"How can you trust any man after what he did to you?"

She had once wondered the same thing. Had despaired of ever trusting her own judgment again.

And yet, here she was. Inexplicably and irrevocably confident that this man would *never* physically harm her.

"Because you're not *him*, Miles. Because you adopt stray dogs. You love your siblings. You take care of your mother. You care about your employees. And I have a sneaking suspicion that if you could safely get away with it, you'd probably liberate all the lobsters in restaurant tanks you can find."

The last coaxed a smile from that beautiful stern mouth.

"I'd release them back into the ocean," he said, with a somber nod.

"Of course, you would," she whispered, and kissed him. She tasted the salt on his lips. "Because you're a wonderful man who hates the thought of anyone or anything in pain."

"Would it alarm you to know that I can very much envision your twisted husband writhing in absolute agony? The way he died wasn't painful enough for my liking. It feels like he got away with what he did to you. I hate that. And I loathe the fact that people are still singing his praises like he was a fucking saint."

"It used to bother me. It doesn't anymore."

He sighed—the sound deep and despondent—and pressed his forehead to hers for a moment.

"The way I feel about you..." his voice was rough and low. "Terrifies me. It also exhilarates and delights me."

She had his jaw in her palms, and it was easy for her to hold him still for her kiss.

"Make love to me, Miles," she murmured against his lips after ending the kiss, and his arms tightened around her waist as he dragged her even closer.

"With absolute fucking pleasure, sweetheart."

Chapter Fifteen

"Why are we at Lia and Sam's at six am on a Saturday?" Charity asked grumpily, a week later, when George drew the SUV to a stop in front of the aforementioned couple's beautiful cabin up on the hill overlooking town.

Charity was cranky because he had awoken her at four-thirty after only three hours' sleep and a satisfyingly exhausting night of lovemaking.

After her initial irritation of being awoken from a sound sleep faded; depression, misery, and regret had hit her like a ton of bricks when she remembered that it was Gracie's birthday. Charity had messaged Faith late Thursday night to let her sister know she would not be joining them for the party.

She would be heading home shortly anyway and, she was happy to delay the inevitable painful conversations she would be having with her family. But more than that, she was acutely aware that time was running out for her and Miles. It had been a difficult decision, but in the end, Charity knew that she wanted to share as much time with him as she could.

Neither Charity nor Miles ever mentioned it, but he was nearly back at full strength. His breathing was a lot easier, he rarely coughed anymore, and he exercised regularly. Charity could see the difference in his color and the lack of gauntness in that lean face. And she could definitely feel it in the way he moved when they made love. The sinuous coiled vigor in that fantastic body was sexy as hell.

He had awoken her with breakfast—well, a stale croissant and terrible coffee—in bed that morning...She had turned her nose up at the less than appetizing offering. Not that she could eat in the middle of the night anyway.

After the failed attempt at feeding her, Miles had then insisted she hurry up and get dressed. He had urged her to pack an overnight bag for an impromptu overnight getaway.

He knew that it was Gracie's birthday today, perhaps this was his way of trying to cheer her up.

Sweet, *sweet* man.

But the curiosity was eating her alive.

Now she watched as Miles cuddled his dog close.

"It won't be for long, girl. I'll be back before you know it. And I'll bring treats. And toys. I promise. Okay?"

It was ridiculous and adorable at the same time. He gave the pup another squeeze that she tried to squirm out of, and commanded Charity and George to stay put while he leaped from the vehicle and flung Stormy's "go bag", as he called it, over a shoulder. The dog was cradled in his other arm like a baby.

He wasn't gone long and, even though it was still mostly dark, Charity was certain that his eyes were gleaming with moisture when he returned a couple of minutes later.

Amused though she was, she curled her arm through his, wanting to offer comfort.

"She has never spent a night without me," he muttered, sounding distraught.

"Miles, she was a stray when you found her, she has spent many nights without you."

"She doesn't remember that life. She's attached, she'll be a wreck without me."

Charity suspected the dog would be quite fine. The *man*, however, was a completely different story.

His phone beeped and he absently glanced at the message and then glowered.

"Well...*hell*."

He lifted the device to show her the screen, and Charity convulsed with laughter. Sam had sent a pic of Stormy in bed with Lia, who was obviously—like most sane people at this hour —having a Saturday morning lie-in. Something Charity would dearly have *loved* to do. The pup was fast asleep in the woman's arms, and they both appeared snug and contented.

Miles muttered something beneath his breath. Something that sounded suspiciously like "traitorous little bitch."

And Charity pressed her lips together in an attempt to curb her laughter.

"Let's get a move on, George," he instructed the older man brusquely, and George saluted mockingly before obeying.

"What is this?" Charity asked suspiciously, when George parked at a private airfield just outside of Plettenberg Bay. Miles had been closemouthed about their destination for the entirety of their twenty-minute drive. Fobbing off her questions with vague "you'll see" type responses. Charity had assumed they would eventually wind up at some scenic and romantic location in Plett. But an airfield was a game changer. Had he chartered a plane to some remote place? The prospect was exciting and daunting at the same time.

"Where are we going?" she asked again, and he must have heard some evidence of the panic that she was trying to tamp down, creeping into her voice, because he paused in the middle of unbuckling his seatbelt to look at her.

His eyes were tender, and he brushed a thumb over her cheekbone.

"I want it to be a surprise..." he murmured. "But if you need me to tell you, I will."

Charity worried her lower lip with her teeth, part of her needing to know where they were going but another, larger, part urging her to trust him.

She swallowed her panic and inhaled deeply, in an attempt to regulate her breathing and slow down her heart rate.

"Lead the way, Miles."

"Fearless," he whispered in admiration, and leaned in to give her a sweet kiss. For a second, she allowed it, until she remembered George, who had exited to get their overnight bags.

"George," she muttered in self-conscious explanation, after withdrawing from Miles's embrace.

He grinned unrepentantly. "If you think George doesn't know what's happening between us, you have a serious rethink coming. That man knows everything. And you can be damned sure that if *he* knows, Amos does as well."

"Oh my *God*," she groaned, burying her face in her hands for a brief moment of chagrin.

"Buck up, Mrs. Cole," he advised her cheerfully. "You don't give a good goddamn what people think about you, right?"

"Sure. Right," she agreed, not sounding at all convincing. "Whatever."

He laughed and undid his belt before leaping from the SUV. He rounded the vehicle to help her down. George was whistling cheerfully as he accompanied them to a waiting helicopter.

Charity stopped and stared at the large, luxurious looking chopper. It was black and silver and had the words *Chapman GPG Inc.* emblazoned on the side.

"Greyson said we could hitch a ride on their company chopper. His brother and sister-in-law have just flown in from Cape Town, and the chopper was on its way back. He said we could borrow it for a quick detour on its return journey."

"Sure," Charity said breezily. "Just borrow a chopper from your new buddy."

"Hey, I'm happy to return the favor anytime he's in London."

"God, who even *are* you people? I used to borrow clothes and money from *my* friends." She rolled her eyes, and he laughed again, curling his arm around her shoulders and leading her to the chopper.

He greeted the pilot with a handshake and exchanged a few words, before the man took their luggage from George and loaded it. Miles helped Charity into the chopper, and she sank into one of the plush leather seats. She had never been on a helicopter before and by now her excitement outweighed her curiosity and nervousness.

Her grin stretched from ear to ear, and she was certain that whatever fancy or exotic location Miles was spiriting her off to, could in no way compete with the mode of transportation he had used to get her there.

The flight was a little more than an hour long. And it was over much too soon for Charity's liking. She had marveled over the sights, seeing the uniquely beautiful Western Cape in an entirely new way. The pilot had kept mostly to the shoreline, and the scenery on this gorgeous clear day had been diverse and absolutely breathtaking.

Miles had been strangely quiet throughout the flight. They had worn headsets for communication, and while she had vocally thrilled over the incomparable sunrise, magnificent pods of humpback whales, craggy cliffs, pristine beaches, and rugged mountaintops, he had barely strung together two sentences.

And once the helicopter began its descent, somewhere close to Stellenbosch in Cape Town as far as she could tell, she had sensed him tensing more and more. Maybe he was a nervous flyer. She couldn't quite imagine that, but it seemed like a logical explanation for his strange mood.

They were landing in the middle of a grassy field, close to what she assumed was a wine farm. She could see a large group of people milling close by.

It was just after eight, and Charity figured most of the people gathered had to be hotel staff to welcome them. Miles Hollingsworth was a pretty high profile guest, and Charity knew that they would pull out all the stops for a man of his caliber.

The pilot set the chopper down gently and flipped a few switches, before looking over his shoulder and grinning at them.

"Welcome to Weltevreden Estate," he said jovially, before returning his attention to the knobs and dials. But Charity—instantly blinded with rage after that cavalier identification of their location—was no longer paying attention to the pilot.

Instead, she turned to glare at Miles, who looked pale and anxious and sicker than he had in weeks.

"How..." Charity shook her head and forced her chaotic thoughts into order before attempting to speak again. "How *dare* you?"

"Charity, please hear me out. I knew you wouldn't make this decision by yourself and—" Words continued to tumble from his lips. Sounding practiced and a little desperate, but nothing he said in this moment could make this right.

She had trusted him. And this was a complete betrayal of that trust.

"This was *my* choice to make. Not yours. Never yours. How fucking *dare* you?"

He swallowed, ashen, trembling.

The pilot, who could hear their conversation through his headset, shot them a troubled glance over his shoulder and removed his headset to give them some privacy.

"I trusted you to never hurt me. And this hurts, Miles." She was beyond livid. "You shouldn't have forced this on me. Take me back!"

"It's too late," he said, dismayed. "Faith knows we're coming. They stayed at the hotel last night because they wanted to make a proper weekend out of this, and she messaged me earlier to say that they would all be waiting at the landing sight."

Charity's trembling hand crept up to her mouth, and her eyes drifted back to the group of people that she had assumed consisted of mostly hotel staff. Through a blur of tears, she could now pick out individuals in that crowd. She knew everybody there. Her parents, Faith, and Faith's husband—Stuart. A few close cousins and their spouses. And nearly lost among the adults, was the tiny figure of her niece, jumping up and down excitedly.

And, of course, also standing among all of those much-loved people was Paul. And Sandra.

At the unwelcome sight of her former in-laws, a huge part of Charity wanted to curl up and hide from the inevitability of this moment. But she tossed back her shoulders defiantly. Refusing to buckle beneath this last remnant of Blaine's suffocating control. His parents no longer had the power to hurt her.

"Charity, I made a mistake but I thought—"

"I'm not interested in what you thought." She was scathing in her dismissal of Miles's frantic attempt at an explanation.

"Charity, I'm so..."

She shot him a disdainful look before deliberately lifting the headset from her ears, effectively drowning him out beneath the noise of the helicopter.

His mouth slammed shut and the look of abject misery on his face would have been satisfying if she wasn't so devastated by what felt like a massive loss.

Miles watched Charity gird herself to face her family. She smoothed her hands down the front of the flirty, pleated chiffon skirt of the lovely dress she was wearing and patted her short tresses nervously. It was a gesture that he hadn't seen her use in weeks and hated that it was back. Hated that *he* was the reason it was back.

Christ, he had fucked up so badly. He should have stayed out of it, he should have let her do this in her own time. She was right...how fucking dare he? It wasn't his place to fix her life. He should have supported her decisions to do what needed to be done at her own pace.

And now, because of his sheer arrogance, it looked like he had lost her.

The pilot hopped from the cockpit and opened the door for her and she stepped down. She looked ethereal and beautiful. The pastel pink of her dress such a gorgeous contrast to the velvet perfection of her brown skin...the downwash from the rotors lifted the skirt enough to give him a tantalizing glimpse of the lacy white panties beneath, before she ruthlessly clamped her palms over her butt and crotch to keep the skirt in place.

Miles wasn't quite sure what to do...an increasingly familiar sensation around Charity, but he hopped out of the chopper as well. After briefly thanking the pilot, he grabbed their bags and followed Charity. She had thrown back her shoulders and was bravely walking toward her family, as if she wasn't absolutely petrified of facing them all again.

She didn't spare Miles a second look but he, nevertheless, followed her slowly. Giving her enough distance to not feel crowded, but making sure he was close enough so that she knew he was there if she needed him.

Not that she would need him. Not that she would turn to him even if she did need him.

The people hovering just yards away, could no longer contain themselves and once she was out of the chopper's downwash radius, they rushed toward her, with joyful exclamations and open arms. Charity was surrounded by them in seconds, disappearing in the middle of the crowd, swamped with love and hugs and kisses.

Miles knew that she would probably never forgive him...but seeing the vulnerable fear disappear from her eyes to be replaced by love and joy almost made this devastating loss worth it.

Losing her had always been inevitable. But at least now he never had to worry about her being alone, or hiding from the world again.

Because she was finally home.

"Mr. Hollingsworth contacted me last Friday," Faith explained twenty minutes later, when everybody had settled down to a sizable family breakfast. "He told me that you took your job very seriously and because he had been ill you were reluctant to leave. But he said he knew you wanted to come and felt bad about your missing the party on his account. That's how he came up with the idea to surprise you by bringing you here today. He said you would never abandon your post so to speak, which meant that he had to do all of this without your knowledge. He's so nice."

Oh, he was *something* alright. But *nice* wasn't the adjective that currently sprang to Charity's mind.

Manipulative, maybe.

Bossy, sure.

Control freak, abso*freaking*lutely.

But *nice*?

Charity allowed herself a sigh as she acknowledged, that despite being all of the above...there was no denying that he was nice as well. Miles Henry Hollingsworth was a complex man. And nice, kind, and gentle...were a few of the *many* layers she had uncovered in him.

But just because he was one of the sweetest men she had ever met, did *not* mean that he got a free pass after this stunt.

In the following half an hour of sheer excitement and everybody talking over one another and hugs and so much emotion, Charity lost track of Miles. In fact—she surreptitiously glanced around the long, crowded family table—he was nowhere to be seen. The still-pissed-off part of Charity told her that she didn't care where he was. That he had no place being here anyway. But the Charity who had melted into a puddle of unadulterated joy at the sight of her family, admitted to being more than a little grateful to him for orchestrating this reunion. And *that* Charity worried that he had left thinking she would never forgive him. Possibly even that she hated him.

And she couldn't hate him. Because deep down she knew that this hadn't been the move of a man who felt the need to manipulate or dictate her life. The fool man had been attempting to help her.

She sighed. Then again...making excuses for a man was something she was good at doing, and that sketchy track record made her doubt herself and Miles's intentions.

Still, she wished she knew where he was.

Gracie, who had left with her father to get dressed for her party, ran into the room, dressed in a pink tutu and a glittery unicorn T-shirt. The girl had been understandably reticent and shy when everybody had pushed her to hug her "Auntie Cherry" hello. But she seemed to have overcome that initial reserve now. She was hugging a plush white unicorn to her chest, and she ran straight to Charity to give her a gap-toothed smile.

"Thank you for my present, Auntie Cherry." Charity stared at the toy the girl was holding and lifted her gaze to the entrance of the restaurant, where Miles now hovered uncertainly. He must have been with Gracie and Stuart earlier, and he had obviously thought of everything. She didn't even know when he'd had the opportunity to buy this toy...especially since he had spent almost every waking—and sleeping—moment with her this past week.

"You're welcome, sweetie. I'm glad you like it."

"This is a unicorn party," the girl happily lisped. "My cake is a unicorn."

"That's fantastic. I can't wait to see it."

"All of my friends are coming. Aaaaall of them." She gestured expansively to emphasize that fact.

"Wow. This is going to be an epic party."

"Super epic," Gracie enthused. "And better than Kyle Stanford's *Transformers* party."

Gracie threw her arms around Charity's neck to give her a squeeze.

"I'm glad you're here, Auntie Cherry." Charity tried not to wince at the nickname and hugged her niece close for a long moment. Loving the sweet smell of her. How could she have stayed away for so long?

"I'm glad too, Gracie," she admitted. The words sincere. She wasn't happy about the circumstances that had led to this moment, but now that she was surrounded by these people who loved her so dearly, she couldn't regret being here.

She released Gracie reluctantly, and Stuart gave her an affectionate smile. "Thank you for coming, Charity, it means the world to all of us."

Charity swallowed past the lump in her throat and gave her brother-in-law a watery smile. He steered Gracie away, telling the excited little girl that she had to get to the venue to greet her guests.

Her father had joined Miles in the doorway and grabbed hold of his hand to shake it vigorously. The older, taller man slung a familiar arm around Miles's shoulders and led him toward the table.

"We have so much to talk about," Faith said, drawing Charity's attention away from where her father was ushering Miles into a chair beside her mother. "But I'm afraid that duty calls. Mr. Hollingsworth told me that he'd booked a couple of rooms for you guys for the night. That's great. We're here for the weekend, and once the guests are gone and Gracie has crashed from all the sugar and excitement, the adults can have dinner and wine and catch up."

"Can I help with anything?" Charity asked, not wanting to watch her parents fuss over Miles any longer.

"There's nothing much to do. The venue has taken care of everything. You stay here for a while longer, catch up with Mom and Dad. And I know Sandra and Paul have been dying to talk with you."

Something in her face must have revealed how she felt about that idea, because Faith gave her a sad, sympathetic smile and squeezed her forearm reassuringly.

"I know it's hard, Cherry," she said, clearly misinterpreting the emotion behind Charity's reluctance. "But they love you too, and they've missed you so much. You're like a daughter to them. And honestly? I think having you around, keeps some vestige of Blaine alive for them."

The thought of keeping any part of Blaine alive was sickening to Charity, and she swallowed down her nausea before forcing herself to smile.

"We all have a lot to talk about, Faith," Charity said in a husky undertone, not wanting anyone to overhear her. "I haven't been fair to all of you. Or completely honest with you."

Faith's dark eyes gave her a lingering once-over.

"You seem so different," she said. "*Good* different. Mellow, self-confident...I haven't seen you like this in so long, Charity. I thought you were hiding from the world out there in the middle of nowhere. But I can't deny that whatever you've been doing over there, has truly worked wonders on the fragile, sad creature who left us three years ago."

"I'll tell you about it later, okay? Let's have fun today."

Miles couldn't ever recall being at a children's party before. The low-key celebrations his mother had given his siblings had been limited by budget. Miles had always been deemed too old for a birthday party.

Vicki's sixth birthday had been the closest any of them had come to having a proper childhood party. She had demanded princesses, poofy dresses, and lots of pink. She had received an acid pink sheet cake with *Happy Birthday, Victorya* piped in white icing across the top. Somebody had attempted to fix the spelling mistake, by turning the *y* into an *i*, but they had only succeeded in making the error more obvious. Luckily Vicki, who at that point could barely spell her own name, hadn't noticed.

Their mother, Hugh, and Miles had made a huge fuss over the birthday girl. And she had been ecstatic in her "princess" dress made from one of their mother's old skirts, the tiara Miles had fabricated with pipe cleaners and foil, and the makeup, Hugh had caked onto her face.

It had been memorable. And nowhere near the scale of this event.

Faith and Stuart Culpepper had rented the entire kids carnival section of the estate. As far as Miles could tell, there were in excess of fifty rug rats, hopped up on sugar and the lukewarm winter sunshine, dashing around the place. There were trampolines, play gyms, a freaking bouncy castle, and a seemingly endless supply of food.

Miles stood apart, watching Charity with the kids. She didn't seem to care that she was wearing a pretty, feminine dress, she had kicked off her shoes, tucked her skirt into her underwear and was on one of the trampolines, having an absolute blast. He didn't like that some of the dads present appeared to be enjoying the view as much as he was, but who could blame them?

"Thank you for bringing our Charity back to us." The words were spoken by the tall, blonde older woman, whom Miles hadn't noticed standing beside him. He recognized her, of course. She had been the author of many of the Facebook posts on Blaine Davenport's memorial page.

He didn't respond to the woman's words but waited to see what she would do next.

"She's my daughter-in-law, you know? She was devastated when our Blaine died. Absolutely *devastated.* She was in a depression for so long, we feared we would lose her too. Feared she would follow him...you know? Because she couldn't stand to live without him." Something told Miles that that was what she had expected of Charity. For her to *follow* Blaine.

Fuck that.

"Charity would never do something so utterly *weak* and cowardly," he dismissed caustically. And watched in satisfaction, as the shot scored a direct hit. Blaine the Arsehole may not be with them any longer, but this woman had been complicit in his abuse of Charity, and Miles wasn't above taking potshots at her.

The woman's expression went frigid, all pretense of civility evaporating in the face of Miles's opening salvo.

"My son was a strong, proud, and honorable man. He adored his wife and she adored him."

"Bullshit, you knew exactly what a monster your son was. You raised him to be that way."

She gasped, an affronted hand going up to her chest.

"I don't know what Charity has told you...but I can assure you it's false. Blaine always loved her so much."

"Yeah, I like to burn the women I love too," Miles replied,

with a cynical snort. "And cut them and hurt them and humiliate them."

"You don't know *anything*." Her voice was an angry sibilant whisper, and she bristled with fury. "Charity was always difficult. I warned him not to marry her, warned him she would make a terrible pastor's wife, but he loved that girl beyond reason. She tested him. Tested his commitment to his faith and his parish. What was he supposed to do?"

"Not fucking hit her! Not mark her with cigarettes, or slice her with razor blades. Not break her ribs. He was supposed to love her for the amazing, spirited, beautiful woman she is."

"Yes, their relationship was very volatile, but there was always love there."

Her eyes shone with tears, and for a second, Miles felt sorry for her, for the mother who had lost her only child. Then he recalled Charity mentioning the times the very woman standing before him had driven Charity to hospital after one of her precious son's more violent beatings. How she had made Charity feel at fault. She had been as abusive as her son and Miles refused to waste another moment of sympathy on her.

He glanced over at Charity, then froze, she had climbed off the trampoline and was staring at them in concern.

Shit.

He was one-hundred-percent certain she wouldn't be pleased to know what they were discussing. He swallowed down the rest of what he wanted to say and smiled frigidly instead.

"If you'll excuse me," he said, with insincere politeness. "I see someone over there I'd much rather be spending time with."

He shoved his hands into his trouser pockets and, without waiting for a response, walked away.

"WHAT DID you tell that horrid, *horrid* man about my son?" Sandra cornered Charity in the ladies' room about forty-five minutes after Charity had seen her speaking with Miles. It had been very apparent from the woman's offended body language during that conversation that whatever Miles had been saying had not been to her liking.

Charity had an inkling of course, but she hadn't been able to pin him down to ask for specifics. Not when everybody wanted to speak with her and spend time with her.

Charity wasn't even sure how she felt about Miles talking to Sandra about Blaine. Angry? Upset? Hurt? Concerned? *Relieved*? It was all jumbled up and left her even more confused and frustrated than before.

Now her former mother-in-law had a hand clamped around Charity's wrist and looked utterly furious with her. Sandra's hand tightened when she caught sight of Charity's bare ring finger. She had stopped wearing the fake ring the day after she and Miles first made love.

"*Where* is your wedding ring? Why aren't you wearing it? It's a family heirloom. I want it back if you no longer intend to wear it."

In the past, Charity may have been cowed by the older woman's strong-arm tactics. Back when they had isolated her from her family, this woman had been the only maternal figure in her life, and Charity had been *grateful* to her for always taking care of her in the aftermath of Blaine's brutal attacks. She had long since recognized it for the carrot-and-stick routine that it had been. And Sandra Davenport no longer held any sway over her.

She yanked her wrist out of the woman's grip and glared right back.

"I told Miles nothing but the truth. And I donated the ring to a shelter for victims of domestic violence." She took a great deal of satisfaction in Sandra's appalled gasp. "It represented years of horrific abuse, and I hated wearing it. My fondest hope is that it has helped other women escape the same nightmare I lived through."

"You had no right! It was Paul's mother's ring."

Charity shrugged carelessly. "I can give you the name of the shelter, and you can try to track it down. But I never want to see the vile thing again."

Sandra blinked, appearing confused by Charity's nonchalance and lack of timidity. She inhaled, before changing the subject. Possibly in an attempt to goad an emotional response from Charity. "How *dare* you speak to that monster about my beautiful boy? And how *could* you sully my Blaine's memory by whoring yourself to a man like that?"

Well...if she had been trying to provoke a reaction from Charity, she succeeded with that. Because it pissed Charity all the way off.

"Miles Hollingsworth is a thousand times the man Blaine was. He's kind and gentle and caring. He would *never* hurt me. And like any sane man would be, he was sickened to hear what your son did to me in the name of love."

"You killed my boy," Sandra snapped. "I've been silent all these years, but we both know that it's your fault he's dead. You were toxic for him. And you drove him to do everything that he did. Drove him to kill himself."

"Your precious fucking son tried to kill me that last night. And the only reason he committed suicide was because he thought he'd succeeded. I knew him well, and I know that he wasn't man enough to face the consequences of what he thought he had done. I'm happy I'm free of him. Free of you. And I refuse to feel any guilt whatsoever about what happened that night. I lived in fear and pain and regret for too long. I left because I could no longer pretend to feel any kind of grief over his death. And because I couldn't stand to watch my parents mourn for him. But I'm back now. And I won't allow them to think of him as some saint anymore."

The woman went gray, and Charity folded her arms over her chest, staring her down.

"What are you going to do?" The words were choked and panic stricken, but Charity had not an ounce of pity for her.

"That's none of your concern. My *family* is none of your concern. I think it's past time that you and Paul gracefully exit our lives."

"Your parents are our best friends."

"Not for much longer," Charity promised grimly.

"Chari—"

The door to the restroom swung inward, and Faith and one of their cousins stepped inside. The two women were laughing, but the laughter froze when they sensed the tension in the room.

Faith eyed them warily. "Is everything okay?"

"Excuse me, I have to find Paul." Sandra said, and hastened past the two women. Faith watched her leave while Melly, their cousin, ducked into one of the stalls.

"What's up?" Faith asked, her voice hushed so that Melly wouldn't hear them. "I know coming back here must be so painful, and it has to dredge up bittersweet memories. I hope you're not finding it all too overwhelming."

"No. Not in the way you're thinking. I'm so happy to see everyone again. We have to have a family discussion tonight, after Gracie has settled down for the night. I have a lot to tell you."

"Anything to do with that lovely man who brought you here today? I confess, after seeing the way he looks at you, I was rather hoping you were moving on from the past. I know how much you loved Blaine...but it's time for..."

"Let me stop you right there, sis," Charity interrupted her quietly. "Miles has been *good* to me. And we've grown close during his convalescence, but what I have to tell you has nothing to do with him. He and I soon will part as friends..." She ignored the painful jab in the vicinity of her heart as she uttered those surprisingly difficult words and continued on. "And that will be the end of it. As for Blaine...I haven't felt anything close to love for him in a very long time."

"I don't understand."

Charity grabbed her sister's hand and squeezed it.

"Enjoy the party. I'll explain later, okay?" Faith nodded, and Charity drew her into a fierce, tight hug. "I'm so happy to be here."

As far as Miles could tell, the party was a (literal) screaming success. After the last excited little guests departed, Faith and Stuart ushered Gracie to their room for a bath and Charity's parents, Erik and Rita, once again profusely thanked Miles for bringing Charity to the party, before heading to their suite to freshen up before dinner.

That left Charity and Miles standing in the foyer of the hotel.

"Faith told me that you've arranged a room for us," Charity

said, her voice cold and curt. He tried not to be disheartened by all that ice and nodded.

"We're in one of the cottages. It has two bedrooms. I wasn't sure if you wanted your family to know about...about us. And I wasn't sure how you would feel after what I did."

She sighed heavily. "Let's go. I need a long, hot shower. We'll discuss this when we get to the cottage."

MILES SHOWERED and changed for dinner, but he wondered if he should fry himself an egg—he could only get the self-catered cottage at such short notice—and give Charity and her family privacy to have their long overdue talk.

After he and Charity had reached the cottage, she had barely given the quaint abode a second glance, instead heading straight to her room...telling him that they would "talk later". They shared a bathroom, and he had allowed her first dibs at the shower, before spending a torturous fifteen minutes in a steamy bathroom that smelled just like her.

Now, nearly half an hour after her promise to talk, he sat on the side of his massive bed and stared at the bedside clock, watching the minutes creep by, and wondering when *later* would be.

Fuck. This was ridiculous.

He picked up his phone to send Charity a text:

MILES
I think I'll stay in tonight.

CHARITY
Why?

MILES
Figured you all should have some privacy.

The staccato rap on his bedroom door startled him, and he frowned.

"Come."

The door swung inward, and Charity stepped into his room, a wry smile on her lips.

"What's funny?" he asked, perplexed by that unexpected grin.

"For nearly two years, whenever you ordered me, or anyone else, to 'come', I'd imagine you saying it in the exact same clipped way to your lovers."

He couldn't quite figure out what she meant and stared at her in bewilderment.

"Y'know," she continued. "During your most intimate moments? Commanding them to *come* on cue."

He felt his neck flush, and the tips of his ears heated up.

"I'm not going to lie..." she said. "I always thought it was a little hot."

"*Charity*!" Miles knew he sounded like a scandalized old lady, but he couldn't help it. To say he was shocked was an understatement. For some reason, because he hadn't thought of her as a sexual being back then, he couldn't imagine her—no... *Mrs. Cole*—harboring such raunchy thoughts about him. Despite logically knowing that all along, she had been this same stunning woman standing before.

And *Christ*, she looked spectacular right now. He didn't think she could outdo the pretty pink of this afternoon, but tonight she looked empowered and sexy in a figure-hugging fire engine red dress that complemented her coloring marvelously. She wore the same vibrant shade on her lips. Her short hair had been slicked down, and she had done something to her eyes that made them smoky and seductive and mysterious all at the same time.

"I know right?" she laughed, in response to his outburst. "I tell you, I shocked even myself every time the thought crossed my mind. I deluded myself into thinking I've only recently started seeing you in a sexual light. But I've always found you attractive. I just wasn't ready to cope with anything remotely erotic before now."

"Are you still pissed off with me?" he asked hesitantly. She was in a strange mood. He couldn't figure it out. Not nervous, though he had expected her to be, given the dinner she was about to have with her family. Not angry, despite what he had done. Not sad.

She seemed almost...*ebullient.*

"I'm not pissed off with you, Miles. Well...I *was*. I was furious. But I had a lovely day, and it's hard to hold onto a good mad, when you're having fun and so freaking happy to be surrounded by your loved ones."

"That's—"

"*But*," she interrupted him, holding up an index finger to indicate that she was not yet done speaking. "What you did was so incredibly unacceptable and just because it worked out for the best, doesn't make it okay."

"I know."

"*Do* you, though? Or was this a matter of thinking it's better to ask for forgiveness than permission? Because, if that's the case, it's inexcusable. This was my decision to make, in my own time. The reason I decided not to come to the party, was partly because, yes, I was being cowardly and delaying the inevitable... but mostly because I wanted to enjoy our extremely finite time together. It's all we have."

She plunged those words into his guts like a sharp knife, reminding him of his place in her life with a succinct twist. While simultaneously offering him hope that their *finite* time together was not yet over.

"I'm sorry. I'm used to deciding what's best for everybody, and sometimes I stomp around like a bull in a china shop, without giving enough consideration to the harm I'm causing. I understand now that this situation required more delicate handling, but I just wanted to do something for you. Something useful. Worthwhile...something that you would perhaps value. And instead, I bollocksed it up. I'll get you flowers next time."

She smiled and left the doorway to slowly walk over to where he still sat on the bed. The sway of her hips in that figure-hugging dress was mesmerizing. Sonnets have been written about lesser things.

She didn't stop until she was standing between his parted thighs. He took a moment to appreciate the fact that his eyes were level with her perfectly pert and delicately scented cleavage.

And she grasped his jaw to slant his head until his gaze met hers.

"Eyes up, sir. I'm over here," she instructed him cheekily,

and he grinned. Her soft hands smoothed the hair back from his forehead, and she held his eyes for a long moment, while his breathing ceased completely, and his heart raced out of control in his chest.

"I'm terrified that if I forgive you for this, it means I'm falling into the same patterns again. Forgiving a man for a wrong he has done to me and thereby allowing his behavior to escalate."

"Not all men are like Blaine Davenport, Charity. Sometimes we think we know best and fuck up. Because we're idiots. We apologize, learn from our mistakes, and move forward."

Miles wasn't a short man, and he had rarely had anyone tower over him in this way before. But he found that he didn't mind it. And he enjoyed the power and control it gave her. Because he knew that, in this moment, she needed the added security. And he definitely didn't mind how close she was standing. How he could feel the heat coming off her, hear the escalation in her breathing, and feel the slight tremor in the soft fingers entangled in his hair.

"What you need to do," he continued, his voice hoarsening with the desire he was trying to keep under rigid control. "Is figure out which men are which."

"How do I do that?"

"You start by trusting yourself again. Stop punishing yourself for Blaine. What happened in your marriage was not your fault, Charity. It was all him and the parents who enabled him."

"I don't want you to stay in tonight," she said, the shift in topic abrupt yet somehow not jarring at all. "I want you with me when I tell them. I love them but I want, I don't know, a neutral party at the table, I suppose."

"Okay. But I have to warn you...I'm not neutral. I'm like 150 percent in your corner."

She beamed at him, and he sighed in relief. Grateful that, for now, she seemed to have let his dumb mistake slide.

"Well, that's okay too. But not a word. I don't need you to make things easier for me. I just...need you."

"You have me."

It was a promise. An oath. An utterly unbreakable vow.

She had him. And she would always have him. Now and forever.

Chapter Sixteen

When Charity and Miles reached the hotel foyer, it was to find her parents and Faith already waiting at reception.

"Where's Stuart?" Charity asked, confused by her brother-in-law's absence.

"He's staying with Gracie. We don't have a 'sitter here. And I'd rather not have a stranger watching my child. He told me to tell you he'd see you at breakfast."

"So, it's just us?"

"Sandra and Paul couldn't stay. She wasn't feeling very well," her mother explained, with a sympathetic smile. "I'm sorry. I'm sure you were looking forward to spending some time with them as well."

Charity bit the inside of her cheek to prevent herself from responding, and she felt the back of Mile's hand lightly brush against hers. The touch was so delicate she was sure no one present noticed. But she noticed...and she sucked in a grateful breath at that silent show of support.

"What's the plan?" Charity asked, with a forced smile.

"Dad's made a reservation at a fabulous restaurant on the neighboring estate," Faith said. "The one here is very nice, but we wanted a quieter venue, so that we could talk and catch up in relative peace."

"Great. Can Miles and I bum a lift with someone? His rental car is only being delivered in the morning."

"We can all fit into Daddy's showboat of an SUV," Faith piped up. "I don't know why anyone needs a massive vehicle like that."

"The only way to safely transport my golf clubs," their father quipped. When their tiny mother jabbed him in his ribs, he winced and added, "And my lovely wife, of course."

Their parents were a sickeningly cute couple. Both were surgeons—their mother cardiothoracic and their father neuro—and yet they were polar opposites in so many ways. Their mother was five foot one, and their father six foot three. He was pale, blond and hazel-eyed. She had a rich brown complexion, a shade or so darker than Charity's skin, midnight black hair and sultry eyes. He was slender and muscular. She was comfortably curvy.

He was loud and jovial. She was quiet and contemplative. He made stupid dad jokes, and she rarely got them.

They balanced each other perfectly.

Charity had never seen two people more in love. And Faith appeared to have found a similar relationship with Stuart. Charity had dreamed of having the same with Blaine...perhaps that's why it had been so hard to accept or admit what was happening at first. Because this was her template, and she had tried to force the abomination of a marriage she'd had with Blaine into this same mold.

Only it would never fit...the jagged edges of that relationship had been too ugly and too sharp and had ripped her fragile mold apart.

Her father enfolded her mother in an affectionate embrace and kissed the top of her head.

"Come on, kids," their father invited, leading the way. "To the dadmobile."

"Oh my God, Daddy. Do you have to be so lame in front of a guest?" Faith complained as they all filed out after the older couple. Charity laughed, enjoying the moment. Knowing that all too soon, there would be only confusion and pain.

Her hand drifted into Miles's...as she silently sought the unwavering support that she knew was right there for the taking. His palm kissed hers, and their fingers meshed.

For now, this would do.

THE EVENING WAS FILLED with small talk, reminiscences, laughter, and sentimentality. Miles enjoyed watching the light-hearted byplay between the older Coles and their daughters. This interaction between father and kids was not something he'd had plenty of opportunity to observe firsthand, and he found himself envious of that affectionate bond. He had lost his dad at an age when he had needed him most.

His mother had tried her best, bless her. His first shave had been with a pink woman's razor and floral scented shaving gel. The horrifically vague "birds and bees" talk after his first wet dream. The awkward condom discussion had involved a cucumber and a lot of accidentally torn condoms. If nothing else, he had learned that condoms were most certainly *not* infallible.

They were all cringe-y, but fond memories...but he occasionally wondered how life would have been with an adult male influence in his life.

As the evening progressed, Charity grew more and more distant. The others were starting to pick up on it, and Miles noticed Rita and Erik exchange a few concerned glances.

"I've decided that I'm moving back to the Cape after Miles returns to London." Charity blurted out over dessert and coffee. Her words effectively silenced all the slightly desperate banter that had been darting back and forth between Faith and the older Coles.

"That's wonderful, darling. We've all missed you so much." Rita squeezed Charity's arm, seemingly oblivious to her tension. Miles wasn't sure if they were just ignoring it and trying to pretend that everything was fine. Or if they genuinely could not tell how stressed Charity was.

"But?" The soft word came from Faith. Miles was relieved that *someone* could see that there was more to be said here.

Charity shot her sister a grateful look before gulping down a mouthful of red wine and then grimacing.

"But...I'd prefer never to see Sandra and Paul again."

"Charity," Rita's voice was gently chastising. "I know it's diffi—"

"Pleased don't say it's *difficult*," Charity interrupted her sharply. She cast a self-conscious glance around the room, but the other patrons hadn't noticed the slight rise in her tone. "The only thing that was difficult for me was having to watch you all cry for him. Miss him. Mourn him. And to pretend that I felt the same way."

Rita's mouth opened and then closed. Clearly lost for words. Erik was frowning, but Faith...Faith had paled. With her drawn face and distraught eyes, she looked like someone who had just witnessed a fatal accident.

"What did he *do* to you?" she asked, her voice pitched low, and Erik made a soft, distressed sound in the back of his throat. Rita still looked confused and horrified. Not as quick as her husband and older daughter...probably too sweet and insulated to even imagine such a thing happening to one of her precious children.

Charity laughed. There was no humor in the awful sound. Only bleakness and despair and anguish.

"Oh God," she murmured, scrubbing her palms over her face. "What *didn't* he do? It was like he followed an abusers' manual or something, because he did it all."

Rita made a choked sound, and her hand shot up to cover her mouth, her lovely eyes glittered fiercely above that hand.

"It started on our wedding night. It ended the night he killed himself. And he only did that because he thought he had killed *me*. He called his parents before he shot himself though.

"Knowing Blaine, he was too vain to allow our bodies to lay there undiscovered possibly for days. So, he called his parents who always took care of everything for him. And they came running. The police were not to know that he had tried to smother me with a pillow, of course. So, they concocted this story about him mistakenly thinking I was going to leave him. And, as a result, he shot himself while I was asleep. I was in shock, and traumatized to find myself covered in blood after regaining consciousness. Numb and confused...it was simpler to sit back and allow Sandra and Paul to dictate the narrative.

"Everything I said and did was always to preserve Blaine's perfect public image. And then his precious memory. I was so...*conditioned* to do what was expected of me by then that I, once again, allowed them to control my thoughts, my words, even my emotions.

"Blaine and I had an argument. He thought I was going to

leave him. He killed himself because he loved me too much to lose me. That was our story. I took the blame and his devoted parishioners hated me for what I did to their precious pastor. I played the victim, the villain, and the grieving widow all at the same time, when inside I was just so...*relieved* that he was gone. But you all were so sad. And I couldn't stand it. I had to get away."

"Why didn't you tell us?" Rita's tears had overflowed, and she was hanging on to Erik's arm as if her life depended on it. The older man also had tears streaming down his devastated face as he stared at his daughter in horrified silence.

"I was so ashamed." Her voice wobbled on the last word, and Miles palmed the vulnerable nape of her neck and squeezed it reassuringly to remind her that he was here if she needed him. "He made me feel like there was something wrong with me. Like I was to blame for everything he did. He didn't want me to work. I know you thought I was wasting my education and when I mentioned possibly joining, or starting, a practice, he... he..." She shook her head, but the starkness in her eyes told its own harrowing tale.

"He isolated me from everybody. Not only because he wanted to control me, but because he was so possessive that he felt threatened and was jealous of any other relationships. I once had lunch with Faith, and afterward, he demanded to know where we had gone. What we had spoken about. What I had worn. None of my answers satisfied him. And he snapped. It never took much for him to snap. He broke a couple of ribs that time, and Sandra drove me to hospital to have them strapped. To this day, I don't know how she explained it away. But she always had a handy excuse available for her clumsy daughter-in-law's silly accidents.

"And the worst part of it all is, that I was *so* grateful to her for always helping me. I didn't even understand until much later, how much she enabled him. She used my dependency on her to control my emotions. It wrecked me every time she told me she was *disappointed* in me for not being more aware of Blaine's needs. For driving him to such extreme measure. For being *so* difficult."

She stopped talking to take a thirsty drink of water. Faith was swearing, a steady stream of angry and impressively colorful invective. Rita and Erik were both still silently crying, and Charity, as if only now becoming aware of how her words had affected them blinked and gasped in horror.

"I'm sorry. I just wanted to get it all out. But I could have eased you into it a bit more—a little less..."

"Charity," Miles murmured, brushing the back of his hand against her cheek. "Give them a second to process."

"You were so quiet and withdrawn after the wedding. We all noticed, but..." Rita paused and shook her head bitterly. "*Sandra* told me you were just nervous about your new role as a pastor's wife. You wanted to make a good impression, she told us. You were trying to tone down your wild streak."

"She never had a fucking wild streak," Erik growled, surprising Miles with the unexpected profanity. Thus far, the cheerful semi-retired neurosurgeon had been silently absorbing every painful hit. Earlier, Erik Cole had struck Miles as a cheery, good-natured man, who rarely had a bad word to say about anyone. Now he understandably resembled someone whose entire world had tilted on its axis. "We entrusted our beautiful, exuberant, free-spirited *child* to them. And they turned that spirit against her. It never sat right with me when they called her wild. But she seemed content. So, settled. Fuck...*fuck*. Charity. I'm so sorry, baby."

"It's not your fault, Daddy," she said, taking hold of his hand and smiling at him through her tears. "None of you are to blame for his actions. And, it took me a very long time to understand this, but it's not *my* fault either. For too long I believed that it was. I believed if I changed everything about myself, I could be what he needed me to be. But he was sick and twisted and he enjoyed hurting me."

"We should have seen what was going on."

"How? I didn't let on. I became adept at hiding what was happening from the world. I withdrew from all of you. And I knew it must have been hurtful and confusing...And I'm so sorry for that."

"God, don't *apologize*!" Faith snapped. "Just don't!"

"Faith..."

Faith shook her head and tossed her napkin onto the table. "I can't deal with this. I just can't. I need some air. I'm sorry."

Rita sighed softly and shifted her chair away from the table. "I'll go speak to her."

"Why don't you three stay and talk?" Miles suggested quietly. "I'll make sure she's okay."

"Oh but—" Rita began to protest, and Miles offered the clearly torn woman, a sympathetic smile.

"It's fine. You stay. Charity, is that alright with you?"

"Yes. Thank you."

He squeezed her shoulders and dropped a quick kiss on her head, appearances be damned. And then went in search of Faith.

He found her outside, leaning against the wall of the building, and struggling to light a cigarette. Her hands were shaking too badly, and the matches kept flickering out in the breeze.

"Allow me," he offered. He removed the restaurant matchbook from her shaky grasp and expertly lit the cigarette, cupping his free hand around the flame to protect it from the wind.

"Thanks," she said, after a long drag. She exhaled, turning

her head to direct the stream of smoke away from them. But Miles still caught the fragrant hint of tobacco floating back on the breeze. "I bummed it off one of the waiters. I haven't touched one of these fucking things since before Gracie was born."

She furiously wiped her damp cheeks with the heel of her hand and huddled against the wall, seeking shelter from the cold wind. She had left her coat inside, and Miles shrugged out of his jacket to slide it over her shoulders.

"I wish he were still alive, so that I could slice off his balls and force feed them to him down a tube."

Miles sighed and plucked the cigarette from her fingers to take a drag as well, before handing it back. He had quit smoking ten years ago, and it wasn't a habit he was ever tempted to resume. But he figured he'd step off the wagon with her for a brief moment of solidarity.

He held the nicotine in his lungs for a beat, but the burn reminded him that this was not the best treatment of his newly healed lungs and he exhaled on a cough.

"I said something similar when she first told me. But I think we'd have to get in line behind Charity. She's strong, feisty and while I didn't know her before this happened to her...I can tell you that I'm in awe of the woman she is now."

"We should have known. Should have seen. She was so quiet. So fucking *perfect* all the time. And that wasn't my sister. My sister was loud and messy and crazy and boisterous."

"*Don't*," he muttered grimly. "Don't do this to yourself. To her. Self-recriminations won't help anyone right now. She may not quite be the same loud, messy, crazy woman you knew before. But she's your sister and she loves you all so much. She needs you to accept the woman she is now. Needs you to move forward with her."

"Who *are* you?" Faith asked, but the question wasn't hostile or angry. It was genuinely curious. "You show up here, Charity's boss, and yet clearly on intimate terms with her. How does that even work? How do we know you're not taking advantage of her?"

It was a fair question, and Miles shifted his shoulders uncomfortably, starting to feel the cold now.

"I get that, after what you've just learned about her marriage, it may be easy to assume that I'm just another arsehole taking advantage of a vulnerable woman. A woman with a history of being manipulated by arseholes. But in making that assumption, you're underestimating your sister and the woman she is now. I love her." It staggered him how easily those words drifted out of his mouth. They lingered on the breeze and—much like the nicotine in the drifting smoke—Miles loved the buzz they gave him. "And I'm here to offer her any emotional support she needs."

"She can get that from us now."

"I know." He kept his tone conciliatory. Wanting her to understand that he wasn't here to tread on toes or run interference between Charity and her family. "Charity and I are very aware that our relationship will end after I leave. We'll both go home to our families and our lives will continue on without each other. And we'll be the better for having had this beautiful thing between us."

"I'm so *angry* with her," Faith unexpectedly admitted, from between clenched teeth, taking another drag before tossing the cigarette to the ground and crushing it beneath her heel. "And I feel like I can't tell her that because she's already been through so much."

"You're her older sister. I reckon you're entitled to speak your mind."

"How can I?"

"Trust me, Charity is not a fragile flower. Fuck...despite

everything she survived with that bastard—no, likely *because* of it—she's one of the strongest people I know."

"I feel like I don't even know her anymore. Three years she was in that marriage, and then another three years after that, hiding out there in the middle of nowhere. And she never told us. We never had an inkling. Meanwhile we ate with those horrid people, cried with them, laughed with them. We fucking *loved* them and they broke our girl."

She covered her face with her hands, sobs shuddering through her slender frame and Miles, after a brief hesitation, enfolded her in his arms. She was similar in height to Charity, but softer, rounder.

He preferred Charity's leaner, sleekly muscled body. A fact which constantly surprised him, since he had always enjoyed soft, rounded curves before.

"They didn't break her. She's in that restaurant, fiercely unbroken, and ready to share her war stories with you. It may have taken longer than you feel it should have...but it's happening right now. And I think you should be in there. To hear what she has to say."

"God." Her voice was muffled against his shoulder. "Your family must find you insufferable. You're such a fucking know it all."

"Yes," he agreed somberly. "And, worse, I'm right *all* the time."

She made a sound, something between a sob and laugh and moved out of his arms.

He plucked his handkerchief from the front pocket of the dinner jacket she still had draped over her shoulders and offered it to her. She took it with a soft murmur of thanks and used it to dab at her cheeks and vigorously blow her nose.

"Hope you weren't expecting this back?" she asked tartly, taking one last swipe at her nose, and he chuckled.

"You and Charity are very much alike, you know?" he pointed out, with a wry shake of his head.

"I used to think so," Faith said with a heavy sigh.

"Come on. Let's get in out of the cold."

"Today was weird." Charity shrugged out of her coat and draped it over the back of the plush sofa in their quaint cottage. Because of her earlier tension and dread, she hadn't paid much attention to the accommodation Miles had arranged for them. This place was simply fantastic. Beautifully furnished, comfortable, and luxurious.

She sank onto the large sofa and absently rubbed the back of her neck, wincing at the knots she found there. Miles was in the kitchen, rummaging through the cupboards. He paused in his search for whatever to stare at her assessingly.

"Tea?"

Charity snorted in amusement at the prosaic question. It was so typical of Miles.

"You do know that's your go-to remedy for everything, right? Last year, when your sister fell and twisted her ankle? You immediately called for tea. When your brother's boyfriend dumped him the year before? Extra sugar in the tea."

"It does cure all ills," he murmured sagely, and filled the kettle.

"I don't need tea, Miles."

He shoved his hands into his trouser pockets and lifted his head to look at her. God, he was so wildly beautiful. It was unfathomable to her that she had once found him anything less than gorgeous. Jaw dark with day old stubble, hair shaggy and in disarray thanks to the wind. His white dress shirt was open at the collar and rolled up to his elbows. The expensive fabric strained at the muscular shoulders, proof of how much he had bulked up since his illness.

He was amazing, caring, concerned...and so damned *present.*

What the hell was she going to do without him?

It was a distressing question, best left for another day, but it still sent a shudder of anxiety down her spine.

She was going to miss him so fricking much. And she didn't want to spend the time she had left with him, nursing anger or grudges. He was here now.

And she loved him.

"I need you."

His dimple deepened. Making an appearance before the actual smile graced his lips.

When he spoke, his voice brushed the air like silk floating on a gentle breeze, "I told you earlier, my love, you have me."

Her eyes welled up, and he made a dismayed sound in the back of his throat. She held out her hand to him, and he was across the floor, and by her side in an instant, his hand in hers.

"Can you just hold me?"

He made a gruff sound and sank down beside her, gathering her close, as if she were the most precious thing in the entire world. She melted into that hold, hating how much it comforted her.

He was humming, his breath stirring the hair at her temple. The notes were melodic, and unrecognizable at first. But the tune organized itself into something familiar.

And a little... incongruous.

"*I'm Too Sexy*?" she asked with an incredulous blink, and lifted her head to stare at him.

He grinned sheepishly. "I used to hum it to Hugh and Vicki when they couldn't sleep. It was the *only* song that ever came to mind. Don't ask me why."

She laughed. "Your mind is a weird and wonderful thing."

She snuggled up against his chest again, her fingers toying with his shirt buttons. After a beat, he went back to humming, his hands gently stroking her back. But Charity couldn't settle down and she sighed restlessly in the middle of what she assumed was the second verse. Hard to tell without the accompanying lyrics.

The humming stopped. "What's wrong?"

"It's all I can think of now," she complained, and his hands stopped stroking.

"What?" His voice was puzzled, and she lifted her head to meet his somber gaze.

"How very much too sexy you are for this damned shirt." Her words startled a laugh from him, and she grinned. "So maybe you should get rid of it. You're too sexy for your pants too, by the way. And definitely way, way, *way* too sexy for your boxers."

"Christ, you're just..." He paused in mid-sentence and swallowed, his eyes devouring her face. The gravity in those gray depths, at odds with the lightness of the moment. "So, fucking adorable."

"Stop speaking, Mr. Hollingsworth," she whispered, framing his face with her palms. "And kiss me."

"Charity I—" She made an impatient sound in the back of throat and covered his mouth. Swallowing the rest of his words as she triumphantly claimed the kiss that she had demanded.

No further words were required after that.

"WHY DO you love these monstrously huge cars?" Charity complained as she heaved herself into the rental car the following morning. This one was a cherry red Jeep Wrangler... big, boxy, and uncomfortably high.

The drive back would take between six to eight hours and they had to leave immediately after breakfast.

The morning meal had been subdued. Her family still reeling after the previous night's revelations. Faith had obviously filled Stuart in, because the first thing he had done upon seeing her that morning was tug her into a protective bear hug. It had been comforting. Stuart had always been like a brother to her. Her sister's high school sweetheart, he had been a constant presence in their family for as long as she could remember.

Faith, in the meantime, could barely make eye contact with her. Her responses to Charity's comments and questions had been clipped to the point of rudeness. Charity was trying to be patient but part of her wanted to grab her sister by the shoulders and shake her.

Her mother was over-compensating, lavishing her with attention and hugs and endearments, while looking on the verge of tears throughout breakfast. While her father had been so *quiet*. Her father who always found the funny in every situation, who was filled to the brim with stupid dad jokes, whose voice was always the loudest and most cheerful in every room, had barely spoken half a dozen words all morning.

In the end, it was almost a relief to leave. But the farewells had been genuine and gut-wrenching. Her father and mother clung to her in a three-way hug that felt like it would never end.

Stuart kissed her on the cheek and made her promise to call if she needed anything.

And Faith...Charity's eyes flooded with tears as she waved her family goodbye and watched them grow smaller and smaller in the rear window. Faith had hugged her fiercely, almost painfully and had whispered, "I'm so fucking angry with you. And Blaine. I'm *pissed* at everything and everyone right now. And I don't know how to cope. I love you, you dozy cow. Okay? But I'm just so... *mad* at you."

"I know."

"I shouldn't be."

"You should, I'm angry with myself as well. I should have told you. Told someone."

"You should have *trusted* us."

"Yes."

"I love you. We'll work it out. And heal. As a family."

"I know."

"Go. Enjoy the rest of your shagfest with Mr. Know-It-All over there. But you *hurry* home. Your life has been on hold for far too long."

The car took a corner, and when she lost sight of her waving family, Charity promptly burst into tears.

She wasn't even aware that Miles had pulled over until she felt his arms around her.

"Charity." His voice was a gruff, pain-filled whisper. "You don't have to leave. You can stay. I won't hold it against you. I just...I want you to be happy."

The thought of staying hadn't even occurred to her, and his words made her cry harder, because with the offer now on the table, she *had* to consider it. She could stay. Give up the little time she had left with Miles, and start the healing process with her family.

What was to be gained by returning with Miles? A few weeks more of tormenting herself with something she could not have? There was nothing back there for her. Her future, her life...it was here.

All she had to do was tell him to turn around.

She pushed herself away from him and stared into his harsh face resentfully. Hating that he had offered her this choice.

Why couldn't he just be selfish for once? Tell her she *had* to return with him? Be a controlling dick? Why couldn't he make this easy for her?

In that moment she hated him a little. Hated him intensely for making her love him so much.

Her body curled into a paroxysm of agony as she struggled with this impossible decision. Only it shouldn't be impossible. It should be easy...

She had once been forced to choose a man over her family. But that hadn't been a real choice.

This *was*...and it killed her that it was so hard.

His phone buzzed, providing a welcome diversion to the intensity of the moment, and Charity glanced over to where he had affixed the device to the dashboard. A picture of Stormy floated onto the screen, and Charity hiccoughed, her sobs lessening. She stared at the picture fixedly, *gratefully*. It was the answer she had been searching for.

This wasn't just about her and Miles.

"I have to go back to Riversend with you," she managed to say between lessening sobs.

He did nothing to hide the naked relief in his eyes. But because he was such a good guy, he still warily asked, "Are you sure?"

"I have to say goodbye to George and Amos, and my f-friends..." New friends, people she had only recently allowed into her heart and life. The thought of bidding them farewell was surprisingly hard. But it *was* the right thing to do. Leaving without so much as a goodbye would be unforgivable. "I have to say g-goodbye to St-St...*Stormy*."

"Okay. If you're sure."

"I'm sure," she said. Strength and conviction in her voice. "I have to say goodbye to *you*, Miles. A proper goodbye. My family? Life here? It's my future. But I'm not quite done with this bit of my past yet."

Even though she said she wasn't done with it, it still hurt like hell to already be referred to as part of her past. But still, he'd take it. And be damned grateful for it. Because for a dreadful, heartbreaking, devastating moment there, he had been so certain that this was *it* for them.

Goodbye.

But it wasn't. Not yet.

It was a reprieve. A stay of execution. All the more painful because he knew that it was temporary...the last gasp of a dying relationship.

He stared into her tear-drenched face. Her nose was red, her cheeks blotchy, eyes red and swollen...and yet she had never been more beautiful.

This was the beginning of the end for them. And Miles was going to make damned sure their journey to that end followed an iridescent rainbow path toward a glorious technicolor sunset.

Chapter Seventeen

"Why do I have to look at these?" Miles glared at the tablet Charity had placed on the table in front of him. He had recoiled from it like it was a venomous snake.

"You need to find my replacement."

She had compiled a list of résumés that she felt were suitable and wanted to start arranging interviews. He acted cagey whenever she mentioned his return to London, and in the three days since they had returned from Gracie's party, he hadn't mentioned a possible departure date yet.

Not that she was pushing him for one. She was dreading it as much as he appeared to be. But she had to arrange for the closure of the house. Had to organize her transportation back to the Cape. Pack. All of that would be much easier to plan if she had some dates to work with.

"You're irreplaceable."

The words were gruff and practically barked at her. But Charity's heart still turned to mush and puddled into her stomach, leaving her feeling warm and fuzzy and a little queasy. Because he kept saying things like that, and she wanted to scream at him to just *stop*.

It wasn't making the situation any easier.

"Miles," she began tentatively. "We're living in a bubble right now. And it's wonderful in here. Everything feels so right between us. But none of this is real. A few months from now, you'll be remembering this in fond confusion and wondering why it all felt so intense."

He shook his head and swept the tablet aside in an irritated motion. She encased his hand in both of hers and gave it a comforting squeeze.

"You know it's true."

"This is real to *me*, Charity. Excruciatingly fucking real."

She swallowed trying to ease the ache that had lodged in her throat.

She was beginning to think she should have chosen to stay with her family when he had given her the option to do so. She could have returned later to say her goodbyes and sort out her belongings.

Because this protracted farewell with Miles wasn't a sweet, romantic interlude filled with warm, wonderful moments.

It was raw and brutally intense.

"Let's go for a walk," she suggested. Pushing to her feet, she tugged at his hand, and he reluctantly allowed himself to be pulled up. "The fresh air will do us both some good."

Stormy danced around their feet. *Walk* was her absolute favorite word, and she went into rapturous spasms every time somebody said it. She dashed back and forth between the kitchen door and Miles, clearly keen to get going.

"Okay, pup, we're getting there," Miles muttered, shaking his head. They grabbed their coats and Stormy's leash and harness.

"She's going to miss the lake," Miles observed, as he watched his dog streak up the shore ahead of them. Lately he had allowed her more freedom off leash on their walks, especially when they walked along the familiar lakeshore.

"Do you think you'll be able to devote the same amount of time to her, when you're back at work?" Charity asked. It was a question that had begun to plague her a lot recently. Man and dog were inseparable, and she wasn't sure how Stormy was going to cope once she wasn't the center of Miles's universe anymore.

He slanted her a surprised look. "Of course, I will."

The absolute certainty in his voice surprised her.

"She'll be coming in to work with me. I'm considering implementing a dog friendly workplace. A lot of companies are doing it. It reduces stress, boosts morale and productivity..."

"You've been reading up on it, I take it?" she said, a wry note in her voice and he wrinkled his nose, before grinning sheepishly.

"*Busted.* Yes. I was trying to figure out how I could get away with bringing her to work every day and then reckoned it wouldn't be fair unless everybody else is allowed the same opportunity. The dogs would have to be socialized, toilet-trained, and we naturally have to consider those with phobias and allergies as well. But it's doable. But I for damned sure am not leaving Stormy without me for long stretches at a time."

"That's fantastic, Miles," Charity said, happy for both man and dog. Well, mostly for Miles. The man was a wreck without his dog.

Stormy was enthusiastically digging a hole in the soft white sand, a few yards ahead of them, and Charity smiled at her antics. She was going to miss the adorable foundling.

"Tell me what you miss most about your home?" she impulsively invited. Wanting him to focus on the good things he would be returning to and obsess less about what he was leaving behind.

He gave a look that told her he knew exactly what she was doing, but he shifted his shoulders restlessly and inhaled deeply.

"My family obviously. And their messy problems. They've been keeping me out of their relationship and work dramas since I've been here, and I admit it's left me feeling useless. Which is odd since, six months ago, I would probably dearly have loved to be left out of their chaotic personal lives."

"I don't believe that. You like being needed by them. Admit it."

"Maybe I do. A little bit."

"Of course, you do. More than a little bit I'd say. What else do you miss? Work?"

"Not entirely. I thought I'd go stir crazy not knowing what was happening with the business...but I've barely given it a second thought. I trust Bryan to keep things running smoothly and I trust Hugh to have my—and the family's—best interests at heart. I think I may loosen the reins once I return, allow Hugh more leeway to try new things."

"What else do you miss? A more active social life?"

He snorted at that.

"How many times do I have to tell you that I'm shit with people, before you believe me?"

"But you're *not* shit with people. I've seen you with the people in town. With Sam and Greyson. George and Amos. They like you, and they all strike me as pretty decent judges of character."

"Half of the people you've listed work for me. They have a vested interest in keeping me happy."

Charity laughed, genuinely amused by that statement. "I mean, have you *met* George Clark and Amos Moloi? Two of the most straight-talking, zero bullshit old men I've ever had the pleasure of knowing? They couldn't care less about keeping you happy. But they do because they like you. More people than you realize like you, Miles."

He stopped walking and turned to face her, his eyes narrowed against the blustery wind.

"What's this about, Charity?"

"I don't know. I just wish you could see yourself the way I do."

"And how's that?" His voice had deepened, roughened. The gravel scraped her raw and left her on fire.

Stormy's loud squeal saved her from replying, and they both looked up in alarm at the sound. The dog had leaped back from the hole and was still yelping, her left front paw held aloft in obvious pain.

"*Shit*!" Miles streaked down the beach toward his still crying dog, with Charity close behind. By the time she caught up, he was on his knees in the sand, the trembling pup held protectively in his lap. He was examining the paw.

"One of the pads is bleeding. It doesn't look too terrible, but I'm not taking any chances, we have to get her to the vet."

"Oh my God," Charity went to her knees beside him and stared at the sluggishly bleeding paw. The blood was mixed with fine beach sand. The wound would definitely need cleaning. "Did she cut herself? Is there glass in there? A nail?"

"No." He shook his head grimly, glaring out at the tranquil lake. "I think she got nipped by a crab. It was scuttling toward the water by the time I reached her." He got up, the shivering, whimpering dog still gently cradled in his arms.

They were all piled into the SUV and on their way in under ten minutes. Stormy, clearly in pain, whined all the way to town and Miles, his eyes stark and his features taut, barely spoke a word during the entire drive.

Fortunately, Dr. McGregor considered the situation enough of an emergency to see them immediately, but after cleaning the wound and examining it, he smiled reassuringly at the still tense Miles.

"It's just a flesh wound, as they say in the movies," he quipped. "I'll apply some salve and bandage the paw, but you won't need to keep it on overnight or anything. It's just to allow the salve some time to work without being licked off. Besides, this young miss is feeling very sorry for herself. A bandage will make her feel vindicated after all this drama. I'll give her an anti-inflammatory shot, prescribe a course of antibiotics, and she'll be right as rain soon enough."

"You sure about that?" Miles barked, but the vet—obviously quite used to being barked, and snapped, and snarled at—merely smiled gently.

"Absolutely certain. I think you were right about a crab being the likely culprit. If nothing else, this will give her a healthy respect for all things crustacean. Sometimes we need to learn life's lessons the hard way."

Miles sagged in relief and after bombarding the vet with after care questions, they finally left. Charity watched as he murmured sweet, reassuring, little nothings to a sleepy Stormy... entirely focused on his dog, but still concerned enough about Charity to constantly check over his shoulder if she was following.

She had once believed that Blaine would be the literal death of her. But this complicated, sweet, caring man...*he* was the one who was going to end her. And the longer she stayed here with him like this, the worse it was going to be. She had to leave.

Soon.

Because if she didn't, she wouldn't have a beating heart left in her chest when she returned home to her family. Miles would have stolen it from her completely.

The drive back to the house was as silent as it had been in to town...but when he parked the car in the basement garage, she broke the silence before he could unbuckle his seatbelt.

"I'm leaving."

His head swiveled, and his intense eyes honed in on her face. "What do you mean?"

"On Saturday. I think that'll give me enough time to say my goodbyes and arrange to ship the bulk of my things to my parents. I'll leave you the shortlist of names and résumés for my replacement. If you don't want to do it, I'm sure Lia will be happy to help. She knows a few of the ladies on the list and can give you some sound advice on who would be best for the job."

"But...what about us?"

"Miles. This is for the best. Before we get too *attached*."

"What the fuck does *that* mean?" His voice rose, and Stormy whimpered, startled out of a sound sleep. "Christ, Charity, I'm already attached. And I *know* you are as well. Why are you cheating us out of the last bit of time we could have together?"

She swiped at a few errant tears, refusing to make this worse by crying. But it was so hard when he looked so unreservedly distraught. Like his whole world was imploding.

"I'm sorry, Miles. I thought I could do this. But I can't. I can't do the long, lingering goodbye thing. I wish..." She shook her head. Nothing she said now could make this hurt less, for either of them. "I'm sorry."

She pushed open the door and trudged toward the staircase. She heard the driver's door open and shut, and his feet pounding on the polished concrete floor as he ran to catch up with her.

Which he did...cutting off her route to the stairs with the bulk of his body.

"You can't do this," he growled, his teeth clenched, and his entire body bristling.

"Miles, please, don't make this more difficult than it has to be."

"Can you at least fucking tell me why?"

"Why? Because you make me feel too *much*. Because I have to have something of myself left when I leave here...and if I stay here much longer I won't. It'll all belong to you. And I'll be no good to anyone then."

"Goddamnit, Charity, you're not the only one who—" His hand sliced through the air, a sudden, vicious movement that came out of nowhere, and Charity flinched reflexively, covering her head with her arms.

It was an instinctive reaction, made in response to the movement and not the man. And she uncurled from her protective huddle within seconds. Feeling sheepish for the overreaction to what she had always known was just an angry gesture, she lifted her eyes, her immediate instinct to apologize to Miles. But he was staring at her fixedly, his throat working, his eyes wide, his skin deathly pale.

He looked wrecked and wretched. "I wasn't going to...I would never..."

That he felt the need to *explain* broke her heart. As if she would ever believe he would hurt her.

As if he could.

"No, Miles. Of course, you wouldn't. I'm sorry. It wasn't you. I just reacted to the sudden movement."

"I wouldn't hurt you." He looked dazed, hurt, shocked.

"I know." She took his hand and squeezed it, wanting to reassure him. "Miles. I know that. Okay? This is not a you thing.

This is very much a *me* thing. And one of the countless things I have to fix about myself. I mean, we can't even have a decent argument without me flaking out on you. That's not normal, Miles, and it's on the long list of reasons this has to end. Sooner rather than later."

He didn't respond. His eyes still had that harrowing, hollow look in them, and Charity wasn't sure if anything she said now could improve the situation.

"I have to get Stormy," he murmured, turning away stiffly.

"Miles..." His name was a miserable whisper on her lips. Not loud enough for him to hear and turn back.

But it was probably better if he didn't turn back. If he never turned to her again.

She stifled a sob and screwed her eyes shut.

Inhaled deeply, threw back her shoulders...

And continued on.

FOR THE FIRST time in over two weeks, they did not share a bed. And Miles found himself unable to sleep because of it.

He missed her. Missed the way she hogged the covers, and that adorable snorting snuffle on every third breath. He missed her warmth, and the way she often curled up tightly against his side, crowding him almost off the bed. He had quickly grown accustomed to her presence, and not having her next to him felt wrong.

The pain of loss was intolerable. And it was made worse by his recognition that this was how the next thousand nights would be. And the thousand after that.

This was what all his nights would be like.

He would be alone. Lonely. Lost.

Forever...

He sat up in bed, propping himself up against the headboard to stare into the black, desolate void of the night. The perfect canvas against which to replay the tormenting memory of Charity flinching away from him, over and over again.

If he lived to be a hundred, he would never forget the way she had curled herself up in fright against the violence of his movement. He had been responsible for that reaction. No matter what she said, the blame lay with him. He knew her history and should have foreseen how she would react to an unpredictable motion like that in the middle of a heated argument.

It had been fucking unforgivable.

He scrubbed his hands over his face. Calling himself every awful name under the sun.

And she was leaving him. So much sooner than he was ready to let her go. But considering how today went that was probably for the best anyway.

His phone chimed, and he glared at its brightly lit face on the nightstand. He reached for it, and then frowned at the message displayed on the lock screen.

VICKI

Hey!!Guess what? 😊

He sighed and swiped the screen to get into his message app. Vicki may prove exactly the diversion he needed right now.

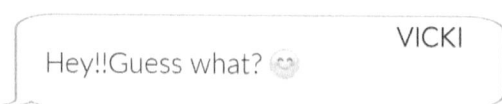

MILES
What?

VICKI
You'll find out soon enough

What the hell was that supposed to mean?

MILES
What are you up to, Vic?

VICKI
Who me?????? Nothing. Just your beloved sister being beloved 😇 Hugs!!!!!!!!!!

MILES
Vicki!!!!

VICKI
Miss you, big bruvva 😘 😘

He sent a few more texts demanding answers, but they remained unread.

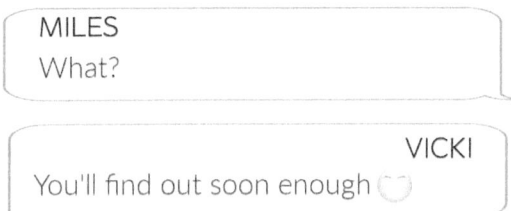

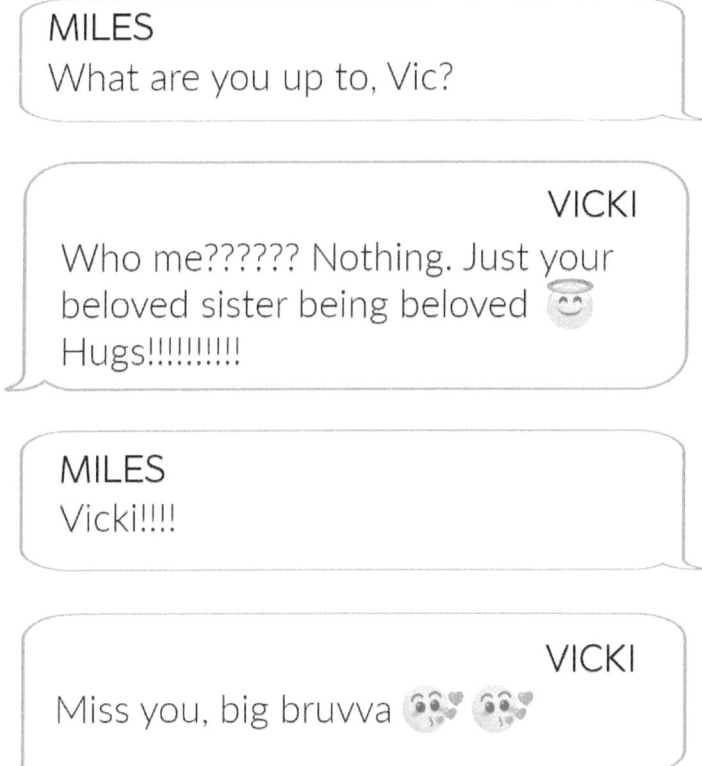

Damn it!

He hoped she wasn't up to something ridiculous again. His sister was sweet, creative, and smart as a whip...but she was stupidly impulsive at times. He trusted that Chambers would keep her from doing anything too imprudent.

He sighed disconsolately. As diversions went, this one hadn't been particularly effective because his mind refocused on Charity all too damned soon.

He should get used to it. Because this was just the start of the rest of his miserable life without her.

Charity was already prepping for breakfast by the time Miles dragged himself out of bed and into the kitchen the following morning. He had succumbed to a restless doze shortly before sunrise and had barely scraped together three hours of sleep.

He was in a dark emotional space, and seeing her standing in the middle of the kitchen back in her Mrs. *Fucking* Cole get up, felt like a shot to the heart.

"Morning," she greeted, eyes averted, as she removed a carton of eggs from the fridge.

He said nothing. Instead he glared at her until she lifted her gaze to meet his.

"Why are you dressed like that?"

She carefully placed the eggs on the island between them and gave him an imploring look. "Miles..."

"*Why*, Charity?"

"I thought it would be easier."

"Easier to use the same shield that worked for you after years of spousal abuse?" Didn't she get what a total fucking affront that was? "You thought you needed it with me? After everything we..."

His voice cracked, and he shook his head in frustration.

"It's not like that," she hastened to explain. "Miles, I never intended to insult or to hurt you. I just feel less vulnerable with a clearly defined role to play. No misunderstandings...no emotions. Just work. Until I leave."

He. Could. Not. Bear. It.

He hated seeing her like this. Dressed in that horrendous armor. As if she needed to physically shield herself from him.

She was breaking his heart to pieces, and she thought *she* was the one who needed protection?

Stormy growled. The sound was low and vicious and so uncharacteristic, it shocked both of them into staring at her. At first Miles assumed she was reacting to the tension in the room, but the little dog was facing the basement door, her hackles up and her lips raised in a snarl.

She looked about as threatening as a mouse, but it was clear that something had upset her. Miles frowned at the basement door, wondering what had set her off.

And then he heard it. Footsteps on the staircase, accompanied by chatter and laughter and...

"*Fuck*," he swore shakily, and pinched the bridge of his nose wearily. Well, this explained Vicki's late-night text. It was literally the last thing he needed right now.

The door swung inward, and Stormy's growls escalated into high-pitched, excited yaps.

The delighted feminine squeal that greeted the barking grated on Miles's nerve endings. His sister was always so *shrill*.

"Oh my God, what's this? A pupper? Who are you, buddy?" Vicki asked, scooping Stormy up into her arms. The dog didn't know how to react. Looking excited and terrified and ecstatic all at the same time. Her tail was wagging and her body shaking and her tongue lapping at every bit of available skin she could find.

"Christ, give her to me, you're scaring her," Miles muttered, possessively taking his dog back and hugging her close to his chest. Vicki had a habit of claiming his possessions. And he would be damned if she thought she could do the same with Stormy.

"Hullo, big brother, did you miss me?" Vicki grinned, launching herself at him and hugging him tightly. Stormy squirmed between them, and Miles shifted her aside before reciprocating with a stiff, one-armed hug.

"What the hell are you doing here? What about the shop?"

"*Surprise*!" Vicki spread her arms and added a cheeky grin and jazz hands to the expansive motion. "You're always so cagey on the phone and truly *pathetic* at texts. And when you refused to send me any proof of health photos, I had no option but to take matters into my own hands. I traded in my winter vacation for a mini summer break, so that I could come down here to see for myself how you're doing. Linda"—her manager—"and I swapped some things around and here I am! Ooh, and check it out." She directed her jazz hands toward the door, where Tyler Chambers, her large, hulking bodyguard, was courteously helping an older woman up the stairs.

"*Mum*?" Miles exclaimed. His face broke into a delighted grin at the sight of the older woman. "But you hate flying."

"Well, I've never tried it before, have I?" his mother, ever practical, pointed out. "I can't hate something I've never tried."

"But you never *wanted* to try it," he said. Overwhelmed by the unexpectedness of this, he still wasn't sure how the hell they had gotten here. Or why nobody had bothered to let him know of their imminent arrival.

"Like your sister said, you weren't very forthcoming in your phone calls. And when she suggested we do this, I did what any concerned mother would do, I packed my bags. So here we are." As if it were the simplest thing in the world. Never mind that she had broken a lifelong vow never to climb into "one of those tin cans that had no business hurtling through the sky at obscene speeds".

"Your sweet friend, Bryan, was kind enough to lend us his aeroplane."

"It's *my* 'plane, Mum."

She gave a disapproving *tut* and shook her head critically. Making him feel about ten years old. "It's not nice to brag, Miles."

"Yes, Mum. Sorry," he apologized, only because it was expected of him

She tilted her head to give him a critical once-over.

"You've gained weight. Good," she said, with an approving nod. "And put on some color. You look so much better. That *very* nice man, George, was telling us on the way here from the airport, that you've been doing well. Now come over here, give your old mum a kiss, and tell her how happy you are to see her."

His smile widened, and put Stormy down, to envelope his pleasantly round mum in an affectionate hug, planting a big kiss on her cheek in the process.

"I'm always happy to see you, Gorgeous. You know that."

He stepped away from her and gave her an assessing once over. Gratified to note that she looked hale and hearty as well.

"Hello, Mrs. Cole," Vicki's cheerful greeting instantly distracted Miles, and his head swiveled to see Vicki smiling up at the taller Charity. "I'm sorry we gave you no advance warning...I know you're probably miffed we didn't give you time to prepare for our visit. But we wanted to surprise him."

Charity gave Vicki a stiff smile.

"It's nice to see you again, Miss Hollingsworth. I trust you've been well?"

"Well enough. Much better than my brother, that's for sure. There'll be three extra guests, Mrs. Cole. For the remainder of Miles's stay. I think you can put the Hulk in Hughie's room."

Fuck. Fuckfuckfuck...*FUCK!*

This was so wrong. He hated that Vicki was treating the woman he loved like Mrs. Cole, the trusty housekeeper.

And yet...Charity had made it abundantly clear earlier, that that was exactly what she wanted.

"I was just preparing Mr. Hollingsworth's breakfast. Are you all hungry? Or would you like to settle into your rooms first, and have me fix you something later?"

Miles glowered at her. Fuming that, without any trace of sarcasm or irony, he had gone right back to being Mr. Hollingsworth.

Chapter Eighteen

"Oh, I think we can settle in and get refreshed before having breakfast," Vicki replied, oblivious to Miles's impotent fury. She invited their mother over, with a wave of her hand. "Mum, come and meet Mrs. Cole. She's a miracle worker. She can get anything you need. At any time of the day or night. I once needed an emergency...uhm... never mind." She went bright red and cleared her throat, and Miles raised his eyebrows, wondering what dire emergency had required Charity's assistance *at any time of the day or night*.

His mother eyed Vicki askance as well, before focusing her attention on Charity.

She smiled warmly and held out a hand in greeting.

"Why you're just a baby," she said wonderingly, and Charity coughed nervously before taking Miles's mother's hand. "I was expecting someone far older, the way Vicki was carrying on."

"Mum," Vicki's voice was almost a whine as she darted an embarrassed look at Charity. Her eyes widened as if she had only now noticed the change in their formerly dour housekeeper. Charity may have donned her Mrs. Cole garb this morning, but there was no denying how much younger she looked with the short hair. And there was a softness about her that had been missing before. In the glow of her eyes and around the fullness of her lips.

"Wow, Mrs. Cole...you do look, uh, different."

"She cut her hair," Miles interjected curtly, hating how discomfited Charity seemed beneath all this scrutiny. "Now why don't you show Mum to her room, while we fix some breakfast?"

"*We*?" Vicki's eyebrows rose clear to her hairline, and Miles met her eyes levelly.

"Did you forget who used to cook all your breakfasts when you were a kid?"

Vicki darted another wide-eyed look at Charity. "Yes, but... Mrs. Cole usually..."

"Mrs. Cole no longer works for us." Miles supplied curtly, and Charity made a soft sound of protest.

"I can stay a little longer to help out."

Of course, she was fine with staying a little longer, now that his family was here to act as an awkward buffer. And she offensively assumed that Miles would be equally fine watching her waiting hand and foot on his mother and sister.

And pretending that they had never been lovers. And friends.

"That's fine, Mrs. Cole," he growled, hoping nobody could hear the underlying note of simmering resentment in his voice. "You said you wanted to leave by the weekend. No need to change your timeline because of this unforeseen hiccup. Mum, Vicki and I can take care of ourselves."

Tyler—who had disappeared back down the stairs obviously to help with the bags—and George entered the kitchen carrying more luggage than seemed feasible for two women staying for a short time.

"Of course, we can," his mother agreed firmly. "I don't have any servants myself, despite this one's constant nagging"—she pointed her chin at Miles—"I do all my own cooking and cleaning. There's nothing wrong with my body or hands. And I'm uncomfortable having others do for me, when I can do for myself."

"An admirable and attractive quality," George interjected, his dark eyes wrinkling at the corners as he smiled at the older woman. She visibly preened beneath the attention, and Miles's eyes narrowed.

"Oh, stop it, George," she said flirtatiously. "You certainly know how to flatter an old lady."

"Old my arse. Fine ladies like you don't grow old, they mature beautifully, like a full-bodied cabernet sauvignon."

Miles's jaw dropped when his fifty-five-year-old mother giggled and preened like a schoolgirl.

What. The. Fuck?

Miles's eyes darted between his mother and driver incredulously. Were they flirting?

"Yeah, *that's* been going on since he helped her into the car at the airport." Vicki muttered beneath her breath.

His mother returned her smiling attention to Charity. "Well, as I was saying...you needn't concern yourself about us, Mrs. Cole."

"Call her Charity." Okay, so maybe he had barked that command louder than was polite, because everybody gaped at him in surprise.

"Only if it's okay with *her*," his mother said, after an uncomfortable beat of silence.

"It's fine with me." Charity said, avoiding Miles's eyes. She had been avoiding his fucking eyes since his sister had walked through the door.

"Well, then I insist you call me Enid." The warm directive was followed by an artful peek at the driver. "You too, George."

Jesus.

This was giving him a throbbing headache.

"Vic, show Mum to her room."

"What about Tyler?" His sister asked, tossing a disinterested glance at the tall, big guy who kind of faded into the background. Admirable quality in a bodyguard.

"I want to have a word with *Tyler*. You too, George."

"Are you going to relieve him of his duties? I'm perfectly safe here, so his services are no longer required, right?"

"Is that why you came?" Miles asked tightly, and Vicki's eyes widened and then shimmered.

Shit. She looked wounded, and he felt like an arse. Especially when Charity made a soft, disapproving sound in the back of her throat.

"I came because I missed you. And because I wanted to see for myself that you were okay. Excuse me, I'll show Mum around."

"Vic..." he began. But she had linked elbows with their mother, picked Stormy up, and led the older woman out of the kitchen toward the family suites. "Damn it. She took my dog!"

He was fucking everything up today. He squeezed the nape of his neck before rounding on the tall bodyguard.

"Why didn't you inform me of her plans to come here?"

"Well heck, sir," the man spoke for the first time since he had entered the kitchen. A lazy, slow Texan drawl. "My job is to keep her safe. Not keep you conversant of her every movement. I'm a close protection officer. Not a spy."

Fair point.

"Well, one of you could have warned me. George, you must have known since at least yesterday."

"Your sister wanted to surprise you. Far be it from me to spoil the surprise."

Miles bit back an expletive and glared at them both for a long moment before shaking his head.

"George, please show Chambers to Hugh's room." George saluted, and the two men quickly exited the room.

"I hate when he does that. And he knows it," Miles muttered. But as soon as he realized that he and Charity were alone in the kitchen, dread bubbled to the surface. He gritted his teeth and slowly turned to face her. She was watching him curiously, her head canted to the side as if she were trying to figure him out.

"So why not tell him not to do it?" she asked.

"Because he gets such a fucking kick out it."

Her lips quirked but her eyes were immeasurably sad.

"Miles, I can stay and..."

"No."

"But—"

"Charity, if you stay, it won't be as the housekeeper."

"What do you mean?"

"I mean that I would want you to share meals with us, go on outings with us. I'd want you to get to know my mother and sister on a personal level. I don't want you picking up after us. Cleaning up...organizing our lives. Fucking getting emergency whatever-the-hells at all hours of the day or night. You would be staying as my partner, my lover...the woman I—"

He swallowed the words. He couldn't say them. She needed to make a clean getaway. And telling her how he felt would place an unfair emotional burden on her.

. . .

The woman he what? Charity longed for him to complete that sentence. She couldn't remember anything she had craved more than to hear the rest of what she was certain he had been about to say. But she knew the words were better left unspoken.

For the sake of her sanity...and his.

"Be nicer to your sister," she advised softly. "Don't push them away, Miles. They love you."

"What do you care? Why are you telling me this?" he asked bitterly, then immediately felt petty.

"We're still friends, aren't we? That was our deal, right? Friends...possibly lovers. But *always* friends."

"Charity," his voice was hoarse with suppressed emotion, and his eyes glittered when he forced himself to look at her. "I don't know how to be your friend."

"You've been my friend all along, Miles. And I...thank you for that."

"*Don't.* Just..." He swallowed loudly, his Adam's apple bobbing with the motion. "You don't have to thank me for anything, Charity. Ever. Okay? That infers a debt that simply isn't owed."

Her lips quivered, and she brought them under strict control, drawing them between her teeth to prevent the movement.

"I have to get breakfast started," she said, hoping the change in subject would bring everything back into perspective. But the man was ever unpredictable, and she stared at him in astonishment, when he lifted her spare frilly pinafore apron from a hook next to the back door and tied it around his waist. He looked ridiculously adorable. "*Whoa*...what are you doing?"

"I said *we* would be fixing breakfast, and I meant it. You no longer work for me. But if you insist on doing things like cooking and cleaning during your last few days here, I'm for damned sure going to help you with everything."

"You're the strangest millionaire I know." She huffed, infuriated and—*damn him*—hopelessly charmed by his insistence on helping her.

"Know a lot of millionaires, do you?" he asked, with a sardonic twist of his lips. He didn't wait for her reply, instead he rubbed his palms together and gave her a manic grin. "Let's get cracking, Mrs. Cole...you know how my sister gets when she's hangry."

Relieved that he seemed in better spirts, Charity tentatively returned the smile. "By the way, I think your mother and George are totally crushing on each other."

He shuddered and shook his head. "There's a thought I do not want to entertain right now. My Mum always had a soft spot for the scoundrels."

"*Scoundrels*?" she repeated gleefully. This man constantly gave her reason to smile. Even with their situation so irredeemably tragic. "Have you shifted your focus from fantasy novels to historical romances?"

"The description is apropos, and you know it."

"And are you going to warn said scoundrel away from your mummy?" she asked, on a teasing note.

He snorted. "Far be it from me to dictate my mother's love life. She can take care of herself. If she likes George, and he likes her, I'm guessing there'll be a holiday romance blooming in no time, and I'm just going to have to deal with it. Besides, George may be a scoundrel, but he's also a gentleman. He won't hurt her."

"You're a great guy, you know that?"

He looked pained by her words and shadows drifted back into his eyes. "Sometimes I wish I weren't. Sometimes I wish I were an arsehole who made unreasonable demands and selfishly took what he wanted. Being a great guy doesn't always work out so well." The bitterness in his voice was palpable, it tainted the air, and she could practically taste it on her tongue.

"Being that guy would make you miserable, Miles. It's not in your DNA to make others unhappy."

"Stop making me sound like a fucking saint, Charity. I'm not. I don't know how to deal with any of this. I'm trying to do the right thing. I'm trying to be graceful about losing you and I..." He shook his head. "I fucking hate it! I hate every moment of this. It's like a painful, lingering death."

He ran a shaky hand through his already disheveled hair and inhaled deeply. Once. Twice...a third time.

It reminded her of her counting.

A coping mechanism she hadn't needed in weeks thanks to Miles. He centered her. Grounded her. Made her feel safe.

And all *she* had done in return was turn him into this wreck of a man standing before her.

And if *that* wasn't definitive proof that she was doing the right thing in leaving, then she didn't know what was. She wasn't good for him. He had to constantly monitor his words, his reactions, in case it brought out the crazy in her. How was that fair?

"I'm sorry." His words were quiet, and she sucked in a painful breath.

"You haven't done a single thing to apologize for, Miles. We found each other at the wrong time. That's all. And I so wish it could have been different for us."

"Where's your shadow?" Miles asked Vicki that evening after dinner. Their mother had joined them for supper but had excused herself soon afterwards to go dancing with George.

"He bummed a lift into town with Mum and George. Said he was going to hang out with his boss, Sam Brand. He's such a slacker. You should fire him."

Miles grinned and shook his head.

"You keep on flogging that dead horse, sis."

Charity had joined them for dinner but had retreated to her rooms soon afterward. In fact, their mother had insisted that her "children" would clean the kitchen, and Charity should get some packing done.

She had appeared grateful for the excuse to leave.

Which left Miles and Vicki in the kitchen, companionably rinsing dishes and loading the dishwasher, with Stormy snoozing in her basket next to the banquette.

"Sooo...what's the deal with you and Mrs. Cole?"

His sister's question was so unexpected, Miles almost dropped the plate he was rinsing.

"Uh...what?"

Smooth. But in his defense, she had completely wrong-footed him.

"You and Mrs. Cole."

"Charity," he corrected automatically, his mind racing.

"Okay. *Charity.* There's something going on between you. She's smoking hot, by the way, so congratulations on your conquest."

"She's not a conquest!" he snapped, infuriated that she would think that. "Don't speak of her like that."

Her eyes widened, and she gingerly lowered the glass she had been rinsing to the drainer.

She whistled. "Well, I didn't expect to hit that nerve *quite* so hard. Miles, what's going on? You look so much healthier than before you left. I didn't say it at the time, but it was terrifying to see you so weak and so obviously ill. But now...you look healthy sure. And you also look so bloody desolate."

Vicki had always been entirely too perceptive. And he loved that about her. He was proud of her intelligence and wit. But right now, because of her incredible mental acuity, he truly wished he were dealing with Hugh, or his mother instead. They usually took everything he said at face value. Vicki never had. And she wouldn't do so now.

"Well," he began, fixating on the ruffled edge of the tea towel he was holding. Worrying at it, he found a frayed stitch and tugged. Anything to avoid his sister's insightful gaze. "She's leaving, isn't she?"

"And that's what has you so miserable?"

"I'm a little..." He cleared his throat, and when the piece of thread he'd been worrying broke, he found another one to tug on. "I'm a little in love with her."

He dared a quick glance at Vicki from beneath his brow, she was gawking at him, her jaw unattractively agape. And he hastily went back to his loose thread.

"More than a little in love actually. I fucking adore her."

"So why the hell are you letting her go?"

"It's complicated, Swish." He hadn't used the nickname in so long it actually startled him when it emerged from his mouth. *Swish*, because Vicki had been such a talented netball player at high school. "She's been through some shit. And she's been hiding from it. She's finally ready to carry on with her life. To be with her family and friends again. I can't deprive her of that. To do so would be selfish."

"Does she love you?"

"I don't think she's quite ready for love yet. I don't even think she was ready for what we *did* have. But it was an irresistible, unstoppable force, and we couldn't fight it. But she needs to heal. To figure out who she is now. And what she wants to do. And she needs to do that without me around to cloud her judgment."

So easy to say those words, to recognize the practicality and rightness in them...and yet so very hard to actually *live* them.

"I'm sorry, Miles," she said, her voice brimming with sincerity.

"It is what it is." He set the tea towel aside and folded his arms over his chest. He eyed her assessingly. His cute baby sister with her dark curls, her pale gray eyes, her slightly crooked smile, and the overly big glasses that gave her the appearance of a myopic owl. He had always adored her. "I'm happy to see you, you know?"

"Are you? Really?" Her voice was small and uncertain and contained the tiniest portion of childlike hope.

"I am, yes. I'm sorry if I made you feel differently this morning."

"It was a pretty dick thing to suggest."

"I know."

She held his gaze for a long while, before grinning happily. "But, I'm so happy you got us a dog! Thank you. She's so sweet."

"I didn't get us anything. She's *my* dog." Best to make that clear right now. Vicki had already claimed far too much of Stormy's time and attention today.

"You never wanted a dog, Miles. I did. And now that you've finally brought one into the family, you're going to hog her?"

"Yes, I'm going to hog her, she's my dog. I share enough with you brats as it is, I'm not sharing my dog."

Her eyes went somber, and she gave him a melancholy smile. "Do you resent us because of that? Having to share or give up your stuff when we were kids?"

"*Never*!" His response was emphatic. He wanted there to be

no doubt about his sincerity. "And don't you dare let that thought cross your mind again. I was happy to share everything I had with you and Hughie. I still am. Just not my dog. I'm going to need her...after everything."

By that he meant *after Charity*. A fact that his sister seemed to tune in to immediately if the compassion in her eyes was anything to go by.

"Oh, Miles," she murmured, crossing the short distance between them to wrap her arms around his waist and hug him fiercely. His arms closed around her small frame moments later as he gratefully accepted the comfort she was so freely offering.

IF CHARITY's life was a leaky boat, time was the water that flooded through the gaping holes faster than she could plug them. All too soon, she was submerged and drowning beneath the weight of everything that still needed to be done before she left in just twenty-four hours.

Three days hadn't been enough time. And with Enid, Vicki, and the taciturn Tyler Chambers to accommodate now too, Charity found herself barely able to cope.

The good thing about them being here was that she rarely saw Miles.

The bad thing about them being here was that she rarely saw Miles.

He took them sightseeing every day. Ostensibly to make things easier for Charity. But she knew that he was avoiding her.

She was grateful for that. But she also *hated* it. He was angry and hurt. She knew that...but a small, impractical part of her had hoped for a friendship at least. She couldn't stand the thought of losing him so absolutely.

But he could barely make eye contact with her, which made even a casual acquaintance after her departure, seem unlikely at this point.

Sam and Lia had invited them all to dinner tonight. A farewell gathering in Charity's honor. Miles had seemed less than enthusiastic about the idea, but she knew he'd go. He had to. It would look odd if he didn't. And—considering that they lived in the same house—it was ridiculous how much she was looking forward to seeing him and spending some time with him tonight.

She had spoken with her parents and sister every day since Gracie's party. She had renewed acquaintances and friendships with people whom she had been close to before her marriage. She had booked her clinical competence exam, was doing job research, weighing partnership practices up against hanging out her own shingle. There were so many great opportunities available to her.

Her future looked bright and exciting and filled her with effervescent optimism.

And yet...she was bone crushingly lonely.

She wanted to discuss all of this with Miles. Wanted to bounce ideas off him. Wanted him to share in her excitement and happiness. She felt a little lost without him. Felt like she had lost her best friend really.

And her heartbreak stemmed from the fact that she knew that the loss was permanent.

Everybody was having a marvelous time at Charity's impromptu farewell. Laughter, drinking, *fucking* merriment. How could everybody be so happy about someone's imminent departure?

Miles was trying his best to put up a *merry* front. He wanted Charity to understand that while he was mourning her loss in his life, he wanted her to be happy.

But it was so fucking hard when all he wanted to do was howl like a wounded beast.

He was being a selfish prick. He knew it. But he felt cheated out of days—*weeks*—more.

"You'd better stop this hulking and sulking in the corner, my boy. This petulance is not a good look on you." His mother invaded the gloriously isolated corner which he had claimed for his—as she had so aptly put it—hulking and sulking. She handed him a beer, and he wrinkled his nose. He had never been much of a beer drinker. His mother, however, *loved* the stuff. Preferably a draught, but a bottle would do in a pinch.

She took a pull from hers, before turning her full attention on him. "The way I see it, you have two choices. Tell her how you feel about her, and let the chips fall where they may. Or let her go gracefully and be happy for her. I can't believe she has been housekeeping for the last three years, when she's a qualified chiropractor. It's *good* that she's finally going to answer that calling."

"You don't know how I feel about her. Or how I feel about this situation."

"Please. I birthed you. And I may not have been entirely present during your childhood, but I know you. A lot better than you think I do, and it's as clear as that oversized nose on your face. You're so in love with that woman, you can barely see straight. And you're *miserable* at the thought of losing her. What

I don't understand is why my ambitious, go-getter of a son, doesn't...well *go get her*?"

"It's complicated and messy."

"Well, uncomplicate it, Miles. If you love the woman, figure it out. I've never seen you look at anybody the way you look at her. To be honest I've despaired of ever seeing you look at someone like that...and now that you've found her, you're just letting her go?"

"She's not mine to keep. She never has been. The best thing I can do for her is let her go."

"Like this? With so much reluctance and surliness and moodiness? What kind of message does that send? She's surrounded by all these people who care about her, who will miss her when she leaves. Who want her to succeed in the future, and all she can do is stare at you with her shattered heart in her eyes."

Her words jerked Miles's head up and he unerringly sought and found Charity. True to his mother's words, she was watching him. Her eyes widened when he caught her staring, and she hastily looked away.

"She shattered my heart first," he said, sounding like the petulant boy she had called him earlier. He shut his eyes and shook his head, irritated with himself for being this way.

"I'm being a prick." It was a statement of fact, an acknowledgment of his ridiculous behavior. Not too long ago, he had promised to be her friend above all else.

And he was being a terrible fucking friend.

"Excuse me, Mum. I have to—"

"No need to explain, my boy," his mother interrupted cheerfully, taking another swig from her beer. "Go talk to her."

. . .

He was coming over.

Charity's breath hitched, and her heart, which had been glumly lurking close to the vicinity of her feet all evening long, leaped back into her chest and tattooed a frantically happy beat against her ribcage. She watched him approach, unable to take her eyes off him.

He moved like a panther, sinuously, gracefully, purposefully...

Would she ever stop loving him?

He glided to a stop in front of her. His eyes boring intently into hers. With his dark brows furrowed into a glower, and his hair untamed, there was a familiar hint of wildness about him. And she found it utterly irresistible.

He held out a hand, palm up. "Dance with me?"

Her tongue was glued to the roof of her dry mouth, and she struggled to formulate her response.

It took so long, his hand started to shake, and the spark in his eyes dimmed.

"There's no music," she eventually managed to croak out, and his eyebrows lowered even more.

"There isn't?" He looked confused by her statement for a moment. But then he smiled. And his face transformed from savage to drop dead gorgeous in seconds. "I always hear music when I'm with you, Charity."

The words were cringingly sweet; but her knees went weak, and her legs turned to gelatin.

"That's hands down the corniest thing I've ever heard you say," she said, with a laugh, and he grinned.

"I know." His palm was still outstretched, and she dropped her own hand into it and allowed him to tug her into his arms. He nuzzled the hair at her temple and breathed the rest of what he had to say directly into her ear, "It's true though."

He was swaying gently, to the beat of some song only he could hear. Charity sighed and snuggled closer, her arms going around his waist, while his hands fisted against her back.

"I'm sorry I've been such a twat," he muttered, and she shook her head.

"I understand that my decision to leave was a shock. I'm sorry too."

"Let's not spend the remainder of our time together apologizing to each other, okay?"

"Okay."

"You all packed?"

"Hmm."

"I'm going to miss you, my love."

"I'm going to miss you too, Miles," her voice wobbled. "*So* much."

"You're going to have a phenomenal life. Because you deserve it."

Her throat and nose clogged up, and her eyes stung. She buried her face in his neck, wishing he could hold her forever.

He started to hum softly into her ear, and she smiled, her arms tightening around him.

"You really need to learn some other songs, Miles," she chuckled, and she felt his lips stretch into a grin against her ear.

"Nah, it's too late for me, darling. Sometimes you find that one perfect thing and then it becomes yours, forever. Know what I mean?"

She swallowed and nodded.

Of course, she knew what he meant. These last several weeks with him had been her perfect thing. And the memory of their time together would live on in her heart forever.

"WHERE ARE YOU GOING?" Charity asked into her pillow, when she felt her mattress shift as Miles got up. He had made tender love to her for hours after the party last night. Worshiping her with his body, hands, and mouth. Lavishing her with praise and endearments.

It had been perfect...but now he appeared to be sneaking out of bed and tiptoeing to the door like a thief in the night. She pushed herself up onto her elbow and glared at him in the dim predawn light.

"I'm sorry," he whispered, coming back to sit down on the edge of the bed. "I didn't mean to wake you."

"Where are you going?" Charity repeated and reached over to switch on the bedside lamp.

"Charity...last night was my farewell to you. I don't think I can watch you leave. I couldn't stand it."

"You were just going to sneak out without a word?" She sat up, tucking the bedsheet under her arms.

He sighed and cupped her jaw between his palms.

"Be happy, my love." He gave her sweetest, gentlest kiss.

And left before she could reply.

MILES AND STORMY were on the beach when he heard the engine of the SUV start up. Despite his conviction not to watch her leave, he couldn't prevent himself from turning around to track the progress of the vehicle with his own eyes. He watched it shakily traverse the dirt road toward the bridge. He was too far to see her face...but he was more than passingly familiar with the elegant shape of her head. She was in the back seat. And judging from the tilt of that head, she had spotted him on the misty beach.

Her body language changed, and he saw her press a palm to the window. He made a tortured sound, something between a keen and a moan and lifted his own hand in response.

I see you, darling. I love you.

The vehicle disappeared around the bend, and the sound of the engine gradually grew fainter and fainter, until all he could hear were the sounds of the birds chirping, the wind rustling through the trees and grass, the waves gently slapping against the shore, and his jagged breathing as he battled to keep the emergent, harsh sobs at bay.

In the end, the anguish of loss was just too unbearable, and he sank down onto the sand, clutched his knees to his chest and grieved.

Chapter Nineteen

THREE MONTHS LATER

"Are you happy, Charity?"

Faith's unexpected question threw Charity for a loop. They were in a bustling coffee shop, having their weekly brunch. Catching up on gossip. And suddenly *this*.

Why was she asking? Did Charity not seem happy? Did her family catch occasional glimpses of the loneliness and yearning she still felt for something she could no longer have?

When they had started family therapy, it had been with the understanding that there would be no more life-altering secrets among them. But Charity didn't feel like she was keeping secrets. Her family knew about Miles. Knew how much he meant to her. Knew that she had to be missing him.

So technically there were no real secrets here. Just unspoken truths.

"Why do you ask?"

"I have it penciled into my schedule," Faith informed her somberly. "The first day of every third month, *ask Charity about happiness*."

Charity's eyes widened. "What? Seriously?"

"Of course not, you ditz," her sister laughed, taking a sip from her chocolate latte, before elaborating. "But I have decided that it's something I need to ask you more often. To allow you space to...I dunno, talk. If you want to."

"I'm fine, sis," Charity said, offering Faith a small smile. "I'm doing well, I'm content. But..." She sighed and shook her head. "No. I'm not happy."

"I didn't think you were."

"I m-miss him so much," she confessed, stumbling over the words in her haste to get them out.

Faith wrapped her palms around her cup of coffee and sucked her upper lip into her mouth as she scrutinized Charity's face.

"It's funny," she began, her tone of voice almost wondering, as she continued to stare at Charity like she had never seen her before.

"What is?"

"After Blaine died, I thought you were sad. Missing him. The usual things, you know? Grieving. But with the gift of hindsight, and seeing you as you are now...Charity, *this* is real sorrow. You had something special and you lost it. And it broke your heart. And I wish I knew how to make it better for you."

"Talking helps," she admitted.

"So why didn't you say something sooner?"

"Because I feel like *that* person, you know? That person who can never be happy and content. Who always finds a reason to be miserable. I'm *supposed* to be happy. I have everything I thought I wanted...I have you all back. I'm starting my own practice. I have old friends and new. I don't feel weighted down by my past anymore. I still have so much PTSD to work through after my life with Blaine...but it no longer feels like the sum total of who I am. I should be happy."

"But you're not. And that's okay."

"Is it? It was supposed to be a fling. Nothing more. I was never meant to be *hung up* on him."

Faith snorted and waved her hand impatiently.

"You're not 'hung up' on him. You're in love with him. Big difference, sis. One suggests an impractical obsession with a past lover. The other indicates depth of feeling, a *realness* that cannot be casually dismissed."

"He helped me overcome so much...but he was also the first man after Blaine, and I thought I was rebounding or something. He took me by surprise, you know. I always thought he was this aloof, terse, tense man with few friends, no hobbies and no concept of how to let loose and have fun. He always struck me as a guy with a giant stick up his butt."

"He was none of those things, I take it?"

"One of the first things he did after arriving at the house for his convalescence was rescue a flea-bitten, skinny pup. I mean, she was a raggedy, sad looking little thing, but he thought she was the most beautiful freaking dog in the world. He named her Stormy, and they fell instantly in love and were inseparable from the very beginning. He lost his appetite at a farmhouse restaurant because some chickens wandered into the yard, and he was concerned that we were eating one of their offspring.

"And don't get me started on how he feels about captive lobsters in restaurant tanks. The man is borderline militant on the topic. He's patient, kind, sweet, understanding. He's also intelligent, funny, companionable, and passionate about the things he loves. He's fantastic in bed. He made me feel safe and—"

"Cherry, stop!" Even though her family tried very hard to

refrain from using that nickname, they occasionally slipped up. But Charity found herself minding less and less. They loved her, they could call her anything they damned well pleased. Blaine had taken enough from her, and she had decided that this was something he could no longer have. "If you feel this way about him, why aren't you grabbing him with both hands and holding on tight?"

"He's there. I'm here. It's long-distance or one of us moves. That's if he even wants to start anything serious with me."

"Oh, I saw the way that man looked at you. He wants it alright."

"And I thought the next part of my life shouldn't be about a man. It should be about me."

"Admirable. But why can't it be about both? Why can't you have your career, your independence, *and* the man you love? Why can't you have everything? You fucking deserve it!"

Faith's questions made her pause, and her brow puckered as she contemplated the words. Words she had never allowed herself to even consider before.

Could this be just another way she was allowing her past with Blaine to manipulate and influence her future? Miles had strong feelings for her. She knew that. She hadn't dared asked him for clarification on those feelings because she didn't want to know. She feared that it would weaken her resolve to be more.

Be better.

But what she hadn't considered was that she *was* already better. Better on her own *and* better with him. She had nothing to prove to anyone except herself, and after three years of near isolation, making herself mentally and physically strong, she already possessed that proof.

Miles had afforded her the emotional support she hadn't even known she needed. Without him, she could very well have remained stuck in that safe chrysalis for many more years. But his strength had bolstered hers and had encouraged her to emerge and fly.

She didn't *need* him to make her whole. But...she damned well wanted him.

CHARITY
Give Stormy a hug and a kiss from me. Tell her I miss her.

Miles—who had been lounging on an uncomfortably overstuffed sofa in his study—choked on the thirty-year-old Richard Hennessy he had been sipping when the message materialized on his screen. He sat upright carelessly spilling the liquid gold as he gaped at his phone in disbelief.

He blinked few times, but the message didn't disappear. Stormy, the world's most spoiled dog, lifted her head from her plush cushion on the sofa beside him, to watch him quizzically. He lifted the phone to show her, before recognizing how nuts the gesture was.

He went back to staring at the message, not sure if he should respond or not. Surely she had sent him the message expecting some kind of response?

He set aside the crystal snifter, and impulsively lifted Stormy into his arms. He took a few selfies of himself hugging and kissing the dog. He sent them all with the accompanying text:

> MILES
> She misses you too.

After he sent the message, he started fretting like a teenage girl. Had he responded too quickly? Seemed over eager? Three months of zero communication, and he responded to her first text within seconds.

That *had* to reek of desperation.

Worse, he now found himself fixedly staring at the screen, waiting for a response.

This was ridiculous. He was a grown man, he had better things to do than sit at home mooning over his bloody phone.

Only...he really didn't. He hadn't done anything remotely social since returning from Riversend.

Work, eat, walk Stormy, sleep, repeat.

Vicki often popped by to visit him at his luxurious Knightsbridge apartment. Hugh and his mother were regular visitors as well. But he knew his mum wasn't wholly comfortable in this place. In fact, given how often she complained about its lack of warmth, Miles would go so far as to say she hated it quite passionately. He was never sure if she meant the heating or the monochromatic décor.

Vicki and Hugh shared a three-bedroomed apartment in Hammersmith. One of Miles's many properties. And their mother lived in a cozy flat that Miles had bought for her in her old neighborhood in Kensington. Miles liked that they all lived in close proximity of one another.

He could keep an eye on them, make sure they were safe. They all had security details. His mum's more discreet. So discreet she had no idea they were there. Tyler Chambers was still on Vicki duty and would be for the conceivable future. His sister hated it, and Chambers didn't seem overly impressed with the situation either. Miles imagined that watching an eccentric florist create animal bouquets all day long wasn't quite on par with the level of excitement the guy must have been expecting from his work.

But Miles didn't care. He trusted Chambers to do the job, regardless of boredom or personal preference. And judging from the amount of complaints he received from his sister every day, the man never dropped his guard when they were in public.

He was allowing his mind to wander because it stopped him from obsessing over that fucking message. Stopped him from checking his phone every five seconds.

He got up and prowled the length of the room, intentionally leaving the phone on the glass coffee table. Stormy watched him for a few moments, before sighing and dropping her head back on her cushion. She was curled up in a tight ball, with her nose practically buried in her arse.

The phone vibrated, and its screen lit up again.

Why the surprising texts? What had changed? He had been so fucking tempted to call her or text her these last few months. But he had told himself that doing so would be selfish and unfair.

Which was partly true. The other reason he hadn't attempted to contact her was his healthy fear of being rebuffed. An alien sensation for him. He rarely doubted himself. He always knew exactly what to do in any given situation.

Until now. Until Charity.

He slowed his breathing. Struggling to calm down. Advising

himself to wait a couple of minutes before checking the message, and then a further five before replying.

He lasted thirty seconds.

It was humiliating.

CHARITY
Tell her I'm starting my own practice. I'll be open for business in two weeks.

Miles glared at the screen, irritated.

What the hell *was* this?

He looked over at his snoozing dog and called her name. She lifted her head, her eyes bleary, her wiry beard flat on one side, and her one ear flipped inside out.

She looked adorable.

Miles smiled and pretended to yawn, knowing it would set her off. It always did. He snapped a pic of her in mid-yawn and sent it to Charity.

MILES
She doesn't care. She says not to interrupt her nap again.

This time he didn't have to wait long for a response. It came five seconds later.

CHARITY
Rude.

MILES
Looks like you're stuck with me now.

He held his breath and watched as she began formulating her response.

CHARITY
...
...
...

Was she composing a fucking essay?

CHARITY
...
...
Looks like it

Oh.

Miles stared at the screen. Obsessing over those three words like it was a code in need of decrypting.

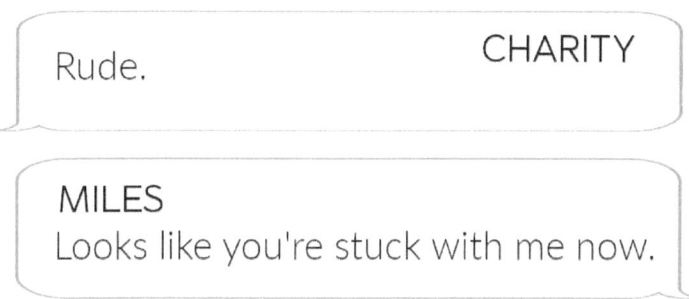

Looks like it.

How was he supposed to respond to that? He felt like he was navigating a minefield and one wrong step could blow him right the hell off the planet.

Fuck it.

He clicked on her number, sucked in a deep breath, and hit the call button.

She answered on the second ring. Her rich, husky voice was brimming with something that sounded suspiciously close to laughter, "Miles?"

"I don't know what that means." He exclaimed, the words out before he could stop himself, and immediately winced.

"I miss you."

Well...there was no mistaking her meaning there. The words, though quiet, seemed to have been blurted out with the same impulsivity of his opening statement.

"It's been three months."

"Now, I'm the one who can honestly say I don't know what *that* means."

"I mean, we haven't spoken in three months. Have you only started missing me now? Because let me tell you, woman, I've been missing you this entire time. And it seems to me that you're a little late to the party."

"It hasn't taken me this long to realize that I miss you, Miles," she told him, that laughter bubbling away beneath the surface again. "I've missed you this entire time as well."

"Damn it, Charity. What the fuck are you doing?"

"I honestly don't know. But I miss having you in my life. I *like* having you in my life."

. . .

He was silent for so long, Charity would have thought the call dropped if not for the soft, uneven sough of his breath in her ear.

Her own breathing was conspicuous by its absence, while she waited for his reply.

He cleared his throat, and her breath escaped on a quiet stream of air.

"You're starting your own practice? That's pretty impressive."

She smiled and allowed herself to breathe. "I wanted to be my own boss. Have you fully adjusted to being back at work again?"

"I've made a few alterations." He didn't elaborate, and she rolled her eyes. Getting him to talk about himself was like pulling teeth at times.

"What kind of alterations?"

"I've given Bryan and Hugh more responsibility and am taking on more of an advisory role in the company. I'll stay on as board chairman...for now. But I'm grooming Bryan for that position."

"But...*why*?"

"I want to focus on other things. My health scare has reorganized my priorities. I don't want my life to be about just work anymore."

"What will you do instead?"

"Make time for family, get out more, travel." He cleared his throat again. Possibly uncomfortable with the subject matter. Or perhaps he was getting a cold. Which she doubted. He continued, "Enjoy life. Maybe even *uh*...marry and have kids or something. I just want more from life. I've spent nearly twenty of my thirty-five years building something I could be proud of. I did it for my mother and siblings. I wanted them to have anything and everything they desired from life. And that was it, my big plan.

My *raison d'être*. I never thought beyond that. And even after I succeeded beyond my wildest imaginings...I couldn't rest for fear of losing everything I'd built. I certainly didn't think I could trust anyone else at the helm, so to speak."

His words tumbled to an awkward halt and Charity waited, expecting him to continue. But when nothing else was forthcoming, she gave him a gentle prod. "And now you know you can trust them? Your friend and your brother, I mean?"

"Yes."

First a deluge of information and now this...monosyllabic tumbleweed.

Perhaps expecting more from him after three months of silence was pushing too hard. She had contacted him because she was ready to explore the possibilities between them. Charity had had time to think, process, plan...but Miles was playing catch-up.

"I've decided to open my practice in Riversend."

"*What?*"

Oh. A roar. Uncharacteristic.

She liked it.

"They don't have a chiropractor in town, they have to drive into Knysna, or farther, for treatment."

"But what about your family? I thought you wanted to live closer to home."

She laughed softly, and sighed. "Turns out, Riversend *is* home. For three years I believed I could live on the outskirts of society, avoid people, and friendships...Be a solitary, self-sufficient island. I was so mistaken. I made connections without even recognizing them. And not just during those last few weeks with you. I found myself constantly wondering if the cheese festival was a success. Everybody in town had been so excited about it. They had been planning parades and raffles and exhibitions. I didn't know that I'd actually been looking forward to it until I missed it."

"And you have friends there," he supplied quietly.

"I do. I reconnected with some of my former friends. The ones from before my marriage...but it's not the same. We have so little in common now."

"What about your family?"

"We talk more. All the time in fact. I've come to realize that it isn't proximity that's important. I can be close to them without being *close* to them. Know what I mean?"

"Yes."

"And this time it's different...I'm not hiding. I'm not running. I'm settling down, carving my own niche in this world. And they fully support me."

"Where are you staying?"

"I'm renting a cottage on the edge of town. It's owned by Lia's youngest sister. It's small but I like it."

"You can..." he stopped speaking, and she held the phone closer to her ear. She could what? He cleared his throat again.

And the silly delay tactic irritated her.

"You should see someone for that," she said pointedly.

"What?"

"That scratch in your throat. It could be a cold. Or allergies. Or..."

"I'm nervous."

Why did he have to be so vulnerable in his honesty? It did painful, clenching things to her already fragile heart.

"I am too." No point in denying it. And if he could be honest, so should she.

"I was going to say, you could stay in my house..."

God, she *loved* this man. She smiled and shook her head,

even though he couldn't see her. "Thank you. That's very generous of you. But...I'm okay for now."

Because the next time she set foot in that house, it would be with him by her side.

"Are you seeing anyone? Dating, I mean?" His hoarse question surprised her. He had seemed so intent on keeping things more or less impersonal, this seemed to come out of left field.

"I've been on several dates. My therapist said it would be good for me to get out with members of the opposite sex. Most of them were setups, y'know? Men my family and friends know. Nice guys that they could personally vouch for. Then again, Blaine was a so-called *nice* guy. So, there's that. But they all seemed decent. I even went on a few repeat dates with some of them."

The silence on the other end of the line was so thunderous it almost deafened her.

"And you?"

"What about me?"

"Have you been seeing anyone?"

"No."

Her lips stretched into a grin so wide, it physically hurt. "Oh? Then how do you intend to meet this future wife you spoke of earlier?"

He ignored her question in favor of one of his own, "Are you still seeing any of those guys?"

"Well, I'm moving. So there's no point really. Lia says she has a few guys she'd like me to meet, but Riversend and surrounds have a much smaller dating pool."

"So you're actively seeking men to date right now?"

"I wouldn't say *actively*...They're just kind of being referred to me by everybody else. To be honest, I had no idea there were still so many single guys in my age group. Some of them were younger than my thirty years, but most of them are in their thirties. They're not even divorced or widowed. Just never been married. That's interesting, right?"

"Not particularly." Charity was *sure* she could hear him gritting his teeth. It sounded painful. Her grin widened. "I mean, *I've* never been married."

"Why not?"

"Work. And I've never met anyone with whom I wanted to spend my life..." She could practically hear the ellipsis in that statement. He had more to add but, *of course*, he stopped talking abruptly.

"Ever?"

"Are you toying with me, Charity?" The question was cold and curt and startled her. God, she didn't want him to think this was some kind of game.

"No, Miles. I'm not toying with you."

"*Don't* ask me questions you're not ready to hear the answers to."

"Maybe I am ready."

"Goodnight, Charity." The words were abrupt. Final.

Her lips quivered and a sob caught in her throat. This hadn't been a good idea. She had believed that maybe if they could start talking again, they could work their way toward regaining what they had lost. But this just felt like more loss.

"Goodnight, Miles." The words emerged on a tremulous voice. Her fingers were so tightly clutched around the phone, they actually ached.

"I'll speak with you again soon."

He disconnected the call without waiting for a response... Totally oblivious to the fact that he had just thrown her a lifeline and saved her from drowning.

Her eyes flooded, and she carefully set her phone aside to bury her face in her hands as reaction set in.

He was going to speak with her again.

Soon.

Thank God.

THIS IS SO STRANGE. The words echoed through Charity's head as she moved from person to person, mingling, chatting... laughing at silly jokes and making even sillier ones herself.

So damned strange.

It felt as if her life had come full circle. Just five months ago, so many of the people in this room had gathered in her name to say farewell. And now they had all assembled at her brand, spanking new consultation rooms, to celebrate her opening in two days' time, on Monday.

After passing her clinical competency test a month ago, Charity had wasted no time renting a couple of rooms in the tiny business center on Riversend's Main Road. The center also housed a tax attorney's practice, an accountant's office, the pediatric clinic, a dentist's surgery, and the vet's office. And since the building was situated right next to the sports store slash gym, Charity was hoping for a lot of referrals.

Setting up a chiropractic practice was an expensive endeavor, and Charity had taken great joy in using the money from Blaine's estate to buy state-of-the-art equipment and the most luxurious, tasteful furniture she could find. There was enough left over to provide a financial cushion if the first six months of business proved slow.

Whenever her gaze swept around the tastefully appointed

reception area of her chiropractic practice, she felt a surge of nerves and the thrill of achievement. It was surreal how much her life had changed in so short a time.

Her parents, as well as Faith and Stuart, had flown in to celebrate this attainment of one of the many dreams she now had for her future. Since it was summer vacation, Faith, Stuart, and Gracie had arrived a few days earlier to help Charity move into her new home, while she focused on setting up the consultation rooms. It had been a busy few weeks. Made even more frantic because they had to race to get all her professional equipment and tools delivered before the supply companies closed for the Christmas vacation.

The country pretty much shut down for the entire month of December as holidaymakers sought to take advantage of the summer weather and many bank holidays. A lot of companies were closed for business until January. Charity had known trying to set up her practice in the weeks before Christmas would prove difficult, but it had been much more frenetic than she had expected.

She had been exceedingly grateful for everyone's help. Lia—on vacation because the kindergarten was closed for summer—had proven invaluable with the admin, while Daff had helped with leaflets and marketing. George had done so much driving for her, his daughter, Nina—an interior designer—had helped with the office décor, despite being just a few weeks shy of giving birth. Amos had insisted on helping with physical tasks that involved way too much manual labor. Not wanting the old man to hurt himself, Charity had instead given him her exact design layout plans, and had tasked him with ensuring the movers got everything in the right positions.

And Greyson's wife, Olivia, had kindly offered to cater tonight's party at a discounted rate.

Coming back to Riversend—*home*—had been the right thing to do. Her family fully supported her. And once she was fully settled and found a larger place to live...they would visit often.

Everything was going phenomenally well.

Except for one thing...

She dug into her skirt pocket for her phone and checked the screen.

Still no messages.

She hadn't heard from Miles in five days. No texts, calls, not even the occasional picture of Stormy. She had grown so used to hearing from him every day for the last six weeks, that his sudden silence filled her with dread.

"Hey, stop mooning over your phone and pay attention to your guests!" Faith, ever the drill sergeant, commanded her. Charity grimaced and guiltily slipped her phone back into her pocket.

Her sister slid an arm around her shoulder and gave her a squeeze, before handing her a glass of bubbly.

"That's better. This is your moment, sis! Enjoy it."

"I am," Charity said. "I just..."

She lifted a shoulder, not wanting to admit she hadn't heard from Miles in a while. Her sister hadn't been too impressed with the strange, chaste cyber relationship they had cultivated.

"And what are you and Miles discussing this evening? How many laps you swam in the community pool last night? Stormy's latest encounter with the French poodle in the park?" The questions were steeped in sarcasm, and Charity narrowed her eyes at her sister.

"Stormy's reaction to the poodle was cute," she responded defensively, and Faith rolled her eyes.

"You guys have been tiptoeing around each other for weeks. Start sexting, for God's sake."

"Shut up! We're doing fine."

Only, they weren't.

Faith threw her head back to glare at the ceiling for a second before levelling her gaze at Charity.

"Charity, at this rate, you're going to text yourself right into the friend zone. Does he even know that you want him back? Or does he think that this weird, impersonal texting friendship is all you have to offer?"

The question made Charity pause. Was that what was happening? Did he think they were just friends? That this was all there was?

"Charity," Faith began. Her tentative voice immediately put Charity on the alert. Her sister was only tentative when she was getting ready to lay a painful home truth on someone. "The longer you delay having a proper conversation about your feelings with him, the harder it will be. And before you know it, all you'll have is a casual, amicable, but ultimately impersonal, friendship. The periods between your messages will grow longer and longer, until you'll be lucky to remember exchanging Christmas or birthday wishes."

"God, that's depressing. When did you get so fricking gloomy?" Charity's voice was teasing while everything inside her was withering up and dying. Faith was right. It was already happening. Five days without contact spoke for itself.

"It's the sad reality. You're setting yourself up to fail, sis."

She blinked into her drink, trying to force the blurriness from her gaze. Not wanting anyone else to see the tears shimmering in her eyes. But Faith swore vehemently, and her arm slid around Charity's shoulders again to give her another squeeze.

"I'm sorry. Ignore me," she apologized quietly. "I just want you to be happy. But that was a douchey thing to say. You've been so brave these last few months, Charity. That's why it frustrates me to watch you lose your nerve in this. When it matters so much to you."

"I haven't lost my nerve," Charity denied. Even though she knew that some part of her was terrified of telling Miles the truth about how she felt. "I was just trying a different approach."

Faith smiled but did not look entirely convinced. Thankfully she chose not to pursue the topic, instead complimenting the spectacular food Olivia 'Libby' Chapman had provided for the modest event.

Charity took her cue from her sister and determinedly pushed Miles and his lack of communication from her mind for the remainder of the evening. And while it wasn't easy, she managed to go the next few hours without looking at her phone.

"Are you sure you're okay?" Faith asked three hours later, after the last of Charity's guests had left.

"I'm fine. You must be exhausted. You guys go and pick Gracie up and head back to your hotel. I'll see you in the morning." Charity could barely stifle a yawn as she spoke with her sister. Faith, Stuart, and Gracie, were staying at a quaint hotel outside of town. Charity's house was simply too small to accommodate everyone. Her parents were currently occupying her shoebox-sized spare bedroom. The older couple had left the party an hour ago, pleading exhaustion.

Lia's parents were watching Gracie this evening.

Faith looked reluctant to leave Charity by herself but also very tempted to take her at her word.

"George will be back soon," Charity placated her concerned sister. "He's just taking Nina and Amos home."

George had been such a godsend these last few weeks. Charity hadn't got around to buying a car yet, and George had happily volunteered his services. He had been unwilling to accept payment from Charity, until she had suggested treating his chronic lower lumbar strain as reimbursement for his chauffeuring services. Both parties felt like they were getting the better end of the deal.

"You're sure?" Faith asked again, and Charity rolled her eyes and directed her gaze over her sister's shoulder to where Stuart was waiting at the door.

"Get her out of here, will you? Before she fusses me to death."

The tall, prematurely balding, good looking man grinned. "Getting that woman to stop fussing is an exercise in futility."

"Hey, watch it, mister!" Faith warned, but her words carried little sting. Testimony to how exhausted she was. As was the yawn that she quickly smothered.

"You sure you're safe alone for a bit?" Stuart asked. "It's nearly midnight."

"George will be here shortly. I'll lock up after you leave, and nobody can gain access to the center without being buzzed in. And even if, despite the security measures, some bad guy still manages to get in here, rest assured I can kick his butt."

He chuckled. "Yeah, we know what a badass you are." He directed his next comment at his visibly drooping wife. "Come on, love. She's fine. Let's get our kid and go to bed."

Faith didn't protest. And after they exchanged a few hugs, with Faith exacting a promise from Charity to call after she got home, they left. Charity made a huge show of locking up behind them, and they waved at her through the glass door before wandering out of the center, hand in hand.

Finally, alone with her thoughts for the first time in hours, Charity slumped down onto the comfortable waiting room sofa and buried her face in her hands for a moment.

She was happy. *She was*. Sink or swim, this practice was everything she had ever dreamed of, and she was proud of getting this far.

Her evening, surrounded by friends and family, had shown her that she was not alone, that people loved her.

So why was she so damned *melancholy*?

Something was missing, and it didn't take genius to figure out what.

She sighed despondently and dragged out her phone for the first time since her earlier conversation with Faith.

No new messages, no missed calls, not even any junk mail.

"Where *are* you?"

The door buzzer to the center's front door sounded, the sound strident and unexpected in the eerie silence of the building, and Charity jumped nearly all the way out of her skin. Reception was equipped with an intercom but not a screen to display street view camera images. It was an additional security measure which she was scheduled to receive early on in the new year, when the installation company reopened for business.

She depressed the intercom button. "Yes?"

"It's me." George's jolly voice drifted through the speaker. Charity smiled and buzzed him in. She hastily unlocked the front door before turning away to gather her purse and one of the three platters of leftover food. If the canapés remained unrefrigerated overnight, they would go bad. Frankly, she was shocked there was any food left, it was so good. But Libby had provided generous portions.

The door opened behind her.

"George, would you mind grabbing these two trays? I can't believe Libby made so much food. I don't know what I'm supposed to do with the rest of it. Feel free to take a tray home to snack on. I know you liked the—" She turned to face the driver, and the rest of what she had been about to say died in her throat.

"You're not George," she uttered blankly. Not sure if exhaustion was playing tricks on her eyes. Maybe she was hallucinating. Seeing what she so dearly wanted to see. Why else would Miles Henry Hollingsworth be standing in the middle of her reception area?

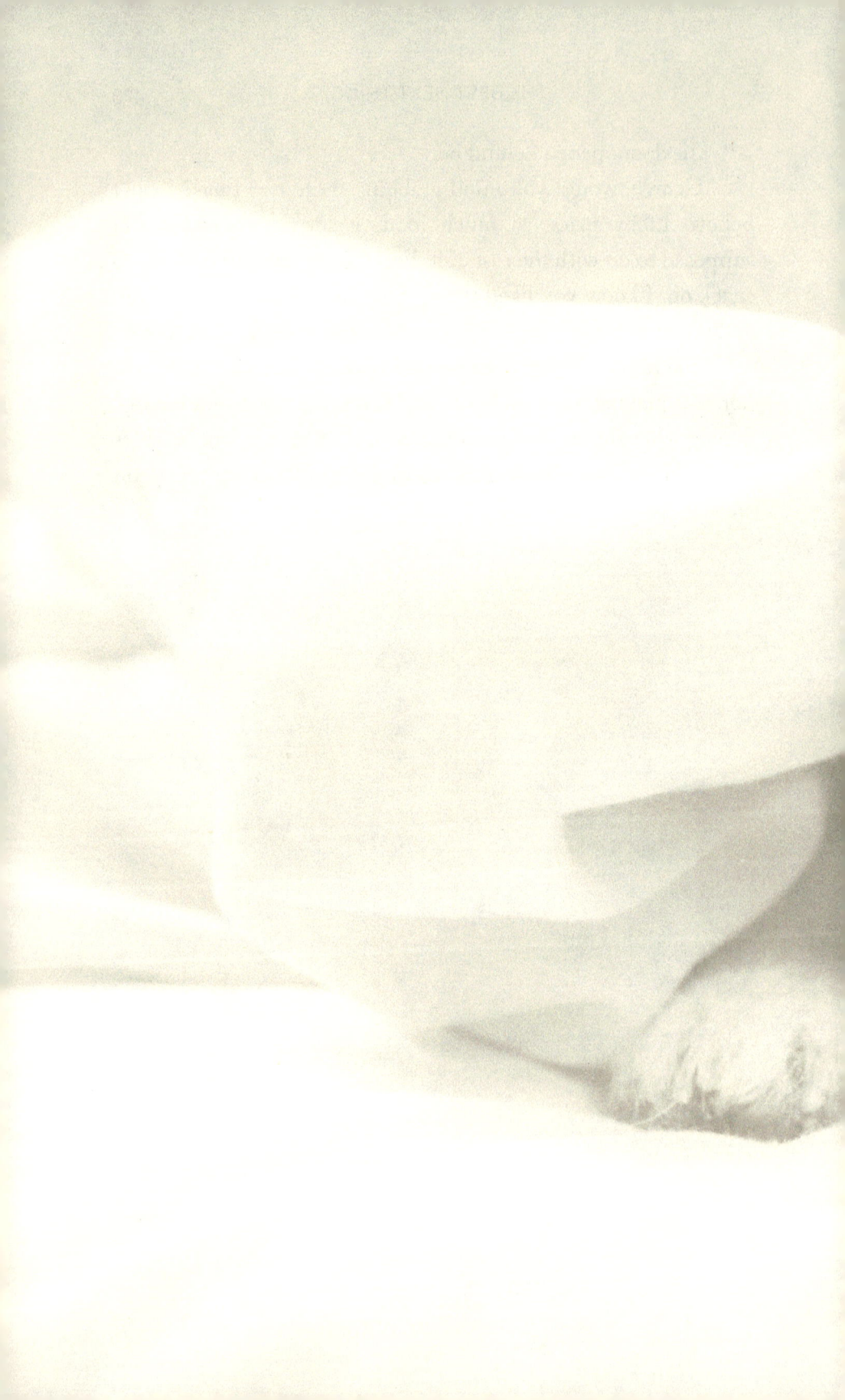

Chapter Twenty

"I'm not George," he confirmed gravely. He looked tired. No, more than that; bone weary. Pale, untidy, and a little haggard.

And so utterly gorgeous it hurt her to look at him.

"You're here. *How*? Why?" She couldn't quite organize her thoughts. She wasn't even sure if she was speaking to an actual person right now or a fabrication created by her exhausted mind.

"I'm here. I think how is fairly self-evident. It's the why that's tricky."

"Why would you think it's self-evident?" she asked, her voice teeming with resentment.

"Fine. If you need the boring details..." He shook his head in exasperation. "Car, plane, car. Can we get back to the why now?"

"Why did you stop messaging me?" Her words held a festering undertone of resentment.

"Turns out, even a semi-retired chairman of the board can't just up and leave his company twice in one year for extended 'personal reasons'." He used air quotes on those two words. "I had urgent business to take care of before I could free up the time to come here. Besides, I didn't think our text messages were filled to the brim with urgent, unmissable content."

Ouch.

She plucked at the hem of her blouse and twisted her mouth as she stared at him for a long silent moment.

"The cat memes were funny," she offered timidly, and his lips twitched.

"Not much you can say about a cat meme. They don't exactly open up avenues of conversation, and I wanted to talk with you."

"We were talking." Okay, that came out sounding defensive. Perhaps because it confirmed everything Faith had said earlier.

"We were *not* talking. We were doing some strange dance, and I didn't know half of the steps."

She stared at him wonderingly, still not entirely sure he was real.

"Charity! Are you listening to me?" Aah, that impatient tone was unmistakably Miles.

She felt her lips part as her face bloomed into a smile.

"You're really here?" She was still clutching the platter of canapés in her hands and, in a lightning fast move, he plucked the tray from her grasp and set it aside. He bridged the distance between them enough for her to feel the delicious heat of his body, and inhale the woodsy fragrance of his aftershave, mingling with the slight musk of his sweat...evidence of the long flight he had just taken.

"I'm here, sweetheart. Hat in hand, heart on my sleeve, wanting to know what the fuck is up with all those cat memes?"

She sobbed and launched herself into his waiting arms.

"You're here! I can't believe you're here!" Her words were

muffled against his neck, and she clung to him tightly, terrified that he'd disappear if she let him go.

"I wanted to be here in time for the party. But we had a weather delay at Heathrow. I'm sorry I missed it. I wanted to celebrate with you."

"George knew all along, didn't he?"

"He did. A driving service took me from the airport to the house, and George picked me up from there when he dropped Amos off."

"I'm so happy you're here."

"Are you?" His arms tightened around her.

"Yes."

"We need to talk, Charity. Are you expected at home tonight? George told me your parents are staying with you. Or... or, do you think we could..."

"Let's go to your place. Oh my God, the house has been closed for months. Did you remember to have the utilities switched on? There's probably no food stocked..."

"Charity," he interrupted her panicked flood of words with an indulgent chuckle. "That's no longer your job. Stop worrying about it. Everything has been arranged."

"How? You're so used to me taking care of ev—" The rest of her words were muffled by the delicious pressure of his mouth on hers. She parted her lips and happily welcomed his tongue home. She groaned when he palmed her face and tilted her head back to deepen the kiss.

He lifted his lips from hers and stared down into her eyes, a tender smile gracing his mouth.

"I've missed you so fucking much." He released her and took a reluctant step back, putting some space between them. "Where are these platters you need me to haul?"

"Uh...you grab those two," she said, pointing to the two on

the reception desk, and lifting the third that he had taken from her earlier.

"What's happening with the clean up?" His gaze travelled around the room. There were champagne flutes and paper plates adorning various surfaces. Confetti and streamers on the floor. A few helium balloons drooping in the corners.

"I have a professional cleaning service coming in tomorrow morning. One of Daff's connections, they're doing us a huge favor coming in on a Sunday. But the place has to be shipshape by start of business on Monday."

"You must be terribly excited." He grinned, his eyes crinkling boyishly at the corners, and she caught her breath at the welcome sight of that familiar dimple.

"Right now, I'm more excited about seeing you," she told him honestly. His smiled faded, and she mourned its loss. Not sure why her words had made it disappear.

"Let's get out of here." He was so somber, and it scared her. Miles was a naturally reserved man, but a lot of his reticence had melted around her during their time together. She wanted that relaxed, happy man back.

She followed him mutely to the door, her movements stiff and mechanical as she juggled her purse and the tray to lock up behind them.

George was waiting for them outside. It was a lovely summer's night and, despite the late hour, there was still a fair number of people out and about. George grinned when he caught sight of Charity and Miles. He looked insufferably self-satisfied.

"Nice surprise, right?" he crowed, his rugged brown face beaming beneath the streetlamp. "I had you fooled, hey? You didn't have a clue what we were up to."

"Nobody likes a gloater, George." Charity chastised, but there was only warmth in her voice, and George chuckled.

"I following orders. Miles wanted it to be a secret."

"*Miles?*" Charity mouthed at the silent man hovering beside her, and Miles rolled his eyes with a short shake of his head.

"He and my mother have spoken every day since she left," he explained beneath his breath while George loaded the platters in the back of the SUV. "I can't very well expect my mother's long-distance boyfriend to call me Mr. Hollingsworth."

"*Boyfriend?*"

"I don't know what else to call him. They're—"

"I'll take this one, Mrs. Cole," George interrupted their hushed exchanged cheerfully, returning for the tray in Charity's hands. She had asked him time and again to call her Charity, but for some reason, he always slipped back into the habit of calling her Mrs. Cole. It was funny that he found it easier to call Miles by his given name than he did Charity.

Miles lightly grasped her elbow. His warm hand on her naked skin sent goosebumps skidding up her spine. She had missed his touch. Thirsted for it. When he released his hold on her seconds after she had settled in the back seat, she disguised her disappointed groan behind a cough.

He rounded the back of the vehicle and climbed in next to her, but remained on his side of the long bench seat. There was a yawning chasm between them...and Charity was tempted to bridge the gap by scooting across the seat and snuggling against him.

She was on the verge of unbuckling her seatbelt and doing just that, when he dumped his briefcase between them. Leaving her with not only a chasm to cross but a mountain to climb.

In the end it was simpler to stay on her side of the car.

George was humming beneath his breath and seemed oblivious to the simmering tension in the back seat.

They sat in silence for the entirety of the drive. Charity wasn't sure what to say. Now that he was here, she found herself uncertain, overwhelmed, nervous, and excited all at the same time.

She toyed with her phone, needing something to occupy her restless hands, and sent Faith a quick message. Her sister's almost instant reply made her grin.

FAITH

OMG! Duck! I mean Duck! That's so DUCKING fantastic! HAVE FUN!! Call me first thing in the morning.

She sent a second message to her mother to let her know where she was.

Her mother responded with:

MOM

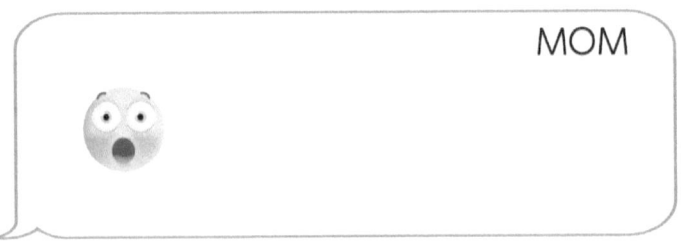

Followed by:

MOM

Let us know how it goes. We love you, angel, and we want you to be happy

After learning about Blaine's abuse, her parents had been understandably mistrustful of the men Charity had dated since her return from Riversend. But they had also understood that Charity had had years longer than them to deal with everything. And she was ready to trust again.

In fact, she *did* trust again. She trusted Miles. And so much of her future happiness hinged on what they would say to each other tonight.

The car took the turn toward the house, and Charity's tension ramped all the way to the stratosphere.

And—if his nervously tapping foot and erratically bouncing knee were any indication-- so did Miles's. His head was turned toward the window, where he appeared to be staring out into the darkness. Possibly to avoid eye contact with her.

They were at the house and parked in the garage less than five minutes later. Charity's heart leaped at the sight of the familiar, brightly lit garage. When she had left here all those months ago, she had never dreamed she would see it again.

And now, here she was, so happy and grateful to be back in this large, open space. They hadn't replaced the dying fluorescent lightbulb yet. It had been on her to-do list, but she had been so distracted by Miles and everything happening to her, that she had forgotten about it.

For some reason, the sight of that flickering bulb added to her sense of familiarity and homecoming.

The sound of the escalating, high-pitched barking from upstairs made her smile.

"You brought Stormy." Her first words to him since they had left town.

"She's a bit of a jet-setter these days," he informed, still alarmingly grim, despite the adorable subject matter. "She even has her own pet passport. She's been to Rome, Paris, Frankfurt, and Tokyo."

The information delighted Charity, whose smile widened at the notion of the former stray living such a glamorous lifestyle. Miles may look like the sky was going to cave in at any moment, but Charity was so elated to be back in his company, that she refused to allow his surly disposition to affect her sunny one any further.

She preceded him up the stairs, and when she opened the door into the kitchen, she squealed when Stormy launched herself practically into her arms.

"Oh, there's my *good* girl! Did you miss me? I missed you." She hugged the dog's excitedly wriggling body tight and planted kisses all over her endearing face. "Nobody brought me presents. *Nobody*. No socks, no boxers, not even a hankie..."

Stormy whined happily and licked her face enthusiastically.

"Ew...stop," Charity giggled and, after one last squeeze, handed the dog over to Miles, who was lavished with the same sloppy kisses.

Miles grimaced but, wonder of wonders, a reluctant smile lifted his lips. Nobody could stay surly beneath such a determinedly adorable onslaught.

"Yes, okay. We're all happy. No need to carry on so," he admonished without heat, and put the dog down. Stormy turned her attention to George, dancing around his legs while he deposited two of the platters on the kitchen counter.

"Keep the third one, George. You seemed to really enjoy those smoked salmon mousse bites."

"Don't mind if I do. That Libby certainly knows how to cook."

He continued to stand in the kitchen, making no move to leave. That was unusual for George. Unless he had some other task to perform, he rarely lingered after he dropped whomever, or whatever, off after an errand. He leaned against the kitchen counter, whistling a cheery tune, and helped himself to a canapé from one of the trays, while Miles and Charity awkwardly stood staring at each other and then the driver.

The reason for his dawdling became apparent seconds later.

"Charity, my dear, how lovely to see you." Charity's eyebrows raised when Enid Hollingsworth flitted into the kitchen. The older woman gave her a warm hug, enveloping Charity in a cloud of fragrant *Chanel No. 5*. Enid was dressed in a loose, colorful, patterned muumuu that floated around her plump frame, and her bottle black bouncy curls were held away from her face with a silk scarf. Her badly applied bright red lipstick stained her teeth and was smudged in the hollow above her lip.

Charity liked Miles's mother. She was bold, brassy, and loud. The complete opposite of her reserved, quiet son. There was no artifice about her. She dressed in off the rack clothing and didn't seem at all affected by her son's hundreds of millions.

The older woman beamed at George after releasing Charity, and gave him a smacking kiss.

"Hello, luv! I'm ready. My bag is in the hallway."

"Where are you going?" Miles asked in some consternation, seeming surprised by his mother's words.

"You didn't think I tagged along to spend time with you, did you, my boy? I love you, but you have other things to take care of." This, with a pointed look at Charity. "I'm staying with George. And we're taking Stormy with us tonight."

"But..."

"I'll take good care of her, Miles," George promised, with an almost lascivious wink. "Oh, and Stormy too, of course. I'll have the pup back first thing in the morning."

Enid picked Stormy up, planted a kiss on Miles's astonished face and sailed out of the kitchen with an airy wave. George followed, carrying a large, brightly patterned hard-shell suitcase.

"G'night," he said, with a nod and smile, leaving Charity and Miles to stare at the closed basement door in bemusement.

Well, Charity was bemused, *Miles*—on the other hand—looked comically horrified.

"So, it looks like your mother found a reason to overcome her fear of flying," Charity said, trying to keep her amusement at bay, but it was hard when Miles looked like he had just swallowed a live eel.

"I knew they were texting each other. But I didn't think it was this serious already. Mum was *very* keen to join me on this trip." He shook himself and lowered his serious eyes to hers, before deadpanning, "Their text messages must have been a hell of a lot more interesting than ours. Less cat memes maybe?"

"Oh my God. What do you have against the memes?"

"Aside from the fact that they don't give me a single goddamned clue about what you're thinking, or how you're feeling? Not a thing."

Oh *my*.

"And you wanted to know those things?"

The sound that clawed its way out of his throat was the mutant offspring of a growl and a sigh. "What do *you* think, Charity?"

He shook his head and turned away from her to slam his way

around the kitchen, opening and closing cupboards at random and seemingly without purpose.

"What are you looking for?" she asked tentatively.

"Where's the bloody tea?"

"Right beside the kettle," she supplied. She slid onto one of the barstools and watched in fascination as his eyes darted to the electric kettle. He glared at the tea, snugly situated between the sugar and coffee.

"Thanks," he grumbled.

"Why are you in such a bad mood?"

He leveled a black look at her. "I'm not in a bad mood."

"Then talk me through what's going on with you. So that we can get past it and move on to what really matters."

Her words made him pause, and he seemed to forget about the tea and, instead, took a step toward her. His eyes laser-focused on her face.

"What do *you* think really matters, Charity?"

"I'd like for you to know exactly what I was thinking and feeling while I was sending you those texts."

Another step closer. "Please...continue."

"I was thinking any contact was better than no contact. And I was hoping that..." It was hard not to lose her nerve with those unblinking, steel gray eyes piercing into her soul.

"Hoping that what?"

"Hoping that it could be the framework—the foundation—for more."

More.

Miles couldn't take his eyes off her, terrified that if he diverted his gaze, if he so much as blinked, he would miss something crucial in her expression. Some tell that would unravel the mystery that was Charity Cole.

He took another step toward her, this one brought him right to the island...an unwanted physical barrier between his body and hers. He flattened his palms on the marble and watched her as she continued to speak. Waited for her to elaborate on that tantalizing *more*.

The tip of her tongue peeked out to nervously wet her succulent lips, and he bit back a groan at the temptation offered by that nimble tongue and that ripe mouth.

It was hard to believe he was in the same room with her. All he wanted to do was wrap her in his arms, kiss her...love her. But that could wait.

It had to wait. He refused to touch her until he knew there was a future in it. Because he couldn't do finite with her anymore.

He needed forever.

"More what?" he prompted impatiently, when it seemed that she wouldn't continue.

"Miles..." she placed a hand on the counter and slid it across the cold, smooth surface toward one of his. When she covered his flattened hand with her smaller one, he shuddered at the contact. "You know that I love you, right?"

His breath snagged in his chest. Trapped by the weight of his expanding heart. The words, long awaited, much coveted, hit him with the force of a ten-ton truck, and he swayed on his feet as his entire body absorbed the impact.

"I did *not* know that," he managed to squeeze the words out despite the expanding heart and trapped breath. They sounded rough, taut...even surly.

"Oh. Well...I do. Love you, I mean. I've been in love with you since"—her eyes went hazy with the recollection—"the day we took Stormy to the beach. Somewhere between our first kiss and the chickens at the restaurant, I fell head over heels in love with you. Only I didn't know it. Because in my mind loving a man meant being weak and helpless. But I didn't feel weak or helpless around you, so it took me a while to recognize the emotion for what it was. The love I feel for you..." She laughed. It was a sound filled with wonder and awe. "The love I feel for you strengthens me. It makes me a better person. It's taken a long time for me to like myself again, Miles. But I find that I like myself even *more* when I'm with you."

His hand flipped over to take her palm in his. He hoped the gesture would tell her everything he currently could not say.

He swallowed, trying to dislodge the obstructive lump in his throat that prevented him from replying. She had stopped speaking and was staring at him with huge, vulnerable eyes. She had laid herself bare, opened herself up to potential rejection and pain. But trusted that he would not hurt her. Or reject her.

Always so fucking brave.

"Thank God for that then," he whispered shakily. The words heartfelt and not exactly what he would have planned to say in response to a declaration of love from the woman of his dreams, if he had been thinking clearly.

He rounded the island, not letting go of her hand, and turned her barstool until her back was to the counter, and he was standing between her thighs.

"I don't know what I would have done if you didn't love me the way I love you. Probably gone back to London brokenhearted...*again.* Only last time, even though it hurt like hell, I told myself I was doing the right thing. Despite my best intentions, I know I wasn't always graceful about it—I was in pain—but I understood that letting you go was the only option available to me. Telling you how I felt would have been manipulative. Unfair. I couldn't do that to you.

"But when you started messaging me, I hoped it meant something. Only you wouldn't stop talking about Stormy and sending me stupid jokes and dumb videos and asking me impersonal questions about fucking work, and I was so damned confused!"

IN HIS EYES was an echo of the frustration and bewilderment he had felt at her bombardment of silly messages. Charity wrapped her arms around his neck and stroked his nape in apology.

While her heart joyfully soared out of her chest and flitted around the kitchen like a drunken, happy butterfly

He loved her.

Despite her regret at her poor handling of the situation with the texts and impersonal calls and voice notes, she couldn't stop herself from grinning at his confession.

"You love me," she murmured.

He was smiling. A beautiful, broad, fully dimpled smile. "You love *me*."

"I do," she confirmed. "So much. But you were right to let me figure it out on my own. I needed the time apart to recognize my feelings for you as deep, genuine, and irrefutable."

"And apparently you needed to shop around too," he muttered, eyeing her askance.

She laughed, "I confess, I had to kiss a few toads before I recognized that I'd already found my frog."

"Waaait a second..." He frowned at the analogy. "That's not how that goes."

"No, it is," she maintained earnestly, before getting up and plastering her chest against his. She hugged him and whispered her next words directly into his ear. "Once upon a time, I had the perfect golden prince, and he was rotten to the core. I don't need a perfect prince, Miles. I need you. You're imperfect and you're beautiful and I love you *exactly* the way you are."

He made a choked sound in the back of his throat and turned his head, his hawkish nose bumping hers in his haste to kiss her. She giggled but was abruptly silenced when his lips latched onto hers fiercely. All thought of laughter fled when he swung her into his arms and carried her from the kitchen without releasing her mouth.

When they next came up for air, they were both naked, sweaty, and sated. Charity was curled up against his chest, her fingers tracing lazy circles through his silky chest hairs. Everything about him was so damned perfect.

"So now what?" she wondered out loud.

"Hmm? I don't know...a shower maybe? I must be getting ripe."

"I love the way you smell," she said on a yawn. "Warm and musky and delicious. You smell like home to me. But that's not what I meant."

"What did you mean then?"

"What happens next? With us? I can't leave, Miles. I have the practice opening on Monday. My life is here."

"I wouldn't ask you to leave," he placated. "No, this is partly what all the restructuring at the company was about. Initially, it was for the reasons I gave, I needed to take things easier, needed my life to be about more than work. But after you contacted me last month, I started hoping that we could somehow find our way back to each other. The company represents my life's work,

Charity. I will continue to chair. And consult. I will probably need to go back to London a few times a year for meetings, but I can do a lot from here with just a laptop and Wi-Fi—barring storms and blackouts of course. In fact, I may have to invest in a satellite phone and a stronger generator. Minor details. The gist of what I'm saying is that...I'm happy to move here, on a semi-permanent basis."

"Miles, you'd be uprooting your whole life."

He tenderly grasped her chin between his thumb and index finger and tipped her head back until she could see his eyes.

"Charity, *you* are my life. And since you're here, that means my life is here."

"Oh, Miles." Her eyes flooded, and she rewarded the beautiful sentiment with a kiss. She was somber when she lifted her lips from his. "Miles, I'm doing well. I'm a lot better and making great strides in dealing with my past. But I'm a work in progress. I'll need therapy for a long time to come. Maybe permanently... and there'll be times a sudden move or an argument will trigger my fight or flight response. I want you to understand that I *know* you will never hurt me. I know you're an amazing, gentle man and on the—hopefully rare—occasions when that does happen, I don't want you to be hurt or think it's about you. It's always about me."

His arms tightened protectively around her, and he kissed the top of her head sweetly.

"I won't pretend that I'm okay with that, sweetheart. It'll hurt. Even though I know where it's coming from. But I'd be happy to attend any couple's therapy sessions you think we may need to help us deal with those moments."

"You would?"

"Of course."

"I don't want you to think you should walk on eggshells

around me. I enjoy a good argument or disagreement as much as the next person. I can't control where or when it happens. But I do know it won't happen all the time. And hopefully with time, patience, and therapy, we'll move past it."

"Well, since we're confessing secrets. Here's one about me you don't know. And I don't want you to look at me any differently...because I know how much of a freak you'll think I am because of it."

Charity's eyes widened, and she levered herself onto her elbow to watch him curiously.

"I'm fucking deathly afraid of heights."

"*No.*" To say she was shocked would be understating it.

"Yeah...your jumping off cliffs and out of planes stories? Terrifying. Why do you think this house is built on one level? When the views would be so much more panoramic from a second floor?"

"But the basement stairs..."

"Oddly, knowing the stairs are below ground, so to speak, makes it less horrifying. I mean, I can stare into a deep, cavernous hole. But I can't handle that exact same distance down, from the top of a building. And flying is fine too. If I'm not sitting close to the window, I can fool my brain into thinking I'm on a bus or something. Weird, right?"

"To be honest, I thought you were weird long before this. I mean, the lobsters, the odd 'wannabe but can't' vegetarian thing, and the only song you know is *I'm Too Sexy*, for God's sake!"

"Absolutely not true," he protested vehemently. "I know plenty of other songs. I just can't ever seem to hum them."

"See? Weird!"

"God, how the hell did I survive so many months without you?" he wondered, abruptly serious.

"We're together now. And this is all that matters. Well this and..."

She allowed her voice to taper off, and she didn't have to wait long for the impatient prod. "And *what*?"

"Well, I need to know what happened with Willow and Delonix."

He shook with silent laughter. "How the hell should I know? I couldn't finish the damned book without you, could I?"

"*Really*?" Hearing him tell her he loved her was one thing... but this right here. This was proof of that love.

"Yes *really*, I missed you and listening to the book made it worse."

She could feel herself beaming and knew her face must have lit up like a Christmas tree. His irritated words made her so damned happy.

"We'll finish it tomorrow," she promised, climbing on top of him to straddle his thighs.

"Yes," he nodded eagerly, whether in response to her enthusiastic grinding against his cock or to her words, she couldn't be certain. Until he added, "And then start the next part of the adventure. Together."

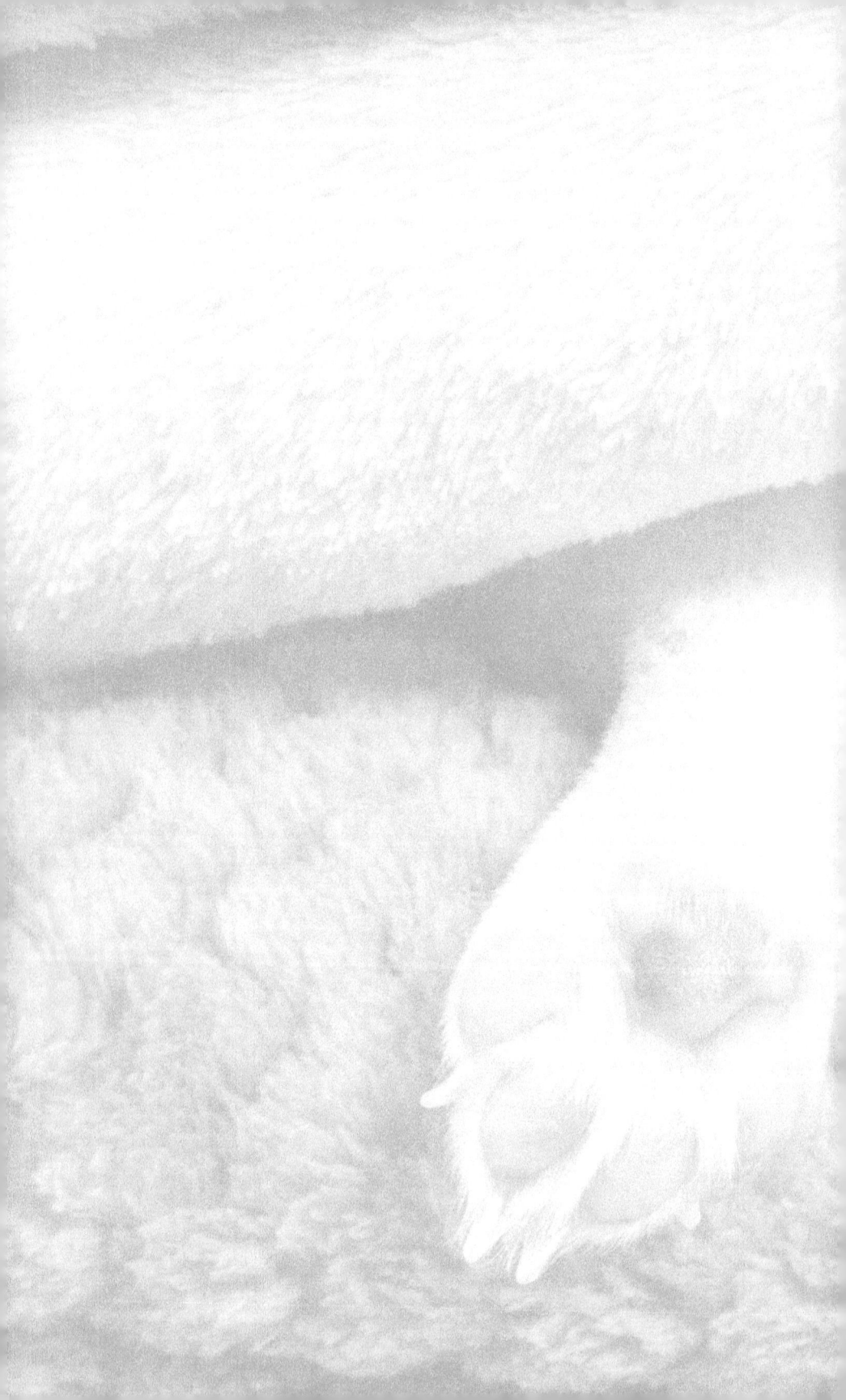

Epilogue

The haunting strains of Wagner's wedding march beautifully plucked from the strings of an elegantly curved pedal harp, swelled to a sobbing crescendo as the bride reached the end of the rose petal strewn red carpet. Her handsome groom, his face a study in reverence, adoration, and love, waited with tightly folded hands. As if he had to physically restrain himself from reaching for her.

"Who gives this woman to marry this man?" The minister intoned seriously, despite the grin on her face.

"I do," the handsome man beside the beautiful bride replied, his voice brimming with pride and emotion. He lifted her veil and planted a sweet kiss on her cheek, before removing her hand from the crook of his elbow and transferring it to her waiting groom's hand.

"You'd better take good care of her, George." The words were thick with warning, and the guests tittered in amusement, even though Charity knew he wasn't joking at all. He took his seat next to hers, his eyes shimmering with emotion he swiftly hid behind a pair of dark glasses.

"Big baby," she whispered in his ear, and he turned his head to give her an impassive look. As if he could fool her with a pair of aviator sunglasses and a downturned mouth. He was a blubbering mess behind that disguise.

After nearly a year of courtship—well, "courtship" was probably too formal a word for canoodling that went on between the two of them—George was finally making an honest woman of his beloved Enid. The woman had pretty much moved to Riversend with Miles. But even though she ostensibly lived at her son's house, she had never spent any significant time there. Instead, she had practically moved into George's house.

Which had suited Miles and Charity just fine because Charity *had* moved in with Miles.

And she had never been happier. Business was thriving, she spoke with her family often, and kept up with her therapy sessions. She had made so many friends since returning to Riversend, and she was becoming a valued member of the community. She had even allowed Sam to coerce her into teaching a few self-defense classes.

Life was good, and at the center of it all was the man beside her. He had traveled more than he'd initially intended to, but always hurried home to her. They were ecstatic. And more and more in love every day.

Her hand crept into his. Because, despite his stoicism, she knew this was an emotional day for him. Her gorgeous, strong man was a little tearful because his mother was getting married.

Charity watched the couple exchange their I do's. Vicki and Nina were bridesmaids, and Hugh the best man. And Miles, duty done, sat and watched as his mother married her beloved George.

"It was a lovely wedding," Charity reflected that evening.

"It was nice," Miles agreed, he had finished brushing his teeth and was watching her moisturize her face with a dreamy smile on his face.

"They were thrilled with their wedding gift. That was a lovely thing you did for them."

"I couldn't have them living in a one-bedroom house. She would drive George nuts, they'd fight, and then she'd wind up back on my doorstep." He folded his arms over his naked chest and shook his head. "Nope, it's better this way. A bigger house will allow them both space to preserve their sanity."

"I didn't think George would accept it." There had been a moment when George had looked on the verge of giving back the title deed of the modest three-bedroom house in town that Miles had bought for them. But in the end, he had hugged Miles and thanked him emotionally.

"George is a wise man. He loves my mum and he knew a bigger house would make her happy. Mum's a humble woman," he said. "And she would have been content in George's old place, but they needed more space. They both knew that."

Charity massaged the excess moisturizer into the skin of her hands and forearms, never shifting her eyes from his somber face.

She got up from her dresser to gift him with a tender kiss.

"I love you, you know that?"

"I have an inkling, yes." He curled his arms around her waist and squeezed her close. He whistled and the incongruous sound startled Charity into looking up.

Stormy came trotting into the room and, momentarily

diverted, Charity shifted her glance down to the dog, and then huffed an exasperated sigh.

"Now what? I thought she was done with this," she groused. She moved out of Miles's arms to kneel on the carpeted floor and call Stormy over. She made a tut-tutting sound and tugged at the random offering Stormy had dangling from her slobbering mouth.

"Ugh, so much drool," she complained, as she investigated the mysterious object. Not sure what it was. She glared at Miles irritably. "In fact, next time you can retrieve whatever gross gift your dog decides to bri—*Miles*?"

He looked odd. Green around the gills and ashen around the mouth and...gray in the face. So many awful shades of hideous colors.

He swallowed thickly and his eyes bugged. Not an attractive look on him at all.

Confused...and more than a little alarmed, Charity pushed to her feet, her intention to touch test his forehead for fever. But when he collapsed to one knee, she gasped, terrified that he was seriously ill.

God! Where was her phone? She instinctively looked down at her hand. No that wasn't her phone it was the thing Stormy had brou—she peered more closely at the item in her hand.

It was a box.

Breathing became the hardest thing in the world. A chore. An impossibility.

She swayed, feeling light-headed as she continued to stare at the beribboned box.

Miles was still on the floor. He could have passed out by now, she wouldn't know. So focused was she on that box.

She slid the ribbon off, wrinkling her nose at how wet it

was...Stormy had carried the box by the ribbon. She exhaled slowly and flipped the lid up.

And then covered her mouth with her free hand as she stared at the stunning, oval, flawless sapphire in awe. The stone was flanked by two smaller diamonds and set on a slender white gold band.

Her confused gaze leaped to Miles's. He was still on the floor. On bended knee. Dressed in a pair of loose gray sweatpants, barefoot, bare chested, with dark stubble blooming on his jaw and lean cheeks, and his short black hair mussed.

He was, and always would be, the most beautiful man she had ever known.

"Charity Ella Cole, I love you more than anything else in this whole damned world. You're my best friend and having you in my life is—quite simply—the most wonderful thing to ever happen to me. I can't imagine being without you. I want to spend forever with you, I want to have children with you. And you would make me the happiest man alive if you wanted those things too. Will you marry me?"

Her lips trembled and her eyes were misty with the tears already streaming down her cheeks.

She knelt beside him and threw her arms around his neck, unbalancing him and sending them both to toppling to the floor. Delighted with this awesome new game, Stormy barked and leaped on top of both of them, licking every surface of available skin she could reach.

They convulsed with laughter, trying to push the dog off, but Stormy seemed to think it was part of the game and redoubled her efforts. They were a crazy tangled mess of limbs, hair, and fur and—in the midst of all that happy chaos—Charity said yes.

Acknowledgments

This wasn't an easy book to write. I had so many doubts about the story, the characters, the subject matter. But thankfully, I had so many who believed in me, encouraged me to go for it, and talked me out of giving up entirely. Completing this story would not have been possible without them.

Rae Rivers for always listening. Hopefully we'll be able to resume our brunches soon.

Jo Watson for your unwavering support, the brainstorming sessions, the fun and laughter. You rock, lady!

Ashleigh Giannoccaro for your invaluable advice throughout the editorial/pre-publishing phase. I can't wait for our wine tour.

My cousin, Melanie Cupido, thanks for reading it and telling me it didn't suck (if she thought it sucked, trust me, she would have told me).

Ilona Ahrens for the beta read. You like to call yourself a fan, but I think of you as a good friend.

Kimberley Whalen – my amazing agent. I owe you everything.

May Sage – for helping me navigate these foreign waters. I appreciate it so much!

Dr. Yomika Venketsamy, Masters of Technology (Chiropractic). I loved our chats. Thank you for sharing your knowledge with me. Charity's chiropractic competence is thanks only to you.

I know too many women who have suffered through domestic violence. This book is for them and for all the others I do not know.

About the Author

With nearly a million books sold, Natasha Anders has been drawing praise and attention as a unique voice in romance since 2012. Her first novel, The Unwanted Wife, was a bestselling sensation and remains a consistent favorite among readers. Her 2017 novel, The Wingman, the first in her new Alpha Men trilogy, was a finalist for a 2018 Romance Writers of America RITA Award.

Born in Cape Town, South Africa, Anders spent nine years as an associate English teacher in Niigata, Japan, where she became a legendary karaoke diva. Anders currently lives in Cape Town with her temperamental chihuahua, Maia; her moody budgie, Baxter; sweet little chihuahua Hana; and her little wingman, adorable parrotlet, Mason.

Readers can connect with her through her Facebook page, on Twitter at @satyne1, or at www.natashaanders.com

Natasha Anders

www.ingramcontent.com/pod-product-compliance
Lightning Source LLC
Chambersburg PA
CBHW021840010726
47493CB00005B/1481
9780620899420